Bit By Bit

MD Hanley

Copyright

Print ISBN 13: 978-1733198622

EBook ISBN: 978-1733198646

Published by MD Hanley

Copyright© 2019 MD Hanley

Acknowledgements

The basis of my story started in 2003, while I was on a scuba diving liveaboard expedition exploring the Great Barrier Reef. One of the dive sites I was on, was the Yongala Wreck. This is considered one of the top three scuba dive sites to go scuba diving around the world.

One person that has inspired me to author this novel is Christine A. Adams. She is a well-known and accomplished author that has been publishing books for the last 35 years. Her experience as a writer, a teacher, and countless edits were invaluable to make this into a great story. My love of stories and great story telling is still as strong as it was when I was 6 years old.

This all started on one of those incredibility long drives to go camping or canoeing in Northern Maine. She introduced me to the world of J. R. R. Tolkien by reading "The Hobbit" to me.

I also want to say thank you to all the family and friends that helped and supported me with this. It is truly appreciated.

Anyone can have a great story, but
you need to be a good storyteller to
make it real and inspire imagination.

Table of Contents

Chapter 1 - Gary McKeown

As witnesses later recalled two small dogs

waltzed into the dance studio,

grabbed the cat and waltzed out

- The Far Side by Gary Larson

200 miles east of the Australian coast.

It's 6:30 AM in the South Pacific Ocean about 200 miles from the east coast of Australia. This early in the morning, there's a breath-taking view of the South Pacific Ocean with the sun climbing ever higher and becoming warmer. The surface of the ocean had what looked like dozens of tiny little mirrors reflecting back to the sun. A familiar tug of war between the sun and the South Pacific Ocean that's been going on since the earth was first formed. The sun continuously beats down on the ocean surface and the response of the ocean is to reflect back to the sun. At the end of each day the ocean and the sun call a truce until the next day. The salty smell of the ocean is strong and pungent. This salty smell is not unpleasant, but it hints there is nothing between the boat and Australian coast.

The triple decker diving boat rocks gently on the water, anchored to a point in the ocean above the S.S.

Yongala shipwreck site. Among most scuba divers, the Yongala is one of the premier dive sites around the world. The SS Yongala was a passenger ship out of Melbourne heading towards Cairns, Queensland in 1911. On the way up the coast, they ran into a severe cyclone and sank. All passengers and cargo were lost. Over the years, the Yongala has become an artificial reef and the home of many species of fish and beautiful coral formations. The wreck sits in an area of sandy shoal about 120 feet underwater at about 4 miles west of the Flinders reef.

The warm sun feels great compared to two days earlier in Boston where a cold winter had a *'Kung-Fu'* grip on New England. Gary McKeown is 48 and physically in good shape. Gary was never the type to go to the gym religiously every morning and lifting huge weights to attain huge muscles. Gary had always liked working out but his attitude toward physical strength was very pragmatic. If he was hanging on the edge of a huge building, would he have the strength to lift his body to the roof or safety without having a huge issue? Could he also do the same if someone was injured and he needed to carry them on his back? Yeah, he figures he could do that but that's it. People at the gym he belongs to are the 'gym rats' getting their bodies ready for the apocalypse and would need the strength to carry eight people on his or her back to get to safety. To each his own, I guess.

Bit By Bit

Gary starts to think about the events that got him here. He had almost cancelled the whole diving trip when he got a call about 3 hours before his flight out of Boston. His friend Ben Costello, who was supposed to come on this scuba diving trip, told Gary that he was in the Emergency Department. He was on a ladder doing some of the last-minute things that his wife had asked to do when he had fallen and broke his leg.

With the prospect of canceling all his plans and staying home over the Christmas Holiday, Gary's business partner, Roger Tillson, mentioned that he might be able to help Gary. Roger still stayed in touch with a mutual friend, Barry Parker, who they both knew from their North Eastern College fraternity. Roger said that Barry had been pestering him to go scuba diving with him so

Gary agreed to let Roger see if Barry was available.

In fifteen minutes, Roger walked into Gary's office and announced that he was the great miracle worker. Roger said he had to call in huge favors. Use some of his contacts with the airlines, use favors owed him. He had to use his amazing negotiating skills to be able to miraculously pull this off. Roger had bought an American /Qantas Airline round trip airline tickets for tonight's flight out of Boston, got all the Visas that were needed, booked a cabin on the Spoil Sport diving boat Gary and Ben were going to take. Unfortunately for

Barry he had to fly coach and share a cabin with one of the crew on the diving boat.

Gary smelled something wrong here. How could all this be done in 20 minutes? Even if it wasn't last minute, it still took a while to book all of these things. At the last-minute Roger was able to book an American Airline/ Qantas Airline coach ticket to Brisbane Australia and then a 3-hour flight north to Cairns, Queensland? And even more surprising was to get a spot on the seven-day scuba diving boat, Spoil Sport. Obtaining all the tickets and visas for this was done in the space of about 20 minutes?

At first Gary thought something was not quite right here. If feels as if Barry already had airplane tickets, visas, and a reservation on Spoil Sport. Even though he was suspicious of this, he was really looking forward to this trip. Reluctantly, he agreed and packed up any papers he was currently working on. He would look at these when he came back. The next 10 days was going to be a great way to just relax and unplug for a while.

Gary went out to the dive deck to see the sun rising. He loved this time of day. Peaceful and calm. The quiet and calming factor of the dive deck is like a house of cards. Undisturbed. No one has broken the silence yet.

Pretty soon, there's a buzz of people going in every direction on the lower diving deck. Some of these are the Spoil Sport diving boat crew. The rest of the people on the deck are the passengers who were there for one thing and only one thing, scuba diving. All sizes of people were here, big, small, tall, or short. The amount of neoprene was obviously abundant!

Almost everyone on board is going on this dive, except Barry. He has not shown up on the diving deck yet. Most people are sitting on one of the three rows of benches. Underneath the bench is a bin that holds all their scuba gear. snorkel, masks, diving fins, weight belts and diving computers. Behind each person is one scuba tank attached to their BCD (Buoyancy Compensator Device). Each tank had been filled earlier that morning with Oxygen, or an Oxygen Nitrogen mix.

On the left and right of the dive deck are a short set of stairs leading to a flat platform, only about a foot above the surface of the ocean. This is where they can put their fins on and jump into the ocean. At the back of the dive deck is a chalkboard that displays the information for their dive. On it is written various depths of the different parts of the dive sight. One of the dive crew starts to get everyone's attention and proceeds with the diving brief.

Whether it was an Oxygen, or a Nitrox mix, it was very important that they be certified to use the right mix. Each carried its own life-threatening ramifications from Nitrogen narcosis or Oxygen toxicity. Incorrectly using the wrong mix can have dire consequences.

Like most scuba diving boats, they have two hard fast rules. Initial when you leave the boat and then initial it when you come back on board. The other rule they have is what they call, 'Peace on the Reef'. This means look all you want, but don't touch. The Great Barrier Reef is one of the world's most beautiful treasures and some of the reef formations take decades and decades to grow that way. Humans can ruin this wonder of the world very quickly and it needs us to respect it and not destroy it.

Since Gary has never dived with Barry before, it was really important to be reading from the same page when they are diving. Over the years Gary has learned the hard way that some people are very safe to dive with and others are not. Gary and his friend, Ben, always approached diving with safety in mind. Gary had not dived with Barry before, so he wanted to make sure they were using the same hand signals. He stressed how important it was to dive as a team. Don't wander off 50 yards away from your dive buddy. What if you have a problem with the tank etc.? If someone gives you thumbs up that doesn't mean 'Ok' but means to ascend. Checking your tanks air supply and communicate when it's half empty and when it is a quarter tank left.

Keep checking your dive computer for how long it is safe to stay at a certain depth. Always, always do safety stops. Stop at 60 feet for 3 to 5 minutes, stop at 30 feet for 3 to 5 minutes and finally a stop at fifteen feet for 3 to 5 minutes. If you don't follow these safety stops then you are not allowing your body to release the nitrogen from the various parts of your body and muscles. Gary would rather abort a dive for safety rather than push the envelope just to see something interesting.

This is the first dive which Gary and Barry are scuba diving together. Immediately, Gary could tell that Barry's diving experience was little to none. If you took a vacation to the Caribbean, there were many hotels that would give you a quickie 3-hour scuba dive class and you would mistakenly believe that you had your official scuba diving license. What you received from the hotel was not a PADI Scuba Certification but was a recreational diving certificate. It was only valid at **their** hotel, and it only allowed you to go to a depth of 30 feet with a certified diver.

It was still light out and the visibility was good. They swam out to the guideline that was about 20 yards from the boat. They slowly released air in the BCD to allow for a gradual descent. Going down slowly helps to equalize the pressure that builds up in the sinus passages. As soon as they descended about 5 feet, Barry just dropped like a rock and let out all of the air from his BCD to help him descend quickly. When Gary reached the same depth and swam over to Barry, he could tell that Barry had a lot of pressure pulsing into his temples and sinus's tissues. When this occurs, you can do one of two things, stop descending or pinch your nose and try to blow air out of your nasal passages. This is called the Valsalva technique. This will help to equalize your eustachian tubes in your inner ears and releases the pressure that builds up. Depending on a person's physiology, some people have a great deal of trouble while others do not.

Gary thought Barry's behavior was a total rookie mistake. He got Barry's attention and asked him if he was ok. He asked him by putting his hand to his nose, as if he was going to equalize the pressure, and then gave an OK signal as a question to see where Barry was. Barry shook his head to say 'no'. Gary said in hand signals, stay for 3 minutes and if the pressure equalizes then they would continue the dive. If not any better, we would ascend to 60 feet and again wait a couple of minutes to see if it corrected the pressure he was feeling. Barry decided that he would just do what he wanted and grabbed the guideline and pulled himself quickly up the guideline.

On his way back to the surface he pushed a girl who was descending, out of his way. As he pushed her aside, he ended up getting his hand under her regulator hose, that connects to the air tank, and yanked it out of her mouth, as he moved his left arm up the guideline. She was a seasoned diver, so she recovered quickly. As Gary ascended to follow Barry, he reached the diver that Barry just bumped into. He tried to pantomime an apology to her. She nodded and accepted his apology.

Later in the morning Gary, and most everyone on the boat, is hoping to do a dive before lunch. Gary is starting to get annoyed that Barry has not come out to get ready for this dive. If Barry didn't show up soon, Gary was going to ask one of the other divers if he could tag along with them on their dive. Gary is partly hoping that Barry doesn't show up for the dive, which would be a blessing. As soon as he was thinking this, Barry stumbled down the stairs to the diving deck.

Shortly after the dive brief, everyone started putting their scuba gear on and trying to get in the water as fast as possible, maximizing their dive time. One thing about scuba diving trips, they follow a consistent pattern of dive, eat, and then dive some more. Generally, you can get anywhere from four or five dives a day. Most conversations people had with each other on the boat were generally about the type of fish or coral that they saw on the last dive, or a hope that they would see it on an upcoming dive.

"Hey, are you up to doing this dive?" Barry asks.

Gary replied, "Yes, I am. You're going to love seeing the Yongala site. Now we are doing a regular air tank dive so hopefully we can stay down on the Yongala wreck for at least 45 or 60 minutes. Also, let's just take our time descending to about 110 feet."

Gary had all his gear on and waited for Barry to put on his equipment. Once he had all his gear on Gary asked, "Ok Barry can you do a scuba gear check for me?"

Barry looks confused asking what Gary wants him to check?

"Never mind I'm pretty sure that my gear is on correctly. Let me do a gear check for you." Gary starts to go through the gear checklist on Barry's gear. This checklist is something that you learn at the very beginning of your lessons for scuba diving. Gary checks for any tangles in his primary regulator and also his secondary regulator. He also checks that Barry's air tank is turned on and open. Gary checks Barry's dive computer and checks that his BCD vest is on correctly and that his weight belt has the proper amount of weights.

Now they are all set and wait patiently to get into the water. When it is their time, they go down the stairs to the flat platform which will allow them to put on their fins. There is a crew member on the platform with a clipboard that each diver needs to initial at the beginning and end of their dives. The crew member also checks that their air tank is fully on. Gary initials the clipboard and hands it to Barry. Barry was hoping for this to happen, it didn't happen earlier. Now that Gary put his initials down, Barry crossed out Gary's initials and initials in the space next to his own name. By doing this he effectively makes it seem as if Gary did not go on this dive.

"Barry let's just take our time on this. We need to stay together and not wander off. We also need to be clear on the hand signals."

Barry says sarcastically, "Ok Gary, I get it. Come on let's go down there."

Barry and Gary swam over to the guideline that they will use to descend. They both started to slowly descend down to the ocean bottom. As they descend, pressure builds up in their sinuses and they must clear this using the 'Valsalva' technique.

Barry was dropping like a rock and not equalizing. Eventually Gary caught up with him and Gary could tell he had a problem with the pressure build up in his ears again. Gary mimicked to Barry to pinch his nose and blow out. After doing this about 4 times, Barry gave him a thumbs up. Wrong hand signal. Thumbs up means go to the surface. Gary mimicked the ok hand symbol which is where you make a circle with your thumb and index finger. Once again, Barry did a thumbs up signal. Gary shrugged his shoulders to indicate that he did not understand. Barry did the 'Ok' symbol realizing why Gary was confused. They continued diving and exploring the reef.

The SS Yongala ship is just amazing. There is every type and size of fish and coral outcroppings. Everywhere you look there is something interesting to see. The boat is tilted to the left and you can see all the compartments and rooms on the ship. The rule that we were told by the crew was not to go inside the ship or to touch any of the fish or coral outcropping.

Gary was looking at a fantastic coral formation at the bow of the ship. Barry swims toward Gary and does not stop his momentum so he bumps right into Gary. Now, Barry is stepping on the coral formations and breaking them off. At one point, he steps on a part of the boat and breaks it off.

Gary is mortified and pissed off. Enough of this guy. Now Barry is chasing a grey reef shark swimming away from the boat, Gary is able to catch up to him and motions him to go back to the Yongala. Barry shakes his head 'no'. Barry reaches over to Gary and pulls his mask off. Gary is surprised and pissed. Once Gary exhales and replaces the water that was in his mask, he again looks for Barry. Barry is now another 50 feet away

Gary thinks why the hell would Roger go diving with guy? Gary catches up with Barry. It's only sand here. Gary looks for the ship, but the visibility is not great, but he is pretty sure if he back tracks, he will be able to find the ship. Barry points even further away from the ship. Gary says no and points behind where he believes the ship is. Barry looks at Gary with a big grin and then pulls his mask off again. As Gary is trying to clear his mask, Barry reaches over and turns Gary's air off. While Gary is dealing with his mask, Barry takes off his weight belt, of 45 lbs. of lead, and puts it on Gary with the release clip in the back so it will be difficult to get off. And then Barry swims back to the ship.

Gary looks at his dive computer and it says that he has been down at 110 feet for too long. He was down here at this depth for an hour and twenty minutes which is 20 minutes longer than he should. Gary starts to have problems getting oxygen and realizes that his tank has been turned off. Gary tries his safety respirator, and it is still bad. Worry starts to creep in from the sides. Gary can't reach the knob to turn the air tank on. Ok well this is what you train for when you get certified. First you need to take off the BCD vest. Gary can't get the weight belt off because it is hooked around his BCD vest and the release clip is in the center of his back.

Nitrogen Narcosis is starting to envelop his body and brain. Gary has felt this before and knows that if he doesn't fix this soon and ascend that he will die. Slowly Gary can feel the different parts of his body start to shut down. As unconsciousness comes marching toward him, he stops struggling and uses whatever air is left. I guess Barry didn't totally turn off the air; Gary takes little sips of air. Unconsciousness won and Gary stops struggling. Gary is trying to not go unconscious, but it starts to win. Just before Gary goes under, he sees a hand turning him over and taking off that bloody weight belt. His last thought was why did Barry do this? Was this Roger's plan from the beginning?

One of the divers on board the Spoil Sport is looking for Gary to show him some of the pictures he had taken on the latest dive. He asked one of the crew members, if Gary had finished his dive or was still under? He says, "No, Gary never left the boat."

The diver that was looking for Gary said he absolutely went diving. He saw him under water by the bow of the Yongala ship. This is worrying for the crew member. He looks at his sheet again and doesn't see Gary's initials. But maybe he forgot. Better safe than sorry. He tells the captain that there is another diver down there and all the other divers have signed in, except Gary McKeown.

Four divers from the crew check in all directions. The crewman, Steve, finds Gary and immediately puts his second respirator for Gary to buddy breathe. He turns Gary's unconscious body so he can remove the weight belts from Gary's gear. He takes Gary and makes a rapid ascent to the surface.

Next, Gary is being carried up on the boat and placed on the top part of the boat. The captain radios the EMT's and they are sending a medical helicopter. The captain asks the crew to clear all the sunbathing chairs and block the steps up to this part of the boat from other divers.

In about 30 minutes there is a medical helicopter landing on the top floor of the boat which is usually used for sunbathing. The medical team carries Gary from where he was laid down, on a stretcher, and then onto the helicopter.

Barry runs up to the helicopter and starts to get in. The first aid people said no way. Barry said that Gary was his brother and he needed to go with them. The guy in the helicopter grimaces and then nods his head for him to get on board. Barry is happy to be done with the scuba diving. It bored him to tears. So tired of pretending to be really interested in the fish or the slimy coral. The only thing that Barry was thinking when looking at those fish was wishing he had a spear gun to shoot at them. The whole time he was underwater he kept thinking about what each fish would taste like.

They are about 25 minutes from Mater Hospital in Brisbane. After they land on the roof of the hospital, Barry follows them to the elevator to take Gary to the emergency department. Barry acts like he is following them there but stops at the intake desk to give the clerk Gary's name and insurance information. He also gives a contact number of Roger's cell phone. Barry asks her if there is a bathroom. She points to the right of the automatic doors to exit; Barry says he will be back in a moment. As he walks towards the men's room, he goes out of the emergency door as another couple is walking through the doors. Barry never makes it to the restroom.

Barry flags a taxi down and asks him to get him to the airport. Roger is going to be pissed that he hadn't finished the job. The little bits he heard in the helicopter was that he was showing signs of an acute nitrogen narcosis coma. This new event may make Roger happy.

Chapter 2 - Lucy McKeown

"Watch out world

I am wearing my sassy pants today!!"

- Lucille Ball

Lucy McKeown, who is 49 years old, has always been in good shape and has a lean body to show for it. Her figure is highlighted with a head of fiery, red curly hair. She has dealt and worked with men who look at her and think that she can be easily swayed or intimidated. Make no mistake on that! Men have tried to act all superior making sure the little women will do what they want. She doesn't mind playing along if it gets her to achieve her goal. However, if you poke the bull then be ready to get the horns!

Growing up with her younger brother, Gary, there were some real knockout fights. He always knew how to get under her skin and push the right buttons. Gary has a special gift in which he has a nearly perfect, total recall of anything that he sees or reads. When they were younger, this could be infuriating. He would correct her about any of the slightest details that she was describing to him or to someone else. Lucy remembers slamming many doors when she was a teenager. Conversely, she knew the way to get him to *toe the line*. Maybe it was a maternal thing, but at times she knew that if she offered any comment toward the quality of their daily chores, he would just short-circuit.

She was almost nineteen and Gary was seventeen, when they both learned about the death of their parents. This was devastating. Every part of their lives turned upside down. This was a turning point for the both them. An unspoken truce developed. They were both hurt, as anyone would be. It became apparent that if one tried to hurt the other, then they were indirectly hurting themselves.

Lucy is usually a calm person and rarely gets very annoyed or angry. Today was not that day. She is feeling extra angry today! It's not that she's in a rush, or there was heavy traffic, she just felt mad at everyone and everything. Lucy turned on the radio and a popular song came on. She liked this song but turning it up really wasn't doing anything to improve her mood.

Lucy navigates her blue Subaru though the winding path to get to Ashwood, a long-term care facility. This is where her younger brother, Gary, was being treated as a patient. Gary had returned from Australia in a type of coma called an "anoxic" coma. This type is largely due to oxygen deprivation. Gary had been in this coma state for the last 2 years.

Lucy pulls into the Ashwood facility and the same thought keeps bouncing into her head. Why do they call it a *long-term care facility*? It's a nursing home. This is a familiar conversation that she has with herself every time she drives the 45 minutes to visit her brother.

Walking through the front entrance, she goes to the set of elevators on her right. On the ride up to the third floor, the feelings of anger and annoyance turn into a feeling of sadness and longing. She misses her brother.

When the elevator door opens, she walks over to the nurse's station. One of the nurses sees Lucy and pushes her chair away from the computer to face her. She could see the monitor the nurse was looking at and it was no surprise that it was her Facebook page. This nurse, Milly, was someone Lucy usually saw when she came here every couple of weeks.

As usual, Milly is wearing light green hospital scrubs and white tennis shoes. One her chest she has a solid blue patch with a white tree in the middle and below the tree it says "Milly Howards, RN".

"Hi Milly. Have there been any changes on Gary's care that I should know about?", Lucy asks.

Milly pulled out Gary's chart, attached are several papers that show all of the blood tests, brain tests, and various care items like feeding, or changing his different linens etc.

"Nope. No changes since last time.", Milly said with a strong emphasis of "last time".

"Has the financial department contacted you? Betsy Richter came by earlier today and said that she needs to talk to you", Milly adds.

Lucy says, *"Nope"* trying to mimic Milly's last response to her. Why does anyone say "nope"? Saying just 'No' is a smaller word and conveys the same thing.

"You can give Betsy my cell phone number if you want."

As Lucy was walking toward Gary's room, she could hear each room's combinations of noise makers. Whir, hum, buzz, or beep. Each room added to the concerto that was being played for the long spotless white hall. It's kind of funny but also not funny. These monitors and machines helped each person's health in some unique way.

Even though it was only about 1:00 everyone seemed to be sleeping. From Lucy's point of view if someone died, Milly wouldn't probably detect that until the next shift came on for the evening.

This was frustrating that the staff didn't see the obvious minimum care they should be giving to patients. She doesn't need to get into the politics of the Ashwood facility, because she keeps on top of Gary's care. She must do this because if *she gave them an inch, they will take a mile.*

As Lucy rounds the corner and enters room 33C, she sees Gary in his bed, hooked up to several machines. Some to check blood pressure, another to give fluids, and others to administer various nutrients to his body. Lucy is not startled or shocked to see her brother like this. She visits Gary often, so she is used to this. However, it does make her feel very sad. She misses talking with Gary. She misses both the laughing and fun that they had always shared and also some of the arguments they would get into. But now is not the time for sadness or self-pity.

Lucy has a routine that she follows every time she comes to visit. She reaches into her pocketbook and brings out a notepad. She lists the things needed to be attended to by Ashwood staff. They have not given him a shave since the last time she visited. He should get a haircut. She walks to the end of his bed and looked at his chart. It's supposed to list anything that the staff has done for his care. She's not surprised to see several days with blank entries.

It annoys her when she sees this. It just highlights that Ashwood is not doing a great job taking care of him. She makes several entries in her notebook.

Lucy pulls out a bottle of skin conditioner and begins to cover Gary's feet, legs, and arms with this. She washes his face; pulls out a razor, bottle of shaving cream and a small hand towel and proceeds to shave the growing beard and mustache on Gary's face. Ashwood really doesn't like it when she does this. They are concerned with liability rather than personal care. The staff here only does as little as they can get away with. Next, Lucy takes hold of Gary's limbs and moves them all around and does little stretching exercises for his tendons and muscles.

After she had finished shaving Gary, and was satisfied with his clean-cut face, she reached into her voluminous pocketbook and pulled out the Stephen King book "Dead Zone". This was a book that Gary had read several times. Lucy never understood why he would reread a book since he has an almost perfect recall or eidetic memory. He said he just likes to go through the process of reading the story. The smells, the colors, the tastes, and the feelings conveyed by the author are a little different each time he rereads a book. She found it ironic that this book was one of Gary's favorites. The story is about a guy that's in an accident and ends up in a coma. The character wakes up after several years and discovers he has a new psychic power of precognition. Maybe Gary ironically had a precognition that he would be in a coma many years later after reading this book.

Lucy finishes the chapter she was reading and collects the things that she brought in with her and heads out to her car. When she passes the nurse's station, she talks to Milly about seeing if she could have someone give Gary a haircut and also to make sure that he was being attended to on a regular basis.

Milly says "Yup."

Lucy walks over to the elevator and starts to make her way out to her car. She was just opening the door to the parking lot when someone from behind her called out her name. She turned to face the person with the screechy voice echoing and reverberating in the large atrium.

"Ms. Hamilton, ah Ms. Hamilton? May I please speak to you?" That voice is Betsy Richter from the financial office. She always addresses Lucy with her married name. She had changed her last name back to her maiden name because it was a constant reminder of her husband, David, who died from cancer 12 years ago.

Betsy asks if she had time, could she come to her office to discuss the financial arrangements for Gary's care. Betsy has one of those super sweet fake personalities that was far from being sweet and far from being real.

Betsy said, "Ms. Hamilton, I have tried several times to reach you regarding the cost of your brother's care. I wanted to alert you that the cost for your brother's care has gone up substantially. Four months ago, the cost for your brother's care increased by five thousand dollars. The money that was being sent to Ashwood for Gary's care wasn't the full amount to cover his care.

Lucy was speechless. Since the day that Roger Tillson called her to inform her about Gary's scuba diving accident, he has been true to his word. She remembers it as if it was yesterday. Roger made a solemn promise to her that the cost for Gary's care would be paid, no matter what the cost.

"Did you speak to Mr. Tillson about this? He's the one who has been paying the cost for Gary to be here. I'm sure that he would be able to take care of this."

Betsy looked a little baffled. "Tillson? I am not aware of a Mr. Tillson being involved in the financial responsibility for your brother's care. I always assumed it was paid by you, or that Gary had set up a trust account to provide for his care. Let me pull up the account and let's take a little *looksy*", Betsy said as she plopped into her chair.

After a minute or two, Betsy said "When your brother was first brought here, we received a letter from a company called Trinity Trust Holdings in Boston. They asked that all financial bills and statements be sent to an account at Trinity Trust Holdings. For the last two years every bill sent to this account has been paid for within one business day. For the past four months the bills were sent but the payment was only enough to cover the cost of his care before it was increased."

Betsy continued, "I am sorry about this, but we really need to find a solution. The current total for Gary is $22,575. At least half of it needs to be paid by the end of the month, which is in two weeks. If payment cannot be made, then I'm sorry to tell you that Gary will need to be moved to a different care facility. For the last several years all, patients that are unable to pay for the full amount of their care are sent to the state-run UMass hospital in Worcester."

Lucy knew the UMass Hospital very well. It's not a place where you would want to be a patient. There have been many stories about different doctors being sued and a high rate of patient deaths over the years. Many have given it a nickname as the *Death Hospital*. People go in, but they do not come out. It sent shivers up and down Lucy's back.

Betsy continued her rambling on about the cost of her brother's care. She said they could accept a credit card, a cashier's check; or if Lucy had a saving's account with enough money to cover at least half of this bill today.

Lucy is only half hearing Betsy. It was taking an enormous amount of energy to get control of the tornado of thoughts and emotions going around in her head. She just kept repeating in her head "that bastard! that son of bitch!" I knew I should not have given Roger any control over Gary's care. Who or what is this Trinity Trust Holdings company?'

She said to herself, stay focused. How can I possibly pay this off? And then it hit her all at once. First things first. Get my brother out of this place. She can take care of him better than they can. Why does Gary need to be here, really?

She and her husband were very good at saving money. Nothing extraordinary. A little bit here and a little bit there started to add up after a while. When David died, he left a lump sum of money for Lucy and the kids. This helped to cover bills for tuition and also to help pay down the mortgage. She felt the cruel irony of his love when anyone called her by her married name.

Why didn't she think of this earlier? She paid off the mortgage several years ago, so paying the money for this hospital was not something that she couldn't have. That's exactly what I am going to do. Busy with the paperwork, Betsy didn't really notice that she wasn't paying attention to her.

Then, Lucy interrupted Betsy in mid-sentence and said, "Betsy I do not want Gary to be moved to the UMass hospital. I will be going to the bank tomorrow, to get a cashier's check for the balance that is due. Please let me know the total amount that is due by 10:00 AM. I will have an ambulance take my brother from Ashwood at 2:00 PM. I would appreciate it if you could have all the paperwork ready for me when the ambulance is here. I will also need to know the address and phone number for the company that has been sending payments for Gary."

Now it was Betsy's turn to be speechless. "Ok, if you want any of the medical records for Gary then please let me know the name of the long-term facility that will be handling your brother's care."

26

Lucy looked at Betsy with a firm commanding face and said, "Betsy, I will be taking my brother home to live in my house. Honestly, it's just easier for me to give my brother the care that he needs. I am quite sure I can do as well if not even better than Ashwood have done."

Betsy made one last attempt with Lucy, "How are you going to be able to take care of Gary? How are you going to do that? You won't have any of the medical supplies or medical equipment that is needed. How will you transport him to your house? I have already called the UMass hospital and they said they would hold a bed for him at the end of the month. Ms. Hamilton. I really think you are making a big mistake. Also, I do not think that moving your brother is legal!"

That was a big mistake for Betsy. She assumed that this would be fine without Lucy's input. Betsy thought that tossing the veiled threat to Lucy about this not being legal would make Lucy comply. Nope, that is not going to happen. If Betsy wants to play this game Lucy thought, then I can also play with her.

"Betsy it is unfortunate that you did not include me into your plans for Gary to move to the UMass Hospital. If you had consulted with me on this, I would not have agreed to it. So legally you are not allowed to move Gary unless I approve it. I am my brother's health care proxy and his legal guardian. This means that all medical decisions for Gary are with me. I plan to bring him home to my house, I can take care of him just as well, if not better than Ashwood has. I have a large room on the first floor of my house that will be perfectly sufficient for Gary's care. These are my brother's wishes when he asked me to be his health care proxy. So, if you could have all the paperwork done by 2:00, that would be perfect" Lucy said assertively.

Betsy was still speechless, it appeared she was having a hard time wrapping her head around this. Finally, she said, "Ok I will get the paperwork ready for tomorrow, but it will be tough to complete on such short notice. Do you want me to see if one of the Ashwood staff would be able to continue his care? They could stop by to help you on a regular basis."

It was difficult to contain her pleasure when Betsy said it would be difficult to get the paperwork done. Ha! Betsy had no problem cornering her and asking her for $22 thousand dollars payable in two weeks. Lucy responded, "No Betsy, I have been in contact with several different hospice organizations that are closer to me. When I spoke to them one woman came out and looked at where I would have Gary and felt that it was not a problem at all. In fact, she said that she would be able to provide a comfortable bed, like the ones used in hospitals, and provide any medical supplies or equipment that Gary would need. I think this will be a better situation for Gary." Lucy hated to tell lies but everything she just said to Betsy was a total lie. The look on Betsy face was all that Lucy wanted. The cash stream that Ms. Hamilton (McKeown) brought in was now shut off.

As Lucy walked out to her car she was smiling. Why didn't I do this earlier? On the drive home she thought, now where the hell will I find a hospital bed for Gary? Her favorite song came on the radio, and she turned the volume up as loud as she could. Lucy was very happy, indeed.

Chapter 3 - Freddie

"Anyone who does anything to help a child

in his or her life is a hero to me."

— *Fred Rogers*

One year later

The late July sun was overhead and felt great. To Lucy, the air and the warmth felt like being wrapped in her most comfortable robe and slippers. The smell of pine trees and pinecones filled the air. The squirrels at the border of Lucy's property were just running back and forth dancing to their own tune. Chasing each other and then running up a tree and then immediately running down. Lucy never really figured that one out, but it made her smile and laugh each time she saw them.

Lucy was in a zone right now. Wearing her ear buds and listening to an eclectic playlist of songs booming from her old iPod. Lucy is wearing a big white and red poker dot hat. Apparently, it's the new 'La Rive Gauche' to make yourself look like a red and white beetle. She doesn't care because the music is turned all the way up, and she is wiggling her butt to the beat of the music as she's tending to her garden.

The smells from her rows of tomatoes, zucchini, and cucumber plants are unique and distinct. The garden has a very musky and intoxicating smell. The soil is a strange color of deep dark brown. Almost black but not quite. The soil looks moist but not necessarily with water. It contains a rich amount of nitrogen, phosphorus, and potassium. Only the best for my garden Lucy thought.

Lucy is so content with her gardening that she doesn't notice the big white and black shadow coming up behind her. When Lucy turns, she sees Gary's 4-year-old Great Dane, Freddie. He has dirt all over his nose and several bits of roses, sunflowers, begonia stems and flowers either in his mouth or on his black and white fur. Lucy can't decide to be angry at him for destroying her flowers or laughing at how cute he is. Freddie realizes that she likes the flowers he brought her so now she's going to give him a treat or play *rip up the flowers* game with him. Lucy can't contain it and bursts out laughing. Lucy feigns with her right hand that she is going pat him and give him some affection. And then the left hand comes down quickly and starts scratching Freddie's belly and long neck. He falls for this every time. But that's ok, he likes it, and he gives Lucy a big, sloppy lick all over her face. Freddie likes this game.

Looking at her watch, Lucy realizes that she needs to go to the grocery store before her two boys come over for dinner tonight. She rushes inside the house and changes her clothes; grabs her wallet, keys, and phone; puts Freddie's water dish outside; and gets in her car.

As Lucy is driving to the grocery store, she thinks about what has happened with her brother since his trip to Australia. When Gary traveled, she always got a message from Gary of where he was. Gary had been looking forward to this diving trip for a while, so it would not be unusual for Gary to extend this trip for a few days or a week. Christmas and New Year in Australia occurred in the warmest months of the southern hemisphere. Lucy thought maybe he would stay longer because it was so far away.

After two weeks of not hearing anything, she started calling some of the people that might provide more information on where Gary might be. The first call was to Gary's friend and diving partner, Ben Costello. When she called his cell number it rang for a long time before someone picked up.

"Hi, is this Ben Costello?" Lucy asks.

"Yes, it is. Who is this?"

"This is Lucy McKeown, Gary McKeown's sister. I was wondering if you knew where Gary is. I haven't heard anything from him since before his trip to Australia."

Ben responds after several seconds and with a little hesitation, "Sorry Lucy, but I don't know where he is. I broke my leg on the day we were supposed to fly out of Logan. I had to cancel my trip, but I thought he was still going anyways."

"Ok thanks Ben. If you hear anything, please let me know."

There was a slight pause when Ben answered her question. Most times that hesitation, even if it is a slight one, tells a lot. Generally, it means that a person is hunting or searching for words. Lucy doesn't buy it.

She went to his hi-rise apartment in the city and could not find him. The man at the front desk knew Gary and said that he had not seen him at all for several weeks. Lucy called Gary's work number and still no one answered. Lucy started to worry. His absence and not checking in with her was very peculiar. He usually calls to let me, and others know that he's ok.

Maybe his assistant, Rose, knows where he is. Lucy met Rose several times since Gary hired her. She liked her and thought she was the perfect *anti-Gary*. She's one of those people that's incredibly meticulous and detailed. She also has no problem speaking her mind about anyone or anything. One night, Rose and her husband had gone to dinner to celebrate Gary's birthday. Rose said jokingly that the four years she had worked for him were such a chore, but she really loved it. He contradicted her claim that he hired her four years ago, Gary said it was five years ago.

Rose just looked at him like he was a little boy, like a foreigner and who didn't know how to speak English. She raised her voice thinking that talking louder in English would translate the meaning of what she was saying.

She said "You really are a lost cause. No, you are wrong. I still have the offer letter that you gave to me, and it has been four years and three months since I have worked with you. You really are very forgetful, where would you be if you didn't have me keeping all this straight for you?"

Gary looked at Lucy and winked. Lucy knew that he was giving Rose a 'win'. Gary has a very uncommon type of memory. This rare gift, an eidetic memory, allows him to have a nearly perfect memory recall of anything that he hears or reads. She knew that he was letting Rose win this one.

Since Rose was always plugged in, she knew where everybody was. Lucy called Rose's cell number. She picked it up on the first ring. Lucy told her that she had not heard from Gary, and he was missing. Lucy asked Rose if she had heard from Gary or if she knew where he is currently. Rose said that she had not heard anything. In fact, she had tried to contact him and just got his voice mail. Rose said that she would look into this and if she finds out anything she will call. She also gave Lucy, Roger Tillson's contact number and said that he might have some more information about Gary's whereabouts.

The next day after talking to Rose, Lucy called Roger. When she dialed the number, the phone rang for a long time. She was just about to hang up when a woman answered.

Lucy asked, "May I speak to Roger Tillson?"

The female voice on the other end said quickly, "Wrong number." And hung up the phone. Lucy redialed but this time the line was busy.

Ironically, Roger called her a couple of days after she attempted to talk to him. He told Lucy that Gary was in a scuba diving accident. He continued by saying that he brought Gary home to Boston two weeks earlier and had him checked into the Ashwood Long-term Facility. Roger also mentioned about how much money he had spent to have Gary flown home. This was Roger's classic sound bite that he likes to play. Implying, all would be lost if Roger had not been there and saved the day.

She had only interacted with him on three different occasions. The first time was at a company sponsored event to celebrate reaching a certain sales target. The event was a huge 'dog and pony' show for potential venture capital investors. Lucy was a master at detecting 'bullshit'. Right from the start she could see through Roger's s smarmy salesman-like demeanor. It was very phony and disingenuous.

Roger asked Lucy to meet him at the Ashwood facility. She agreed to meet the next day. She met Roger at the Ashwood facility and he wanted her to sign several documents concerning Gary's care. She confronted Roger with why he had not called her almost a month ago when this happened. Roger stammered a little bit, but he told Lucy that immigration was difficult because Gary did not have his passport. Lucy half heard Roger because she knew that she would never find out the real truth about this.

Of all the documents Roger wanted her to sign, two of the documents she would not sign. The first was a form that named Roger as the power of attorney. Gary already had a signed a document that made Lucy his power of attorney. Another document was to make Roger his Healthcare Proxy. Again, Gary already had a signed document that named Lucy and her son, Peter, as his Healthcare Proxy. The last document named the person who would be responsible for the financial charges. Lucy said that she should be the named person on the contracts. Roger looked at Lucy and made a solemn vow to her that he would take care of all the finances. He just wished for Gary to get better.

Lucy was not going to give Roger any type of power with respect to Gary's health. Once again, people thought that her good looks and pleasant personality were a sign of being ditzy or just a dumb woman who would just sign whatever was put in from of her. Nope, that will never happen.

Lucy remembered that meeting with Roger from time to time, but today she had errands to do, and Gary needed to be cared for.

Later that day....4:00 PM

When Lucy got home and unloaded all the groceries, she had time to go through her normal routine daily care for Gary. As usual, Freddie follows Lucy into the former office where Gary is staying. Several machines and IV tubes are connected to him. She starts to wash his face and arms. She puts a couple of towels under his head and does her best to wash his hair. Usually, she did this when either the kids were here to help her, or with the help of the strong hospice nurse, who stopped by twice a week. She checks that all the fluids are properly connected; and checks his blood pressure, temperature, and oxygen levels. Everything looks good.

Freddie can't stand it any longer, he wants to see his friend Gary. Freddie stands up on his hind legs and sees that Gary is sleeping. He takes two big licks of Gary's face thinking that Gary will wake up and play. He goes back down on four legs and looks at Lucy and nudges Gary's hand. Nothing happens. Freddie doesn't understand. If he does that with Lucy or her sons and if he is persistent enough, he will get a belly scratch or a treat. He likes both of those options and sometimes he gets both a treat and a belly scratch. What a life.

Lucy rewashes Gary's face and hands. And then she goes to the kitchen to make dinner. Freddie usually would follow because he would always get scraps. But today he decides he's going to stay here in his dog bed until his friend wakes up. Freddie's dog bed was actually a full-size couch that Freddie had claimed as his bed. Within 15 minutes, Freddie is asleep and having dog dreams of running though fields trying to catch rabbits or something.

…. After Dinner

"Mom, that was great, thanks. I wish the cafeteria at school had something like this. The food there doesn't even come close to this" says Patrick McKeown as he gets up and helps his brother Peter clear the table.

"Don't worry Patrick, I made two extra pans of lasagna. One for you and one for your brother."

Patrick looked at Peter with a little grin on his face. He was hoping that she would make extra "left-overs" to bring back with him to college.

After dinner was cleaned up, Lucy asked her boys if they wanted some desert.

Peter said, "I can't right now, I'm too full." Patrick nodded in agreement.

"Ok, let's sit down and catch up. Tell me what's going on with you two. How's the new job working out, Peter?" Lucy said. Peter McKeown was 22 years old and had recently graduated from North Eastern College in Boston. He had just started working at a software company in Cambridge, MA. Usually, he stayed at his girlfriend's apartment, but occasionally he would come back home, even if Lucy had to bribe him with Lasagna.

"This company is awesome. People are super friendly. They assigned another developer to shadow me and show me the ropes. We get along great. He's an older guy, like 35, and he's a wicked gamer", Peter answered.

"That's great, I'm really happy for you. My credit card is also very happy that you're working," she said and gave Patrick a wink.

Peter started to say something, but Freddie starts barking and whimpering. Freddie comes rushing around the corner forgetting that he's a really big dog and that his momentum does not stop his forward motion. Freddie slams into the wall but is unfazed and keeps running at full tilt toward the couch that Lucy and Patrick were sitting on. The whole time, Freddie was barking and whimpering.

Immediately, Lucy thought Freddie had to go outside. Peter was ahead of her and opened the door to let Freddie out. Freddie didn't make a move to the door. Freddie's barking was getting more insistent. Freddie looked at Lucy and gave a big growl bark. Ok, something is up. Freddie races out of the room and down the hall to the room where Gary was staying. Lucy is now worried. Freddie never acts like this.

Patrick, Peter, and Lucy ran into Gary's room. The lights are off but most of the machines throw out a green glow and make tiny noises. Lucy turns on the lights and looks at Gary's bed. Some of the noises that the machines are making are actually alarms to signify that it was not receiving any of a dozen vital signs. Lucy looks at the bed and Gary's eyes are wide open, and he is sitting up in the bed. Lucy is too stunned to say anything. Patrick doesn't hesitate and blurts out, "Holy SHIT". Gary looks at Patrick, Peter and Lucy and says, "Hi guys!" Freddie sticks his nose in between everyone and looks at Gary.

Gary gives a little pat on Freddie's head. "Hey buddy, WOW you have grown."

Chapter 4 - Grandpa Joe

"...no good can ever come from spoiling a child like that, Charlie, you mark my words."

- Grandpa Joe Bucket in the movie Charlie and the Chocolate Factory

It's been about a week since Gary woke up from his long coma. Lucy and the kids still wear a face of incredulity, disbelieving that he's awake. Freddie wasn't surprised at all. He was just happy beyond belief that his friend was back.

At first on that night, there was absolute silence after Lucy and her boys entered the room and saw him sitting up, and awake. Freddie broke that silence with a big loud yelp. After the initial shock, everybody was talking at the same time. Lucy looked at Gary's face and knew that he was getting into a sensory overload with questions coming at him all at once. She told Patrick and Peter to take Freddie out for a walk, so she could talk to Gary. Freddie wouldn't budge one inch, so Patrick and Peter, understanding the situation left the room to watch a little TV.

As Lucy had noticed, she was right that he was trying to take everything in all at once. His brain was overwhelmed. Gary started to feel like he was going to go back to sleep. This is not what he wanted. With tremendous effort, he is trying to maintain his focus on being awake. Going from a constant state of "unconscious" to "conscious" was difficult but if you really focus hard on being awake it is possible. He realized this is very similar to driving and forcing yourself to stay awake.

Slowly, as he became more and more awake. Looking around his bed, he couldn't quite name or recognize things, but each item had a feeling of it being familiar, or not familiar. The rush of looking at his surroundings and just trying to figure out where he was at the moment. There was no reference point to navigate from. One thing at a time here. He looked at the woman in the room with him and he immediately knew she was his sister Lucy. That was easy. Freddie was his buddy and faithful companion. Peter and Patrick were his nephews, but when he thought of their names it was a little fuzzy. When he focused his mind on his nephews and their names, a picture of him running along a beach and throwing a frisbee with them. More and more things started to come back and rush in.

He was really struggling for each and everything that his mind could classify. Across the room there was a squarish box and a screen. he looked at it and instantly knew it was a computer. But for the life of him, he could not "name" the thing that the computer was sitting on.

It felt like he was swimming in maple syrup. He knew that there were parts missing. Almost reflexively, his brain started to create a catalog of items that he knew and a catalog of the things that he doesn't know. For instance, Gary recognized this room because several years ago, his reference point was that he had helped Lucy paint the room. He even remembered the stupid paint color it was painted in, "sassy grass green".

He looked at Lucy and just instinctually knew they were related, and she was his sister. Memories of growing up with her and their parents came easily. All the times of laughing and all the times of the fighting were so clear. He recalls a lot of good times and the laughter that they shared. And, also the bitter knock down fights and arguments. Parts of his memories came in a flood and were "in focus". He could recall every word that was said. So why are these memories so sharp and clear and a lot more are not?

It seems sort of contradictory that he was getting tired and felt that he needed to rest. His brain went from almost nothing to exploding rockets and chaos all at once. He knew that this was not normal for him.

Lucy went out to get him some ice cream and some water to drink. Freddie was still there, a cement statue, vigilantly watching Gary. Freddie would not let his hand go out of sight and at all times was within petting or licking distance. He smiled at Freddie. Freddie was constantly checking that he was awake, and always in reach of a pat on the head or belly.

Looking at Freddie was adding to his confusion. Freddie was only 6 months old when he adopted him from the animal shelter. Now, he was fully grown and about a 120 to 140 pounds, so much larger since he last saw him.

Lucy came in with a big, oversized coffee mug filled with black raspberry ice cream and a large glass of water. Again, he thought, what's the name of the flavor of this ice cream? He knows that he's eating ice cream but can't remember the flavor name. It was delicious even if it was unnamed.

For the next 15 minutes, Lucy tried to bring Gary up to date. At first, she started to tell him that he had been in a coma for 3 years. How is that possible? She talked about their family. He recognized Lucy as his sister and recognized her two sons. Some parts of the story will come later but she wanted to stay away from the discussions of scuba diving, Roger, Ben, his company, and even his unique memory gift. First things first! She stressed that he was safe here. He was only expected to be here and recover in as much time as he needed to.

The shock of waking up and being very disoriented started to slowly dissipate, However, there were many questions that still needed to be answered. He remembers Lucy and their parents very clearly. He also remembers his childhood and school. He remembers Lucy's two sons. He remembers Freddie. All these experiences and people he can recall immediately. But there are some parts of his life that are just blank spots in his mind. No matter how hard he tries to recall people or events they just remain blank spots.

He started to get frustrated. Why can't I remember why I woke up in Lucy's house? Why can't I remember big parts of my life that are hiding? He kept asking Lucy to help fill in the gaps. Some of his questions were about family and growing up. Both Lucy and Gary had a very good childhood. Their mother and father were great parents and always put their children first. They talked about the holidays they shared. Again, Lucy was purposely avoiding any conversation abo the scuba diving and his trip to Australia that put him in this state.

He may have had big chunks of memories missing, or locked up, but he could always tell when his sister was reluctant to talk about something, or how she avoided conversations.

"I know you've done so much for me, but I can always tell when you're evading or not telling the whole truth.," he said with a slight grin on his face.

"What do you mean? We have covered a lot of information tonight. How about we talk more in the morning?" Lucy said, evading his question altogether.

He knew that she was evading his questions, but how he got to her house didn't seem like the most difficult answer for her. How he ended up in Lucy's house kept gnawing at him more and more. A big piece of the puzzle is missing, and he can't find it.

In the weeks that followed, He started to become a little famous around town. Several doctors and nurses volunteered to come over to Lucy's house to check him out and run him through a multitude of physical and cognitive tests. Everything appeared to be fine with no abnormal findings. The doctors and neurologist's that came to see him all explained that each person's mind has a funny way of remembering things.

Most people go through their day, and if asked to recall something, it will usually be just a tiny bit of information that was recorded. Usually, it will be a small piece of visual memory.

For instance, if someone asked you to tell them what it was that you bought at a coffee shop last Thursday, the typical scenario is that you would focus your mind on Thursday and try to see the coffee shop. You will probably see the coffee shop and will remember that you bought a coffee and a muffin. There are probably other details you could dredge up like the size of the coffee and maybe the type of the muffin you bought.

Someone with an eidetic memory like Gary's records everything. It records what is felt, seen, heard, touched, or tasted at the coffee shop. He could tell you the exact time, the exact size and kind of coffee, the number of different flavors of muffins or donuts; if the muffin was bland tasting; that it is freezing cold rain outside; that the coldness is leaking into the coffee shop; that the girl at the counter had fifteen tattoos on her forearms, that her nose had a ring pierced to the right side of her nose; and the guy behind him smelled like he had taken a shower in his cologne this morning. Every single detail was recorded and stored in his memory.

Freddie started to relax his ever-vigilant watch. Gary was awake, and it did not look like this was going to happen again. Of course, he growled and barked when nurses and doctors were underfoot and ran tests on him, but slowly Freddie started to relax a little more and felt sure that the long nap wouldn't come back.

After several weeks passed, the nurses and doctors came over to Lucy's house to make a final house call for Gary. They came and disconnected all IVs, electrocardiogram probes, and, generally removed everything else that needed to be disconnected. The doctors and nurses were all very grateful to be allowed to see him. He'd become somewhat of a medical miracle. Usually, it's rare for someone in a coma that long to completely come back physically and mentally.

The next stage of his recovery was going to be physical therapy to help him start to regain some of the muscle mass that was lost in his comatose state. His weakened muscles were a big problem at first. Lucy, the watchdog, insisted that he not get out of bed unsupervised, unless helped by Lucy, or one of her two sons.

The first time he got out of bed unsupervised he felt ok at first but navigating across the room, with nothing to hold onto for balance, proved to be too much. Lucy heard him fall and crash on the floor. She rushed in and helped him to get back to bed. The whole time scolding him for doing such a stupid thing. At the same time, she was really concerned about him.

"Gary, are you daft? You were in a coma for 3 years. You must let your body heal. It's going to take time," Lucy said in a stern voice. Gary knows this voice and knows it well. This is the older sister telling her younger brother to '*cut the shit and do as you are told*'. This is a voice not to be trifled with.

Each day left him feeling just a little bit better. The first few days, he was only able to eat simple things like cereal or oatmeal. He knew that it would take time for his body to heal. He told himself that his strength like his appetite are just not the same. He allowed getting help from Lucy or her sons. No matter how hard he willed it to be, it doesn't happen overnight. Baby steps, right?

The bed that he was sleeping on was comfortable, he could raise or lower different parts of his body. Some people would think it was great to have one. I know Lucy had to really scramble to be able to get this for him.

He despised and hated this bed. It represents weakness and confinement. I think I have slept enough to last many lifetimes.

One day, Patrick helped to get him back from the bathroom into the dreaded bed. He still felt a little bit dizzy at times, but that would go away soon. Or so the doctors said.

Patrick sensed that his uncle was chuckling at something. "What's so funny? I missed that, what is so funny? Come on tell me." Patrick asked.

"I feel like Grandpa Joe, from Charlie and the Chocolate factory."

Peter looked at his uncle and it was obvious he didn't understand the reference. "Grandpa Joe was the bedridden Grandfather of Charlie Bucket from the movie 'Charlie and the Chocolate factory'. Didn't you ever see that movie?"

"Nope, I don't ever watch any movies that are in black and white. It sounds like a kid's movie."

"Ok, buddy, we're going to have to educate you in movies made before the year 2000."

As he said these things to Patrick, something in his brain started to move around and alert him that there's some memory that should be known to him. He just can't quite connect the dots that will become the key to knowing why this memory keeps gnawing on him.

Like a metal detector He started to dissect each word that he had said. Movies? The year 2000? Grandpa Joe? Charlie and the chocolate factory? He started to take each word apart and see if it helps to remember something, anything. The one item that seemed to be a little more familiar in his mind was when he said, "Grandpa Joe". That name, "Joe", somehow feels familiar. The more he focuses on the word the more it seems to be just that, a word.

As days started to become weeks, he could feel his strength and stamina getting better every day. Appetite came back slowly and most things physical started to coalesce and become more normal. The physical part was on the mend, but his memory was still a patchwork of clear and unclear memories. That memory of the word "Joe"' still had not revealed anything. There were still big gaps in his memory.

Later that day, Lucy came in to let him know that dinner would be done in about 30 minutes. One thing about recuperating at Lucy's house was that you were never left hungry. She was a really good cook. Anytime she made lasagna or beef stew, you did not miss it. Her sons knew that only too well. Tonight, Lucy is only cooking lasagna because he really liked it and it was the favorite for her sons too.

"Hey Gary, I bought something for you when I was out shopping. Do you want to see?" Lucy asked.

Regretfully he said, "Ok sure, but by the look on your face I can tell this is probably some joke, or something I'm not going to like. Is it a pair of depends or some denture cream?"

Lucy brought out a bright purple cane with glitter on it to assist Gary in walking. Every time you put downward pressure on the cane the rubber stopper at the bottom of the cane, lit up in purple for a few seconds. On the side of the cane was a little bell. Lucy couldn't stop her laughing and had to sit down for several minutes because she was laughing so hard. It was even worse at the store where she bought the cane. She was just in tears laughing so hard. The clerk rang it up and told Lucy that it was $29.99. The beep of the register gave her another idea.

Still laughing, it took a while for her to be able to ask the clerk, "Do you have a bell like the one that a child would put on a small bicycle."

The clerk nodded that they did and pointed to the back of the store. Lucy got out of line but had to sit down for a minute. The picture of Gary with a purple cane and a little bell on the side just sent wave after wave of laughing the more she thought about it.

He also laughed at it a lot when she gave it to him. He could just imagine how Lucy had been in the store buying this. It felt good to laugh again. His life started to feel a little more normal.

"How would you like to move into a real bedroom?" Lucy asks.

"Ok, yeah sure, but what about Peter or Patrick? What about school holidays when they come home?"

"Don't worry about that. Peter volunteered his room for you to move into. Besides, Peter doesn't come home that often. And if both Peter and Patrick sleep here, we have a convertible couch, so one of the boys could sleep there. Really, don't worry about it, they will be fine." She said.

"Ok if you're sure about this."

"I did a lot of shopping today. Just routine stuff, groceries, towels, sheets etc. Do you want to know what I bought for Peter's room?"

Lucy pulls out a set of bed sheets, pillowcases, and a blanket for Peter's bed. Each one of these items is plastered with Star Wars characters and figures. She smiles at him knowing that she has had enough fun for the day. Again, they laugh together.

Chapter 5 - Moving…

You can only lose what you cling to.

— Buddha

In the coming weeks, Gary started to feel a little more normal. The physical therapy he went to three times a week really helped him physically. His strength and stamina came back. Although he was starting to get much better physically, this was only half of his issues. The memories of certain events were just a bunch of images and pictures in his head with no connection between them. Every time he looked at an object or tried to remember a conversation he once had, his mind would just go blank. It felt like déjà vu. He knew deep down that something was familiar to him but the harder he focused on it, trying to retrieve a specific memory, the more the memories retreated into the background.

For the next six months Gary worked very closely with physical therapy to return his muscles back to a state that would allow him to walk. He also needed balance for him to walk around. Lucy had done an incredible job of keeping his muscles moving so that he did not lose a lot of muscle. The other thing was the food that she was giving him was very nutritious and helped him to maintain healthy levels of vitamins.

The women that came over to help Gary with his physical therapy was a woman with incredibly piercing eyes and a very serious demeanor. He knew instantly that she was a no non-sense woman. Her thick Haitian creole accent was difficult to understand at first, but he started to understand bits and pieces. From what he could tell she was laughing at him while they were doing the physical therapy. She was making fun of him and would keep doing so until he understood. He picked up small phrases like,

"You be sting big man, luke at ya now.

No strong and no big man. Ya daat's right,

I keeps it up til u understands

yu is string and be string."

He interrupted her and said, "Hey, I am big, and I am strong!"

She looked Gary in the eye and said in perfect English, "Good! Now we start the work. SHOW me how strong you are. Push my hands forward, lift your leg up. Do that for me and I will help you to be strong for yourself. I have worked with many men that I help to be stronger. Don't do this and you will not be able to help yourself."

After a couple of months of physical therapy, restlessness was starting to boil in the background. It's gotten to a point where he started to look forward to something, or someone new, to break up the routine. He knew something was wrong when he started looking forward to 'The Price Is Right', or 'Jeopardy' on TV.

Bit By Bit

He would never be able to payback Lucy for how much she had helped him. They both have their own little quirks or style, but they got along well, as they always have. Lucy made Gary and Freddie always feel welcome, but he knew that being here, in his sister's house, was only temporary. He needed to do something else and to move into his own place. But if he wanted to move out; that would require money.

It really never occurred to him to ask his sister what she did with any of his belongings before his trip to Australia. He wasn't sure if she still had them, or if she sold them. Actually, he would have been fine with that. Later that night, he asked Lucy about it. He was really expecting her to say that it had all been sold to pay for the time he was in the Ashwood facility. Lucy said very nonchalantly, "Oh yeah, I forgot about that."

He was waiting for her to finish her statement when Freddie came in. Freddie was giving the signal that he had to go outside. Gary grabbed Freddie's leash and Lucy said, "Hey wait, let me get my shoes on and I will go with you."

As usual when Gary took Freddie out it was because he really urgently needed to go outside. However, this time Freddie really just wanted to go outside and stretch his legs. Maybe he would pee or maybe he wouldn't, he wasn't sure yet.

The air outside was a little chilly. All the signs of the coming winter were starting to methodically show. It was the beginning of October and all the leaves in each tree were in a fierce competition with other leaves to surpass each other with their surreal colors. This night it wasn't just the color changing on the trees, it was a beautiful song that was softly playing in the background.

For Gary in this moment the leaves started to show more and more colors. The song in the background became louder and louder. Everything was building into an incredible finale. The finale was an explosion of color, and a beautiful crescendo of music.

Lucy continued their discussion, before Freddie had broken the moment, by saying, "I'm glad you asked. I wasn't sure if you would be mad at me for doing this. All of your stuff from your apartment was put into storage. I have room in my basement, but it just seemed like they would get destroyed in the basement."

"Really? I would have thought you sold everything in order to pay for Ashwood. I don't remember what stuff I have, so if you had sold it then it would be OK."

"First of all, your business partner, Roger Tillson, told me that he would cover any charges for your care. But I haven't heard one thing from him since you came back from Australia. There was one odd thing though. A couple of weeks after you came back, I received a letter from a bank in Boston called Trinity Trust Holdings. I was just about to throw it out, but it was addressed to you personally. I opened it and the bank wanted me to sign a document for the release of your health records. It looked normal enough to me. So, I signed it and sent it back"

"Hmm, I don't remember that bank or having anything to do with it," Gary said. He would just have to add this to the growing stack of things he should be able to remember but couldn't.

"When I took you out of Ashwood, Betsy, in the financial office, said all your bills were paid by Trinity Trust Holdings in Boston. She didn't know who Roger Tillson was."

He did remember Roger Tillson from before his trip, but many of the memories of him were foggy and vague. A strange thing happened when Gary thought about Roger, immediately his mind went to the "Danger, danger, don't trust this person" category in his head.

Lucy continued, "I wasn't sure whether you were going to come out of the state you were in or not, but I was thinking that if you ever did wake up that you would need some money to move into another apartment since your lease with the apartment in the city ended. I had power of attorney for your finances; the leasing company sent me the security deposit you gave them and also any money that remained in the leasing account that was set up with the apartment building. I put that money into ..."

"Wait a sec!" Lucy stopped mid-sentence. "How did I miss that? Both checks from your apartment were sent to me and made out to me. They were all coming from the same bank, Trinity Trust Holdings. I can't believe I missed that.," Lucy blurted out.

"Anyways, the money is in an account, and you can access it anytime you want."

"Really? I would have thought that you sold everything to at least help with the cost of a huge Great Dane and your younger brother."

"Gary, if I was in the same situation, you would do anything to help me. You did that for me when Mom and Dad died, and you also helped me going through David's cancer. Right?"

"Yeah, ok I guess you're right. I still think that I should be looking for a job and an apartment right now."

"Well, you have about $5,000 that could probably get you into an apartment. The job will come soon, I'm sure of that. I can help you look for an apartment tomorrow, when I get back from work." Lucy worked at Boston University, as a Professor of Archeology, so she would naturally have access to a lot of students who are constantly moving into or moving out of apartments.

That weekend, on the third apartment they looked at, Freddie decided that he would make the decision for

Gary. He wouldn't budge from the front door to exit the apartment. The apartment that Freddie picked out was really decent. It's near one of the local colleges and also a nice park for Freddie to go to. It was on the bottom floor of a three-story building. Just a simple one-bedroom apartment, rent was $1300, and they allowed pets. Lucy said that she and her boys would help him move stuff from storage into this apartment.

While he was at Ashwood, Lucy, would go periodically into the city to check on Gary's apartment. But she didn't have the key for the elevator. This elevator key fob was needed to go up to the many floors above the city- ideally overlooking Boston Harbor. She had to ask the security guard sitting at a small desk in the marble lobby to run the elevator to the top floor.

When Lucy entered the beautiful marble lobby, she was holding two cups of coffee, one for herself and one for the security guard. The heavy-set guard, Frank, recognized her as she walked in, and he reached for one of the drawers in the desk and pulled out a special key fob. Frank was always very pleasant to her and asked Lucy if she was going up to Gary's apartment to water his plants and pick up Gary's mail. She nodded yes, and she handed over the extra coffee she had brought with her. Frank's eyes lit up as this was a nice treat for him sitting behind his desk all day.

"Thank you so much, you're an angel. What kind of coffee is this today?"

Lucy's coyly smiled and said, "You know I'm not actually sure. I just asked the girl in the coffee shop to surprise me. So, I guess it will be a surprise!! Ha-ha."

Frank and Lucy played this scene out every time she brought him a coffee. She told him it was a surprise. Sometimes she just made up a special name like, 'Pegasus decaf latte with steamed grape jelly foam.' Frank would play along with this conversation and acted like it really was going to be a surprise. Lucy knew what kind of coffee Frank liked. He liked really strong coffee, no sugar, and no cream. Lucy smiled, and Frank gave her the elevator key. Lucy took the elevator to the thirty-third floor.

On this floor there were only three very large apartments. She walked over to apartment 'C' and opened the door to Gary's place. She had been here a couple of times and each time it really took her breath away. Floor to ceiling windows yielded a fantastic view of Boston harbor! She never noticed, or ever needed to talk to him about his finances, or the banks that he used. She knew he was doing well, but this apartment was really over the top.

Now, every time she came over to Gary's apartment, a mixture of emotions came over her. She felt hopeful that he would recover and be able to leave the Ashwood facility. She didn't want to think about all of the 'what if's' for Gary. It took a lot of energy to be hopeful. It was very easy to trip on the sadness of his condition. Keep moving forward. Sadness or despair didn't do anything good for her brother, or for herself.

Gary's lease was due to run out three months after Gary returned home. At the time, it seemed unlikely Gary's condition would improve. Lucy called a moving company and moved everything into storage. There really wasn't that much stuff that needed to go. Gary was not the type to go out and buy anything unless it had a specific function. A big screen TV, a surround sound system, two couches made of soft leather, a nice bed, and countless numbers of bookcases. Each bookcase was jam packed with books of all types, mostly technology books, but also books on flying, scuba diving, sailing and on and on. These bookcases held all of his books and manuals on just about everything

Roger was true to his word. She never received any bills from the Ashwood facility, and they were not sent to her. The only cost she had to pay was the monthly storage costs. She also assumed that Roger had gone into Gary's bank accounts and drained them out to pay for the cost of the Ashwood facility. There was still a lingering question when Betsy Richter said that all costs were paid by a law firm in the city.

It was hard to believe that three and a half years had passed. Now it was the end of October, Gary signed the necessary paperwork and gave his new landlord a check for the first month and last month deposit on the apartment. His nephews, Peter, and Patrick asked a

MD Hanley

couple of their friends, Oscar, and Brent, to help them move their uncle into the new apartment. Fortunately, Peter and Oscar both had pickups, so it was a lot easier with less trips. Peter, and his friends did most of the moving. Gary just had to point to where something needed to go. Freddie made it his mission to follow every person that took something into the apartment. Freddie was intently watching Oscar and Brent, moving the couch from Lucy's office, the one he had claimed as his bed. They asked Gary where they should put the couch. He told them to put the couch on the far side of the living room. Freddie did not like that and growled loudly at the two boys.

Gary thought, "Ok I guess Freddie doesn't want it to be moved there. Freddie was standing in a spot near the door into the apartment. He asked the boys to move it closer to Freddie. When they did, Freddie's, growl turned into a happy woof. When Oscar and Brent put the couch down, Freddie licked each boy's hand as his way to say, *thank you*. By late morning he was all moved in.

Lucy took everyone out for a big meal to thank everyone for helping. Oscar and Brent said it was not a problem at all. Oscar gets asked to help move people a lot because he has a pickup truck. Some of those moves were all day long and back breaking. Oscar said this was the easiest one he had to do. Peter and Patrick grinned when their mother said *thank you* to Oscar and Brent "for their hard work". Both brothers were thinking the same thing. Did we have a choice in this? We were *told* to help, not *asked* to help.

After Oscar and Brent left, Lucy and her boys started to open and unpack boxes. Freddie as usual was trying to get into everyone's way. As each box was unpacked, Freddie would take the empty box into Gary bedroom. No one was in here, so Freddie gave himself the permission to tear and rip the box into pieces. After doing this several times, Freddie got tape wrapped around his nose. Suddenly, from the living room, he heard a big thud and then peals of laughter.

When Freddie came into the room, everyone was laughing uncontrollably. Lucy had picked up a box of books. As she lifted the box up, she didn't see the piece of tape under her sneaker which was connected to the taping on the bottom of the box. As she picked up the box, the tape came off the bottom of the box and the contents fell loudly on the floor.

This was the only box that Roger had sent to Lucy. It contained only the personal effects from his office. At the time, Lucy thought it was odd that Gary's personal items from his office were all contained in one box. Three framed pictures, 8 hard covered novels, 15 or so manuals and two coffee cups. Lucy asked Roger if there were more of Gary's things in his office. Roger said that all papers and laptops were company property; and everything else that was not company property was in the box he had sent her. Lucy didn't really think about this until now. Why was there such a small number of items from an office that Gary had worked at for 7 years?

The manuals, books, and two of the three framed pictures fell to the ground unscathed. The glass in the picture frame of Freddie, when he was a puppy, had broken into two big pieces, as well as several little shards, but the glass broke in a way that it was all contained and broken in the frame. Lucy picked up the frame and broken glass and put it into the waste basket. She promised Gary to buy a replacement. He just smiled and said not to worry about it. It was just an ordinary frame and nothing special.

It was a long day and Gary was glad that he didn't have more furniture in his apartment. After Lucy and her boys left, he was pretty much done for the day. Most of his stuff was unpacked so now the only thing left to do was put everything in the right place. Putting the few dishes that he had into the cabinets; and putting all the books and manuals he owned into several of bookcases that he had in his previous apartment. Since he was getting hungry, he thought he would kill two birds with one stone. He grabbed Freddie's leash and found a little sub shop close by where he got a large Italian submarine to go. Then he took Freddie out to a nearby park. He let Freddie go off his leash and do his business while he found a nice bench to sit down and eat half of his submarine. He gave the other half to Freddie. Italian subs are probably not the best food for a dog, but Freddie was the size of a normal person in height and weight. It was starting to get dark, and they both headed back to the new apartment.

Freddie was thoroughly exhausted when they got back home. It had been a long day of ripping up boxes. Freddie was on the couch and fast asleep in about 5 minutes. Gary looked at the frame with the picture of Freddie. There was something odd about that picture. At first, he figured it was just another memory in the long list of uncategorized memories he was accumulating. He sat down on his couch in front of the coffee table. There was some connection here that he was missing.

All at once, Gary saw why the picture of Freddie looked strange. The picture was taken exactly where he was sitting right now. The coffee table was in the background and Freddie was sleeping on the floor. The coffee table in the picture showed that one of the rectangular legs was not aligned correctly with the sides of the table. The table leg looked like it was not completely "screwed" in. It probably could have been turned a little more so that it was flush with the sides of the table. He wouldn't have noticed it if the table leg was aligned correctly. He turned the table over and found that one of the four legs could be unscrewed from the table. The table leg was hollow and by the sound of it the leg contained something inside.

He took the table leg into the kitchen and emptied the contents of the leg onto the sandy-white faux-granite looking countertop. Three items fell out of the coffee table leg. A small bronze colored key with a white key ring attached to it. On the white tag was written two lines. The first line said Trinity Trust Holdings and below that was handwritten in blue magic marker, 33C. The second item was a large green paperclip that held two pieces of paper neatly folded. The last item was a large stack of crisp one-hundred-dollar bills with a currency strap that said $10,000. Gary let out a laugh and Freddie raised his head off his couch/bed. Everything looked Ok, so he went back to sleep.

Totally stunned by this event, Gary went back to the couch and sat down. The three-legged coffee table was in front of him upside down. Not really sure what made him think of this, but he thought if one of the legs contained something, maybe the other legs had items hidden there also. Sure enough, each leg was able to be unscrewed from the table. Each of the three table legs contained a similar stack of crisp one-hundred-dollar bill with a strap around it that said $10,000.

Gary was just stunned. On his kitchen countertop was $40,000 dollars in four stacks of $10,000. Gary just kept saying silently, "Wow!!" He looked at Freddie and said, "No more cheap crappy dog food for us, it's just steaks and lobsters now!"

Chapter 6 - Learning

"Education is the most powerful weapon

which you can use to change the world."

-Nelson Mandela

Sleeping last night was difficult after finding $40,000 in his coffee table. Trinity Trust Holdings keeps showing up. There must be a link between himself and this Trinity Trust Holdings. Gary made a note to himself about going there soon when he went to the city to pick up some of the items he needed for the new apartment.

First things first. Freddie needed to go out and He needed a cup of coffee. On the way to the field where Gary and Freddie went last night, he stopped at a little 'mom and pop' variety store. A lot of stores did not want a dog running up and down the aisles. Freddie was used to this and when Gary told him to sit, he always obeyed him 100% of the time. As he was opening the door to the store, an older gentleman opened the door for him.

"Good morning to ya. Hey, bring your buddy inside, I have a treat for him," the store owner told him as he opened the door.

"Thank you! That's very nice of you. He is a really well-behaved dog. Most people are leery of him because of his size."

"Hmmff", the owner went behind the counter and went over to a glassed-in cooler that contained a small supply of deli items - ham or roast beef and cheese slices. Freddie was watching him very, very closely. The owner reached in and took several pieces of ham and roast beef and cheese. He rolled the cheese and a couple of slices of ham together and then did the same for the roast beef. He looked up to Gary and said, "I'm Bert Lancaster. Do you mind if I give your friend a little snack?"

"Sure. Wow! Thanks for this. My name is Gary McKeown, and this is Freddie. I just moved into the apartment up the street. 33 Hill Road, apartment C. The building is on the left side of Hill Street"

"I think you just found his weak spot." As Gary said that Freddie licked Bert's hand.

Bert chuckled, "well he is welcome here anytime."

Gary remembered why he was out on this early Sunday; to get coffee and go to the park. He got a large cup of coffee and Bert wouldn't let him pay for it. He thanked him again and said that he will definitely be back again.

When they got to the park, Gary finally had a couple of minutes to enjoy his coffee and make a plan for today. He was still stunned about the money he found. This morning he looked at the duffel bag where he had put all the items that he found last night. He just had to check to make sure it was real and not just imagined. He was so tired last night he put everything in his duffel bag and was asleep in minutes after he laid down. Lucy said that she would stop over about 1:00 to take him out to lunch and pick up some groceries and other odds and ends that he needed for his apartment. It was about 7:30 AM so he could go back and start to make a dent on the unpacking.

Gary looked up from the bench where he was pondering these things and looked for Freddie. Freddie was a large dog, so he was very difficult to miss. He looked around the field and saw Freddie on the other side of the park. He called out to him, but Freddie didn't hear him. He started to jog over to where Freddie was. As he came closer, he saw what was capturing Freddie's attention. There was a woman sitting on a blanket and her little daughter was waving to Freddie and making faces at him. Freddie was about ten feet away from the girl. Freddie and the little girl were having a staring contest. She would put her hands in front of her eyes and then take them away and look at Freddie. She was giggling uncontrollably. Well, she was smiling so Gary took that as a sign that she was not afraid of the huge dog looking at her. Ahh, the innocence of children, always just treat everyone the same way, with love and smiles.

"Freddie. Come!", he said in a voice loud enough to reach Freddie.

He wanted to be closer, so proper introductions were made and that the mother was not afraid for her daughter. The mother looked over at Gary and waved hi. She had made the connection that Freddie was with Gary. Freddie was at his side when he finally reached the women.

He asked the women, "I hope Freddie here was not bothering you? He's very good with kids. He's just really, really big, and uncoordinated. But he's very passive with everyone he meets. If you pet him or scratch his belly, he has been known to give people big sloppy kisses."

The women on the blanket, introduced herself, "My name is Theresa Barnes, but everyone calls me Terry. And this is my daughter, Erin. She is still learning the difference between big people and big animals. When I first saw Freddie, he was as fascinated by 'peek-a-boo' as Erin is. My grandfather had a Great Dane. He was a big dog but a big creampuff and very affectionate. I wasn't worried. I suspected that he got loose from his owner."

"Yes, he did. My name is Gary McKeown. I just moved in yesterday and wanted to let Freddie get a little exercise this morning. I am really sorry, if he was bugging you."

Terry shook her head and said that Freddie was fine. She saw the coffee cup in Gary's hand. "I see you have met Bert. Bert and Betty have been running Lancaster's Store forever. I'm not sure how long his family has been in this town, but he literally knows everyone. He also plays a big part in keeping all the students well behaved. He may get some new kids into town, usually the freshmen, who may not care for him or his store. However, when these kids are sophomore's, they will do anything for Bert. It has happened so many times I have stopped trying to understand it. The winters are pretty cold up here, after it snows, and sidewalks and parking lots are covered in snow. There is always a different kid every morning, before their classes, out early shoveling Bert's parking lot and all the walkways around his store."

Terry continued, "I am not sure, but I think it is a little bit of a status thing with a lot of the students. As I said he has been here for a very long time and he knows everyone, students, teachers, police officers, town council, and on and on. Did you meet his wife, Betty? She is a real hoot! Be careful though, if Bert or Betty disagree about something. Run away. They will put you on the spot and drag you into the disagreement. Ha-ha, it's only harmless stuff. Should they sell lemon squares or lemon pastries in the summer or all year round? I have been pulled into the middle of their different opinion spats too many times to count."

Gary said, "Well, he met Freddie this morning. Giving Freddie a piece of cheese and slices of ham is all it takes to make Freddie like you. Bert was friendly and nice. I'm sure I'll be in there a lot since it is so convenient for me."

Gary continued, "By the way, I moved into 33 Hill Road in the bottom apartment, yesterday."

Terry said she was three houses up the road from him and if he needed anything to not hesitate to ask. Gary said he needed to get back to unpacking and said goodbye to Terry and Erin. Freddie gave Erin a little goodbye by walking over to her, so he was in petting range. Erin patted Freddie's head a couple of times and then burst into another fit of giggling.

As Gary came over the top of Hill Road, it was a strange feeling seeing his new apartment down the street. It was an odd sense to walk down the street and keep saying to himself that this was his new place. Freddie, however, was as happy as a dog is supposed to feel. His master/friend was getting back to the same person he met when he was a little puppy. As a dog, he was constantly doing a tight rope walk between his instincts as a Great Dane to protect and keep safe and the opposing instinct of just pure bliss. Freddie doesn't keep it a secret that he loves to play and be 'playful' in a group of humans. Freddie became more relaxed that Gary was staying and not going away.

As they entered the apartment, Gary saw all the boxes of books that he needed to organize and put into the bookcases that were moved from the storage unit from his apartment in Boston. He was hoping and half expecting that he would see some book that would trigger all of his old memories. He saw just books. It seemed to make more sense to organize the books based on topics.

Several hours later almost all the books were in the bookcases, nicely stacked and 'semi' organized. He sat down on the couch with a cold drink of water and looked at all the work he had done.

Almost an entire bookcase was filled with dozens of computer books. There were many books describing a multitude of different software languages, many different methodologies of software development, several complex design and pattern theory, and an assortment of program management books.

Another bookcase was almost entirely filled with aviation books and manuals. He noticed that many of the aviation books were manuals about training for different pilot ratings. The list included manuals for a private pilot rating, instrument rating, commercial rating, multi-engine aircraft rating, and certified flight instructor rating. He also grouped and ordered by year of the Aeronautical Information Manual (AIM). Several different types of maps, high altitude, and low altitude maps of several different parts of the country.

The last two bookcases were filled with many different hobbies it seemed he enjoyed. Just like the aviation manuals, Gary had several different manuals for scuba diving and scuba diving ratings. This list contained topics like Open Water Diving, Advanced Open Water Diving, and Enriched Air Diving mixtures commonly referred to as Nitrox. Many manuals about attaining different sailing certifications. Coastal Cruising, Advanced Coastal Cruising, and also a manual for Bareboat Cruising. Books on every conceivable knot that could be useful on a boat. Manuals about all the parts of a boat and many others.

The last bookcase was just a hodgepodge of travel books, hard and soft cover novels, and other miscellaneous books. The shelves of all four bookcases were filled except for one shelf. Gary absently sent a 'Huge Thank You' to whoever it was who had the task of packing all of these books up and putting them into the storage unit.

The whole time he was putting the books onto the shelves, he had a strong feeling that these were his books and, of course, that he owned them. As perplexing as it was, he just could not remember one thing about the subjects or contents of these books. Sailing a boat or piloting a plane? Once again, add this to the pile of unknowns in his head.

He walked into the kitchen and saw the two pieces of paper that he had also removed from the coffee table.

He had almost forgotten about these. The one piece of paper had two lines of cryptic text printed on it. Two lines of just hyphens and what looked like bullet points you might see in a list of items. It looked very strange, and he couldn't make any sense of it. The absence of memories that he knows he should know were becoming very frustrating.

```
. -- .- .. .-.. / -...- / --. -- -.-. -.- . --- .-- -. .-.-. .-. . .- .-.. . -
- .- .. .-.. .-.-. .-.-. -.-. --- --
.--. .- ... ... .-- --- .-. -.. / -...- / -.... .- -. -.-.-- -- .
-.. .
```

The second piece of green, thick paper stock was folded up. In the folds of the paper, Gary saw that the paper was folded around a white and purple business card. On the piece of paper there was a line of numbers written in blue ink, **13.8.148.11**. The business card had a solid line of dark purple with white text in this section. Below that written in black text was the name, address, email, and telephone numbers of Joseph Daly. The text at the top of the business card was "Trinity Trust Holdings Corporation". Next to the title were the initials 'TTH' in a very elegant script font.

On the back of the card were 4 lines of text. The first two lines said:

- Go to TTH.
- Ask for Belinda.
- Give her your key

The last line was the signature of Joseph Daly.

Putting the two pieces of paper in his pocket, he saw Lucy out the side window as he was walking to open the door. Lucy, looking like she was gardening this morning, came inside. Freddie sensed that there was someone new in the apartment and by the slightest hint at gardening smells, he knew exactly who it was. He couldn't wait to see Lucy and tell her about the new apartment he was living in. Freddie came over to Lucy and was so excited to see her, he galloped over to her. As usual he didn't know how to stop and crashed into Lucy making her fall onto the couch. Lucy and Gary had seen this happen many times in the months since he woke up from his coma. They both laughed. Freddie still has not mastered the run and stop thing yet.

Looking at the bookcases Lucy said, "You have been busy this morning, I see. Let's get some lunch. Are you hungry?"

He nodded yes, and Lucy continued, "There is a little fish restaurant about ten minutes from here. Nothing fancy, just good food. They also have a big menu to choose from if you're not in the mood for fish.

He laughed a little and replied, "Sure that sounds good, but it's my treat. I really owe you so much for taking care of me for all those months."

"No Gary, I'm ok with paying. Save it, there will be a lot of things to buy to get back to a normal."

He reached into his pocket and pulled out one of the hundred-dollar bills. Lucy stared at Gary a little surprised and she didn't really understand. He put down some more water and a little bit of food for Freddie saying, "Lucy, I will fill you in over lunch. I am starving. Some fish sounds great."

Thirty minutes later, Gary and Lucy were sitting in a little out of the way booth. Since He showed Lucy the $100 bill, Lucy kept asking him about every five minutes about what had changed. Gary really didn't know how to explain it and needed time to figure out his answer. He just solemnly looked at Lucy, smiled and said, "After we order, I will fill you in on everything." Twenty minutes later after the waitress left took both of their orders, Lucy was about to explode.

Gary said, "Ok. Last night I did some more unpacking. Freddie and I found a little sandwich shop and a nice park for Freddie. When I got back, I sat on the couch. In front of me was the coffee table that we had moved yesterday. On top of the table was the picture that was taken from the photo frame that broke earlier. So, on the coffee table was the picture of Freddie sitting next to the same coffee table. I probably wouldn't have noticed it, but something just didn't look right. One of the coffee legs looked like it was 'screwed' into the table itself but was not fully 'screwed' in tight in the picture. I found that I could unscrew each leg of the coffee table. There was a little surprise in the hollow in each of the coffee table legs."

Lucy was thoroughly stunned by this, as He had been. At this point, the waitress brought over their meals and said 'Enjoy!".

Gary decided to stop here now and dig into his food. Lucy just stared at him and said, "So, what did you find?"

With his mouth full, he pointed at his plate to say that nothing else was going to be discussed until he finished his meal. Lucy was just incredulous. It did not change his mind as Lucy started to sullenly eat her lunch.

He looked up at Lucy and said, "OK, I can't stand it. I have wanted to tell you since I woke up this morning. But I've been trying to understand it myself. I knew you were coming over to get some lunch, so I figured it could wait."

He told Lucy about finding $40,000 in cash, the velvet bag with the key and he reached in his pocket and brought out the two pieces of paper he had found.

Everything on the pieces of paper had no meaning to Lucy.

He mentioned that he had met a few people here in town. He told her about Bert Lancaster at the convenience store, and also about meeting Erin and Terry in the park. Lucy, smiled. This is her brother again. She had missed this for a long time. Dialogue between us was always so easy.

"What? Do I have something in my teeth?" Gary said when her mood changed.

Lucy just smiled and said, "You remind me of a person I grew up with!"

Gary thought about that for a minute, and it hit him for the first time, "Yeah, I guess it is going to take a bit of time to get caught up on the time I lost."

His face changed from very relaxed to very serious. "Lucy, I have a couple of questions that sprang up this morning. You have to promise me you will answer me honestly and not try to protect me. I know that face you make when you are trying to protect someone and not hurt them or cause further hurt or confusion. Don't forget, I remember when you wouldn't let me go out for Halloween to commit social suicide when I wanted to be dressed as President Nixon.

Lucy laughed and giggled, "Yeah, that was not a good choice for you. Yes, I will answer anything you want, I'm an open book." Lucy said 'oh shit' to herself.

Gary smiled. He knew this was a code phrase between them to mean that she would be open only to a point. No more and no less. He was stubborn, but Lucy was more stubborn by a factor of ten if she wanted to be. The 'big sister' rule, I guess.

He told Lucy that as he started unpacking boxes of books, they seemed to fall into about six or seven different categories. He couldn't figure it out or remember what they were for. So, the first question he wanted to find out about are the computer languages and technology books.

Lucy smiled, somewhat relieved that they were having this conversation. She knew it was coming but didn't want to push and wanted to let him recover as much as possible. "Gary, programming software and any kind of technology was very easy for you. Before you and Roger started your company, you were very well-known around the world as a distinguished technologist. You were well respected and considered the authority on certain technological topics. For the last ten or fifteen years, you have been traveling to many different parts of the world to consult on large projects or be the keynote speaker at some of the largest conferences in the world. Companies came to you for advice about investing in an area of technology that was not well covered; and if it was something that their company could exploit to gain profit. I supposed they wanted to corner the market or something. Hey, by the way, did you actually look at the authors or co-authors on some of those books you unpacked?"

He was listening to every word Lucy was saying. His memory still registered as 'out to lunch' and no connection could be made, he replied, "Sorry, no I didn't notice them, why?"

Lucy, said, "Well you wrote 4 of them and 3 others you co-wrote. A couple of companies and some astute leaders in technology wanted to speak to you while you were sick." Lucy added, "Many were very stunned by the news of the diving accident. You also got dozens of get-well cards from your different contacts. I mentioned this every time I went into Ashwood, to ask if there were any messages. I know they got several calls, but they always said '*nope, no calls*'. Only a few of previous contacts were able to reach out, and get past Ashwood, to contact me directly. I still have all the messages and notes that were sent to you back at my place."

Just as Lucy finished that statement, the waitress came over to the table to take away their plates. She asked if they wanted desert or coffee. They both got a cup of coffee. The waitress said just let her know if they needed a refill or the check.

After the waitress came back with two cups of coffee, a sugar holder, and some cold cream in a little pitcher. Gary asked Lucy the next question.

"Why are there so many books on aviation and piloting?"

Lucy smiled again. She was relieved but a little hesitant to tell Gary about his extensive knowledge of flying and aviation. He asked so it was too late now. Lucy confessed, "Gary, since you woke did you ever think about flying or being a pilot? Wasn't there a James Bond movie we watched the other night? The opening part is when Bond dives off a cliff and is able to catch a plane in free fall and jump in the pilot seat? I thought for sure that might open up some memories for you."

Lucy continued, "You have been flying airplanes, of all different types, since you were 23 years old. Don't you remember going to Martha's Vineyard, or Atlantic city? You flew Mom, Dad and me there several times."

Gary responded, "Yeah, I do remember going to those places, but I don't think I remember flying there. What was the name of one the airports?"

"I can only remember a couple. The one on Martha's Vineyard was a grass airfield called Katie or something. No, wait, it was called Katama. Yes, that's the name. Atlantic City was in a little airport, I think it was called Bader Field, yes that's the name."

He looked at Lucy and it felt like when you know you are going to sneeze, but don't. He remembered these airports. The one thing that popped in his head was Bader Field. You had to go through New York City airspace to get to it. That was it! The flying and aviation started to come into focus. New York City Airspace pulled the final 'Jenga' piece and like an avalanche so many memories popped up. He remembered all the destinations he went to and also remembered all of the mistakes he made while he was learning. The mistakes were good, provided you didn't kill yourself, or anyone else. Those mistakes are really how you become a better pilot. When he thought about New York City, he had so many memories of just amazing things. He was flying through New York City and witnessed the last flight of the Concorde Jet. The Concorde, also called "Speedbird", was taking off from JFK airport and Air Traffic Control made the 'Speedbird' fly 500 feet **below** his plane at 5000 MSL. Having a plane like that flying 500 feet below you is one hell of a sight.

While all of this is going through his head, he still had not responded to Lucy.

"Lucy yes! Yes, I do remember flying! Wow, this is like a dam breaking, I can remember all of the trips flying to lots of different places. I don't think I remember everything at 100% full detail, but I do remember a lot of it."

The next question threw Lucy a little off guard. He asked, "Do I own a plane? I feel like a lot of these flights I took were in mostly one aircraft."

"As a matter of fact, you do have a plane and it is hangered at an airport close by. I am not going to tell you how to get it or give you the keys. I will **ONLY** give you the keys when you are fully checked out and all your aviation knowledge and skill are at the same level it was before you woke up. Gary this is going to take time. You have all the time in the world. Please do this one favor for me. Don't fly until you spend several hours with a flight instructor; and the aviation doctors sign off on it."

"Ok, Lucy I promise. To be perfectly honest, I can remember doing the piloting but knowing is different from doing."

Lucy said, "OK. The open book is closed for the day. We will talk tomorrow about this some more. Let's get Freddie a doggie bag and get back to your apartment."

I guess the open book is closed now. On the way back to his new apartment, they stopped at a grocery store to pick up some food to fill up his empty cabinets and pick up some food for Freddie. Gary really tried really hard to not spoil Freddie, but he usually lost that argument.

On the way back to his apartment, they started to talk about what the next steps are for him. Lucy said that she had an extra laptop computer at home and if he wanted to use that once his cable and internet were connected, he was welcome to it. She also mentioned that since she was a professor at the college, he could take any day or night classes that he wanted to take, and it would not cost anything except for the cost of the books. He suspected that this was her subtle hint to tell him to get off his ass and start participating in the world. It always amused him that his sister could say the most innocent or non-judgmental statements in a way that was disguised as a very soft tap on the head but was really saying 'either you do this my way or come up with a better plan.'

On the way back from the supermarket, they stopped at Lucy's house and picked up the extra laptop computer; and she also gave him a flyer for all the classes that were offered at the college. After all the groceries were put away and Freddie was taken out for a walk, Gary just fell onto the couch.

The next morning around 9:00 AM there was a knock on the door. The cable technician came in and started to hook up his cable, telephone, and internet service. About 45 minutes later he turned on his TV to a local news station. Most times when he watches TV or reads the paper, it just further reminds him how many things happened while he was in the coma. A lot of the current events were interesting but some of these items were just mind-numbing. He was glad he was not subjected to a daily overdose of reality TV or presidential campaign nonsense. It was a futile exercise to worry about what things he missed or not. He was asleep, he was lucky he was alive, and more importantly he was surrounded by people that cared about him, so move on and don't dwell on it.

He turned the TV off and started to make himself a cup of coffee. He brought his "Lefty's do it better" mug over to a small end table and started to look at all the books on computers and computer languages he had in the bookcase. He found the books that Lucy mentioned that he wrote. One book called <u>Cryptology and Steganography Made Simple</u>. To Gary, this did not look simple or easy. He thumbed through the different pages. Some looked a little familiar and others were just lines of text. He was having the same feeling when he was out to lunch with Lucy yesterday. He felt he was about to sneeze but then it went away.

If he wrote the book, then surely, he should know what the terms inside the book mean. Cryptology is taking characters or symbols that are just random characters put together and will not really mean anything until you use a key or phrase to unlock the encryption code and get the message that is contained within. There are many different ways of doing this. Sometimes you can say or write a message that either will be just jumbled up characters, or a pattern that you had to follow to extract the message. An example of this might be a phrase that you would unlock a message from a piece of text that will be unlocked by writing down the second letter of each word.

The following message was actually sent by a German Spy in WWII:

> *Apparently, neutral's protest is thoroughly discounted and ignored. Isman hard hit. Blockade issue affects pretext for embargo on by products, ejecting suets and vegetable oils.*

Taking the second fetter in each word the following message emerges:

"a**P**parently n**E**utral's p**R**otest i**S** t**H**oroughly d**I**scounted a**N**d i**G**nored. I**S**man h**A**rd h**I**t. B**L**ockade i**S**sue a**F**fects p**R**etext f**O**r e**M**bargo o**N** b**Y**products, e**J**ecting s**U**ets a**N**d V**E**getable o**I**ls. "

Pershing sails from NY June 1

This is just one of the ways to encrypt information. Another way could be via steganography. This is pretty similar to cryptology, but your message is hidden in another way using an image or music files to hide your message. The beat of a song could be a code. The numerical values of a particular color in a picture, or even a barcode, with thick and thin vertical lines are all forms of steganography, hiding messages.

As he was thinking about this, another idea came to him. The dashes and dots on the piece of paper he found, was that some kind of coded message? He thought that he had seen this type of writing or code before. One place he was sure he could find out was in one of his aviation books. Sure enough, in the appendix of his

Private Pilot manual, he found a table of Morse code symbols. He was starting to get really excited here.

Using the appendix, he applied the dots and dash to the letters in Morse code. The message he got at first didn't make any sense to him.

The first line read:

FNBJM

This did not make sense. He looked at the page with the table of Morse characters. He saw that he was off by one in his translation. He went back to decoding the two lines of text to be:

EMAIL =GMCKEOWN@REALEMAIL.COM

PASSWORD =   6An!Mede

The set of numbers on the other piece of paper was an internet address. Gary powered up the laptop that Lucy had given him and went into a browser window and typed:

13.8.148.11

When He pressed the enter key the page that initially opened up was a webpage for www.realemail.com. It then popped up a box asking for the user id and the password. He used the ones he had figured out this morning. It accepted it and when the page loaded it was a simple email program that had a list of emails. There were two emails. The first email was an email welcoming him to this e-mail program. The date of the message was about fourteen days after he had returned from Australia. Hmm that is odd. That means that someone else setup this email account.

The second email was a message sent directly to him, it read

Gary, I really hope that you find this message. As of today, I put into action the contingency plan we had discussed many years ago. Follow these instructions and when you meet Belinda, she will ask you a question that you would need to know the answer to. I am positive that you will know what it is. If for some reason you do not know the answer, then I am sure that Lucy also knows this too. After the signature, the message also said

- Go to Trinity Trust Holdings
- Ask for Belinda Porter
- Give her the key that was hidden

Gary thought ok, well I know what I am doing tomorrow. Gary smiled at this. He felt '*directionless*' and this was giving him some more direction.

Chapter 7 - Joseph

*There is always some kid who may be seeing
me for the first time. I owe him my best.*

- Joe DiMaggio

The next day, he got up early, made some coffee
and was sitting at the small table that was half in the
kitchen and half in the living room. Freddie knew this
routine and was anxiously waiting for his big over-sized
biscuit he was going to give him. He smiled at Freddie
and gave him a second biscuit. He put his sneakers on,
grabbed Freddie's leash and started to head over to the
park. On his way there, he passed by Bert's store. As
soon as he came into Bert's view, he grabbed a cup and
filled it with some coffee, sugar, and grabbed a couple
of bear claws pastries. Bert came out and said with a big
smile, "Good Morning, Good Morning! how is my
favorite guy today?"

Bert looked down at Freddie and Bert continued,
"And ya I like your master too! Freddie, you can bring
him with ya anytime."

Bert now looked at him and said, "Here are some
bear claws and some coffee. on the house. I assume you
are taking Freddie to the park."

"That's right, thanks for the coffee. I really
appreciate it."

"Early mornings in that park are really nice and quiet. Hey, stop by anytime or if you need anything. We have a little bit of everything in the store. If we don't have it, then we most likely can get it in a day or two. I gotta go, or the town regulars will revolt. They can't go to the darn bathroom unless they have a paper to read. Like the world will end if they don't have their paper. You should have seen them last year when the price of the paper increased by 5 cents. I half expected them to come out with pitchforks and shovels. Well, it was nice seeing ya Freddie, bring your master anytime." He could hear Bert cussing out the two people lined up to pay for their paper and cup of coffee. He heard Bert saying, "Keep your pants on, you both are as old as dirt, and you can wait the extra thirty seconds for me to do my 'ambassadorial' duties for the town. My goodness!"

He chuckled a little after hearing that. Bert was correct about how quiet and peaceful the park was during the week. Maybe he might stop here later when he got home with the business in Boston. The apartment he was in was great because it let Gary leave a door to the porch open for Freddie to sit out on the porch if he wanted or needed to make sure everyone was behaving correctly. Lucy brought over Freddie's dog bed that was at her house. Freddie preferred his own couch, but he could do the dog bed thing in a pinch.

After going to the park, he showered and walked over to the subway line. He remembers bits and pieces of being on the subway train. He thought it might bring up some more of his locked memories. He gets on the train and like most things these days, it felt very familiar. He must have been a passenger on the subway system if he lived in Boston. His office was in a different part of Boston, so it would make sense that he would have been a frequent rider. He was really hoping that riding the subway system and the different stops would stir up some more memories. Unfortunately, it was like all the other jumbled memories. Once again, throw these into the pile of familiar memories.

Yesterday when he was at lunch with Lucy, he could see himself on a lot of these flights. He saw the controls, the instrument panel, and various aircraft that he had flown. He could call up dozens of images in his mind quite clearly. At the time he was with Lucy, and she had mentioned aviation he felt that he was having a real breakthrough with remembering his past. He is glad that he could remember these pictures and events, but unfortunately that was all they were. Nothing more than just a bunch of pictures and a jumbled set of memories.

Last night, he had started to look at the Aviation books. It was disappointing that all this information he had learned about flying and aviation did not shake loose anything more than the memories he had the day before. It just felt familiar. The same was true for all the computer books. So many books on computers and technology, it was staggering. Even the books that he had supposedly authored were, again, just pictures and text. None of these images, like so many others, were missing the 'context' of the memories. Seeing pictures or remembering events is only half of the memory. The other part of the memory is the context of these pictures and events. It's just not enough to remember a picture or a vague sense of something familiar, you must also have the understanding, or context, behind the memory.

Gary got to the Trinity Square Stop and found the Trinity Trust Building he needed to go into. It was one of the older buildings in that area. It really gave it a lot of character to be shoulder to shoulder with many of the newer buildings. This building was steeped in history and just oozed of earlier times. Fortunes were made, and fortunes were lost in this building. The lobby was beautiful with an off white and maroon veined marble floor. A security guard sat at a little desk next to the elevator. He was early. The guard told Gary that the offices he wanted opened at 9:00 AM.

This gave him about an hour to explore for a bit. Even though he was just wandering around, he set off in search of a coffee shop. As he walked down the street, again the streets just felt familiar. This is getting so frustrating! In a way it was like having a blindfold on and walking around your house. You can feel the furniture and tables, and they are familiar to you. You can identify them as your furniture, and you identify where they are in the room and where your position is relative to the furniture. If you bump into one of your tables, you naturally change your context of where you are in the room. Your position now is the current context.

He came to a stop at a small local coffee shop, Morissi's Café, which does a huge business in the morning. You could tell that this shop has been here for a long time by the scuffed and peeling black and white checkered linoleum floor. The coffee shop was small. Only about 5 or 6 people could be inside at any one time. On the left side of the shop was where the cashier, baristas, and coffee apparatus were located. On the right side there was a long high counter that was for customers to sip their coffee and get ready for their workday.

There was a smell in the background of the ambience of this little shop that contained a rich and smoky coffee smell. A line of customers came out of the small coffee shop and lined up in the street. The four people behind the counter were able to quickly take the orders from the customers and get them their purchases very quickly. Most of the people didn't really order anything, the person behind the counter just asked, "the usual?" which the customer just nodded. As he got closer to the front of the line, there was a cooler with three shelves of amazing looking pastries and a large assortment of different concoctions of fruit or yogurt. He wasn't that hungry because of the bear claw Bert gave him earlier but he was very tempted to try some of these gorgeous pastries. He thought to himself that if his meeting this morning did not go on too long, he would come back and bring some home for later. Once he got his coffee, he found an empty space on the back counter to drink his coffee. The first taste of his coffee told him why he walked over here. He wished he could make coffee that was even halfway close to the taste of their coffee. Evidence of this was easily recognizable watching the patrons start to drink their 'go-go' juice. It appeared that all of the customers were experiencing an almost sexual experience with their coffee. One cup of this got you through the day, a double shot made you the financial banks CEO for eight hours. For those that dared, a concoction with three shots of expresso transformed you into a king and you had unlimited magical power to rule the office, if not rule the world, for eight hours between and 9:00 AM and 5:30 PM.

It was only about 8:30, so he allowed himself to take his time and drink his coffee at the counter. It also let him corral his thoughts together over the puzzling events over the last couple of days. He had no idea why he was coming down here. He hadn't called or made any arrangements about coming in today, so he tried to just keep an open mind.

Coming down to this building in Boston would hopefully give him some more information about events of his past. The email message he received was very cryptic. And let's not forget about the $40,000 dollars in his coffee table. Maybe this was a mutual fund manager that had some investment he wanted him to get into. He thought it might have been better if he called first rather than just show up. Well, it wasn't a total waste of time, he always liked being in the city. It also 'reintroduced' him to that great little coffee shop.

He went back to a building in Trinity Square and this time the security guard recognized him and told him which elevator to take up to the fourth floor. As he stepped out of the elevator, he wasn't expecting the whole fourth floor to be Trinity Trust Holdings. There was a little reception desk behind a large all glass wall with a glass door with a big bronze handle. He walked up to the woman that was sitting at the desk, gave her his name and he asked to see Belinda Porter. Within a few minutes a very striking and smartly dressed woman came from the wall behind the receptionist's desk. She looked like she was in her mid-twenties or so, but in today's world it is hard to tell. Her long blonde hair is certainly noticed in any room she entered. Gary could also sense that this was a woman that was assertive and commanded attention.

She introduced herself and asked him to follow her. They walked down one side of the office where on his left was cubicle after cubicle or glassed conference room. On the other side of this walkway, there was floor to ceiling glass windows. It was a spectacular view. At the end of this row was a glass office where she went to and asked him to have a seat. Her office was on the corner of the building overlooking Copley plaza with the old and beautiful Trinity Church. It was a spectacular view.

"Mr. McKeown if you don't mind could I take a copy of any ID that you might have with you," Belinda asked.

"Sure, no problem."

Belinda left and returned briefly into the office and handed him his ID. She asked him if he wanted any coffee or tea. Gary said that he was fine, and he also mentioned that he had gone to Morissi's little coffee shop before coming to this building.

She gave him a big smile and said, "Many people that go to Morissi's have been going for years. They also protect Morissi's fiercely. They don't want anything to change. I think that you have to be invited by one of the regulars to even get noticed there. Mr. Daly invited me one morning and I have not gone anywhere else for the last 7 years. There is a strange dynamic that exists there. If they don't know you or you don't have your order ready the instant they say "next;" then you go on their secret board, they keep. First time ok, second time you are warned, and if you unfortunately are put on the board three times, they will give you the 'Morissi's sweet service" label. Basically, they ignore you and will only serve you after everyone else is served. I think, well at least I have heard, that the only way to get off this board is to donate to Children's Hospital, charity, work at the Pine Street Inn for three shifts of serving the homeless people that go there. or to donate to the Pet Hospital in south Boston. They must have recognized you because it sounds like you have been 'sworn' in."

Belinda sat behind her desk after she closed the door. "Mr. McKeown how can I help you today?"

For some reason, He thought it would be best to be a little cautious here. The first thing is that he wanted to know how he is linked to Joseph Daly.

"I came across this business card when I was moving into an apartment this past weekend. I feel a little foolish asking this but, the name, Joseph Daly on the card feels familiar to me. I am sure that I knew him, and it also feels like he was a friend but I cannot remember why or how. I was hoping you could perhaps give me some more information." he replied.

Belinda smiled, but it was a serious little smile similar to two warriors on a battlefield challenging their opponent, 'give it your best shot, because if you miss, then I will win'. "Mr. McKeown, may I call you Gary?"

"Sure"

"Well, you are correct that you do have a connection with Joseph Daly and his younger brother Michael. They have given me very explicit and detailed instructions if you were to come into this office. Now, they were very clear on this part of the instructions. I will ask you one question and if it is the correct answer, then we will continue our discussion with all the information Joseph has told me to give to you. If the answer you provide is incorrect, then I will say good day and security will escort you downstairs. Do you have any questions before I proceed?"

If he substituted the words security guards with 'oompa-loompas' it really did sound like something from Charlie and the Chocolate Factory and Grandpa Joe, the time he had told Lucy's son Peter about the movie. He nodded yes and said, "The email message I received mentioned that my sister would also know the answer to this. Does she need to be here today?"

Belinda again gave him that little smile which was a very good 'tell' for her. It meant that she was incredibly serious and very deliberate in the way she responded. He also knew that she wouldn't hesitate to have him removed from the office if needed.

Belinda replied, "No, Lucy does not have to be here, however if you want to wait until she is here to discuss this, we can reschedule this for a later time when Lucy would be available. Would you like to do that or to proceed further?"

"No, I am anxious to find out more information and how I am connected to Joseph. I have been in the hospital for a long time and my memory is not as good as it was before."

Belinda's expression changed from very serious to one that was very soft and caring. "Gary, we have all been praying and hoping that you would get better and be able to recover your health from the scuba diving situation in Australia."

Belinda realized a little too late, that she had said too much. "Gary if you are ready, then here is the question. Who, where or what word that comes to mind when I say, *GOD, will provide*?"

He didn't even really think about what was asked but it was a phrase very familiar to him. Before he knew it, he reflexively replied before he really even thought about it. He answered, "**BRIDIE!**"

Belinda gave him a big smile and looked genuinely pleased with the answer that he gave to her. She asked him if he could wait here for a few minutes. Gary nodded ok, but he was a little anxious about what Belinda was going to do. Was she going to call security? He felt a little out of place and alone in Belinda's office.

Belinda returned after about five minutes, sat back down behind her desk, and said, "Mr. Daly is in New Zealand right now. I called him to let him know that you came into the office today. I spoke to him briefly, but he told me to convey how very happy he is that you were able to get his message. Joseph is eager to see you. He is disappointed that he's not here today to see you and asked if you could have some patience; he would like to see you as soon as he can. Joseph arrives back to Boston in about one week. He also asked me to give you this."

As Belinda was talking, she was also opening a small door on the right side of her desk. It sounded like she was trying to open a safe with a number pad. She reached in and handed him a thick greenish packet held tight by a string that wrapped around the two pads on the flap of the packet and on the packet itself. Before she handed this to him, she unwound the string that was in a figure eight pattern. The packet itself contained many different dividers and was expandable like an accordion. She reached in and pulled out a thick folder with what looked like legal contracts. She pulled out several different contracts and placed them in a pile in front of Gary. At this point he is a little baffled. Belinda reached in her desk and handed him a beautiful expensive pen. He read the writing that was etched on the side of the pen, '*Et prout vultis ut faciant vobis facturus esset.*'

"Interesting, the golden rule?" He muttered out loud. Belinda said that this was a special pen and was something you always carried with you. You had accidentally left it here at the office before you went to Australia. Belinda leaned back in her chair and said, "Gary, I didn't ask this earlier but when you came to my office and said that you had received the email message from Joseph, it also asked for you to bring something with you.

Gary had completely forgotten about this. He almost left his apartment without taking the items he found in the coffee table leg. He snatched the bronze key, the business card and also the message with Morse code written on it and put these in his pocket. He reached in his pocket and handed Belinda the three items. Belinda frowned when he gave her the key but then started to chuckle. Apparently, there was some inside joke that he was not privy to.

"Gary, I am sorry about this. My father, I mean Joseph, tells people all the time to be careful with information. I am also chuckling because he used Morse code to encrypt the email credentials. No offense, but it's not that hard to figure out the dots and dashes represent Morse code. I have to give him some extra points at least for trying to be clever and used this form of communication." Belinda picked up her phone and called another girl from the sea of cubicles outside the office and asked if she could come to Joseph's office. Another woman came in and introduced herself as Barbara. She said that she is the one that handles, exclusively, Joseph and Michael Daly's various business affairs.

Belinda asked Barbara if she could do her a favor and go into the main records room and retrieve the box that says GMcKeown on the front of it. Barbara quietly left the office. and Belinda asked Gary if he was sure that he didn't want some coffee or something to drink? She said that she needed to get a bottle of water. He changed his mind about something to drink and asked Belinda if he could have a bottle of water too.

Belinda returned and gave a bottle of cold water to him and sat behind the desk.

Belinda began, "Ok, let's start from the beginning. I know that you are still grappling with some memory blocks but, if you have any questions just let me know. Gary, you met my father during his third year in college. Something happened during that year that my father has never forgotten, and you were involved in helping him. It had a profound effect on my father, and he has said that he is very grateful to a man that helped him at a time when he desperately needed help. My father has mentioned this a couple of times, but he rarely wanted to talk about it. After college, my father went to Harvard Law school and earned a degree that specialized in IP, or Intellectual Property. This is where you and my father started to create a long and lucrative business relationship. The company that you both started was Trinity Trust Holdings. At first my father worked with you after your parents died. There was a modest inheritance granted to you and Lucy. You called my father to help you manage this money for Lucy and yourself. The original amount of $85,000 is currently at approximately 9,000."

He had to stop her. "Belinda so you are saying that whatever money that was inherited has decreased in value by $76,000? I mean $9,000 dollars is still $9,000 but from what you are telling me is that it really took a hit. I would have expected more based on the money I found in my coffee table."

Belinda eyes narrowed, and the Cheshire cat smile again came over her face. Belinda, responded, "There was money in your coffee table? Hmm, that is unexpected, but I guess that is something my father would ask you to do. Gary, I am sorry, but my brain sometimes gets ahead of my voice. I said 9000, but what I did not say is that it is currently at a factor of nine thousand times $85.000. So, the original amount of $85,000 is currently at a balance of $765 million. Two hundred million of this money is in a trust fund for your sister, Lucy."

Gary just sat there awestruck. Belinda continued, "my father helped you to file various patents that you own. There are 12 of them and they have added a significant amount of money to your portfolio. My uncle Michael, my father, and you have created and invested in several different business ventures that span around the world. There's quite an impressively long list of assets and investments that you, my father and my uncle have taken on. The Trinity Trust Holdings name represents a trust between my father, my uncle and yourself.

The Trinity Trust handles about 75 different charities around the world. This is my favorite part, and it is also the most rewarding part of my job. Every person outside this office is a creator or contributor for these charities. One of the job requirements for this company is that you have to create or contribute in some significant way to a charity. Money doesn't count. Alright, I think that covers it, do you have any questions?"

His mind is so stunned, he didn't even really hear anything Belinda said after she said $765 million! Thankfully, Barbara broke the silence when she knocked on the door and brought in a box with Gary's name on the front.

"Great! perfect timing." Belinda thanked Barbara for retrieving the large box. Barbara's face lit up like a Christmas Tree. She had a huge smile on her face. On her way out, Barbara said to give her a call if she needed anything else and exited the office.

Belinda took the box and placed this on the right side of her desk. She opened the box and pulled out a large black backpack. There was only one distinguishing feature, it was a small white patch with large red initials TTH on the front of the backpack. After she opened the main zipper in the backpack, Belinda took out two metals cases, a large blue case and a smaller red one. The blue case looked like it was about the same size as a normal briefcase. The red metal case appeared to be half the size of the blue case and was approximately about the size of a postcard. This red case was twice the thickness of the blue case.

Belinda reached down into the safe on the right side of the desk and pulled out an additional box that contained what a looked like a device that an eye doctor would use to check your eyes. He mused if devices like this were used in medieval times as a torture device. She also took out a small pad that looked like a fingerprint scanner. Belinda grabbed the power cord and plugged one end into a power strip on the floor and the other end had two connection chords, one for the eye scanner and the other end for the fingerprint scanner.

She asked him to place his forehead and chin into the little indents provided by this apparatus. He had been to several eye doctors, mostly for regular checkups so this was not that much different from the tools used in an eye doctor's office. Once Gary was all set, she pressed a button that started the device to do a retina scan. When that finished, she asked him to place his thumb in the fingerprint scanner.

Once both scans were complete, Belinda took a very small micro memory chip from base of the scanner device. She took the blue case and put the memory card into the handle of the case. Next, she flipped open the locks on the case in a special pattern. Left lock open, right lock open, left lock close, right lock close. She then repeated the same pattern. A little blue light flashed next to the base of the handle. When the light stopped flashing, Belinda removed the memory card. She then also performed the same set of operations for the red case.

Belinda had been silent during the whole procedure, and he did not want to distract her with silly questions that might make her do the entire process over again. After Belinda finished with the red case she looked up and smiled at him.

She said, "I know this looked a little tricky, but it really is simple. Both of these cases are now locked and cannot be unlocked until both a retina scan and a fingerprint scan are passed. You only have five tries at this. After that it is locked, and you will need either this memory chip or you perform another retina scan or fingerprint scan using this device here."

She continued, "Below the handle you can see that there is a set of rollers to enter in a number to the case. Numbers are there only as a decoy because they do not open the case. They do have a function however, if you press on all four numbers they will recede into the case, much like a button press. Once all the numbers are pushed in you can turn the handle ninety degrees. Turning the handle reveals a fingerprint scanner. If the fingerprint passes, on the side of the case you can pull up what looks like a small mirror. In the middle of this mirror there is a red bulb. Place your eye about 6 or 12 inches from the little mirror. This is what you will use to pass the retina scan. The case locks itself in 30 seconds after the case is closed and the locks are closed. Ok, why don't we test this to make sure that it is working properly."

After she said that last part about 'working properly', she chuckled a bit. Belinda explained, "If it doesn't work then who do I call? Support? You invented this, so I suppose that is the best support I could get!"

He laughed a little in return. Actually, he felt embarrassed by the fact that he has no memory of creating this type of case. He took the blue case and went through the process of unlocking the case. It worked flawlessly, He also did the red case and it also unlocked without out any problem.

Belinda said, "now the last bit of business here are some documents that I will need you to sign."

"The next document is to change your account status with Trinity Trust. What this means is that after you sign this you will once again be the primary holder of your accounts. My father and my uncle changed the status of this account after you came back from Australia. They did this to protect you and Lucy. They made themselves both become the primary on the account and your status was changed to make you the secondary owner of the account. This document will change that. You will be the primary and they will become secondary. This agreement between my father and my uncle has always been this way and was only in place to be able to protect each other if something unexpected happened." He briefly looked at the document and signed it in the four places that needed to be signed.

The last 4 documents were to authorize 4 different credit cards. Two black and silver credit cards with his name on them and two cards with Lucy's name on them. After the documents were signed, Belinda asked Gary to open the red case. He opened the case and inside were two passports, one for Ireland and the other one for the United States. Below the two passports he found two wallets. Each wallet contained a Platinum American Express card, and a Visa card from GMJ Credit. He later found out that 'GMJ' were the first initials of Gary, Michael, and Joseph. Belinda told him that these cards had extremely high limits on them. There are a couple of checks in place, so purchases that are above $50,000 will be flagged. It doesn't mean that the charge will be declined. It is just there to make sure that it is really Lucy or yourself. There is a PIN associated with both of these cards. The pin for both you and Lucy is 02116 or in other words the zip code of Trinity Square. Please try them out by using an ATM and using this number."

When all the documentation was signed, Belinda took a copy of each document and placed the originals into the safe below the desk. The copies she put into the blue case. She put the passports, the wallet assigned to

Lucy and the memory chip from the eye scan device into the red case. She then placed both cases into the backpack and handed this to him. She also gave him the credit card wallet assigned to him.

After everything was completed, she looked at him in a peculiar way. She broke the silence and said, "Well Gary, it looks like we are all set at least initially. One thing that my father wanted to emphasize is that big purchases will be noticed. This is definitely your money. You and Lucy are free to spend it anyway you wish. However, using this money will attract attention. Don't run out and buy a Lamborghini because a purchase like that will be remembered."

"My father is anxious to sit down with you and discuss a plan for going forward. Also, if you have any questions at any time call my cell phone number here. If for some reason I am not available, here is my uncle Michael's cell number.," she added.

As she was saying this she reached into her pocket and retrieved a business card with her cell and her uncle's cell numbers on the back of the card.

He replied, "No, I think I am all set. I have a lot of information to digest here. Thank You for helping get through all these documents. I am still in quite a bit of shock over the amount of money you said that are in these accounts."

Belinda said, "Just one last thing, I have one question for you. I thought you might remember me. I spent a lot of time here with my father and you have known me since I was in sixth grade. You always called me 'Beebe' or 'Lindsey'."

As soon as she said the two names, a firecracker went off in his head. He then connected the dots and smiled back at Lindsey. "It wasn't until you said the names that connected everything together. I do remember you now. We used to play cards a lot. Gin Rummy was the one you always like to play because we played 5 cents a point. A lot of my memories since I woke up are very scattered. Mostly I have a feeling that something or someone is familiar to me. When I saw you earlier this morning, you did seem familiar, but I couldn't explain why. Now you connected the dots."

Belinda walked Gary out to the elevator and said if there are any problems to give her or her uncle a call.

He looked at a clock in the lobby and it was just 11:00 AM. He thought well there was one place that he could try to use his new credit cards and that was a trip to Morissi's.

Chapter 8 - Severe Clear

Oh, I have slipped the surly bonds of earth
And danced the skies on laughter-silvered wings;
Sunward I've climbed, joined the tumbling mirth
Of sun-split clouds ... and done a hundred things
You haven't dreamed, wheeled or soared or swung
High in the sunlit silence. Hovering there,
I've chased the shouting wind along, and flung
My eager craft through footless halls of air.
Up, up the long, delirious, burning blue
I've topped the windswept heights with easy grace
Where never lark, or even eagle flew.
And, while with silent, lifting mind I've trod
The high untrespassed sanctity of space
Put out my hand, and touched the face of God.

By John Gillespie Magee, Jr

It was a hot and muggy day in August. The air felt as if you were swimming in a pool. Gary had taken a shower before coming over to the airport. In the ten minutes it took to drive to the airport, his shirt was damp with sweat. He looked up at the sky and was rewarded with a stunning pockmarked quilt of blindingly bright blues and white fluffy marshmallow- like clouds. After he drove through the gate, Gary drove to the hangar where his plane was stored in. He was eager and anxious to be airborne. Flying an airplane allows you to have a rare view that very few people are able to see. The air is also a lot cooler the higher you fly so that would be a bonus today in addition to that rare view.

However, it didn't matter how anxious he was to be airborne, you still need to go through several different checklists and perform visual checks of all the flight controls. He needed to check that he had ample fuel and that the fuel didn't have any water in it. Overnight condensation can form in the fuel tanks and water from the condensation will sink to the lowest part of the fuel tank. Typically, this is the area of the wings that were closest to the bottom of the tank. Water is heavier than AV (Aviation) Fuel, so it's pretty easy to see if you take a sample of the gas and look for water in the bottom of your sample. Pilots keep repeating this until there's no water in the bottom of the sample cup.

The flight instructor Charlie, who Gary had been working with for the last few weeks really reinforced this sort of diligence to keep checking everything on the checklist before every flight. Check everything you can on the ground, because it's not possible to stop in midair to fix something. This reinforcement was really helpful. Somewhere in his mind he vaguely remembered doing these checklists. As he was going through the various checklists with Charlie, each item that he performed felt familiar to him.

Gary started to feel a little more comfortable taking control of the airplane from Charlie. In a few weeks, Charlie cleared Gary to fly solo and practice some flight maneuvers in a practice area that was about ten miles south of the airport. Charlie wanted Gary to practice several flight maneuvers that would simulate a 'stall' and execute the correct 'stall' recovery procedure. The reason that pilot's practice this is that when you are taking off or you are landing an airplane you are very close to the point of being in a stall configuration. This configuration is when the nose of the plane is raised up at a steep angle to either allow the plane to take off, or to slow it down enough to land. If you raise the nose up too high when landing or taking off, then the wings of the plane lose the ability to provide lift.

A different way of trying to understand this is to imagine you are driving on a highway at 65 MPH and you put your hand out and keep the angle of your hand horizontal. Now, if you change that angle of your hand slightly up or slightly down, then you can feel a force from the air pushing your hand up or pushing your hand down. Now, if you are in a plane, the wings of the plane are like your hand being held out of a car window. Now, if you change the angle of your hand to be perpendicular with the ground, there is no longer any force to push your hand up or push your hand down. Your hand will only feel force from the air to push your hand and arm back.

In an airplane, if you apply the same analogy, then the wings of the airplane are like your hand out of the window. Slight changes in the angle of the wings cause the plane to ascend or descend. Finally, when an airplane stalls it is very similar to your hand being held perpendicular. There is no force to ascend or descend. As a consequence, the weight of the engine in the front is the heaviest part of the aircraft. This weight forces the nose of the aircraft to go below the horizon and it will start losing altitude. The main reason that pilots practice this recovery procedure of a stall is that every pilot comes extremely close to a stall configuration of the wings when you land or your take-off. Many airplanes have crashed because they encounter a stall when they are taking off or landing. If a plane is stalled with sufficient altitude, the pilot recovers from the stall and the plane only loses some altitude. Landing or taking off you do not have sufficient altitude to recover, and the plane will crash. This procedure must be second nature for a pilot.

Twenty minutes later, Gary was over the practice area about ten miles south-east of the airport. When he arrived at the practice area, the altimeter was showing an altitude of 5500 feet. He didn't need to go any higher, but it was such a beautiful day, with many huge cumulonimbus puffy clouds, that he wanted to fly higher. If he was lucky, he might be able to fly over the tops of these giants, even though he was not supposed to.

Cumulonimbus clouds can form very quickly. The bottom of these towering masses can start forming at low altitudes of perhaps 3000 feet and grow into a towering mass of up to 40,000 feet.

He started doing climbing turns to gain more and more altitude. He found the top of one of these clouds at about 14,000 feet. Gary got to an altitude that was just about a couple hundred feet from the top of the cloud. This view never ceased to amaze him. What he was seeing was just pure power.

Looking at this puffy marshmallow cloud, it was very easy to be persuaded into thinking that this cloud was nothing of substance and its only value was to be looked at and admired. That is where many people have been so wrong, and unfortunately, they have been met with dire or fatal circumstances. A large cumulonimbus cloud like this is created by having warm moist air rising rapidly. Once it cools down it does the same thing and descends rapidly. The strength of the updrafts are easily 3000 feet per minute and the downdraft is descending at about 3000 feet per minute. These clouds are pretty to look at, but the power it wields **must** be recognized and be respected.

As Gary was flying over the top of this cloud, he could see that it was literally growing right below him. The surface at the top of the cloud was bubbling and changing. It was similar to watching boiling water. However, this was not water boiling, this was a cloud forming right in front of him.

He looked at the altimeter and it read as 14,600 feet. The view outside of the cockpit was incredibly surreal and terrifically beautiful. The plane needed to keep a steep angle in order to stay at this altitude.

He started to feel a little strange. He was admiring the view, mesmerized by just how beautiful it was, but his vision started to fade and became tunnel vision. He felt that it was starting to become difficult to breathe. He felt his brain changing. He felt a sense of euphoria and his mind started to race at lightspeed. He was trying to keep up with the barrage of thoughts coming at him. He felt that he was only catching about half of the thoughts that his brain was throwing at him.

Very softly, he could hear his mind saying over and over, "this is not good!". Then it changed, and it became louder. His mind kept saying over and over again, "**this is hypoxia – YOU NEED TO DESCEND!!**"

It took a little longer than usual for his brain to process this. Before Gary could start to lower the nose of the plane, the plane went into a stall. He had the plane at a very steep angle of attack for the last 45 minutes so that he could keep flying at such a high altitude.

The stalls that he had practiced over the last several weeks were all preceded with a physical buffeting of the nose of the airplane and then a gentle lowering of the nose to be lower than the horizon. The altitude was descending. To recover from this condition, you need to change the attitude of the plane in order to bring the nose of the plane level with the horizon.

When his plane was on the verge of going into a stall, he was at 14,000 MSL. There was no slight buffeting of the of the plane and a gentle lowering of the nose. This was very different. This stall was not gentle, it was violent. This type of stall is called a 'spin' or a 'tailspin'. The plane felt like it had been roughly turned upside down. Every little scrap of paper, pen, or anything that was not tied down in the back of the plane was violently thrown into the front of the plane.

He was really starting to feel the effects of the hypoxia that made his thoughts sluggish and slow. It seemed to be an agonizingly long amount of time for his brain to assimilate that the plane was in a spin. His reactions were too slow. His mind was screaming inside his head now, "**do something! Do something, anything and do it now!**"

He was having a lot of difficulty trying to determine what to do next. He knew that somewhere in his mind, and locked away for some reason, was the answer that would tell him what to do next. For every spin, the plane was losing about 2000 feet of altitude. He thought, "if I don't fix this I will die."

The plane was losing altitude quickly. Something needed to be done right now. His altimeter was now showing 6,000 feet above the ground. Somewhere deep in the recesses of his mind, something changed. Something snapped in his mind. It felt like a door that was locked was suddenly unlocked. His mind suddenly and unintentionally brought up a picture of the checklist to follow for the recovery from a spin. The picture in his mind was crystal clear and very vivid, almost as if he were looking at the page in a manual right in front of him. The steps to follow were an acronym called P.A.R.E.

Power to Idle.

Ailerons put into a Neutral position

Rudder – FULL rudder opposite the direction of the spin

Elevator – Push forward to "break" the stall.

Slowly he pulled the throttle back and set the ailerons on the wings to a neutral position. The ailerons' single purpose is to make the plane turn and yaw so putting them into a neutral position stopped that. The plane was spinning vertically in a clockwise rotation, so Gary pushed the left rudder pedal in as far as possible with his left foot. Next step was to push the control yoke forward. This would put pressure on the rear of the plane to push it downward. This also forces the nose of the plane to raise up from below the horizon and become level with the horizon.

He is now at an altitude of 4000 feet. The plane now flying straight and level and maintaining a static altitude. He was really shaken up about what just happened. He wanted to assess what happened. Not now, he would have time later. Now he wanted to get back on the ground. He put all his focus and attention on landing. Even though he had just been through a terrifying event he was able to land the plane. Not perfect but safe on the ground now. He taxied over to the hangar and parked it inside. In a corner of the hangar there was a simple red colored metal table, a fold up blue metal chair. On top of the table was a coffee machine. Gary made a pot of coffee before he took off so there was still a lot left. He sat down at the table with a cup of coffee. He took out his brand-new logbook and started to fill in a new entry for this flight.

Once the logbook was filled in, he got an idea. The reason that he had a new logbook was that he couldn't find his old logbook. A logbook is not something you **ever** toss out when it's filled up. He wondered if the logbook was in the plane. It never occurred to him to look. Behind the pilot seat there was a small pocket to put maps or logbooks, or whatever you wanted to have with you in the plane. Sure enough, when Gary looked in the pocket behind the pilot seat, he found his old logbook.

He took the logbook back to the little table and started to thumb through the pages. Each page had approximately 20 entries that were filled in describing the details of a particular flight. Each entry had space for the date, the time flown, the route, plane type, and plane number, day/night hours, and any special maneuvers that happened on that flight. Every page in the logbook was filled out except the last 3 blank entries on the last page.

As he read the first couple of entries several things started to happen in his mind. Memories that were locked up in his mind, were now unlocked. If you ever have a muscle cramp, and your forearm or your calf muscles are tight and tense it is awful. Eventually, these super tight muscles will relax. That feeling of relaxing the muscles is what Gary started to feel within his mind. A small part of his memories that were trapped and inaccessible were now available.

Each entry he read brought an avalanche of information about that particular flight. Every detail regarding that flight came into sharp focus and was incredibility clear. The details of each particular flight rushed into his mind as a picture. From this picture in his mind, he was able to see the faces of his friends as they arrived at the airport to go up with him. Every detail was right in front of him as a picture and all he had to do was look at the image. In addition, other aspects of the event that the picture related to were not necessarily in an image form. These extra details came to him as a *'sense'* memory. All of his senses were related to that detailed image in his mind. Every sense, touch, feel, taste, or smell was recorded alongside the picture.

He continued reading his old logbook. Every entry brought a rush of details that would *pop* into his mind. The information he was receiving for each entry had an additional curious effect. Somehow, they unlocked many other events and memories that were happening in his life at the time the entry was made. This one entry triggered all the details of a flight he took up to Burlington, Vermont for a conference where he was going to be the speaker. Every detail was there. The weather flying up to Burlington, the temperature, the name of the person who was going to fill up his plane with Aviation Fuel, the hotel he was staying at, and on and on. He also remembered other events that were happening in his life at this point. He remembered a good friend of his had died in a car crash. This made him relive the sadness he had felt when his friend died; but he also remembered so many great laughs and fun that he had shared with his friend. This flight was taken 8 years ago, and he remembers it like it was yesterday.

Other memories came bursting through. He remembered how incredibly excited he was on the day that he went on his very first solo flight. He could remember how upset his parents were when they found out that he was taking flying lessons. He remembered how his sister mocked him when she found out. Lucy would say, "Pilot Gary, when are we going to land. Pilot Gary, can we take the plane to McDonald's drive-through and get a couple of Big Mac's and French fries? I'm hungry, Pilot Gary." The more logbook entries he read brought additional memories or events in his life.

Everything was opening up in his mind.

Over the last several months Gary had tried every way he could think to unlock the memories of his life but just couldn't. All of these unnamed items were thrown into a huge pile of memories that did not have an association of any other event in his life.

In the course of about 20 minutes, he had gone through the huge pile of things he couldn't remember, and now he could associate it with a particular chapter or event that happened in his life. He could remember many more details of his childhood and his teens. He remembered the friends he had. School and college were the more adult memories and perspectives. He had loved two times and those memories could still be hurtful if he let them. Memories again of college and friends. Exciting things to learn about. His appetite for learning and knowing "*how things worked*" gave him an incredible satisfaction. This quest for knowledge and understanding had been a direction in his life that always

126

kept him asking the most valuable question of '***what if…?***'

He had been in the hangar now for about an hour and a half and 3 cups of coffee; so, it was time to stop and go home and let Freddie out and get something to eat. Before he left, he gave Lucy a call to see if she wanted to come over for some take out dinner. He was bursting inside and needed to share this breakthrough with Lucy. She is gonna freak!!

Chapter 9 - Roger Dodger

"I enjoy being a highly overpaid actor.

It's easy to sit in relative luxury

and peace and pontificate on the

subject of the Third World debts"

- Roger Moore

A stunning navy-blue high-end Mercedes Benz sedan was navigating its way through the streets of Boston. Roger Tillson sat behind the wheel of this luxurious, expensive car. He loves it when he sees that envious look people give him as he drives through the neighborhoods of Boston. He gets a real charge when he is at a stop light and the person in the car next to him is looking him, and his car over. He always floors it the moment the light turns green. He never gives way to pedestrians or bikes. His view of pedestrians and bicycles is just "clutter that gets in his way". In essence, Roger is an important person who does important work.

Roger, who is 47, is very meticulous in his appearance. Retaining his wavy strawberry blonde hair from his college days. A little bit of grey is creeping in, but he can change that with a good hair stylist. As he gets older a few extra pounds have started to creep in. But he is not afraid of working hard to maintain his appearance. On the other hand, if he needs to go into his office building, why would he ever take the stairs when a perfectly good elevator can get you there quicker?

For Roger, everything is about looks. If he looked like he was so "important" that the world revolved around him, then his expectation was that everyone must bow before him. He considered himself one of the titans of the corporate world. Now he sees his building and drives up to the little punch screen to enter in his passcode. The red barrier gate opens, and he drives up to the parking garage second floor and parks in his assigned parking space. Pressing the lock on the key fob, he hears 2 quick chirps telling him his car is now safe and protected. The concrete in the walls make every sound like an echo, chirping over and over. Boston is constantly building something in the city, so construction and noise are always present just adding to the melody that these concrete walls sung every day. Every morning he says to himself as he is walking to exit the garage, "GOD it's good to be the king!"

Parking in Boston is always at a premium. Ironically, the MBTA subway was directly across the street from his office, so driving into the office was not really the best thing for his commute. Roger didn't care because the thrill and adrenaline he received in the morning, or afternoon traffic, justified his choice to commute.

Bit By Bit

At 8:30 AM, he steps off the elevator at the 33rd floor and walks towards the glass wall of his company's office. This wall of glass was mostly clear but in one section there was a large rectangle of smoked frosted glass with the name of the company, Bit By Bit. Each letter was carefully etched into the rectangular box.

Roger had the master key for the main entrance door and when he opened the door, he looked at the clock. Then, he looked at the empty reception desk. Even though the receptionist is not expected to start until 9:00 AM, he always made a mental note that "she should be here at least an hour or half hour before the companies' outside lines turn over to a live person". This is a glaring and obvious issue to him. What if a customer came here early? Apparently, they would be expected to wait by the door until the main receptionist was here. This would make the company look bad. Mentally, he notes how he needs to have a talk with his executive assistant, Joanne Druci, to speak to her about coming in early. Why isn't it obvious? I would think that she would get in early every day to demonstrate loyalty and impress the executives.

His business partner, Gary McKeown, might not like it but the person who was hired to do the receptionist job fell under his scope of management. At the start of this company, Gary abdicated all the details of the organizational structure to him. Gary would only manage the engineering staff and the product roadmap and release dates.

This had worked well for the company. Roger was very good at being the front man. There was one exception to this organizational structure. Gary insisted that he have his own executive assistant. He didn't want his "admin" reporting to two managers. Reluctantly, Roger agreed to this. He hired Joanne Druci for his "admin" and Gary hired Rosemary Pillentz as his "admin". It didn't happen often but both Joanne and Rosemary would sometimes have a conflict with something they were working on. Most times they could work out a compromise. Rarely, did Rose and Joanne need to get further direction from both Gary and Roger. Usually however, he and Gary discussed a problem, and a decision would be made that would resolve it. The receptionist fell under Roger's jurisdiction, so he was perfectly within his discretion to have her come in early. A lot of times he or Gary might have an early meeting and it would be nice to have some coffee and a few muffins or bagels to have before the meetings.

Roger walked down the hall towards his corner office. Just like his car, how his office appeared to others was always paramount. It is very large and elaborate. He sits in the chair at the back of a mammoth mahogany desk. The desk looks like the desk you might see in the Oval office. Dark mahogany with lots of hand carved filigree accents. The chair, behind the desk, is an incredible feat of engineering. It has a base that is the normal star shaped five legs with a castor roller. It allows him to swivel, tilt, raise up or lower the chair. The flat seat part and the entire back of the chair is held by a long thick vertical column, from the top of the back surface to the bottom of the back surface. Sprouting out from this vertical column were dozens and dozens of horizontal slats or vertebrae much like a person's spine.

If you were to look at it from the front or the side, you would think it is trying to emulate the shape of the human spine. This is interesting but not nearly as interesting as all the mechanisms that could be set for each person who sat in the chair. Even though the office was very spacious and had a great view of the city, the elaborate chair was the real showpiece of his office.

Every morning he brewed a cup of coffee from his ultramodern coffee machine. He sat down in his chair and leaned back. Every morning he allowed himself a few minutes overlooking Boston Harbor. He watched the city wake up as more and more people came into Boston. Looking out over the city helped him to plan his day ahead or to continue to plan out his long-term goal of accumulating more wealth and power. This had been his goal ever since college.

The one difference was, as he increased his bank account, he would pawn off jobs to others, paying them to get their hands dirty so nothing could be traced back to him. If someone were to look at all his acquaintances over the years, it would be easy to guess that he used other people to do his "money-making" dirty work. He paid these people very well, so it was relatively easy to stay anonymous.

Later that afternoon.

Roger's Accountant - Brent Fisher

Roger had been planning for months, his final play so that he could totally disappear. Everything was coming into play now. Next week his accountant, Brent Fisher, working with Joanne, would create the last 25 shell companies to make it a total of 100 different bogus companies. Each company was strategically scattered across the globe. Brent Fisher was a friend and an accountant. Roger had been working with Brent for the last 8 years and he was helping him perform his grand finale. He used one rule for all his dealings, never overpay for anything.

Roger broke his own rule with two people. Joanne and Brent were doing a lot of things that kept his hands clean. Joanne was his right-hand person and knew all the dirty secrets of stealing money from the company, and from the customers that used the company software. Brent made all of the money going through many different accounts over and over in shell companies so that it was impossible to trace. He paid Brent very, very well. He never knew why Brent rarely bought anything with his own money. It was scattered all over the world, but he rarely saw him spend it.

After you create about 50 or so it starts to become difficult to produce different company names of and all the proper details for a pseudo company. Each company would need a location which could just be a PO Box in a foreign country. All of this could be written in legalize to be able to have the filing not attract any attention. He still gets a chuckle when he thinks of the company that was formed in New Zealand. They were in tears laughing so hard because this new company was called, "Suzy's Lemonade".

Suzie's Lemonade.

Suzy's Lemonade was named after a girl who lived across the street from Roger when he a kid. She had a lemonade stand directly across from Roger's house. Suzy sold Lemonade for 25 cents to people, or cars that passed in front of her house. At some point during the day, usually about noon time, she would pick up her the sign, her table and chair placing it across the street in front of his house. Roger did not like this and told her to get out of his yard. Suzy said that his parents told her it was OK. He went in and asked his mother about it. She told him that it was OK for Suzy to do this. His mother also said that if he was nice, she would probably let him sell Lemonade too. Roger thought if he was going to allow this, then Suzy needed to share any money she made; and also, he would charge a 'land tax'. Roger told Suzy that the only way she could do this on his lawn was that he would help, and she had to share any money she made. Suzy didn't like this, but she finally relented. She was very cunning. Suzy would ultimately get what she wanted and take all the money. She just had to wait a little bit. She saw her chance when she noticed out of the corner of his eye, that Roger parents were in the driveway.

This was her chance. She was calmly sitting in front of the table and saw Roger's parents in the distance. She called him stupid and said peevishly that she did all the work. As if on cue, the tears started to come out and a sobbing wail erupted the second his parents turned into the driveway. She said that Roger was stealing all her money and she was trying to save up for the new "Barbie's Playhouse". After this, his parents made him give all of the $3.75 back that he had made. She packed everything up and went back to her house. Just before she left, she stuck out her tongue and said he was stupid to fall for that trick.

He went back into his house angry. His anger was so great he started to be a little nervous because he had never been this angry. He went to bed that night and he was still very angry. He vowed to never let someone cheat him out of money that he thought was owed to him. She was very cunning, but he would be more cunning. He also made a vow to never let anyone think that he was responsible, was at fault, or did something wrong.

Over many years he never forgot this. Everything he did was to look better than he was. Everything he did created a persona around him, that people would gravitate to because he was going to help them in some way. He did this so many times, he could have 10 or 15 of these relationships going on at the same time, each with different lies and subterfuge. This took a lot of energy to keep everything straight and not be stepping over the lies, keeping it all together.

Logan Airport, Boston, MA

One other trait that Roger possessed, was the ability to jump into the limelight with people that he knew, or people he needed to get acquainted with. He was always in the pictures that went to the Boston papers and magazines. Ostensibly, he was there to give credit to the other person whom Roger was sharing the limelight with. He would share but he always made sure that he got the most credit. If you broke down what he was saying, it became easy to recognize that "the emperor has no clothes."

For example, right after college he bumped into a guy who was in his graduation class at North Eastern University. He was getting off a TWA flight coming from Miami, Florida. In the flight gate area, there was a bank of payphones on the wall. One of the people at the payphone turned around when his call was finished. The only reason Roger noticed him was his North Eastern University backpack. He was only 25 at the time and they both recognized each other from college. He tried to remember his name and slowly it popped into his head - Malcolm Burton. They both shook hands and said 'hello'. Malcolm introduced himself.

"Weren't you a friend of Barry Parker?", Roger asked.

"I knew Barry, but he was not my friend.", Malcolm replied.

Malcolm added, "Barry stole my American Politics final paper right off my computer. The professor told me I had copied Barry's paper word for word. I had to take a summer course to make up for that. It was the first, and the only, course I ever flunked."

He knew exactly which paper Malcolm was talking about. He was not in Malcolm's class, but he took the same course at a different time. Both of them used Malcolm's final for the course. He changed a couple of parts that would make it seem like his own creation. Barry was lazy. The only change he made was to put his name instead of Malcolm's.

Barry ended up dropping out that year. He only went to college because he thought he would be able to get drunk and high every day. He drank and drugged every day but forgot that in order to stay you had to maintain at least a 1.0 GPA.

He could tell that Malcolm was troubled and was trying to decide what he was going to do next. He suggested they get a cup of coffee to catch up after North Eastern. Malcolm said sure but was thinking "I can barely afford a small cup of coffee."

When they sat down at a small table with their coffees, he asked Malcolm if he was doing ok?

"I came here today from Baltimore to go to the U.S. Patent office in Boston. I'm going to file a patent application for a new type of athletic apparel that I created. It's a cotton and nylon mesh material that helps athletes to wick away perspiration and helps to keep the body cooler. The patent application cost was $300."

Malcolm continued to explain why he was so troubled. He said, "I brought $300 in cash with me to the airport in Baltimore. When I went through the security at the Baltimore airport, I put my wallet, watch, and everything else I had in my pockets into my backpack."

He continued, "Even though it's a short flight, I fell asleep for about 30 minutes. After I got off the plane, I remembered that my wallet and watch were in his backpack. When I opened the backpack, the wallet and watch were not there. Someone on the plane went into the overhead and stole everything out of my backpack."

The wheels started buzzing in Roger head. First, the obvious question here was how he can get a piece of this wind fall. Before he had any time to think, he told Malcolm that he would give him the money for the patent filing-fee and pay for a room that night at a nearby hotel. The only thing he had to do was just change his flight back to Baltimore from later this evening and go tomorrow morning. He told Malcolm he would give him a ride to the patent office and help him with the filing.

During this process of filing the patent documents it was necessary to have a witness sign the patent application. Right above the witness signature line was a signature line for a co-inventor. He signed a middle name and last name on the co-inventor line. He signed it using his middle name, Thomas, and last name. It was written so that it was illegible and very difficult to read. He signed the witness line with his first and last name in a way that was very legible and did not look like it was the same style of writing that was written on the co-inventor signature line. Later, if he was ever asked about the success of this company, he would take all the credit for this and attribute the success to his amazing financial wizardry.

Most people would see this type of behavior as sleazy and self-serving. He did not do this just for enjoyment. Roger at his core was a person who was driven by money and power. If you laid bare and stripped down all the walls, all the mental barriers, and revealed the essence of who he was, the only thing you would find is an insatiable need for power and money. Some people might see this and view this as an emotional immaturity. But he would never admit to this because to him he was always able to escape any blame or fault.

Meeting at the Bank of Boston

Several years after college Roger bumped into Gary on the front steps of one of the tall skyscrapers in the heart of Boston's financial district. He was coming out of the building and spotted Gary McKeown walking quickly up the front steps going into the building, lost in thought.

When he called out to him, Gary looked up and at first, he didn't quite recognize him. A second later a smile came across Gary's face and he walked over to him. Gary was carrying a laptop bag and a backpack stuffed with papers. Roger put on his best 'you can trust me' smile, that he had been perfecting for years, and shook hands with Gary. After a minute or two of small talk, Gary looked at his watch saying he needed to get inside for a presentation with some of the executives at the bank. Roger said it was good to see someone from their college days and they should go out some time to catch up. A normal pleasantry that people say to each other as a way of being polite. He wasn't expecting Gary to say yes. But Gary said if he wanted, they could meet that night at BD's around seven. He agreed to meet but again he was surprised so he agreed more out of reflex than anything else.

As Roger stood there on the steps, he watched Gary go up into the building. Gary seemed a little different. In pretty good shape as he had always been. His clothes were rumpled and very casual, A nice Polo shirt and some beige Khaki's. He remembered that this was basically Gary's entire répéteur of clothes. The new office dress code. He didn't understand this code. He only knew one way to dress and that was to dress for success. A dark suit, white dress shirt, and a tasteful bold colored tie; no exceptions and definitely no white sneakers.

Yes, this was typically the way he remembered Gary, but there was something different. He couldn't quite put a name to it but eventually he realized that Gary had this 'aura' of self-confidence that oozed from every part of him. This was very intriguing to Roger!

Having several hours to kill, he went to a local internet café where he decided to search the internet for any information about Gary McKeown. He hated to use computers, but he got by. He asked the guy behind the desk if he could help him to look up a person and any other relevant information. The young kid, with lots of tattoos, said "sure". He could tell that he was asked this a lot.

The kid went over to his assigned computer, opened a browser, and helped him start his search. He told him," type in any question that you want to retrieve information on. For example, if you want to find out where this 'dude' was born, just type in his name and then type in the words 'place born'. He told him he could ask it anything, but he cautioned that it automatically locks the computer if he's searching for porn. Roger thanked him and started to compile a list of information about Gary McKeown.

To his surprise, there was quite a bit of information about Gary. He clicked on several of the links and from what he could tell, Gary had a large following and the reputation of someone who was asking a lot of technical questions. Each time Roger looked, it listed page after page of questions that Gary was asking. Roger didn't understand most of these. Some of the topics kept repeating over and over. Most were about networks and this thing called a 'firewall'. He didn't even want to know what that was about. Other topics were about security and "hiding your information". Another topic which had about 150 questions that Gary had asked were about a thing called encryption and decryption.

Roger realized that he needed a good definition of these terms. The kid at the counter said to type in any information you wanted to search for. Ok, this seemed like it would be pretty easy. He opened a new window, and at the top was a box to type so he typed in "define encryption and decryption."

After a second or two the screen came back with this:

encryption (i[nˈkripSH(ə)n, enˈkripSH(ə)n])
NOUN

> the process of converting information or data into a code, especially to prevent unauthorized access.

decrypt ([dee-kript, di-]
VERB (used with object)

> to decode or decipher.

Roger went back to the page that contained the list of links that mentioned Gary McKeown. He noticed that Gary was talking to some of the top CTO's or Directors at huge corporations. Some of the huge corporations were companies like, Bank of America, GE, IBM, SSA (Social Security Administration), or JPL. And that was just a fraction of the companies that Gary worked with. Quite a long list. Is that how the internet worked?

It looked like Gary was gaining a positive reputation in the technology field. He only comprehended about 2% of the topics Gary was talking about. Most of the complex topics were around things like computer security, or like "what are the best practices to safeguard information, or how to use encryption and decryption properly".

One site that caught his attention was a link to something called 'GM Blog' and underneath the link it said, "Welcome to Gary McKeown's Blog". Clicking on the link, he saw it appeared to be a log of the list of questions that Gary asked. There were hundreds and hundreds of questions over the last couple of years. Why would anyone want to list the questions that Gary asked? It seemed useless and a big waste of time. He thought, how do people earn real money on the internet?

After a couple of hours, he started to realize that he had it all wrong. He mistakenly thought that Gary was listing questions he was asking, it turned out to be Gary that was providing answers to these hundreds and hundreds of questions. Ok, now this makes more sense!

He reread some of the answers Gary was providing to these companies. It seemed that Gary was considered an expert in several different fields of software and hardware engineering. If Gary has all these technical skills, why isn't he making a ton of money off that knowledge? Gary was helping some very large corporations.

If this were me, I would be asking to be paid top dollar by these large companies like Proctor & Gamble, GE, IBM, Lockheed, AOL, Bank of America, Boeing etc. Companies this size have more money than they know what to do with it. It would not be uncommon if you charged top dollar for this service. Charging $1000, $10,000 or $100,000 for services to a blue-chip stock company in this stratosphere, they didn't even flinch if you were charging prices like that.

Why isn't Gary cashing in on these relationships? The wheels of profit and greed started to turn in his mind. Gary's knowledge could be leveraged to produce a real product. Something that could be leveraged in a very lucrative way. The only issue that he saw was that Gary needed to be onboard with this. If he wasn't, then this wouldn't go anywhere.

He started to formulate a grand plan. Gary knew a ton about computers and software, and he could sell ice cubes to an Eskimo. The more he read about Gary's post college years he felt certain that they could put something together that would make them both rich. When he thought about this, he knew this was a gold mine and would make them both very wealthy.

Roger had this tingling feeling. His brain was working at top speed, and he was a little giddy with the rush of possibilities and the money that could be made. People usually set a goal that is realistic for the time and resources available. He never thought like that. He only knew of the weapons he would need to crush anyone or anything that was in his way. This was a technique that he used in business on a daily basis.

Later that night.

He arrived at BD's, a restaurant bar near North Eastern College, at a little before seven, and spotted Gary in one of the familiar booths in the back. A lot of college kids spend time together here, usually to study or write assigned papers. In the winter this was a real haven to be able to focus on work and keep warm. Dorms were always freezing. New England winters can be relentless. BD's, as it was known, was a great place to do some school stuff, get warm and out of the cold and also eat some good food. BD's actually stood for Bez Dupków which means 'no smartasses' in Polish. Food and drinks were cheap. The owner, Stan Kasistki, had a funny reputation about patrons having proper manners. If you were rude or showed any disrespect to Stan or the employees, then Stan was not so nice. Drinks were slowed down, food came out cold or not cooked enough, or the staff just plain ignored you. Most people weren't sure if this was true or just urban myth.

Stan was old school and some students suspected that Stan was actually the person that fueled the urban myth. However, no one that he or Gary knew ever dared to test it. If Stan liked you and you were short on money, he might ask you to do something very trivial. He might ask you to explain an English phrase in the newspaper; or ask you to move a small box to the back of the kitchen. He would complain about his sore back and thanked you for helping him. No one left BD's hungry, or too drunk to drive. The only remedy to get off the bad list was to remember to say, 'thank you' or 'please'. That went a long way to how Stan felt about you.

When Roger walked into BD's he saw Stan who pointed to where Gary was sitting. He gave Stan a smile and asked if he could get a drink for Gary and himself. Stan didn't really trust Roger. No specific reason but his gut did not trust him. He followed the politeness rules, so Stan let him come in and get what he wanted.

Pulling out 2 frosted mugs, Stan filled one with the current draft and the other with Ginger-ale. He had a great memory when it came to the drinks people usually ordered. Roger thanked Stan and put five dollars on the counter for the two drinks. Stan gave it back and said that Gary had already started a tab. He had expected that. Sometimes people are so easy to read.

He picked up the mugs and walked over to the booth where Gary was sitting reading the Boston Globe. Seeing Roger, Gary waved him over. He sat down with a big smile and asked how he was, what he had been doing, etc. After a few minutes Gary, who was starving, wanted to order some food. Gary told Roger to get whatever he wants, he was buying.

After they were done eating, Roger asked Gary what he had been doing since college. Gary's eyes lit it up and a big smile bloomed on his face.

"After graduation I went out to California to take a couple of classes at the University of California – Berkeley. Some of the courses I took were in topics that I really liked; but a couple of classes were about network security and how to protect a company's data and trade secret," Gary said.

"The California lifestyle is just not for me. Weather is nice but there are so many millions of people trying to make it. Not me. Even though we have frigid winters here, LA or San Francisco are not my cup of tea", he added.

Gary said that while he was out there, he noticed a specific weakness of many companies, "There's is so much information 'out in the wild' and no one is taking that information and making it work for them. Companies with huge customer databases never use that information to help them make money. Their approach is one sided. They would see an uptick in sales of a particular item. Their response was to carpet bomb every customer, or residents in a local town, with flyers or mass mailing. There was no targeted way to reach these customers. So out of 100,000 thousand people in a given area they would send out a flyer or call each one of them. Of those 100,000 prospects there might be 50 people that became interested in what was being sold. This is a huge waste of money and resources."

He continued, " To make matters even worse, they have no way to find out whether their ads or flyers are working or not. I knew I could do a better job by taking a large chunk of data to generate very targeted lists."

Roger stopped him at this point to ask a couple of questions. "Most people I know don't use computers, or don't see any use for them. Buying stuff online just seems like it is more expensive. They will charge you at full retail cost and then add shipping to it."

Gary said, "I know that many people think a computer is more of an annoyance and really only good for playing Solitaire or Chess. We have opened Pandora's box with our current technology and there is no going back."

"How so? I don't use a computer and I really don't see the need to have an email address," Roger said flatly.

Gary threw a smile at Roger and replied, "Roger, this is my point exactly. In the grocery store when I get to the 16-year-old cashier, the clerk will ask me what my phone number is, before she rings anything up. Slowly, these bits and pieces of data are being generated and getting more valuable and expensive by the day. Gathering demographic information is getting more and more popular. It would not take that long to create huge lists of very targeted lists of demographic data."

Gary continued, "There's a couple of companies out there that are in the business of collecting demographic information. I think I could do as good, or even better than the other companies trying to find little nuggets of information about people. I also think that large companies have all this demographic information already. They just don't know how to get it in a form they can use. They can't see where there would be an opportunity to sell additional products to their customers."

Gary paused a second and said, "One of the reasons I was at that bank today was to pitch this idea to some of the advertising executives. They can take all of that data just sitting there and make it work for them. For a bank, their products are different flavors of accounts and services. Ask them to provide a list of the percentage of their customers that bounced checks in the last six months. How many of those customers that bounced these checks were on fixed income and deposited a check once a month? The bank can't do that quickly or efficiently. To solve this the bank could do a number of things."

"They could look at each account as a whole. For example, the bank might have several customers who have been at that bank for 25 years. They have always had a positive balance but in the last four months they've overdrawn their account. The overdrafts occurred during the coldest months during winter. The bank could work with them to create a kind of escrow account," Gary added.

"For example, if you're retired and get a Social Security check on the 25th and it's something like

$1000. The bank could see that everything paid out was exactly the same amount as the month before. There are two variable payments like electricity, and gasoline. If this bank knew that this was coming, then they could deduct an average amount from the account each of the last 12 months. In winter, the electricity is high typically about 55 dollars and, in the summer, it is a smaller amount of $45.00. If you were to average for the past 12 months you could say that on average, what they paid was $50.00. Every month this amount would be deducted from the available balance. This service could be an add-on for their checking account for let's say an extra $2.00 per month. This helps both the Bank and their customers. All you need is a good way to create very specific lists that banks could use," Gary concluded.

Roger was really struggling to comprehend all this.

Suddenly, Roger had a "eureka" moment, "OK, I think I get this now. Wouldn't this take months and or years to create? How would you do this? It seems like this would be very specific for a particular bank?"

Gary took a deep breath and took a moment to respond. "Well actually there's a couple of companies that go out and gather these lists of data. A list is a list, right? No, it's not. The company that bought a list from one of these list sellers doesn't know the first thing about the data they just bought. All they care about is the number of items that were on the list they bought. They don't know whether the people on this list are all male or female, don't know how old they are, etc... I think if I had access to their servers, I could generate the perfect list for them."

"OK, Gary I think I see where this is going. Bear with me, I haven't really spent that much with computers and stuff, so it takes me a little longer to get what you are saying."

Gary continued, "No absolutely I understand. This would not have to be a huge project. I would start out by working 'inside the box'. Call this phase one. When I say, 'in the box', what I mean is that we have immediate access to their data and their servers. Everything is done within the company's networks. We are helping them to reuse information that they already have."

Gary continued, "I have been thinking about this a little and I think that a phase two of this project would be 'outside the box'. Companies are starting to create websites which allow them more accessibility and potentially more sales. Ok, now can you imagine if every airline company allows us to put an advertisement on their website for rental cars. The airline might pay us a penny or two for this ad. If the user clicks on this ad, then we carry them to the rental car company that the airline has a relationship with. The rental company pays the airline one penny for having one of their customers go to the Rental Car company. Here's where it gets interesting. The rental car company pays us 4 pennies to carry them from the airline website to their rental car reservation site. It would also add to the rental car companies' servers this information that could be used at a future date for a future promotion they are running. Things like departure and arrival dates, destinations, flying first class or coach, etc. If we pass on the information that the airline customer flew first class that would flag the rental company to offer the best and most expensive car they can."

Again, Gary takes a breather and drinks some of his ginger ale. "Ok here is where it starts to give even more opportunities. The example of the airline and rental car can be drawn out even more. What if we had an ad for a hotel on that rental car website? Or what if an advertisement took the person to a flight insurance company? Each time that's done you could expect to be paid anywhere from 1 cent to 10 cents for these ads. But the best part of this is that we are keeping the data we collect from the airline, rental car, hotel, or travel insurance. And the cherry on top is that we get paid regardless of whether they buy airline tickets, rental cars, hotels etc. Every click can make us money," Gary concluded.

Roger asked, "Correct me if I am wrong but this could develop into thousands of different types of companies. You get paid to put the ad there and you get paid for 'carrying' the user to the next step. This could be used for thousands of different scenarios. At the same time, you are doing this for the company where you placed the ad so this allows you to accumulate demographics of the users of these sites. Wow! This can branch out into so many places like, big department stores, hair salons, restaurants, grocery stores, and on and on. Large companies have the money to do this, so it could be an endless supply. How much do these other data brokers sell their lists for?"

"Well, that's a good question I think I saw somewhere a company that was selling massive lists of people in Canada for $900. The first part of this is what I was pitching to the bank today. I left that meeting and they had a lot of questions. I'm going back tomorrow to provide answers to them about how much it would cost. I haven't created anything yet, but I have some ideas that could make this work. One key part is that the bank must agree that I can have access to many of their servers, but with this bank I am not worried. The meeting I went to today was arranged for me by Joe Daly. You remember him, right? He left after sophomore year and went to Fordham."

Roger said that he didn't remember him, but that was not true. He did know Joseph Daly from college. Roger was involved in a prank that went bad. He never was blamed for this, or even associated with it. Gary, or Joseph for that matter, didn't know that Roger was involved in it. He looked at Gary and shook his head indicating he didn't remember Joseph.

"Hey, I remember from college that you were really good at selling stuff. What are you doing tomorrow? Maybe you could help me pitch this," Gary suggested.

Roger paused for a moment to give a little drama to the conversation. Then he exhaled loudly and said, "Do you really think so? I don't know a lot about computers, but I think I do get the part about having good, verified lists. Ok, yeah count me in. What time is your meeting?"

Roger suddenly got goosebumps running up and down his arms. That was the start of his profitable relationship with Gary. He remembers this day very well.

He left with a big grin on his face.

Chapter 10 - Uber Moron

You can't make a good guy out of an asshole!!

- Anonymous

As autumn starts to fade from the spectacular colors of vivacious reds and exploding oranges to succumb to the inevitable greys and blacks of winter, many people in New England know that there's no fighting against this. Your options are to spend the winter in a warmer place or accept that winter is coming. There's a peculiar love or hate of winter. Cold is pervasive, it's everywhere and there's no escaping its clutches. Your only defense is to bundle up in thick warm clothing and respect that winter is a very powerful force.

The first snow, and those days when it's snowing so hard that everything is white, are oddly a very pleasing sight. Skiing and skating are prerequisites for winter. Heed the "put on your tire chains" signs, drive slowly, give way to plows and salt trucks. Always expect that the other person on the road is not a good driver in snow. Car accidents are much higher in winter, usually it's caused by someone not driving safely for the road conditions.

Conversely, most people start to have a high anticipation of the activities that come with the winter months. Skiing down beautiful, picturesque slopes; skating on large frozen lakes to play a game of hockey, or just skating for the fun of it; speeding down hills in a toboggan full of your friends, or racing each other in silver saucers; sitting near a crackling fireplace with a warm, comfortable blanket while sipping hot chocolate; or joining friends and families in the many winter holidays and "get togethers". Eventually, despite all your reservations, you must give in and resign yourself to accept that winter is coming.

In the weeks after his flying incident, Gary could feel that something was different with him. When he woke up in the morning, he followed a familiar routine. Walk down to Bert's store. Get his usual coffee and a muffin, or something sweet that would be great with his cup of coffee. As usual, Bert said it was on the house as long as he brought Freddie with him. He appreciated the kindness, but he didn't feel right about it.

One day, he saw an AOPA (Aircraft Owners and Pilot Association), sticker on the side of the cooler where Bert kept the ice cream and popsicles. He asked Bert about it. Bert said he'd done a lot of flying in his time. He was trained in the Air Force when he was getting close to the end of his tour of duty. His friend and wingman was killed when his plane crashed landing on a short runway. Gary could see this was a sad memory.

"Would you be interested in going up with me to practice touch and go's, or to go to one of those $100 hamburger, or breakfast places, at one of the airports in the area?", Gary asked. A $100 hamburger or breakfast is approximately $85 for aviation fuel and then $20 for food. He instantly saw that wanderlust of flying put a sparkle in Bert's eyes. He knew there were a few decent $100 burger joints around.

"I remember having a good time at the restaurant at the Nashua airport. " Bert pitched in.

Gary agreed. He had been there a couple of times and the locals were a pretty cantankerous sort. " Betty's welcome to join us if she wants."

"I'd love to go up with you. It's been many years since I've been up in a small plane. Betty doesn't like me going up, but maybe some morning we can sneak away." Gary left Bert thinking about a flying trip.

When Gary got to the park, there were only a handful of people out this autumn morning. Most of them were students at the college who were trying to get in a morning run before classes or trying to stay fit for the track and field team. He occasionally saw Terry and Erin and every time he was amazed at the change in Erin after only a few weeks.

Once Freddie was done with his morning 'business' and he removed it from the field, Freddie ran off to say good morning to each runner on the track. Most of the students had met Freddie before but some just politely avoided him. Some people were 'dog' people, and some were not. Gary thought, I can respect that.

Many mornings he would come to the park because it was peaceful. It also gave him a little time in the day to process all the memories that were coming out from the shadows - all showing up front and center in his mind. They wanted attention!

At times, when he woke up in the morning, it would feel like a firehose of memories and sensations. He felt like it was impossible to keep up with the information overload. Bit by bit, each memory or sensation would start to make sense becoming a little clearer.

These memories came at him all disjointed and out of order. Sometimes a memory would also bring up other memories. For example, a memory of a particular time being at the ocean with Lucy and her kids would come into his mind. This triggered some memories of scuba diving. It wasn't just the memory, but it was also many of the sensations attached to the memory. This gave each memory more context.

A memory of the beach could be anything, maybe a picture in a movie or an image in a magazine. However, that particular beach might not be familiar, the memory needed something more. The smell of salt in the ocean, the feeling of a sunburn on his shoulders, the heat of the sun, the salty sweet of an orange slice, and the coldness of a bottle of soda. The raw power of the waves crashing on the shore would bring up memories of being pulled or pushed towards, or away, from the beach or gliding or fighting against strong currents underwater. There was a very distinct feeling about it all. Going to the park in the morning helped him to process all of the activity going on inside his head.

Processing all these memories was mentally and physically taxing. The coffee and the peace gave him a tiny little anchor to the present, to connect his past. Since there were so many memories and feelings that would wash over him, it was easy to be overwhelmed. One memory in particular was a random feeling and image that he couldn't decipher.

It was very different than the rest. Most of his memories were made up of two parts, a mental picture of something and the other senses giving that mental picture the context. The reason that this memory was different was that the visible picture was like looking at something through water. He remembered a game that he played with friends in a pool. Tossing rings out in the middle of a pool and racing to be the first to grab the ring from the deep end of the pool. The other details of this memory contained feelings of sharp pain in his temples, breathing became slower, body felt cold, his brain went into a hyper thinking mode. Bit by bit different parts of his brain went into a shutdown mode and finally the loss of consciousness.

At this point, he usually stopped trying to process the firehose of memories. It gave him a slight reprieve until the next day, He got up from the park bench, called Freddie over and went back to his apartment, to shower and get ready for the rest of the day. Lucy was coming over today and they planned to go to lunch.

He didn't tell Lucy about his meeting with Belinda. He wanted to tell Lucy on the day he went into Belinda's office, but decided to wait a bit. He'd asked Belinda for a couple of things to be in place before he told Lucy. Belinda had advised caution about bringing any attention to himself or Lucy.

He became very aware of this warning. Every question he asked himself was how he got to where he was now. Why did someone try to kill him? Who was behind this? He almost always ended up at the same place, Roger Tillson! Barry was just a pawn in all this, if given enough money he would do anything, even kill someone.

Events and milestones of the past four years

While he was getting ready to meet Lucy, his mind went into autopilot. Washing, shaving, putting on clothes was not something he had to think about doing. It was just a routine of something we all do every day. While his brain was on autopilot mode, he started to backtrack all of the events he'd gone through over the last 4 years. Some of this information was second hand from Lucy.

Four years ago, he had flown to Australia to go on a scuba diving trip in the Coral Sea off the northern coast of Australia. It was on this boat trip, Lucy told him that he had a failure of his air tank and he succumbed to nitrogen narcosis and became unconscious at the bottom of the dive site which was at a depth of 40 meters or 131 feet.

Roger had him flown back to the United States at the end of January, almost a month after the diving accident. He was taken to the Ashwood Facility and checked in as a long-term patient. Lucy had contacted everyone she could think of to see if they knew where he was and if he was ok. Nobody could help solve this.

At the end of January, Lucy received a box, it contained several items that she recognized as his. There was also a letter from his business partner, Roger. The letter explained how sorry he was to tell her about Gary's condition. In the letter he told Lucy that Gary was checked into the Ashwood Hospital, a long-term facility. It also gave the number of the facility and who Lucy should speak to. Roger went on further and said that the company was taking care of all the costs for Gary to stay at the facility and any costs for medical treatments that were incurred. Finally, he mentioned that all transportation costs to bring him back to the United States were also paid.

Over the course of the next two years, he was a patient in the Ashwood facility. Roger was true to his word; all costs were paid for or, so it was assumed based on his letter. He hated that he put Lucy through this ordeal for two years at the facility and also another two years at Lucy's house. Miraculously he woke up from the coma state. It was a total of three years that he was in a coma.

For the next six months Gary worked very closely with physical therapy to return his muscles back to a state that would allow him to stand and to walk. He also needed balance for him to walk around. Lucy had done an incredible job of keeping his muscles moving around so that he did not lose a lot of muscle tone. The other thing was the food that she was giving him was very nutritious and helped him to maintain healthy levels of vitamins.

The woman who came over to help him with his physical therapy was a woman with incredibly piercing eyes and a very serious demeanor. He knew instantly that she was a no non-sense woman. Her thick Haitian creole accent was difficult to understand at first, but he started to understand bits and pieces. From what he could tell was that she was laughing at him while he was doing the physical therapy. She was making fun of him and would keep doing so until he understood her words.

He picked up small phrases like,

"you be sting big man, luke at ya now. No strong and no big man.

Ya daat's right, I keeps it up til u

understands yu is string and be string."

He interrupted her and said, "Hey I am big, and I am strong!"

She looked him in the eye and said in perfect English, "Good! Now we start the work. **SHOW** me how strong you are. Push my hands forward, lift your leg up. Do that for me and I will help you to be strong for yourself. I have worked with many men that I help to be stronger. Don't do this and you will not be able to help yourself."

Each day he would back track the events and the people of the last four years. It helped him to stay grounded in the present.

Lucy knocked on the door and he went to answer, but as usual Freddie got there first needing to know who it was. Lucy brought with her some Starbuck's coffees and a couple of muffins. She brought it over to his makeshift dinner table, which was really just an old card table. He grabbed a notebook and pen. He was still trying to make sense of his past and the warning from Belinda.

As they started to sip their coffees, he took the notebook and started to write while he talked. "Ok, first thing here are the players involved, or who appear to be a part of this"

He drew one vertical line down the page. Above these two columns, He wrote at the top of each column, "Who" and "What". Underneath the "Who" column, he wrote the following names: Roger Tillson, Barry Parker, Joanne Druci, Ben Costello, Brent Fisher, Joseph Daly, and Milly Howards.

He looked at Lucy and she said, "You should put your name and my name also. We are both part of this subterfuge, so our actions might help draw a line around the mystery."

"Well, look at you, I guess all those Nancy Drew books are starting to pay off," Lucy gave him the look that if she had laser eyes, she would be slicing him in pieces, right now.

After about an hour of discussion, it appeared that several people on the list were not who they pretended to be; and there must be a reason why both Roger and Barry disappeared. Now Belinda said they were looking for Roger.

Roger Tillson

- Met in College
- Met a few years after college and they started a software company called Bit By Bit
- Roger is nowhere to be found

Barry Parker

- Met in Collage.
- Dropped out in Junior year in college because of him cheating
- Was expelled from the university for cheating and plagiarizing one of his final papers

*Joanne Druci

- Roger's Administrative Assistant
- If anyone knew where Roger is, then she would know

Ben Costello

- Was supposed to go diving but dropped out at the last minute.
- Like Roger he has also disappeared. Was he part of this?

Milly Howard

- Nurse at Ashwood Facility
- How is she involved? Is there a connection back to Roger?
- Was she telling someone what his physical state was?

Ashwood Facility

- Roger dumped him off there and then left town
- Roger only paid for the cost of transporting him from Australia

- Joseph, not Roger was paying the monthly charge for his care at Ashwood

☑Joseph Daly

- Good friend from college. Worked with him for 20 years
- Roger and Barry nearly killed him in a fraternity hazing stunt

☑Lucy McKeown

- Took care of him while he was at her house
- Roger made all the arrangements for Ashwood
- Informed only after receiving the letter from Roger which was a month after he had been transported to Ashwood

☑Gary McKeown

- Worked with Roger etc.

☑RoseMary Pillantez

- Gary's Administrative Assistant
- She has worked with Gary for the last 5 years

☑Alexi Restorz

- Worked with Gary on the total rewrite of the software to a new product for bitcoin and blockchain security. Very hard worker
- Gary and Alexi shared many late-night pizza's

As the morning started to change to afternoon, he looked at what they had written. There were still a lot of questions but at least it was a start to unravel this mystery. Everything all pointed back to Roger. Some of the people on the list he was absolutely sure were not trying to harm him. The people he trusted were all marked with a checkmark ☑. For the people that he didn't trust or were people that he wasn't really sure about. Those he marked with an asterisk *.

After looking at the list he told Lucy, "Before I left for Australia, actually it was the day that I was leaving for my trip, I was looking at several accounts that were just not making any sense. I typically don't get into the finances, but I was getting some calls from many longtime customers who were not happy about the security and potential information that had been stolen. Many of them said that our software was leaving their networks vulnerable to being hacked."

Lucy seemed interested.

"Do you remember when Roger and I first started our company, we were in the business of collecting information for companies, and also for individual customers. Companies really started to rely on our software so that they could start to quantify information about their customers, and potential new customers."

Lucy listened intently.

"Our software was able to collect and create targeted lists and was able to spot different trends for all kinds of marketing and direct selling. We also had the trimmed down version that we sold to regular customers themselves. Do you remember those discounts, and cheaper prices, when you would buy stuff?"

Lucy interjected, "Oh yeah, I forgot about that. That was great software. I bought a lot of birthday and Christmas gifts for a lot less using the coupons and promo codes it collected. I loved it. I haven't used it lately though. What is it called again, 'Honey' something?"

"Honeycomb Discounter."

Lucy smiled and continued enthusiastically, "No wait, oh yeah, I forgot about that. That was the morning you came over when Peter was sick with a cold. He named it when you asked him 'what you should I name my new software?' He said 'Honeycomb.' Remember he was hungry after an awful night being sick. He had only one thing on his mind, and it was the was Honeycomb cereal."

"At the time we were selling the software, people didn't even think twice about giving out their email address, phone numbers, or really any information that companies would ask for. Everywhere you went you would have to open up an account and create a profile for a website, or get a specific newsletter, or something.

"I do it all the time." Lucy added.

"Remember at first it was easy to give bogus information but eventually it became more difficult, and you had to enter real information in order to gain access. The questions that people were being asked to provide might have sensitive identity info. The majority of people using the internet thought well this is a good company, I can trust them with this information'."

Lucy nodded with her understanding.

Gary continued, "Social media, privacy, terms of conditions overloaded internet users. This information you used to create an account started to slowly become a commodity that could be used or sold for whatever purpose. Often this information was used for bad purposes."

He looked at Lucy and her eyes didn't have the eyes *glazed* overlook yet, so he went on, "The internet in the beginning was really designed for connecting computers and sharing information. That has totally changed now. Information is the currency of the internet. So, your email address in the early days of the internet was only worth about $0.01 to $0.05. Today it is much more. Your email address might be worth anywhere from $5 to $65.00. Imagine if you had a list of 30,000 email addresses and each address is worth $65.00 - if it is a qualified lead email address."

Lucy said, "Ok, yeah, I get it. You invented junk and spam mail. Wow, do you have any other tricks?

He smiled at her. In a way Lucy was right, even if the intent was not to do that he thought. The legacy might be to have these automated pieces of code going to thousands and thousands of websites and gathering any kind of profile information it could. In the early days of the internet, different standards and protocols were really brilliant, but there were also some parts that were easily used for bad purposes. It's very easy to find out what the name of the servers are that handle all the email going into a company. There are some tricks that you can use with this mail server. For instance, I can send a message to Lucy and make it seem like she was receiving an email from anyone. Maybe it is the US president, the IRS, Bill Gates, Santa Claus, or anyone I wanted.

He was lost in thought and Lucy broke him out it, "Hey do you want to get some lunch or something? They decided to go to a favorite local Chinese restaurant.

After they ate lunch Gary and Lucy were sitting at the table just sipping some tea. Gary's new cell phone rang. He dug it out of his pocket while Lucy gave him a curious look. It took a couple of moments before he realized it was Belinda Daly. After a brief conversation, he thanked her and hung up.

He said, "That was Belinda Daly, she's the daughter of my friend Joseph. Do you remember Joseph, from college? He's on the list we did this morning."

Lucy thought about it, "Wasn't he the guy that we would go to dinner within the city? He was incredibly nice. Belinda is Joseph's daughter, right? She came with him a couple of times. I remember that she was very insistent that her father call her 'Lindsey' and not 'Belinda'. So, was that a social call or business?"

He hesitated for a moment in order to get his thoughts together. "Well yes and no. She wanted to ask if I could meet her father, Joseph, for dinner next week. Are we all set to leave? I should probably get home and let Freddie out."

When they arrived at his apartment, Gary asked her if she wanted to go for a walk. About twenty minutes later, they were sitting on the park bench that he usually goes to in the morning. Freddie went off to make the rounds, meeting all the new people in **his** park and also his friends. There was always an unlimited supply of smells and scents for Freddie.

Gary looked at Lucy with a very serious face and said, "I didn't say this at the restaurant, but I have some very, very, very big news. Don't worry, it is all good news, I promise."

"Gary there's very little you could tell me that I would be surprised about. Go ahead, I promise I won't freak out."

"Well, you might not say that after I tell you. Ok, I went to my friend Joseph's office about a week and a half ago. That money that I found in the hollow leg of my coffee table and the key I found was a clue that Joseph left for me telling me to go to meet him at his office in Boston. Well Joseph and his brother Michael, were away on business and wouldn't be back in the office for a couple of weeks."

"So, you met Belinda or Lindsey?", Lucy concluded.

"Yes. I went into Boston and went to the offices of Trinity Trust Holdings. Belinda told me a lot about my financial relationship with both her father, Joseph, and her uncle, Michael. I don't know if I ever told you this but both Joseph Daly and Michael Daly were in the same class as me at North Eastern. We have been friends for a long time. Michael and Joseph both went to Harvard Law, and they were the very good contract and IP (Intellectual Property) lawyers that helped me with all of the contracts and legal filings that I was involved in. The three of us created the company Trinity Trust Holdings. Well, Trinity Trust Holdings is a lot bigger than you can imagine."

"Ok. I remember after you graduated that you were working at a friend's company. I suppose I didn't connect the dots."

"They have helped me in so many ways both with making some great investments and also helping me with several legal issues that I was running into. When I went into Boston, Belinda wanted me to sign several documents. As the name of the company suggests, the three of us had to operate on a level of 'trust'. Hence the name Trinity Trust. We wanted to have a way to protect each of us if something were to happen.

When we started this company, each of us was the primary owner of one third of the value of the company."

Gary continued to explain, "When we started Trinity Trust Holdings, we created a contingency plan for each of us. We did this to protect ourselves and also if something happened, we could be assured that the money was given to a named person, in my case, I put your name as the benefactor.

"My trip to Australia and being in a coma, forced this contingency to be executed. Documents were signed by Michael and Joseph to change my ownership of any assets in Trinity Trust Holdings from a primary owner to become the secondary owner."

"Now that I am awake, the same thing happens, I become the primary account holder and Joseph and

Michael become the secondary account holders. Joseph and Michael and I all have the same contingency plans in place. If I had not woken up, or drowned in Australia, God forbid, Joseph and Michael would have contacted you and made you the primary account holder."

"How much are we talking about? Enough for a pizza and beer?", Lucy said with a quick retort.

"Well, it is a little more than that. Do you remember the money that Mom and Dad left to us? At the time neither of us were in any shape to think about the $85,000. Joseph helped with selling the house and any legal issues during the closing of the house. Joseph said that he could take care of it for a while until we both got on our feet again. I gave him the $85,000. Joseph took this money and started to make some investments for us. He did very well on these investments."

Lucy interjected, "I got statements from Fidelity each month. I saw that amount growing over the years. Whatever the amount was I always split that figure in my head knowing that this money was for both of us. The last time I looked at it was about $149,000 now. Is that money ours or is Joseph taking a piece?"

"No Joseph never took a dime from that. That $149,000 is the interest that is generated by some of our investments. We invested in several properties and also several technology companies. After college, I became involved with a lot of very large companies. I was also writing and publishing many articles. I spent six months working on creating a new piece of technology that was missing in the tech field. This piece of technology was something I was able to get patented. Many large companies around the world were using this software illegally. We sued two companies for an astronomical amount of money. We won the legal battles, and it took several years but we were awarded the full amount of the lawsuits. One company was obligated to pay us $500 million dollars. Another was for $250 million dollars. The total of this was $750 million dollars. We divided the amount between the three of us and that came out to $250 million dollars. I split my share with you because the money we inherited was $85,000 and this was used to litigate these cases. Therefore, half of the money is yours. This amount is $125,000,000 dollars."

Lucy looked at him in a funny way. She looked confused and asked timidly, "I don't know if you are playing a joke on me or are you really saying that I have $125 million dollars?"

"Yes, Lucy, you own $125 million dollars. A lot of this was happening at a time when David was going in and out of the hospital. I didn't want to distract you during that time. Right before David died, I talked to him to get his advice on telling you about this. He asked me to do a couple of things. Make sure the boys are taken care of for school and put some of the money in a trust for them to be paid out when they are 25 years old. He said he wanted them to live normally and not be spoiled. Of course, he winked at me when he said that and told me I could spoil them a little bit. David was heartbroken that he was putting you through so much of his sickness. He asked me to make sure that you would be financially secure. He also asked me to do another thing. He asked me to wait a while before I told you. David was very aware of what this disease was doing to you. He told me that he trusted me to tell you when the time is right."

"So why is now the right time? Have you known about this for the last 12 years?", Lucy said with a little bit of sarcasm.

"I did tell you about this 10 years ago. We were in the car and going out to dinner with Joseph, Michael, and Lindsey. The reason we were going out that night was to share in the victory of winning the two cases of patent infringement for $750 million. Later, at the restaurant, I made a toast of winning the cases and each of us making $250 million from that. Even though we won those two cases, it took years to collect on those cases."

Lucy was just awestruck. She thought that trying to understand all this was quite a lot for her to take in. Lucy was annoyed with Gary and for some reason she couldn't quite figure it out.

She said, "I wish I knew about this sooner. My life might be different, who knows. But you should have told me very soon after David died. I mean not on the day he died but a short time after. Not two years."

Gary's expression was totally blank. He couldn't quite figure out why she was mad at him.

"Gary, I understand that you were trying to honor David's request and you felt you were doing the right thing. You did tell me about this 10 years ago, great. But you didn't follow through with telling me how to access this or really any other details about this. Gary, you should have told me sooner."

"Lucy, I am sorry I didn't tell you earlier and provide more details. I should have given you this information earlier."

Lucy replied, "Ok. It's just so surprising to me. It's a lot to digest all at once."

Gary reached into his pocket and gave Lucy an envelope that contained two cards. One was an American Express card and the other one was a blue MasterCard. He told her, "These two credit cards are in your name and have incredibly high limits. The cards are from GMJ Holdings which stands for our first initials, Gary, Michael, and Joseph. There's a limit of $75,000 per purchase. It's only there to make sure that it is you that's making the purchase. If you want to splurge and buy a $100 million-dollar mansion; then fine, have fun. But Joseph and Michael have cautioned both of us to not make big purchases because large purchases will be remembered and might attract unwanted attention. Roger Tillson is looking for me."

He looked down at his feet where Freddie was comfortably lying. Gary looked normal to Freddie, but he was a little worried about Lucy. Her face was giving off weird signals to Freddie. She didn't look mad or sad or hurt, but it looked like she was confused. Freddie thought well that's ok, I get like that sometimes too.

Gary looked at Lucy and they both just sat there for a minute as Lucy was still trying to absorb the news, he told her.

He finally said, "I have been thinking about this for a little bit now and Joseph is right to be cautious. Where was Roger during all of this? He rigged something up with that guy Barry, to murder me, I suppose. The only thing Roger did was have me shipped back home on a freighter. This is when Joseph and Michael started to act on our contingency plan. Did Roger say that he was going to pay for that long-term facility? He didn't pay one cent. Trinity Trust paid for that place for two years. They were very suspicious of Roger and Barry and suspected that they had someone on the inside that worked there giving them information on my condition."

At this point, Lucy realized that she needed to trust her brother and stand by him just as she had always done.

One Week Later

Bit By Bit

Gary was in the lobby of the Boston Harbor Hotel at about 6:30. He found a nice comfy chair in this busy high-class lobby to wait for Joseph. He knew that the lobby would be comfortable with it's expensive finishes. This night the Boston Harbor lobby was buzzing with all the sounds and noises that most big hotel lobbies have. It's interesting sitting in a lobby with so much controlled chaos and it's easy to eavesdrop on the people nearby.

A couple was arguing with the man behind the reservations desk about the room they wanted and what kind of view they would have. Obviously, the rooms on the upper floors would have a fantastic view of the harbor and they would be able to sit out on their little deck to watch the sunset or sunrise. It's clear that the person at the reservation desk was unflappable to the "not so nice attitude" the couple was giving him. After he was able to find something palatable for them, the couple left the desk.

Gary didn't realize that the reservation person was looking at him. He smiled and nodded to him as a way to say silently that the couple was "very bitchy", and he handled it like a professional. The man smiled back at Gary as if to say "thank you" for noticing and as far as rude guests they were barely registering with him as being a problem.

Boston Harbor Hotel was very memorable. Only a couple of blocks further inwards on the marina was the Boston Sailing Club. Gary spent a lot of time sailing into and out of the Boston harbor for different sailing destinations. Summer times were great fun taking several friends, or Lucy and the kids, sailing over to Martha Vineyard or Nantucket. He understood that one of the really great perks of sailing is to be competent enough to go "bareboating". Bareboating is essentially going to some nice vacation spot in the Virgin Islands, the Caribbean, or the Mediterranean; chartering a 60 or 80 foot boat for a week to sail around anywhere you wanted to go. Traveling with a group of friends, it's a great way to vacation in the warmer climates.

Gary looked at his watch and noticed that it was now 7:00 PM. Belinda, or Lindsey, told him Joseph would meet with him at 6:30. He didn't mind him being late, but it was very unusual for Joseph. He continued to wait but stopped listening to the conversations in the lobby and instead watched the main doorway.

It was now 7:30. He was getting nervous worrying if Joseph had a car accident or something. He thought about calling Lindsey. Just as he was getting his wallet out to find the business card, she had given him with her cell number, Joseph came into the lobby. He saw Gary and was almost running toward him. Something was wrong, very wrong!

"Joseph, what is going on? You look stressed, are you alright?" He said as he got up. Joseph's raincoat was dirty, almost like he had fallen into a large puddle. Joseph reached into his raincoat and pulled out a small journal book. It looked like it been through a lot of wear and tear.

"Gary, it's really great to see you. I've missed you, my friend. I'm sorry but I can't stay. I have to get away from you so that whoever is following me doesn't see us together. Take this and do not show it to anyone except Michael. I'm sorry about this, but I'm sure someone saw me coming in here. Keep this book safe. This has all the accounts and where they are and how much is in them. I really am sorry. Gary, guard this book! I'll call you as soon as I can." Joseph leaned in and spoke to him in a hushed way,

And with that Joseph rushed out of the back entrance of the hotel to the marina. There's a long deck all along the marina behind several of the hotels. He was walking very fast, almost a run to get to a hotel about three blocks down. When he reached it, he went out front. While he was walking, he punched into the Uber app on his phone and the address for this hotel. When he got to the front of the hotel, he immediately saw the black Lexus with the Uber decal. Joseph jumped in and asked the driver to take him to his place in Cambridge.

Traffic was light this time of day, so the driver was not without the banter of small talk. He talked about the Red Sox, the Patriot's. Joseph was only half listening and thinking about the guy in the parking garage who appeared to be following him a couple of hours ago.

Joseph had already taken two different subways to make sure someone was not following him. As he was thinking about this, the banter from the driver started to stir up old memories. He never really looked at the driver when he was getting in the car. But he knew this voice of the driver. Now, he was positive when the driver laughed at something. This is when Joseph knew that he was caught.

It took a second or two, but Joseph would never forget that face from his college days. Barry's laughter was unique, very loud. He kind of snorted like a pig. Barry turned to him and said, "Now, you remember me, right?"

Barry turned into a dead-end street with a bunch of large dumpsters. He had a baseball bat on the front passenger side of the car. He got out of the car and opened the back door where Joseph was sitting.

"So, where is your smart-ass boyfriend? I've been looking for him. Tell me now and I won't hurt you too much. Don't tell me and I will kill you, 'capeesh'?"

"I thought you would know. Gary's in that shitty long-term nursing facility you and Roger put him in," Joseph lied.

"Nope, wrong answer!" Barry took the fat end of the bat and pushed it into Joseph's face, a feeling similar to being punched in the face by someone's fist. Joseph's nose instantly started to bleed.

"I was at that crappy place looking for him. He ain't there, jackass! I have a little honey in there that said he was taken out of there about two years ago. So, I'll ask you again, where is your boyfriend, Gary! If I don't get a good answer, I am gonna crack your skull."

Joseph thought Barry would do this no matter what he said now. He had two options, tell him the truth, or tell him to piss him off. Maybe it was even a little pound of flesh for him.

"Barry, I really never thought you would be so stupid, or then again maybe I did. You and Roger thought you were putting on this big con-job. Gary and I have made millions, no actually it is billions of dollars. Gary got out of that place after just two months, and the last I heard was that he was living in Spain or sailing around the Caribbean. We knew about Milly and your contact with her, so we paid her very nicely to keep you and Roger in the dark. Ha-ha, you thought she was your little squeeze that you could do your thing and then leave. Actually, it was the opposite. You were her little plaything and when she got tired of you, she was done."

Barry's face was getting more and more red. He screamed at Joseph, "You and Gary think you are so friggin smart, well let's see how this baseball bat feels about that."

Barry grabbed Joseph out of the back seat and kicked and hit him with the bat until Joseph was bleeding from several places. He suspected his nose was broken. While Joseph was on the ground, Barry picked up Joseph's left leg and kept hitting and hitting it with the bat until he felt and heard a snap as if his leg was broken. Barry wasn't done there, He picked up Joseph's right leg and hit it with the bat. This sounded and felt different to Barry. It felt like he was hitting something metal or hard plastic and not flesh. He raised the bat and hit his leg again, but this time the leg Barry was holding separated from Joseph. Barry wasn't expecting that and fell back and landed on his ass.

Joseph saw this and started to laugh hysterically. It was painful to laugh, and blood and pain was everywhere. Joseph said to Barry, "You forgot about that, didn't you? You forgot about what you put me through in college? I lost that leg because of you, don't you remember! You tied me to that pole in the park during that blizzard. You and Roger left me there in my underwear. I lost my leg that night because of you. You really are a moron. Hahaha! You are the UBER MORON." Joseph couldn't stop laughing when he said that.

Joseph knew that this was going to be the end of it for him. Barry was breathing very hard, and spittle was coming out of his mouth from the rage that was boiling in him. Barry took the bat and hit Joseph on the head. He kept hitting him everywhere. Leg broken, ok well let's break your arms too. Then, Barry stopped and thought he had gone too far. Joseph was not breathing and was bleeding in a lot of places. Barry quickly got into his car and started to drive away.

Chapter 11 - Michael Daly

In a world filled with hate, we must still dare to hope.

In a world filled with anger, we must still dare to comfort.

In a world filled with despair, we must still dare to dream.

In a world filled with distrust, we must still dare to believe"

- Michael Jackson

    Gary sat back on his chair. In his left hand, was the book Joseph had handed him. He didn't fully understand the reason Joseph asked him to do this, but he shoved the book carefully into his coat pocket. He thought he should get out of the hotel lobby, so he wouldn't stand out. His first thought was to go home but, something in him decided that he needed to go to a quiet place and process the event that just happened. He crossed the street to the entrance for Boston's subway and walked down a flight of stairs. At the bottom of the stairs was an arrow pointing left with many of the stops outside of the city. Another arrow pointing to the right to go to further into the city. He went to the right taking the subway to the Prudential stop. He went up a short set of stairs and exited the subway station into the lobby of the Prudential Center. Most of the locals in Boston called it "The Pru".

The front of the building opened to a large and dramatic presentation of opulence and luxury. The Westin hotel reservation desk was on the first floor. There was also a ticket booth to take the elevator directly to the Skywalk Observatory, or the very expensive restaurant called, "Top of the Hub". One side of the building faced Fenway park. Therefore, during World Series or Playoff Games, the top twenty floors turned office lights on to spell out, "**GO SOX**"

As he rode the escalator up to the first level, he took note of the multiple levels of shops and stores above him. The lobby was really a combination of a hotel, office space, and a mall all in one. It felt like a grand old Georgian style entry way. Very dramatic and huge. It was hard not to be impressed at how large this lobby was. Marble floors and a large set of wide marble stairs ascending to the first level. On either side of the wide marbled staircase was a set of escalators. Multiple levels of stores and shops added to the opulence of this large entryway.

A sign pointed in the direction of the hotel reservation desk. He went to the first person available and purchased a ticket for the Skywalk Observatory. Walking over to an elevator that took you to the top, which was on the 50th floor, he rode to the 50th floor. It took a couple of minutes to clear his ears from the rapid ascent in the elevator. Pulling out the ticket that he purchased downstairs, he handed it to a young girl who was waiting by the elevator to collect tickets. Gary found a quiet area where there were very few people and sat down on one of the flat padded benches that were laid out at varying spots along the walls of glass.

He had come here for a couple of reasons. First, he needed to think about what just happened with Joseph and this was his quiet, private place to think. He started to replay what happened at the hotel in his mind almost frame by frame.

Gary remembered he had been watching the door looking for Joseph. The noise in the lobby was very chaotic. People were coming in and out of the lobby door continuously since he had been there. Every time the door opened; cold air rushed into the lobby. The cold air contained its own set of noises and smells from outside. Cars honking, the salty smell of Boston Harbor. Someone was smoking a cigar outside the entrance of the lobby area. He spotted Joseph even before the valet opened the lobby door for him.

At that moment he remembered, he stood up still looking at the door. Joseph came in and he immediately saw Gary. He replayed that last part of seeing Joseph walking into the lobby in his mind. When that lobby door opened, he saw a big heavy-set person who was following Joseph. He could tell that the man was very muscular and didn't quite fit into his green t-shirt and black jacket. It looked like this man was constantly keeping an eye on Joseph.

When the lobby door opened the man in the black jacket completely turned around and walked away from Joseph. At the time, Gary was thinking about seeing an old friend, so it didn't fully register yet in his mind. As Joseph came closer, he could tell that something was wrong. Joseph had a panicked look about him. His eyes were darting everywhere around the lobby. Then Joseph said he was sorry and that he had to leave. Before Joseph left, he shoved a small black journal into his hands and told him to only give this to Michael, no one else. Joseph was out the back door towards a walkway that ran along the harbor. He looked toward the front door of the lobby and could see the man running towards a busy street that ran parallel to the harbor walkway that Joseph had just gone to.

While he was sitting on the bench in a corner of the Observatory, all the images of the past hour started to roll over him. He got a fleeting look at the person behind Joseph. It was only a tenth of a second that he saw this person. This face was familiar to him. Where had he seen this face before? Instantly, he remembered that this was the same face that he saw on the bottom of the ocean so long ago. Barry Parker! He was sure this is who it was.

He took the book out of his pocket and thumbed through the pages. Every page contained three columns, an account number, a password, and a dollar amount. In the password column it was almost the same password,

Jade Unicorn. Many of these entries were the same or had some variation of the password, like Unicorn Jade, or Uncorni Jade. On the last page was a hastily written message which was almost illegible. Gary had seen this scribble many times and knew how to read it. The message said, "Call Michael" and below this was the number for Michael's cell phone. One of the trademarks of Joseph was that his penmanship was atrocious, barely legible. However, when Joseph wrote down numbers, they were almost perfect. It looked like it was typewritten.

He reached into his jacket and took out his cell phone and was about to call Michael. He hesitated for a second, was he overreacting? Seeing Joseph looking so nervous and panicked, the hastily scrawled message on the back, and then Barry Parker. He knew that he needed to alert Michael.

When he dialed the number for Michael, it rang for a long time; but just as he thought it was going to go to voicemail, someone answered the phone. Before he could say anything, the person on the other end said, "Gary?"

"Yes, this is Gary. Is this Michael?"

Michael said very quickly, "Gary, we need to meet as soon as possible. Can you meet me at the Brown Derby restaurant at Faneuil Hall? I'll be there in 30 minutes at the bar in the back part of the restaurant."

He agreed and hung up the phone. Quickly, he went downstairs, got on the subway to go to Faneuil Hall, or Quincy Market as it was also known. Typically, it's a big tourist draw. Quincy market has many gift shops, or a variety of food counters to buy authentic Boston or New England cuisine like Maine Lobsters, New England Clam Chowder, fresh Atlantic scallops, saltwater taffy, or Gino's Boston's North End artisan pizza and on and on. Of the several restaurants here, the Brown Derby is about halfway down the main corridor of vendors selling their goods. There was a small set of steps to go underground and into the restaurant and bar.

Gary walked in and went over to the bar. He didn't see anyone sitting there, so he went to the far end and sat down on a hard-wooden stool. He ordered a glass of cranberry juice and soda water. A TV on the wall was blasting the latest Patriots game. There were only a few tables in this little bar/restaurant and most of them were full. The noise of the TV and the background noise of other patrons was surprisingly not all that loud. If anything, it drowned out the din above him of the busy Quincy Market main corridor of people.

It was not that long before he saw Michael come in. Michael took a seat next to Gary. It always surprised Gary how close Michael and his brother Joseph were in looks. Biologically they were twins, so the resemblance wasn't a surprise. They were twins in looks but they each had different and distinct personalities. Joseph rarely got angry. He had a quiet logical approach to business. Michael on the other hand, could at times be impulsive and quick to decide an outcome based on how it felt.

Joseph and Michael were both exceptionally smart. In a weird kind of way, that oppositeness of their personalities complemented their physical similarly. Listening to their banter of snappy comeback lines was amusing to experience. Joseph had a way of overstating the obvious to Michael. Michael, in response, was very quick to give Joseph one of his endless snappy replies.

Gary stood up and shook hands with Michael.

"Gary, I'm really glad to see you again after such a long time. When you called me, I had just finished talking to the Boston Police. They just told me that Joseph was hurt very badly this morning. They think it was a mugging gone wrong, but I don't believe that. Joseph is currently in critical condition at Mass General. He's in surgery right now with a lot of internal bleeding. Belinda is at the hospital now, but I need to talk to you first. Did you talk to Joseph? Did my brother give you anyth..."?

Gary interrupted, "Michael sorry, but I need to tell you something. I was waiting for Joseph and when he walked into the lobby, Barry Parker was right behind him! I'm positive that it was him. Joseph gave me a little black ledger book and said to trust no one. I should only give this to you and no one else."

Michael just sat there silently for a couple of seconds before speaking. "Oh, shit. We thought Barry would show up soon, but not this soon. He's been following Joseph for the last two weeks. We thought we shook him off the trail but apparently not."

Michael's cell phone rang, and Michael pulled it out of his pocket. When Michael hung up, he looked a little relieved.

"That was the doctor in the emergency room. Joseph had to go to surgery immediately because of the internal bleeding. He also had his leg and two arms broken, a broken nose, three cracked ribs, and a broken collar bone. He's recovering from surgery now but is still in critical condition. Joseph is being moved to a different part of Mass General under a pseudonym of Trip Odds."

Michael continued, "Gary, I'm sorry that we don't have more time but there's some information you need to know. Why this is happening and how we got to this point. Ok?"

Gary was stunned and just nodded yes.

Michael picked up the book and explained, "Gary, this is a list of accounting irregularities which we started to look into before you went to Australia four years ago. On the day you left on your trip, you had several documents that were crucial to finding out the extent of money in these accounts and who was doing it. Roger has disappeared and now Barry is showing up. I'm almost positive it was Barry."

"A long time ago, you created some software libraries where you could go to a website and bypass their firewall and have complete access to any of the internal servers within a company. These libraries were something we were able to get a patent for. This was all done before you and Roger started Bit By Bit," Michael added.

When you and Roger started your company, you tried to incorporate your software into the first version of 'Bit By Bit'. The first version of the software had a critical flaw. It could break into almost every computer network out there. The 'Bit By Bit' software was originally meant to gather demographic data, like how many males or females were spending time on a company's website, what the average age was, and on and on. The assumption was that a company would place this on their own web site and not anyone else's. Well, several companies were doing this and stealing financial data, customer data, source code repositories. This became a huge liability and if it was released like that, your company could be held liable for any damages. Your company never released that version of software. Do you remember Alexi Restorz?"

He remembered Alexi and how they worked non-stop to create a new version of the software in just a couple of weeks.

"Yes, I remember him. Very good developer. Lots of late nights, arguments, and pizza rewriting that version of the software. We also changed the software from going out and gathering information to a model of protecting that information."

Michael interrupted, "Yes, the first version that had this flaw was not released. But someone made a copy of that software version that contained the flaw. Roger had somehow created about fifty copies of that version. Roger's copies were sold at an absurd cost which Roger pocketed. Every disk he sold gave him anywhere from 5 million dollars to 25 million dollars. He hid this from you and put this money in several different offshore accounts. We suspect that Roger and Barry had something to do with this. Also, Roger's admin, Joanne Druci helped."

Gary offered an explanation, "Most likely it was Joanne. Roger could barely staple two pages together, never mind burn DVD disks. She also has Administrator privileges, so she could access to any servers she wanted."

Michael was trying to not overload Gary, but it was useless.

He continued, "We sued five large companies and won based on Patent Law. This was a pivotal case. It wasn't just one company, it was many companies using your software to unlock and steal a competitor's source code, or they could change their competitors source code with crippling bugs."

Instantly, he understood the seriousness of Michael's words.

"All three of us, benefited from those cases. However, it also posed a security risk. The companies that lost these lawsuits were not that happy at all when they had to pay us. There was a threat of violence from these companies. When it became clear our safety might be at risk, we decided that we needed a way to get out of town quietly and quickly. We stored three backpacks with sufficient money, passports, phones, credit cards and any documentation, or visas, which needed to be put in place."

Michael had brought this black backpack with him. He handed it over to Gary.

"Where do I need to go?"

"I'm sorry that this is so last minute. Gary, you must move very carefully and quickly. There's a jet on standby for you which will take you to a safe place. You need to leave tonight. If you can convince Lucy to go with you, that would be great. Go home and talk to Lucy. It's her call but I think she might need or want to get out of town quickly too. Don't pack anything, just bring a warm coat. If you need anything, then you can buy it anywhere you go."

Michael took out his wallet and handed Gary a business card. As he was putting on his jacket to get ready to leave, he said, "Call this number and a car will be sent to your house to pick you up. The driver's name is Amy, and she will come to you any time, day, or night. Amy is very good at keeping people safe. The Jet remains on standby. Give Lucy the number if she wants to go at a later time. Good luck! We should only communicate through the email address you found in the note from your coffee table leg, at least for a couple of days. I will keep you apprised of Joseph and Barry."

With that Michael hurried out of the Brown Derby into the sea of tourists enjoying Quincy market. He left the small black journal on the top of the bar. Gary was a little confused that Michael did not take this with him.

Chapter 12 - Going Rogue

"The Point Of Serving Your Country Is Not

To Do Your Own Thing Or To Go Rogue, But

To Work As Part Of The Process."

- Kal Penn

Gary sat there a little stunned. Tonight? Lucy? It was almost 10 PM. Gary expected this to be a long night. On the train home he called Lucy and asked if he could stop by and talk to her. She said sure, but he knew that she sounded concerned. Freddie was staying at Lucy's house while he was in Boston tonight, so Lucy probably thought that he was coming over to get him. When Gary arrived, Freddie came running at him. Freddie is always so glad to see him and in his klutzy way he came full tilt running at him. Freddie's frenetic bounding pushed throw rugs to the side and luckily, he did not break anything. His exuberance has on several occasions knocked stuff off shelves or tables, so Gary got used to this and without even thinking made any room Freddie was in "Freddie proof". He suspected that Lucy, who also did the same, was used to it.

After all the commotion, Freddie settled down and Lucy sat at the kitchen table with two over-sized coffee mugs filled with chocolate caramel ice cream. For the next twenty minutes, he told Lucy about Joseph and

Barry in the lobby of the "Boston Harbor Hotel." He then told her about his conversation with Michael. The look of concern was visible in her face.

Gary was stalling a little bit because he knew that the next part of what Michael had told him would be a difficult to talk about. It was not just him that was at risk, but it is also possible that Lucy and his nephews could also be in danger and that they also needed to leave tonight. As he expected, the last part for Lucy was not easy. At first Lucy, said no way. It's not going to happen. Knowing Lucy as well as he did, if her mind was made up, then there was little that would change it.

"Lucy, I'm really so sorry that you're once again getting put into a situation that I have caused. Leaving tonight is a lot to ask. The Christmas break is coming soon, maybe you could get everyone out to go on a vacation somewhere. Please, just think about it," he said.

Gary continued, "I can't really take Freddie with me, tonight. I mean I could, but I'm not sure if I'll be able to do the normal routine things for him."

"Sure, don't worry about Freddie. I like having the goofball around here and so do the kids. So, do you think that Michael is overreacting?"

"No, I don't. About 13 years ago Michael and Joseph won a huge victory in a lawsuit against several companies. Those companies were not happy about this, and some threatened they would hurt us physically and also anyone that we cared about. That is when Michael, Joseph, and I put in a contingency plan if we needed to get out of town quickly. Barry was following Joseph and he hurt Joseph badly from what Michael told me. Roger and the nurse at Ashwood are the only people that know I have a sister."

Lucy did a doubletake, "Which nurse at Ashwood?"

"The nurse they told me about was a woman named Milly. Michael and Joseph paid Milly a lot of money to string Barry along feeding him all kinds of false information. She was kind of like our spy. She told Barry that I was still at the facility almost a year after I had left," Gary explained.

Lucy said incredulously, "Milly? Seriously, Milly was working for Michael and Joseph? She was the worst nurse I have ever seen."

Michael told me that you pissed her off every time you came in to look after me. I'm not sure how Milly got this information, but she found out that our company, Trinity Trust Holdings, was paying for everything. He laughed a little. Actually, she called up to complain about how you were treating her. She thought that she would shake the tree a little bit and try to get some more money. Of all the people to talk to, she ended up talking with Belinda. Belinda took her to lunch one day, at a bar/restaurant near Ashwood. After several drinks, she told Belinda that Barry kept asking her about me. Well

Belinda, thought that this would be a way to keep tabs on Barry or Roger. We paid Milly $10,000 to keep talking with Barry and tell him that Ashwood was still treating me. Every month we gave her an additional $2,000 to continue the ruse.

"Now this brings us back to the original question, any chance you be able to go with me tonight?"

Lucy shook her head, "Gary, I really can't. I think you knew the answer to this before you came over. I will think about it, though. The winter break for school is in two weeks. It would be difficult to leave tonight but maybe we could go somewhere safe and go skiing or something like that. OK?"

Gary stood up and grabbed a piece of paper and wrote several items on the paper. When he was done, he gave it to Lucy.

"This has the number of the driver that is picking me up now. This is also the email that Michael and I are using to communicate. I also wrote down Belinda's, I mean Lindsey's, cell number. Call her anytime if you need anything. She is pretty plugged in here so I'm sure she can help you if you need it. Finally, I wrote down Bert Lancaster's phone number. Bert can help you with Freddie if you get into a jam and need some on take him for a few hours. Bert and Freddie are the best of friends, but I think Freddie is using him to get cheese and ham slices. I haven't talked to Bert yet, but I'm sure that this arrangement would absolutely make his day.

He called the driver, Amy, to pick him up at Lucy's address. Amy said she would be there in about 20 minutes.

Putting on his coat, and looking at Lucy, Gary said, "If anything looks weird or out of place, get out of town. Also, one last thing. Use your normal bank account for the miscellaneous stuff like groceries. If you do want to get something big or pay for something out of the ordinary use the credit cards, I gave to you. Or use cash from an ATM to pay for stuff. You are a 'millionairess' now, so you can order steak or lobster, but just don't buy a red Lamborghini."

He gave Lucy a big hug and knelt down and gave Freddie a hug. He told Freddie to watch out for Lucy. Freddie licked his face as if to say, "Roger, wilco! I will keep her safe."

2 hours later, 36,000 MSL over Michigan

Amy drove Gary to the Bedford Airport. The Bedford Airport had two entrances. The first was the entrance for all the general aviation pilots and plane storage. The other entrance was for 66th Air Hanscom Air Force base, but most people called it Hanscom.

Amy, his driver, drove to a gate that was for the civilian side of the airport. As the car pulled up to the gate, she rolled down her window and punched in a set of six numbers on a keypad that opened the gate.

Gary had been to this airport many times because this is where the hangar for his plane was located. These hangars are not that big, so you were only able to just barely fit an aircraft and that was about it. Gary expected Amy to drive over to that part of the airport, but she went past the rows of the hangars and drove over to a part where all the bigger planes and jets were stored. One aircraft, a Bombardier Learjet 75, was out in front of one of the hangars. I guess "stand-by" really does mean anytime you want to go.

He thanked Amy for driving him and when he stepped out of the town car, the pilot of the Jet came over and introduced himself as Frank Douglas. After the plane reached about 5000 feet, Gary still didn't know where it was that he was going. He got up and went into the cockpit to talk to the pilot.

He instantly forgot his question as he looked at the ultra-modern avionics that was splayed all over the cockpit. Frank knew that Gary was a pilot and asked if he wanted to sit in the right seat. The position of where you are sitting in the cockpit has traditionally always been that the Pilot In Command (PIC) sits in the left seat and the co-pilot sits in the right seat. Frank pointed to a set of David Clark headsets to communicate above the noise made by the jet itself. For the next two hours, he and Frank did a usual thing between pilots; they pilot talked. When two pilots get together, generally all conversation is about any aspect of aviation - a wide range of topics from FAA rules, landings, flying tough weather conditions, instrument approaches, planes, and on and on. Gary finally remembered why he had come up to the cockpit which was to find out their destination. Frank told him that they were going to stop in Seattle.

He said that they were still about four hours out and suggested that if Gary wanted, he could go in the cabin and get some sleep. The chairs laid flat like a bed and he said there were some blankets and pillows in the top closet in the rear of the cabin. Gary agreed that he was tired and would do exactly that.

Once he got all settled and was trying to fall asleep, he was restless. Many of the past events and information were scrambling for attention. After about an hour, he fell into a restless sleep. He would fall asleep for about 10 minutes and then he would start to wake up, and then he would fall back asleep for 10 minutes. This porpoising of sleep, awake, sleep, awake did not allow him to feel anymore rested than he was before he lay down. He stopped fighting this and put the seat back into its normal position. Then, Gary went back up to the cockpit.

Frank told him that if he wanted coffee or something to drink, there was a little refrigerator in the front of the plane cabin on the left side. It contained chilled water and soda and above the little refrigerator was a coffee maker. He asked if Frank wanted a cup of coffee and Frank gave him a thumbs up.

Gary went into the cabin and brewed two cups of coffee with the little French Roast K-Cups. He handed the coffee to Frank and asked if he could come and sit up front again. Frank said sure. Gary got into the right seat of the cockpit and put his coffee in a drink holder. Once he was all set in the right-hand chair, Frank asked him if he could just watch the plane for a few minutes while he went to the bathroom. Frank said everything was on autopilot so he wouldn't need him to do anything. It seemed silly, but the aviation part of him was very excited as he looked at all the controls in front of him. Frank was back in a few minutes and sat back down in the left pilot seat.

In a few hours, they landed at the Seattle Airport, or Sea-Tac, which is shorthand for SEAttle-TAComa. This is typically how people refer to this airport. They took a cab to downtown Seattle and checked in at the "Inn at the Market" hotel. Gary pulled out the credit card that Michael gave him. The girl behind the reception desk said that she did not need his credit card because the rooms were paid for in advance. She handed one keycard to him and one keycard to Frank. Finally, she asked him what size pants, shirt, and shoe size he was. He wasn't expecting that question but, he told her the sizes that fit him. She smiled and said a new set of clothes would be brought up to him at about 11 AM.

Gary thanked her and put his new credit card into his wallet. At the last second, he saw that the name on the card was "Gary Tolland" and not Gary McKeown. He and Frank both got into the elevator and pressed the eleventh floor. Frank said that he was in room 1110 and if Gary needed anything to come and get him. Gary said, "good night" and headed down to his room at the other end of the hall.

Putting his jacket and backpack on the little couch near the window, he noticed the beautiful view of Puget sound and Seattle. He took out the passport, license, and credit cards Michael had given him a couple of hours earlier. All the identification documents said that he was Gary Tolland.

He is going to have to make sure that he remembers that. After taking a quick shower he was asleep in about five minutes.

Chapter 13 - Crazy Ivan

"Seaman Jones, sonar! Crazy Ivan!"

Capt. Bart Mancuso: All stop! Quick quiet!

[the ships engines are shut down completely]

Beaumont: What's goin' on?

Seaman Jones: Russian captains sometime turn suddenly to see if anyone's behind them. We call it a "Crazy Ivan." The only thing you can do is go dead. Shut everything down and make like a hole in the water.

-The Hunt For Red October (1990)

Several hours later, Gary woke up to someone knocking on his door. When he opened the door, a bellhop was standing next to a luggage trolley with various small boxes and bags.

Looking inquisitively at him, Gary asked him to come inside.

"Good afternoon. I'm Tim, I was told that you would need a couple of days' worth of clothing and a shaving kit. The front desk gave me all the sizes you wear. I didn't have much information to go on, but I think I was able to get you some comfortable clothes."

The bellhop looked like he was probably about twenty-five or so. As he was telling Gary that he picked out the new clothes, he saw for just an instant a devilish smile on his face. He raised his eyebrow as Tim was talking.

The young bellhop caught Gary's look and chuckled. "Sir don't worry, I didn't pick out any 'Tie-dyed' or whacky t-shirts." He could tell Tim really liked doing these kinds of errands, so he took them very seriously.

Now it was Gary's turn to chuckle. As he opened the boxes, he was pleasantly surprised. Almost everything was exactly the type and kinds of clothes that he usually bought for himself. His taste in clothing was usually just very simple clothes, nothing really loud or strange colors.

"Tim, you did a very good job here. The style and colors are right on. The Nike cross-fit white and blue sneakers you brought are perfect. Thank you very much."

"Thank you. I'm glad you like these. I was a little nervous since I really didn't have much to go on except the sizes the front desk gave me. I also put a few other things like socks and undershirts, underwear, and a bunch of other toiletries I thought you might need."

Gary picked up a pair of white boxers with small red hearts all over it. Tim smiled.

"Well maybe I got carried away on those, but the only other choice was white with teddy bears. It was a judgement call. If you need anything, please give me a call." Tim said handing him a small business card with his name, Tim Triton, and a cell number on it. On the back of the business card was another cell number.

Tim continued, "I know Seattle inside out. Many of the other bell hops and concierges work together as a little network to help each other out. We trade favors with each other so if a guest at a hotel has an unusual request, we can almost always find a way within our network."

As Tim started to take the luggage trolley out of the room, he reached for his wallet. He only had three singles and five one hundred-dollar bills. He thought this kid did a great job. In his current situation, he may need someone that can be very discreet and knowledgeable in the area. He loved the look on Tim's face as he gave him a $100 bill as a tip.

Gary put on one of the outfits. When he caught a view of himself in the mirror, he thought these clothes looked quite good. He felt a little silly. Memories of elementary school and getting all dressed up for the class picture day. He was not really fond on getting dressed up. Some people live for that and are more interested in being seen in new clothes. He was more interested in comfort.

To Gary, clothes have a certain personality. Anthropomorphizing his clothes might be construed as being someone that talked to his clothes. Some people or phycologists would say that he has lost his mind and should be taken to the mental asylum if he talks to his clothes. He doesn't talk to his clothes. But his clothes, to him, contained memories and multiple contexts. His navy sweatshirt reminds him of many memories of baseball games, cold subways, or skiing. Or a suit coat that just never felt right. The sleeves were too long, the shoulders felt tight. That suit reminds him of the times when he had worn it. Special occasions like a christening of his nephew, a friend's wedding, and a few funerals that he attended.

It was a little after 9 AM and Gary was starting to feel hungry, so he went down the hall to Frank's room. When he opened the door, Frank was talking on his phone. He motioned for Gary to come in. When Frank was done on the phone, Gary asked Frank if he was hungry.

Frank smiled and said "yes, I am."

Ten minutes later, they were sitting in the bar area of the hotel. The restaurant was made up of a long bar shaped like the letter 'U' with all the different brands of alcohol in the middle. They opted to sit in one of the booths. After they ordered food, the bartender came over with two enormous burgers and fries.

Bit By Bit

While they were eating, Frank asked, "Have you ever been to the Seattle area before? There is a lot of interesting places to see and things to do. Just outside and down the street, is 'Pike Place Market'. People go to 'The 'Fish Market' for just caught fish. The guys running that fish counter are known to throw whole salmon out to the various fishmongers taking orders from customers. There are also many vendors selling different food items or selling various arts and crafts. There's also the 'Space Needle'. Today, is cloudy so it probably is not a great time to go up to the top of it."

To Gary, Frank seemed like a genuine person. Pretty down to earth type of person. Most people acted on rationality and were usually logical in their behavior. There are so many small clues you can tell about a person's personality. How did they treat the taxi driver? How did they approach the reception at the hotel? Respectfully or were they just tolerating the role of the reception? If they were walking into or out of a building, did they hold the door open for someone? Smalltalk is also very telling. Did they interrupt when you were talking? Did they try to "one-up" you? Did they laugh inappropriately if they discussed the misfortune of another person? Did they contradict themselves by saying things that make them out to be so honest and pure but at other times would be negative about things?

MD Hanley

One clue that was important to him was when he watched Frank's interaction and how he interacted with the Sea-Tac Air Traffic Controller. Like most aircraft landing at an airport, a pilot is busy during this part of a flight. They must adjust the aircraft speed, the vertical descent, the glide slope, and putting the plane into the proper configuration to land. There is no 'hey, I kind of landed'. Every landing is full of its own special uniqueness. The training and experience of thousands of landings come into play. No one else is going to land the plane. Not air traffic control, not passengers, just you. A landing must be precise.

When they turned onto final approach, another plane incorrectly taxied onto the current runway that they were assigned to. The Air Traffic controller asked us to slow our speed so that we could give the plane on the runway more time to takeoff. As it turned out, we slowed the speed down, but this still was not enough, and the Air Traffic Control asked us to perform a 'go around'. Frank was calm as a cucumber, and he flew in a published flight maneuver that brought us around for another approach to land. It caused us an extra twenty minutes of flight before the Learjet 33C landed. The Air Traffic Controller told us that he appreciated our help and patience for asking us to perform a 'go around' maneuver. Frank's response was polite and respectful. Many pilots wouldn't be that happy to do this maneuver because of the increased use of jet fuel and the time delay that rippled out for all the flights after this.

"Frank, why are we here in Seattle?"

Frank looked at Gary a little perplexed and said, "Gary, I thought you knew why we flew here. I was only told to have the Lear prepped and ready to go. I wasn't told exactly where to fly to until about one hour before you arrived. The girl that called me, her name was Belinda, told me to plan a flight to Seattle and be ready for a takeoff in an hour. I have a son that lives north of Seattle. I thought she wanted me to go northwest here because I've made several trips here. I didn't get any other information. I've worked with Belinda and her father before, so I didn't really question it. Have you ever met Belinda? Did you know that she has an ATP pilot certificate?"

Now that surprised Gary. His memory was much better since his scuba diving experience four years ago. When Frank told his this, Gary remembered many years earlier, he was flying to Baltimore with Joseph and Belinda. During the flight, he asked her if she wanted to take over the controls for a little bit. She said no and seemed uninterested.

It takes several years of many hours of flying and endless time training to become an Airline Transport Pilot (ATP). Belinda must have had a pilot's license when he asked her if she wanted to take over the controls of the plane several years ago. Why was this a secret?

He noticed that Frank was still waiting for his answer and said "No I wasn't aware of that. But I guess I'm getting old, and the memory starts to fade a little."

"She must have called you right after I spoke with her uncle Michael. This was all last minute. She asked me to go with you. She mentioned that Joseph was coming out next week to look at a piece of property next week," Gary said.

The last part he was making it up on the fly. He didn't think it was wise to show his cards of the real reason he was here just yet. After all, his ID said he was Garry Tolland in Seattle.

"Where is your son located?" he asked Frank to quickly change the topic.

"Scott, my son, is living with his wife and their 8-year-old boy on Bainbridge Island. I wasn't sure where you were going today, but if you want, we could go over there for some fresh caught king salmon. If you have not had fresh salmon from Puget Sound this will be a nice treat for you. We can take the ferry over there. Scott said that you are more than welcome to come over."

Gary said that he'd be glad to go over to his sons for dinner.

Frank smiled and said it was still early so asked Gary to meet him in the lobby later this afternoon at 4PM.

It was a little cloudy today, but the view from the ferry boat of Seattle and the surrounding mountains were spectacular. Mount Rainier in the distance was surreal. The sheer power of that mountain was daunting and humbling. Those who climb or live near Mount Rainier know that respect must be given to it. The mountain has claimed many lives since its birth and will continue to do so. If you're prepared and wish to climb the difficult terrain, your reward will be a life changing and spectacular opportunity to view the entire Olympic Mountain Range. Gorgeous and equally as mighty are the Cascade Mountains to the east and Mount St. Helens off in the southern distance. He was very impressed by the view! Frank smiled at him and told him he had that same sense of incredible beauty and power when he first saw these mountains.

Frank's son, Scott met them at the ferry disembarking area and drove us back to his house. It was a nice ranch style house, and their lot was surrounded by trees. Scott's wife, Mary, came out to greet them. She gave Frank a big hug as Frank introduced him to Mary. Then Mary also gave Gary a big hug.

Laughingly she said, "We are big huggers, sorry about that. Dinner will be in about twenty minutes.

Gary, do you like Salmon and do you like Brussels sprouts?"

He nodded and said, "Yes, that sounds delicious."

Scott motioned for Frank and Gary to sit in the living room. He asked if they wanted anything to drink while waiting for the meal.

"Ginger ale if you have it." Frank replied. Gary noticed that Frank did not want a beer like his son was having one. Probably an old habit for him to not drink anything if there was a possibility of flying anymore today. Scott looked at Gary and he said that he would have the same thing as Frank.

"Scott, what kind of work do you do?" Gary asked.

"I used to be a software developer but changed careers about 8 years ago and became a lawyer specializing in Intellectual Property. This part of the country is loaded with tech firms so there's always a lot of work here."

"I agree Seattle, San Francisco, Austin, and Boston are right in the middle of the bubble with technology growing so fast," Gary replied.

Scott continued enthusiastically, "Many companies in technology are shifting their focus from doing the work in the USA to outsourcing to other countries. The labor cost is only about one third of what it costs here. I'm amazed at all the laws in different countries and their interpretation of IP, patents, or copyrights. Some countries don't even have laws against pirating. You have to be very careful of what you give engineers in other countries."

He knew from his experience with Michael and Joseph, a lot about patents and intellectual property. This topic was getting a little too close to Gary. Thankfully, Mary came in the room and said that dinner was all set.

As Frank had promised, the king salmon was incredible. Probably the best he can remember. After dinner, they all sat in the living room with some after dinner coffees. Mary's cellphone rang. She stepped out of the room to take the call. In a few minutes, she returned to sit down. She told Scott that her sister, Amy, had called to tell her that she just returned from her scuba diving vacation on Grand Cayman in the Caribbean. Amy had uploaded a bunch of the pictures on her Facebook page.

"Have you ever done any scuba diving?" she asked him.

"No, I just snorkel around a bit and get a horribly sunburned back," he said. He was not sure why he was lying about scuba diving. Some of the conversations about patents, Intellectual Property, and scuba diving were just hitting very close to home. He remembered what Michael had told him and that he needed to go away and be anonymous.

As Mary was sitting next to Gary, she was absentmindedly scrolling through the pictures that Amy had just posted.

"What do you think about the cloudy rainy weather we have here? Sometimes it can be three or four months in the winter before we get a couple of clear days together." Scott interjected.

Something on Mary's cell phone caught his attention. He wanted to see if he could get a closer look at that picture.

He almost forgot that Scott asked him a question. He smiled at Scott, "Well it is not quite the same as New England, but we also get our share of cloudy days in the winter."

He looked at Mary and asked her if she would go back a picture or two, there was something that he saw that he recognized. Mary said sure and when she got to the photo that Gary wanted to see, he asked her if he could take a look closer. She gave her phone to him. He took the phone and zoomed in on one part of the picture that caught his eye.

The picture he was looking at was a picture of a couple standing in front of a short stone wall. In the background was a beautiful expanse of the Caribbean beach and ocean. On the left side of the photo, a man's leg was caught in the frame. It appeared that this person was sitting on the small rock wall.

Bit By Bit

All you could see was his left leg. There was a long vertical scar on the calf muscle. A set of purple neon fins rest against the wall and the man with the scar had a purple neon dive knife attached to his leg, He knew this person that had gear exactly like that and the same scar. He froze. That person was Ben Costello!

Luckily, he was able to keep his face absolutely neutral and didn't reflect on his shock at seeing Ben. He handed the phone back to Mary saying it was beautiful spot where your sister took that shot.

After about five minutes, Gary knew he needed to get away from here. After about another ten minutes of small talk with Frank's family, he asked Frank if he could get a ride to the ferry spot, feigning that he was very jet lagged. Scott volunteered that he could sleep here if he wanted. He politely told him that he really wanted to go back to his hotel and thanked him for his hospitality.

Scott said he'd be happy to give him a ride to the Ferry. Reluctantly, Frank said it would be a good time to head back to the hotel for himself also. But Gary insisted that Frank stay here with his family. After a minute or two Frank finally gave in and said ok. All he needed to do was give him a call if he needed to go anywhere. He waved goodbye and thanked Mary for the dinner. Twenty minutes later, he was sitting on the Ferry motoring to Seattle on Puget Sound. He walked straight to the hotel thinking about what his next step would be.

Ben disappeared and never even called about him after the scuba trip in Australia. He always wondered about that. He felt that Ben must be involved into this mess with Barry and Roger.

The ferry was approximately four blocks from the hotel. As he walked, he was so deep in thought that he bumped into people a couple of times. He walked past a little tourist shop that had pictures and flyers of things to see or do while visiting the "Emerald City" or Seattle. One flyer had a picture of Vancouver city. A good place to be anonymous. He decided right there that this was where he was going to go but would need some help.

As he had hoped, Tim was standing behind the concierge desk, busily filling out some paperwork. Tim greeted him as he walked over to the desk. Tim was filling out a newspaper sudoku puzzle. Tim wasn't quick enough to hide it, so he just smiled. Gary asked him if he could help him with a couple of special requests.

"Certainly, Mr. Tolland, I would be glad to help in anyway I can." Tim said.

He took Tim aside so as not to have anyone overhear what he was going to ask him. "Tim, I need your help with some transportation. I'd like to get out of Seattle and go to Vancouver tonight if possible? I need to do this in a way that the hotel still thinks that I am still checked in. I want to do this very discretely and quietly. Is there someone you trust in your network of other hotels that could get me up to Vancouver via a ferry or some other form of transportation?"

Again, Tim smiled with that mischievous and devilish face. "Mr. Tolland I can definitely get that done for you. Is there anything else you would need before you leave the hotel?"

The backpack Michael gave him included a cell phone. That phone can still be tracked, so he thought it was best to get another phone that was totally anonymous. Also, he reminded himself that he would also need to take the battery out of that phone. He thought about that for a second and said, "Actually there's one other thing I need to get is a cell phone, like a TracFone or Net10 so that it cannot be tracked or traced on. Does the Gift Shop sell those?"

"The gift shop does sell those but if it were me, I would not get one there. I tell you what, there is a little convenience store about a block down the road that sells a lot of tourist knick-knacks and such. Give me about 45 minutes, go to that store and I'll meet you. Is that ok?"

"Sure, I can meet you there. I'm going back up to my room, wash up, and get my stuff from the room. Ok, I'll meet you there in 45 minutes. Thank you."

He rushed upstairs to his room and grabbed all of his things, took a quick shower, and headed downstairs. It was a little before seven when he walked into the convenience store. He nodded to the man behind the counter and went into the back where the cold drinks were. He grabbed several different drinks for the ride to Vancouver. He also picked up a couple of snacks like chips or what have you. Just as a lark, Gary asked the cashier to give him twenty $10 scratch tickets. He thought he would give these to Tim since he was being so helpful. After he finished paying for everything, and putting the drinks in his jacket, he walked out of the store. A nice navy-blue Honda Accord car pulled over to the curb in front of the convenience store. The passenger side window rolled down and he could see it was Tim. In a couple of minutes, they were driving I-5 North to Vancouver, Canada

"I'm surprised you are taking this long drive on," Gary said.

"Well, you said to get someone you trusted. I do know a lot of the people that could do this, but I felt it'd be the best to do this quietly and quickly. Besides, it's a little mini-road trip for me."

On the drive north, Gary got to learn a little more about Tim. He is the youngest of five brothers and lives with his girlfriend a little north of Seattle. He started working on a boat for a couple of seasons working on an Alaskan king crab boat after high school. Gary could tell that Tim missed doing that because of the lucrative cash. He saved all of it and was able to pay for his college and was hoping to start law school next fall.

At first, he was trying to be very guarded about his past, considering all the recent issues that kept coming up. At one point, they were talking about technology and computers. Tim was incredibly eager to learn as much as he could. The conversation turned to talking about cryptography and cryptographic currencies.

"Bitcoins and blockchains seem to be the buzz word these days. You must have heard about Bitcoin or heard about this," Tim said.

He was a little surprised that Tim mentioned this topic. He was very knowledgeable about this type of technology and currencies. Before the scuba accident, he was on the forefront of these technologies. Cryptographic currencies like Bitcoin, were changing the way that people understood currency. Currency is now electronic and not physical. The company that he created with Roger, was starting to become well known in the area of crypto currencies and protecting people and companies using this form of currency.

Tim cut him off. Tim's face lit up. He got very excited and said, "Oh shit! Why didn't I see this before? It's you. You were the keynote speaker at several of the technology events in San Francisco or in Seattle several years ago. When I first brought up the clothes to your room, for a split second I thought you looked like Gary McKeown and not Gary Tolland. I went to one of those seminars that you were presenting about Bitcoin and Blockchain technologies. I remember this because some of the things you talked about didn't exist or were on the rise for future growth. Don't worry I will keep this secret."

"Ok, Tim, you found me out, but please just keep your eyes on the road."

"Yeah sure. Sorry if I got a little excited there. But really, I can't believe it is you. What happened to you? You just seemed to disappear over the last 3 or 4 years."

Gary liked Tim, so he thought, ok I got found out. He felt that Tim was reliable and wouldn't say anything about his being here in the northwest. "Ok, this is kind of a long story, but here goes."

For the next 45 minutes he told Tim about the scuba diving accident, the coma, and how his memory is coming back to him now, bit by bit. He was vague about Roger and Barry because he didn't want anything to go back on Tim or jeopardize his safety.

When they reached the border, they were able to pass through to Canada without any special border fussiness. They asked Gary about the scratch tickets he had in his pocket. He had completely forgotten about this. He told the border officer that he had just picked them up on the road at a gas station. Other than that, there were no hassles. When they were back on the road, he told Tim that he had bought the scratch tickets for him because he was helping him to get out of the city.

Tim was very thrilled about this and the chance of winning some money.

It was now close to 11:30, and Gary asked if there were any really nice hotels that Tim could recommend. Tim said, "I have a friend that works at the Rosewood Georgia hotel. It is a very nice place to stay but they are a little pricey. My friend can probably give us a good discount."

"Ok, let's go there and get a couple of rooms. I wouldn't feel comfortable having you drive home this late. If you don't mind, I don't want to get your friend to give us a discount because I really don't want anyone to know that I'm here."

Tim nodded in agreement and said, "You know that you don't really have to check-in on a real name. People do this all the time in Seattle. If you want, you can check-in under any name you want, like Mickey Mouse or John Smith. The hotel wants to get money for the room, and they don't care who the person is. Also, my friend can make that happen without you even needing to talk to the desk clerk."

Chapter 14 - Wellington

New Zealand is a country

of thirty thousand million sheep,

three million of whom think they are human."

-Barry Humphries

A lonely, black-tipped sea gull flies back and forth over the coastal beach. Instinctually the little bird is searching, hunting, listening, waiting, diving; constantly looking for food. Movement of any kind will make the bird dive in for a kill. The success of these dives was almost always rewarded. This simple pattern occurs daily at sunset and sunrise. That instinct to eat or be eaten was paramount. Survive or die!

A man sitting in a lounge chair on a large penthouse deck watched this activity with boring contempt. A small white table on his right held a long-stemmed wine glass half filled with red wine. Next to the wine glass was a greenish glass ash tray that held a thick cigar. Occasionally, little curls of smoke were rising from the end of the cigar. The temperature was pleasant and only required shorts and a t-shirt. His skin was weathered, coffee colored. But his neck at the top of his t-shirt was reddish and white which betrayed the true color of his skin.

The view was magnificent, overlooking the Wellington Harbor, with an amazing panorama of luxury resorts, ridiculously expensive apartments, and endless beaches. Daniel Ortis groaned as he got up from the lounge chair. He wasn't looking forward to the party he was going to tonight. His attendance was required, unfortunately.

Four years ago, the person who was known as Roger Tillson disappeared. In his place a new identity was created. Roger Tillson became Paul S. Schneider from London, Ontario, Canada. After a year passed, Paul Schneider was given Canadian citizenship. After two years, Paul Schneider, disappeared and in his place emerged Daniel Ortis from Wellington, New Zealand.

The reason that Roger Tillson, aka Paul Schneider, aka Daniel Ortis, changed his identity several times was relatively simple. He was a thief. For the last 4 years, his Roger Tillson identity disappeared as the new identity of Paul Schneider from Ontario Canada made him able to get full Canadian citizenship in the required year and a half. Once citizenship was established, Paul Schneider disappeared and now he was Daniel Ortis, a citizen of Wellington, New Zealand. He hated the identity of Paul Schneider because he had to verbally spell his name out every single time that he was asked his name. He couldn't understand why everyone that tried to spell it on their own, more often than not, spelled it *Shiniter*. Now, he was glad to drop that identity altogether. Each identity was a deliberate move to obfuscate any connection to Roger Tillson.

His life took a lot of planning, but he had started to put a grand scheme into place about two years before Barry and Gary went to Australia scuba diving. During that last year, most of the stealing money from the company and the customers was done, sort of. Naturally, the money couldn't be deposited into a regular bank. During that last year Roger and his accountant, Brent Fisher, had created hundreds of different shell companies scattered all over the world.

The shell companies were very simple. Look for an office in a building with the lowest rent or lease possible. Get a P.O. Box. Have electricity connected. Get a phone line. Create a sign to put on the door and that is it! If someone from the building tried to enter this tiny office space, their master key wouldn't unlock the door because a magnetic lock was put on the door. The lock required a special magnetic card. Anyway, if they were able to get inside this office, all they would see is a phone sitting on the floor and that was it. Simple and easy.

Each of these shell companies were all part of a process to keep money moving away from Roger Tillson. If you moved the money several times, it became virtually untraceable. For example, Roger and his accountant, Brent, created a company that buys or sells expensive artwork. Well, the artwork really wasn't your classical artwork. Each of these paintings were from Brent's kitchen refrigerator. Every week his kids created a masterpiece of Crayola crayons. To Brent these pieces done in Crayola crayon were priceless. Beauty is in the eye of the beholder, they reasoned.

Once that company was set up, another company was set up that would insure priceless works of art. So, the picture with 2 larger stick figures (mommy and daddy) holding hands with the smaller stick figure that represented Brent's son, fell off from the refrigerator one day and got wet. It was filed as flood damage and the insured value was $150,000 dollars. This bogus insurance company sent the money to another anonymous owner of the Crayola painting.

So, every month, a lot of money was being put into the insurance company and then a lot of money was being sent out. This money was sent to realtors to buy several pieces of property or sent to casino's that could take 2% of the money and then send it to an offshore bank. All proceeds eventually were deposited into accounts held by Daniel Ortis.

These accounts were all in hidden locations around the world. It was surprising how many countries allowed banks total impunity by allowing for bank accounts and bank transactions to be relatively hidden and exempt from paying taxes.

His money laundering schemes were employed in different locations with many different companies. It might be artwork, real estate, casinos, or bogus inventions of things that just didn't exist.

Roger still got a kick out of one of the companies he was investing in. It was a company that was responsible for negotiating with an extraterrestrial council about sharing several decades of music and tv for access to alien weapons. The more Gin and Tonics, the more fantastical the types of shell companies became.

The system of moving money in and out of the companies happened at the beginning of the month. This was called "*layering*" or "*smurfing*". Every month money was moving from one layer to the next. At the end of this process, the money was untraceable back to Roger.

In the beginning he couldn't wait until the first of the month. For each identity, he needed to hire several people who had the discipline to be discreet. One was Brent Fisher, his accountant and longtime lawyer friend-the person he worked with while he was Roger Tillson. Having Brent meant having someone who could be trusted and discreet. Brent was very good at hiding money in various accounts all around the world. He knew what Roger was trying to achieve. However, Brent was also in a position to hurt him greatly. It was because of this liability that he made sure that Brent was rewarded handsomely. Probably a lot more than other financial lawyers, but because of the length of time working together over the years they developed a measure of trust. However, even though it was never voiced, trusting another person with all of your secrets, also contains an equal measure of distrust.

Discretion was paramount here. He paid or even overpaid these people to help keep his money rolling in and out of the cash laundering conveyor belt. There was one truism that Roger could rely on. If you pay the key people that have the ability to *hurt* you, make sure they are paid well. They won't even think about doing anything to hurt you. A couple of times, he knew that a couple of people were skimming off the top. He'd expected that! However, if people were taking more than one or two percent, he couldn't tolerate that.

Over the years he'd acquired many people that were tasked with finding out information that could be leveraged if anyone took a little too much. For example, when someone was asked to scout out and set up a shell company in Rio de Janeiro. The scout billed for two weeks work to find one rental in a building in the metro Rio de Janeiro area. It should've taken at most 3 days. An envelope of pay for three days work was hand delivered to the man. Also, in the envelope, with the check, were several intimate, compromising pictures of the scout kissing a lover, and doing a few things that wouldn't be appreciated if these pictures were sent to his wife. Included were pictures of his two small children going to school. That was all it took to secure his silence.

Bit By Bit

Changing his identity closed any credit history that he had as Roger Tillson - no history of bad credit. Creating a positive credit history is very easy to do, 'just lie'. Roger changed his identity to Paul Schneider. After he had a good credit record and Canadian citizenship, he needed to change identities again. Thus, Daniel Ortis and a new credit history was created.

New Zealand is a funny place. Citizenship isn't that easy to get. Some countries don't even require you to be present. In New Zealand, they are very rigid requiring one year of residence with attendance at a citizenship ceremony.

About a year ago, he tried to attain New Zealand citizenship which was promptly denied. He became enraged. He hadn't felt this feeling since he was a child, and Suzie-Q's lemonade stand. He couldn't stand it when someone told him he couldn't have something. This rage had been boiling in the background ever since he was a child. So, he retained a New Zealand lawyer who would help him gain citizenship. Not unlike a lot of countries around the world, citizenship could be attained and expedited by requesting citizenship by grant. Ordinarily, it's rare for a Minister of Internal Affairs to grant citizenship. However, making a large donation to a New Zealand charity would expedite the matter. Roger's lawyer suggested that he donate to the Wellington Regional Hospital located on the North Island of New Zealand.

Donating 2.5 million to the hospital to help fund the child cancer center to help sick children and their families, was a big part of getting citizenship quicker. Typically, donations, should be free of any encumbrances. But his donation included a few provisions. First, the hospital was to host a party for fundraising. He gave the hospital a list of names that needed to attend saying his hope was to raise more money for the hospital. Roger didn't care about more money for the hospital, this was a "networking" party. The more exclusive something is the more that people want it. The last provision was that he remained completely anonymous. The Hospital agreed to both conditions.

The only things that Roger cared about was money and power. But he didn't just want power. If all you have is power, then it can change in a second-if you show any type of weakness. You become the dog with the loud bark, but you have no bite. Kind of like "decaf" coffee.

If you just have money, then it's a little trickier. Roger found out that being rich allows you to hire smart people to do your bidding and protect you. One problem with that is if they are like him, inherently greedy, they aren't loyal. If they protect you once or twice and are compensated well; then what will happen on the third or fourth time? They will want more money to do the same job. Or even worse, you risk all your money on a bad investment or two and you are done for. Going to this party risked his maintaining his anonymity, but it was necessary.

About a month before the party, he sent out personal letters to five people that were very well connected and would be able to make a little excitement for the party. The letters described the different levels of donations that were suggested. The people that committed $100,000 would be given a colored bracelet to wear to show their support of one of the charities that Roger made up. If they donated $500,000 for that particular charity, then you got the same colored bracelet but only it was a brilliant *neon-like* color.

He had created 5 different holding companies for each of the charity causes. Each colored bracelet went into a corresponding holding company. Roger couldn't believe how easy this was to do. The payoff would be huge! If you looked at where this money came from, it was almost impossible to trace the origin of the $2.5 million dollars that he donated to the hospital.

It was not surprising that some of the people who attended the party weren't on Roger's original list. The attendees were very rich and considered the untouchable elite. The gluttony aspect of human behavior

is so predictable. Roger predicted that attending this party would cause a stir in the "*who's who*" of the wealthy. Attendance was fantastic! There were about 100 people attending that night who had donated a lot of money. Most importantly, no one knew that he had given the hospital the donation.

As he walked around the party mingling with many guests, he smiled when he saw people wearing various colored bracelets. The charities that were being donated to tonight were some of the most ridiculous charities. Some charities were real, but some were just made up. The charities that people donated to were EFFO (Provide food for cows to make them less flatulence), B.O.R.P. (Create a Bill of Rights for Plants), F.E.E.L. (Federal Ecological Empathy for Lobsters), NSM (Negative Portrayal of Snakes in Movies), and finally MARYHAB (Creation of a Livable Resort Habitat at the bottom of the Mariana Trench).

The colored bracelets were either light blue or neon blue; light red or neon red; light green or neon green; light purple or neon purple; light yellow or neon yellow. There was one additional bracelet that was a mix of all the colors which was reserved for people that had donated to more than one charity.

Roger wore two multicolored bracelets. Many people came up to him to offer congratulations for doing such a philanthropic act. During these conversations almost, everyone wanted to know what business he was in; of course, noticing he donated so much. This was the true reason Roger wanted to have this party. If he could convince some of these people to invest in his other projects, or the real estate he supposedly was going to invest in; then, they could be on the forefront of helping to save the world and help the poor. That is the way that they could justify their greed. If they were all honest, their attendance for charity was only done to increase their wealth.

Roger had that covered. One event staffer walked around the crowd. If people wanted to buy a bracelet, then the staffer needed to get a check or preferably a credit card of $100,000 or $500,000. and he gave them one of the coveted bracelets. Anything higher than $500.000, he gave them the very much coveted multi-colored bracelet. Not surprising, peer pressure caused several of the party goers to write a check for $500,000 to collect the multicolored bracelet. Roger sensed a ripple go through the party as more and more people were collecting the multicolored bracelets.

Several times, that night Roger had to excuse himself. He would go to the men's room. Make sure no one was in the bathroom, or in the stalls. He kept thinking that he spent $60 for a box of 200 colored bracelets. People at this party tonight were either wearing them proudly, or actively looking for a way to get their own bracelet. He couldn't keep it in anymore. Finally, he went into an uncontrollable fit of laughter. The more that he thought about the grand-dames attending, in their perfectly bespeckled and bejeweled attire who were wearing a "Lavender" or "neon Purple" bracelet, the more he laughed. Several times that night he almost lost control and burst out laughing in front of the guests. Luckily, he hadn't done this.

The party started to dissipate after about 11 pm. On the way home, he thought about tonight's big success. He gave the hospital the $2.5 million plus another million from tonight. So, the hospital received $3.5 million. This was perfect because it helped him make his dirty money untraceable and irreproachable. He told all the holding companies of the bogus charities to send him a text at 11 p.m. to update him on the money that was being collected. The range went from $1.8 million up to $5.3 million. The total was $14.1 million dollars. He couldn't believe how easy this was.

When he got home, he opened a very large magnum of 2004 Bollinger Champagne. At $1100 a bottle, this would barely register in the amount of money he just accumulated. This is extravagant, but after a payday like that, it was worth it. The more champagne he drank, the more he laughed. Finally, exhausted from laughing, he went to bed.

Twelve years earlier

Twelve years ago, Roger Tillson and Gary McKeown, started a small startup software company in Boston. The software they created and sold was a program that could create huge lists of data that marketing, or sales teams could use to sell to. This was not a new concept.

Several large companies had been doing this for a long time. Wasting money on mass mailings, or big full-page ads that weren't giving back a large return on their marketing costs. was common. It wasn't that difficult to sell this software program. They could provide very targeted and fully vetted leads that the companies could exploit. Companies were skeptical at first, but the results were like liquid gold for the customers they sold it to.

He often thought of those days twelve years ago! He vividly remembered how he and Gary got started.

Project 1 – Lists of Bits

In the early days of our company, Gary and I were laser-focused on each of our roles. I was the sales department, and he controlled the engineering department. The two-year anniversary of our company was cause for a little celebration. Both of us were just surprised that we were still a company and making money. Occasionally, we would go to lunch together at a little diner near the office. Cracked leather seats and several dingy little booths but if those weren't available you could always find a spot at the counter to order lunch.

He remembered a day that was different when we planned to go to one of the fancy restaurants in the city. While they were waiting for their food, Gary said, "we might be able to add a new product." Roger showed his interest by nodding in his direction.

He said, 'I'm seeing a new trend happening on the internet. The information we used to make the lists for companies is all in the public domain."

He moved in closer to the conversation.

He continued, "Mail systems and websites are making more and more private information available if you know what to look for. Personal information is starting to become something of a commodity that could be traded all over the place. It would be harder to sell this if everybody is jumping into the pool. Too much competition."

Product 2 – Protect the Bits

Now Gary lowered his voice and moved closer to Roger, "Many of the mega large cap companies have "piously" said, 'we respect your privacy and won't give out your information'. Bullshit! Every one of these large companies has captured your information and sold it fifty times on the first day you signed in - or gave away your email address, credit card, social security, phone numbers or any other information you gave them. These companies went out of their way to make promises about privacy. Again, this is just a lie."

Eventually Roger knew it was because of this lie that their company earned its bread and butter. Gary was a phenomenal whiz when it came to writing software. Most companies big and small, all have websites that could be accessed online to sell things or provide information like latest lottery results, their banks, stock trading account, or public transportation schedules etc.

Gary said, "My idea is to create a new product that would protect this private information. Many people think that once your computer is turned off any personal information is deleted. But more and more companies are going online creating accounts for customers - like social media accounts for example. These accounts could easily give up your personal information, if someone knew how to find it by asking the right questions to the websites and mail systems."

Gary started to ramble on about banks, credit card companies, social security numbers, company passwords etc. This was where Gary lost him in the conversation!

As his new idea started to sink in, all he could think about was how easy it would be to get and sell this information. His thinking, by no means, was benevolent and benign but leaning more to bribery and ransom. Wheels in his head were on overdrive.

He asked, "So how would you be able to protect this information?"

"Well, if you think of it like a safe. You're the only one that has the combination. This could be a way to store all of your bank account numbers, SSI information, social media accounts and about anything else you wanted to protect."

"So, how long do you think it would take to create this?"

"I would estimate probably about 12 months give or take 2 or 3 months. If I could get some help with this, I could really make this bullet proof in about 9 months. We could start out with engineers on a contract basis. If they were very good, we could think of hiring them full time. Don't forget that I'm working round the clock and weekends to keep our current product alive." he said ending with a little smirk.

Roger concluded, "Ok Gary I'm sold. Let's start calling some of the contract agencies to get this started." At that point he realized he'd need to have one of those little nerds be a double agent working for him. But let's wait and see, he thought to himself privately.

He continued to scheme. The one thing that our software could provide was a way to protect customer's privacy. But you can learn a lot about a person by looking at their browser history. Our software would only let you or the person that has the combination be allowed to look at it.

He thought the trail of websites a person typically connects to is huge. It doesn't take a rocket scientist to piece it together. There are so many places on the internet that are quite benign and are just websites that you normally wouldn't care who knew. But there might be something on a site that you might not want to be broadcast. Maybe you were looking at laxatives or hemorrhoid cream. What if you had prescriptions for an illness? The person that is piecing the trail you followed might draw wrong conclusions. There are so many questionable websites on the internet. It's a virtual mine field!

Many people would be crushed if this information got out. People could lose their job, friends, status in a church etc. Roger was overjoyed by the fact that he might be able to access any of this information - or even just stealing money from people's bank accounts. He knew that Gary's ethics wouldn't even think, or entertain, the idea of using this private information for a gain.

Making a lot of money from this information was something that he desperately wanted. He thought about this everyday as he drove into work in his banged-up Ford Taurus. Capturing this information and using this information for other uses could be a cash cow if used correctly. He felt so close to being able to acquire this information, but it always seemed just out of reach. So, he was in!

Gary started interviewing prospective candidates the next week. They decided to add six software engineers and three quality test engineers on a contract basis for a period of six months which may be extended to one year. Working with a reputable talent agency in

Boston they were able to hire six software engineers and three quality engineers.

He had a bitter argument with Gary over the price per hour for the contractors. He wanted to pay the new hires with the lowest rate possible per hour. Gary want to pay $10 over the rate the talent agency was asking for. Reluctantly, he gave in to what Gary wanted to pay for them.

By adding more people to their little company, the office started becoming very claustrophobic. Gary didn't care so much about it. Roger said, "It's important to put out a good image."

Finally, Gary agreed that they needed to move to a bigger office. Gary let him take the lead and do whatever he thought appropriate. Gary didn't want to get bogged down in the logistics of moving. Two months later they were in a new office building in the financial district of Boston.

Leasing this office space was very expensive per month, but they got into an office on one of the lower floors with a cheaper lease price. But they were in!

The building had a fulltime information desk support for the tenants. It had a great underground car park for employees and guests. Fulltime mail service, building maintenance and IT support for the tenants. It had a lot of nice "extras" and was in a very desirable location. At first' Gary was against it but he let Roger make the financial decisions. The office had a fantastic "Wow!" factor which was something that couldn't be beat.

Once everyone was in the tiny office, Gary laid out all the details of this project. He assigned different deliverables for each team member.

Product 3 – Transactions with Bits

"Roger, can we meet for lunch later today?" Gary asked with a sense of urgency.

Roger agreed but he had a bad feeling about this request. They went to their usual place. Gary looked upset.

"Gary, what up? What's eating you up?"

"I think the program we are working on, can be a really good product. I firmly believe that this product will be a big hit and money will soon start coming in. I've been thinking about this all night. I think our program is going to be great, but I don't think we are hitting the right target. Don't get me wrong I think the product we are working on now will sell and bring in a lot of revenue, so I don't want to stop this."

"So, what's the new target?"

"I think we can be ahead of the game and on the cusp of a part of an absolute global tidal wave. This trend is exploding everywhere. Roger, have you ever heard about Bitcoin or Blockchain technology?"

He didn't want to sound like he was stupid and not knowledgeable about a new trend in software, but he figured Gary wasn't expecting him to know this. So, he shook his head no.

Gary continued, "Ok, well Bitcoin and Blockchain are kind of complicated but there's nothing that exists in the market that really compares to this. Stop me if you aren't following or have questions, ok?"

For the next forty-five minutes Gary explained to him about cryptocurrency. The first and biggest topic was Bitcoin. This new product could take advantage of a growing explosion in investment markets using cryptographic currencies or cryptocurrency. Bitcoin was at the top of the stack with virtually no competitors.

Cryptocurrencies and Blockchain were an area of technology that many industries just started to look at. Banks wanted to get into this monetary boom. It was gaining a lot of attention! This new software project Gary was proposing was broken down to two pieces of functionality. The first part was that they would create a *digital wallet* for users that wanted to complete monetary transactions with bitcoins. Each bitcoin has two unique encrypted signatures of a private "key" and a public 'key'. This information would be stored in the digital wallet they provided.

Gary explained, "The digital wallet would be used when we want to buy something with Bitcoin or receive money in Bitcoins. So, if we wanted to buy something in Bitcoin, then the vendor would give us their public key and we would send back a message to the vendor that combines our private key and their public key. This transaction is unique and cannot be modified."

Roger listened intently about the transfer of money.

"The transaction signature of our private key and their public key is validated against other nodes on the internet. If you receive a positive validation of the Bitcoin transactions, then you will be able to complete the transaction. If a person or vendor is sending you money, then the same thing happens just in reverse order. Vendor sends their private key to our public key. Once this is validated, it becomes money."

Again, he perked up at the idea of money.

Gary asked him if he understood what he was saying or wanted him to explain it in another way. "This is where blockchain comes into play. As an example, imagine that you are in a global grocery store. You pick up a few items and go wait in line to be checked out. There are 4 checkout lanes which are the express 13 items or less. You have less than 13 items, so you go over there and get checked out. You supply your credit card number. This credit card is shared by all members of your family so you think it should go through ok, or at least you hope it will. The cashier puts your items on the conveyor belt and starts to bag them. If no alarms go off and everything is checked and validated, then, this money will be charged to your credit card. So, in essence the payment of your groceries was entered into the general ledger."

"Ok, the same scenario, but this time you have 14 items. You must wait in the longer line of shoppers. There ten people ahead of you in line. Eventually, you will get to the cashier and make a transaction for your groceries. Suddenly, the light goes on over a register near you that says 14 items or less. You jump over to that line and now your transaction will go into the general ledger quicker than the last line you were in."

He was beginning to lose track of understanding this.

"Now since this transaction is anonymous, it must be checked and rechecked by many different sources. If everything is ok, then the transaction still needs to be written and recorded as a transaction for that exact bitcoin. Once the transaction is recorded, it can't be changed. This is done to guard against '*double booking*', For example, you can think about this as buying a cup of coffee and a muffin at Starbucks in Seattle using your Starbuck's account. If you were able to coordinate with 100 of your friends to use your Starbuck's account at precisely the same time, the first transaction that gets to the server first wins. All 99 other transactions would be denied."

Gary tried to clarify further! Roger listened.

"Essentially the same thing is enforced by the blockchain. Blockchain will look at a thing called a node (sometimes this is referred to a data miner) on the internet and look at the 10 transactions that are ahead of the transaction you want to create. Then it will look behind 10 transactions before your transaction. If your transaction on that internet _node_ is positive that it is unique, it will send back a positive reply. Now it doesn't just do this one node but will also do 10 or more additional nodes. If they all come back positive, then your transaction is created. Everyone else around the world is doing the same thing so people in Africa might see your transaction and return a positive reply because they check it thoroughly. However, if this transaction already exists then the data miner in Africa might send back a negative reply to whoever called them to check."

Gary asked him if he was still following him, and Roger nodded.

"The cryptographic signatures that are recorded out on the general ledger have gone through some sort of validation of each transaction. Checking these signatures are heavily computer processor driven. A single computer is sometimes called a _node_. This could be a dedicated machine that is performing a lot of these calculations. These computers or sets of computers are called _data miners_. It might take anywhere from 4 days to a couple of weeks to complete the validation. They are rewarded with a small fraction of a Bitcoin. If you received ฿0.001 of a Bitcoin and Bitcoin was trading at $8,000, then you would get $8.00."

Gary went on!

"One computer doing this type of work was not paid enough to justify the electricity to run the computer. However, if you have a massive network then it's justifying the cost for the electricity. For instance, if the Social Security Administration stepped into this area of technology by using their server farms overnight. Remember this is thousands of high-speed computers. They could theoretically make SSA have a positive cash flow for retirement funding. It could easily generate maybe 300 to 500 Bitcoins per week. Three hundred Bitcoins might be valued at approximately $8,000 per Bitcoin. That comes out to be $2.4 million a week and $120 million per year."

Roger was about to explode hearing these numbers.

BANG!!!! That was it. That is what Roger was waiting for. This "*data mining*" could be a great way to skim off the top. He would need to enlist a developer that could be a double agent for him. His double agent was going to really earn his or her keep now. As they came into the office to start learning their codebase, he would assess the developers to see who could help him. He hadn't approached them yet. Soon though, soon he schemed silently.

For this new product Gary wanted to create, they decided to hire three more developers and one extra quality engineer. This group of contractors needed to have some additional skill requirements. The Bitcoin and Blockchain code can be very math intensive. They also needed to be well versed in many of the different encryption algorithms models. The first group of contractors that came in were exactly what Gary wanted. All very hard workers, all with boundless energy, and all eager to help us create a product that would be on the *cutting-edge* of technologies.

One developer stood out. He saw it in a second. Gary was clueless to be able to spot the signs. He spotted these signs because they were familiar to him. The person he saw would work hard but only if certain requirements were met. The requirements were simple. Nothing is done without a reward. If I do this, how does this increase my value as an indefensible member of the team?

One afternoon, he felt that now was the best time to enlist his little spy. For the last couple of weeks, while they were getting started, he caught one of the developers sitting in front of Gary's computer. Gary rarely used his office during the day. He typically bounced around to different members of the teams to check in with them to offer support or help with some of the nasty parts of the software or testing that needed to be done. If you wanted to find Gary, he was most likely out on the floor sitting at a developer's desk. After hours or early mornings, was really the only times that Gary was in his office. Mostly to get caught up on emails or approve some necessary spending.

So, it was unusual to see someone in front of Gary's desk. Roger walked down the hall, passing Gary's office. The thing that caught his attention was that she was going through all of Gary's email. Many messages to Gary were generally just perfunctory. There were several messages that were confidential that Gary needed to reply to. For example, one message that he saw open on Gary's laptop was an email to approve a purchase of more parking spaces in the garage. She also had a spreadsheet out that listed everyone's current salary.

Her name - Kimberly Ambrose. She was always the kid in school who would ask if they could have more homework over the holiday, or the weekend. She never did the homework but made someone else do it. She kept secrets, a lot of them. These were always used to give her leverage against fellow students.

Roger walked into the office and politely said, "Those spreadsheets can be tricky. Change one number and that will change all the fields on it."

Startled by Rogers presence, she quickly pressed a key that made the screen go black and turned around to see Roger. She stammered, "Umn, eh. Yes, they can be very tricky."

He smiled and thought that was perfect.

"Kimberly, right?"

"Yes, Kimberly Ambrose. I was hired a few weeks ago."

"Ok. Kimberly. Why were you looking at Gary's emails? He won't be happy about that. And again, why were you looking at the spreadsheets with everyone salary?" he asked.

Kimberly was caught red handed. It was doubtful that she would be able to continue with this breach of privacy. Roger was still standing in the doorway. "Ok, Mr. Tillson, I will empty my cubicle and leave in about 30 minutes. Thank you for everything."

"Kimberly, finish the rest of the day and tell no one that this happened. I mean no one! There is a Starbucks around the corner from here. Let's meet there at 6:30 PM tonight."

"Uhm Ok. Sure.," her voice had a subtle timidity to it.

He caught that look and laughed a little. He said, "Kimberly, don't worry. This is just a talk and nothing untoward. I promise. We have several different software products we use in the office and I'm having a difficult time with some of them. Ok?"

She nodded approval and practically ran out of Gary's office.

At approximately 6:30 PM, Roger walked into a very busy Starbucks. It was not that big and sometimes it was difficult to hear people. Most would say that is a detriment, but today it was very helpful to not have other people overhear what was discussed. He spotted Kimberly sitting at a little table in the back part of the coffee shop. He went over sitting down holding his newly purchased cup of coffee.

"Thank you for meeting with me tonight. You do know that what I saw you doing in Gary's office wasn't good. Right?"

Kimberly had thought about this all day. Trying to find a plausible reason why she was on Gary's computer. She could've said that Gary asked her to get something off a spreadsheet or find and print a particular email. She knew that if she did go with that excuse then all Roger needed to do was ask Gary.

In the end, she knew she was caught. She said, "Yeah, I suppose. So why am I here? I could be hanging out with my friends instead of being here tonight. If you're wasting my time, then I am outta here."

She started to stand up as if to leave. Roger said in a very stern commanding voice, "**SIT!**"

This startled her and immediately she sat down.

"Kimberly, I'll give you two options tonight. First is to be fired right here, right now," he said calmly.

"The other option is to help me with changing some of the bitcoin code to create a little trapdoor that would allow a person to get into their network without being detected. I also want the datamining code to be changed. I want the code changed so that when a *data miner* is supposed to receive payment for data mining, they will only be receiving one third of what they should be getting. I want the other two thirds sent to a location that I will give you. Do you understand what I am asking for?"

After a moment, she said, "Ok, I think I understand this. The product that was released three months ago, you want me to provide you with a trapdoor for this program so that it can leave a way into the customer's network and gather many different types or information. We are planning on an update soon so I can put that in there, right?"

Roger nodded his approval.

Kimberly continued, "And also for the new program we are writing, you want me to change the code. Make changes so that the data miners only receive one third of the payment they are supposed to get. The remaining two thirds will go into different location that you will provide me."

"That sounds about right."

Kimberly smiled and with her most sweet voice, "Sure, I think I can do that, but I need to get more familiar with the codebase before I can put this into place. Mr. Tillson, I understand what you are trying to do but since I am the one changing the code, I was wondering if I could possibly earn a little money for doing this?"

Roger took a long pause and wanted to draw this out to be dramatic. He exhaled slowly and said, "Was that why you were looking at the salary spreadsheet earlier today?"

She nodded yes. Roger thought for a minute about this. It didn't surprise him that she asked him this. The thing that surprised him was the boldness and sheer audacity to ask. She held no advantage in this deal. He finally said, "Kimberly, that's a good question. If you were in my shoes, how would you answer this question?"

The sweet smile she had quickly turned to a frown. Her brow furrowed. She was scrambling in her mind to find the best way to answer this question.

Kimberly hesitated and for some reason she thought of her father. She remembered that it was a bitterly cold winter one year and a pipe burst in the basement of their house. It was a mess. Her father spent several afternoons getting quotes from various plumbers. Four of the quotes were generally around the same amount. One of the quotes was astronomically low. Her father went with that one. It was about 2 weeks later when another pipe burst in the basement. Then, he called one of the four quotes he received earlier. This new plumber did the work necessary and corrected the prior plumber's work. It cost a lot, but they never had pipes burst again. She remembered that lesson.

Finally, she replied, "Well, I think you can go about this in a couple of different ways. You could have someone do this work, but how confident will you be if the work isn't easily detectable? If it were me, I would want to have this work hidden very deep, so it won't be easily seen. I can do that for you! Or if you just want the code changed, I can do that also. I would just hope that it doesn't show up with QA or even worse, have the customer encounter this."

As loud as it was in the coffee shop, everyone stopped for a millisecond to see where this loud laugh was coming from. Roger had to admit it but, that was a great answer. He thought that she was going to be very rich someday.

Roger said, "Kimberly, I wrote up a document earlier. I gave it to my lawyer. We copied your signature from one of the pieces of paper you signed when you started working here. I also had my lawyer notarize this. I will pay you for the work that you will be doing for me. If you can complete this work in one month, then I will give you an additional bonus. Any payment to you will most likely be in cash to an offshore bank or if you prefer, Bitcoin. If you help me with this, then I will destroy the document that was notarized today. If you have a change of heart and wish to 'not do this', then that is your prerogative. However, this document will be sent to Mr. McKeown and my attorney to press charges for stealing intellectual property from our customers. Do you understand?"

"Yes, Mr. Tillson I do understand."

He got up from his chair and left Starbucks. Kimberly gave her a little smile as she took the top of her coffee cup off. Inside the coffee cup there was a little voice recorder. She got up and put the voice recorder in her jacket pocket and got a nice hot caramel macchiato. As she walked out of the coffee shop, she was thinking how ironic this was. A thief asks another thief to steal and says if you don't steal, I will frame you. However, it never dawned on the original thief that the second thief had just recorded the entire conversation.

Chapter 15 - Vancouver

All hockey players are bilingual.

They know English and profanity.

- Gordie Howe

It was about 5:00 AM, and Gary woke after just a couple of hours sleep. He had to remind himself that he was in Vancouver Canada and that he was on PST (Pacific Standard Time) now. Time in Boston was three hours ahead. Opening the large heavy light-blocking curtains revealed a city that was just waking up.

With the light starting to brighten up the room, he was able to take a closer look at the hotel room. It had two queen sized beds, a nice flat screen and the bathroom that was a masterpiece of marble and gold finishes. Next to the TV was a small coffee maker. All in all, this was a nice, albeit a medium sized hotel room.

He made a cup of coffee and noticed a chaise lounge in the corner next to the window. The lounge was made of an azure velour material. Not sure if it was the velour material, or the stuffing inside the pillows but, it was very comfortable. Sitting here and sipping his coffee, he had a great vantage point to look at the full expanse of the city. The Vancouver Harbour could be seen at the far end of the city with the many boats bobbing up and down at every mooring as if on a glistening flat pan of water.

As he sipped his coffee, the recent events started to unroll. He felt that he was at a crossroads of what to do next. It felt like someone with a handful of different colored confetti threw it up in the air and then told him to catch all the red pieces. Ok, he said to himself, first order of business is to look at and analyze a list of the recent red-hot issues.

Mentally his mind relaxed. When he grew up, every sense came to him all at once. Every sight, every smell, every feeling, every sound heard, or every taste needed to be put somewhere. Sometimes this could be overwhelming. Everything, like this morning, came at him as a sight, a smell, a taste, a sound, or a feeling,

When he was overwhelmed, all his energy went towards recording and putting the information into the proper box in is mind. He mentioned this to a teacher that gave him an F on an English paper. This teacher taught other classes that he was in, so he knew that something was going on. This teacher had mentioned that meditation was something that he did every day and it helped him to be more centered. He recommended a daily meditation class at a church near the school. Gary decided to take him up on the offer.

He was very surprised when this helped him. After a while it became second nature to him. However, he had not meditated since his scuba diving trip to Australia. Sitting on the chaise lounge was comfortable so it was not hard to fall into this meditative space. He was able to calm his thinking and feel every part of his body relaxing. Looking at recent events helped him to slowly analyze them.

Thoughts started to bubble up from the mix. Joseph in the lobby of the Boston Harbor Hotel looking frantic and frenzied. Michael telling him that Joseph was hurt. The hurried flight and exodus to Seattle. Driving north to get away from Seattle into Vancouver Canada. All these thoughts and feelings all screaming for attention at the same time. There was one thing hidden in the background of his mind. This one thing started to rise to the top and increase in urgency. Roger Tillson!

He laughed at himself a little. Of course, it was Roger Tillson. Why didn't he arrive at this earlier? Then he gave himself a little slack on this because he had been in a coma for three years. Tim said that he recognized me because of the work I had done with cryptographic currencies. Like a gigantic "Jenga" game, Tim pulled the one piece that made everything come down and fall into focus.

The company that Roger and he created was almost totally devoted to safeguarding its customers cryptocurrencies. Even though their company was small, they had been doing extremely well. After all, he went around the world giving "a dog and pony show" of their software and the security it had. Many publications were printing very flattering articles. We were said to be a "shooting star" in this small market that was going to explode exponentially in the next 5 to 10 years. Roger was a good front person because he was a perfect salesman. He talked the talk and made people believe that they were at tremendous risk of being robbed without our software. This was not really a total lie. It was a good pitch, and we were getting the reputation of an up and coming star. Gary did not want any part of that, and he let Roger do his thing.

The question was why? There is no other person that could have done this. Suddenly, he saw the big picture. His friend Ben couldn't go to Australia with Gary. Roger almost instantaneously had Barry all booked with an airline ticket, and a spot on the scuba boat. It all smelled rotten.

Gary got up and took a shower and turned on the TV. He shut it off as soon as he turned it on. Why did Roger do this? The more he thought of it, the angrier he got. Rarely, did he give into anger. This was different, this was attempted murder. It may have been Barry underwater, but he was certain that Barry was doing this at Roger's behest.

Barry was responsible for Joseph losing his leg. He thought about that cold winter night walking by one of the streetlights on the edge of the Northeastern University campus. He saw Joseph tied to the light pole wearing only his boxers. He was shocked by this. Gary ran over to Joseph, untied him from the pole and put his jacket on him. Joseph was shivering uncontrollably. He called 911 and told them to meet him on campus at this location. Joseph looked at him with just incredible gratitude.

The ambulance came around the corner and got Joseph inside quickly to start to warm him up. When Gary jumped in, he got a better look at him, and his lower, right leg was badly discolored black. He stayed with him. When they got him to the hospital, Gary went over to the intake nurse and gave him Joseph's information; then, he asked the nurse if he could go in and see him. She led him over to the bed that Joseph was on. Joseph looked at Gary and tried to say 'thank you' to him.

One of the ER doctors took Gary off to the side to ask him some questions. He asked how long Joseph was exposed to the cold temperature. Gary didn't know the answer, but he called 911 as soon as he saw him there. "I tried to warm him up with my coat."

The ER doctor told Gary, "He was lucky when you came - and saw him. "I don't think Joseph would have lasted another 15 minutes."

The doctor went back into the mix of the chaotic blur of each person fulfilling his or her role. Joseph looked at Gary and tried to say something to him. Joseph stuttered out the word, "Barry!"

Gary understood completely what he was saying. This act was done by a fellow student named Barry Parker.

He asked Joseph, "Is there anyone you want me to call? Is there anything I can do for you?"

Joseph was trying to get the word out, but his body was shaking uncontrollably. Finally, he mouthed the word "Michael" and then found his voice and said, "and hot coffee, black."

"Me too!" said one of the nurses. That was followed by several other people working on Joseph to echo what the nurse just said.

The doctors working on Joseph, started to pack everything up and started to move Joseph upstairs to Intensive Care. The doctor told Gary that he would get him when he knew more about Joseph's condition. He knew Joseph's younger brother, Michael.

"I will be in the waiting room, and I will call your brother,", Gary said as he left the room.

Again, he got that incredible look of gratitude. Gratitude is something that's not easily faked so Gary knew that this was sincere - and life changing for both of them.

Michael came to the hospital as soon as Gary told him. Around 4 AM, one of the hospital's surgeons came out from a side door of the emergency room and asked for Michael Daly.

"I am Michael Daly," he said as he stood up.

Gary also stood up to listen to the doctor tell Michael the status and extent of Joseph's injuries.

"Mr. Daly, your brother Joseph was really lucky that he got here when he did. If he had been exposed in the cold weather much longer and he would have died. Everybody has an internal core temperature typically in a normal person is 98.6°F. If your core body temperature goes below 95°F this is when you start to see problems. Your brother's core body temperature was 88°F."

Letting this sink in for a second, the doctor continued, "The human body has an amazing way of transporting blood throughout the body. If one of your veins gets blocked, the body will try to find a different path. From what we saw in the CT exam, your brother had a previous surgery or injury to his knee. Joseph's leg was not able to get blood to his right leg below his knee. We tried everything to raise his body core temperature and get blood circulating into his right leg. The injury sustained was too severe. We had to take aggressive action to save his life. His right leg was amputated below his knee. Your brother is in ICU and is still in recovery, but he is being monitored and made as comfortable as possible."

He looked at Michael and said, "Why don't you go out and get some breakfast. Your brother is resting comfortably. Come back in a couple of hours. In my experience with these types of injuries, it is very shocking for someone to wake up with the loss of a limb, but family and friends can help a great deal in their recovery."

The surgeon left the waiting room, and Michael sat down on one of the chairs. Clearly stunned. In the past several hours of waiting, Michael and Gary didn't really talk too much. The stress and tension were just too great.

"Michael, I am so sorry to hear about this. Is there anything I can do for you?"

Slowly Michael raised his head from looking at his shoes to look at Gary and said, "Get me outta here. I can't process any of this right now. Let's find a place to get some breakfast. I just can't be here in this waiting room any longer."

Gary nodded and grabbed Michael's arm to help him get out of the chair. Twenty minutes later, they were both in a local diner booth that was quiet at 4:30 AM. This place would be a madhouse in a couple of hours. For right now, this was what they needed.

After they got some coffee and toast, Michael said, "Gary, I can't tell you how much Joseph and I owe you for helping. If you hadn't come along, Joseph would be in worse shape and could have died. Thank you so much. I don't know why, or who, would do something to Joseph like this?"

Gary had been reluctant to tell Michael anything more until Joseph's condition was known; but now he knew Michael needed to know who did this.

"Michael, Joseph told me who did this." He mouthed the word, *Barry*. "Barry Parker is a classmate of Joseph and me. Barry was recently kicked out of the fraternity. He was caught cheating on a paper for an English course. The college hasn't finished its investigation of this charge and is still trying to figure out what to do with Barry. The fraternity didn't want Barry's cheating incident to reflect on the fraternity. I heard that the frat kicked him out last week."

Michael was half listening and just nodded.

"I never really knew Barry and occasionally I would see him in a class or a party. He hung out with a lot of the 'stoners and party animal crowd' at school."

Again, Michael just nodded but he took in what Gary told him.

Gary remembered that morning with Michael as if it had just happened. Michael was a person that was usually very stoic and unflappable. That morning, they both gave into the sadness, the anger, and the uncertainty about what the next steps would be.

That summer both Michael and Gary worked with Joseph every day helping him to get stronger and more capable. Gary chuckled a little and thought about the times in the gym with Joseph and Michael. Michael was unrelenting and pushed Joseph hard on being able to do everything without a normal right leg. As hard as it was, Joseph knew his brother wanted to help him get through this and not be a person that was limited in any way.

Now Joseph and Michael have helped Gary so much over the years. He thought if someone was pushing me as hard as Michael pushed Joseph, they might end up with a punch in the face. But Joseph was getting stronger and could get around on his own and didn't need to depend on anyone. Michael being a hard ass was, the best thing for Joseph.

Sitting in the early morning and sipping coffee in a nice Vancouver hotel room helped him to remember and focus.

New questions popped in his head. Why in the world would he go scuba diving with Barry? Those accounts and spreadsheets he was looking at before he left for his trip. He never really figured out why these accounts were showing up as withdrawing large amounts of money. Every time money was withdrawn from the companies account it was quickly deposited into many different offshore accounts. There was only one thing that he could see that looked similar or semi consistent was a term, Jade Unicorn. It wasn't as simple as that though. Every account had some type of variation, like Unicorn Jade, Unicorni jade, unicornijade, jadeunicorn, and on and on. He immediately recognized that whoever was entering information for these accounts was not that savvy with computers. Using the term, Jade Unicorn, and rearranging or putting in a space or taking a space out, was someone who thought they were so clever. But they left a very easy trail for tracking it.

It was 6:30 AM in Vancouver and 9:30 AM in Boston. Time to make some calls. His first call was to Belinda. She answered on the first ring.

"Gary? Where are you calling from?"

"Good morning. I am in Vancouver Canada at the Rosewood Hotel Georgia."

"I got a call from Frank this morning and he said that you checked out of the hotel in Seattle. Are you OK?"

He sheepishly said, "Belinda, I went with Frank over to his son's house on Bainbridge Island. His daughter-in-law was showing some Facebook photos and I saw my friend, Ben Costello's, purple gear. I am positive it was his gear."

Before Belinda could say anything else, "How is Joseph? Michael said that he was in ICU."

There was a slight hesitation before she answered, "Gary, my father is recovering but he was badly beaten up. His left leg is broken, both his arms are broken, one of his kidneys might be failing. Hopefully, his kidney will recover, if not then it, will have to be removed. They were going to have him go to dialysis for a little while. There's a lot of bruising, but the doctors are keeping him comfortable in the ICU. We are all pretty shaken up about this."

"I'm so sorry about this. I'll get on the next plane out of Vancouver to Boston."

Belinda said quickly and assertively, "No. Don't. I know my father would like to see you, but he's in no condition at the moment."

"Should I call Frank and tell him where I am?"

"Gary, give me the phone number you can be reached at. My phone says you're using a burner phone with no caller id. Give me about twenty minutes and I'll call you back. Ok? I will call Frank and let him know about where you are. You said that you saw your friend, Ben Costello's scuba gear. I'm not sure why Ben's gear was in a picture of his daughter-in-law. Did Ben ever tell you where he worked?"

"No, I don't think so. He did mention that he was doing a lot of stock trading, so I assumed he was a 'Day Trader'. Why?"

Belinda started to laugh a little. She said, "Ben is by no means a stock trader. What Ben neglected to tell you is that he works for a part of the FBI that has agents working in both the NAS and FBI. Sort of an information sharing thing. Ben was interested in you because your name kept coming up in any discussions of encryption. Ben was working with my father to help decipher how and where most of the money from your company went. I know he was getting close. Listen, give me your cell phone number and let me call you back in about 20 minutes."

Gary sat there looking at the phone in his hand. He felt more confused than he was before he called Belinda.

True to her word, twenty minutes later his phone rang.

"Gary, I just talked to Michael and Frank. Frank has the location of where he will be taking you to next. He'll fly up to Vancouver to pick you up. The General Aviation at the Vancouver area is called Airport South.

She continued to explain, "Also, there's a part of the airport that services General Aviation planes, small jets, sea planes, helicopters etc. When you go to the airport follow the signs that will get you to an area called South Terminal. Coming into the front of the South Terminal building, look for a little coffee spot, called 'Aroma Joes'. This is good coffee but a close second to Morissi's coffee. Frank said he can meet you at around 2:00 PM. He will be looking for you at 'Aroma Joes'. If for some reason you don't see each other, or if there are any changes, here is Frank's cell phone."

He thanked her and hung up. Then, he called his sister, Lucy, to let her know what was going on. As he suspected she was not happy about Joseph getting hurt. He calmed her down, somewhat, and told her that he thought he would be home soon.

Looking at the clock on his nightstand, it was 7:30 AM. He went down the hall and knocked on Tim's door. Tim, looking like he had finished showering and shaving, was up for breakfast and ready to go. They headed down to the lobby and grabbed a table at the small restaurant slowly filling up with hotel guests.

The breakfast was a typical buffet style of different breakfast foods like fruit, cereal, and scrambled eggs. A chef was near the end of the table taking orders for different omelet ingredients. He was efficient and mastered about 8 different fry pans for each omelet. This chef was like most hotel chef's he has seen before. They were part entertainer and part chef. The entertainer part was fine with Gary. A little corny but he shuddered to think of how this line of people would like his omelets if he was the chef. He was sure that it would have been a great disaster.

The server brought them a couple of coffees and asked if she could get anything else. Gary looked at Tim and they both said, "We're all set."

After they loaded their plates with an abundance of food from the buffet, Gary asked Tim if he was heading back to Seattle. Tim had this ear to ear grin on his face.

"Well, when I woke up this morning, I saw the scratch tickets I left on the table last night. I know you probably wanted to scratch them. I'm sorry and I hope you're not pissed but I scratched 14 of them. I'm sorry. I should have given them to you."

Now it was Gary's turn to have the huge grin, "Tim, you didn't understand what I said last night. Those are totally yours. Did you win?"

Tim's face totally changed to a grimace, "Wait Gary, you bought those, and they are yours."

Gary repeated the same statement, "No Tim those are yours. Did you win?"

Tim sheepishly said "yes" as he lowered his voice, "Gary, of the fourteen I scratched, all of them were winners! They won big! Just the fourteen tickets I scratched won $63,500 hundred dollars. Gary, I can't take this money from you. You bought those tickets. Really, that money is yours."

Gary repeated in a very emphatic way saying, "No. Tim, I gave those tickets to you because I was in a jam and needed to leave Seattle quickly. You got me out of Seattle on the spur of the moment. I thought you could try the scratch tickets but if you didn't win any money,

I was going to pay you a couple of hundred dollars for going out of your way to get me here."

"I'm ecstatic that they won and can give you and your fiancé some fun money. I'm sure that it can help if you want to go to law school. If you have the unscratched tickets on you, let's see if they can increase your wallet?", Gary continued.

Tim pulled the scratch tickets from his pocket, smiled at him, and started to feverishly scratch off the latex film covering numbers and prizes. Tim was almost jumping out of the chair. The first three tickets won $6 and two $60 squares. The next two tickets were not winners. The last ticket that Tim scratched was the biggest win yet. The ticket was laid out in a table. In that table there were 5 rows and 5 columns, next to the table were two numbers. Tim furiously scratched off the whole ticket. When he was done, he pushed it to Gary. He picked up the card and saw one number at the top that contained a 60.

7	3	4	9	XXX
13	14	X	5	2
XX	60	33	60	44
1	66	98	77	60

XXX	60 x 10 x10x10	$60,000
XX	60 x 10 x 10	$6000
X	60 x 10	$600
60		$5
60		$5
60		$5

Tim had a great ticket. The number at the top was number 60 and in the 5 squares below that, Tim scratched off the whole ticket and the total of this one ticket was $66,615.

As Tim and Gary watched and it slowly dawned on them that this would be huge, Tim was vibrating with so much excitement he looked like he was ready to shoot up and out of his chair. With all the tickets, he won $130,115 in total. This was a nice bonus for Tim driving him up to Vancouver. Tim could hardly stay still in his chair. Gary loved this and laughed along with Tim.

Gary told Tim to put the tickets out of sight for a moment when he called the waitress over. He asked for the check and a pen. When she came back, Gary signed the check. He caught himself as he almost started to write McKeown but quickly changed it to Tolland. He gave the pen to Tim.

"Sign those tickets right away. One hundred and thirty thousand one hundred and ten dollars is a nice bonus for you. I 'm really very happy for you"

MD Hanley

Tim insisted that he needed to give him a portion of the winnings. He wouldn't have it.

"Tim, I'll tell you what, I am going to need a ride to the airport to meet someone at two. If you give me a ride there, then we'll call it even." Gary stuck out his hand to shake on it. This is old school stuff that his father had taught him. If you shake someone's hand during a deal, then you are honor-bound to live up to the deal. A handshake was your bond and something that was not broken for any reason.

Tim smiled at this. He knew what Gary was doing because his father had taught him the same thing. Growing up with five brothers could sometimes be chaos. But if you make a deal with someone then you had better stand by your word. For some reason, he could tell that Tim knew this unbreakable bond as he shook hands with Gary.

Later that day, Tim dropped him off at the airport.

As they were in the car heading over to airport He said, "Tim I 'm really glad we got to know each other. It was fun. Hey, are you still interested in pursuing a law degree?"

"Yeah, I am. Taking on another degree and paying for it was sort of a big question mark but I was hoping that I could go part time at first and full time later on. This money from those scratch tickets is really going to help me a ton. I wish I could share some of this with you.

280

You do realize that you are paying me $25,000 for each mile to the airport?"

"It's probably the best money I've spent in a long time. A close friend of mine in Boston has a very successful law practice. I'm going to give him your contact information. He might be looking for an intern next year, or someone out here in the Northwest to work for him. He's always looking for smart people starting in a law career. He's top notch and handles a lot of Intellectual Property and Contract Law. He's helped me through a lot of legal minefields."

Gary waved goodbye as Tim left. Then, he walked over to the coffee kiosk where Belinda told him to be.

After a couple of minutes, he saw Frank, his pilot, coming towards him. Frank had a big grin on his face when he saw Gary. He was worried that Frank would be upset about leaving Seattle, going to Vancouver and now someplace else. Thankfully, he wasn't. Frank told him that he had the jet fueled up and was ready to go. After a brief customs check, they headed over to where the plane was parked on the tarmac.

As they walked over to the Lear Jet, he asked Frank where they were flying to. He thought it might be back to Boston. Frank told him that they were going to New York City and flying into JFK.

Gary was very excited. Flying into JFK is rather different than flying over JFK. This would be a first for him. Right now, the sky was wiped clean of all clouds with just blue sky everywhere. Today, definitely qualified as a "severe clear" day for flying.

Chapter 16 - Excelsior

"New York is the only city in the world where you can get run down on the sidewalk by a pedestrian."

— *David Berger*

It was about 11:30 PM when Frank and Gary checked into the "The Westin New York Grand Central". He checked both Frank and him into a couple of rooms on the 33rd floor. As the receptionist was handing him the room keys, she said that she had a message to give to him. She handed over a reddish colored envelop.

He took the piece of paper out of the envelope and read the message as he walked over to Frank to give him his room key. The message said simply, "We will give you a call in the morning when we get to New York. Lucy is coming with me." It was signed "Lindsey".

He and Frank got in the elevator and went up to their rooms on the 33rd floor. Gary was hungry as he realized the last time, he ate was breakfast this morning with Tim. He smiled as he recalled how excited Tim was. That energy is very intoxicating. Gary grabbed a can of Ginger Ale from the mini bar. He hesitated on grabbing a big Hershey's bar or a bag of granola and mixed nuts for $25. He hated to get robbed like this, so he passed on it. He thought he would get a good breakfast tomorrow morning. After taking a quick shower, he went right sleep.

Next Morning...

After a relaxing sleep, Gary woke up around 6:30 AM. He got out of bed. On the little table/desk next to the window, was a set of magnetic keys for the room and a reddish colored envelope that contained the message from Belinda. He made a mental note to stop calling her Belinda and to call her Lindsey.

He looked in the knapsack where he kept his clothes. He noticed that there was only one set of shirts, socks, underwear, and pants left that were clean. Everything else in his backpack needed to be washed and cleaned. He called downstairs to the laundry service in the hotel and asked them if they could take and clean his clothes. Someone from guest services came to his door after what seemed just one or two minutes. They were glad to help him.

.   They asked, "Can we return with these clothes at around noon?"

"That's fine. I wasn't expecting to get same day service."

After he showered and shaved, he put on the today's clothes and sat on the small beige padded couch near the window. The view from the window was spectacular with the Chrysler Building and the Empire State

Building so prominent in the New York Manhattan skyline.

There was a light knock on the door. It was Frank. When Frank came in, Gary noticed that he had his heavy cold weather jacket on, so he was most likely heading off somewhere.

"I'm leaving to take care of some business with maintenance and certification of the Learjet."

Many planes required certain maintenance after so many flying hours. Checks on the engine or other parts of the plane. The FAA is very strict with regards to this. If it doesn't pass these specific tests, then the aircraft could be grounded and not fit for airworthiness.

Frank continued, "I wanted to pass on a message from Belinda. She said that she will be in the lobby in an hour with your sister."

Also, he said, that he enjoyed the trip back and forth with Gary as his co-pilot. Gary also expressed that he liked being his co-pilot. They shook hands and said goodbye.

Gary went back to his perch by the window. He was grateful to experience this view which many people never get to experience. His parents were steadfast in teaching both he and Lucy, to be grateful for all things in our lives. Be grateful for all the little things, and all the big things. Roger Tillson was the antithesis of what his parents taught him. Now that he thought about this,

Roger qualified as hitting just about all the seven deadly sins, or the seven vices. *Pride, Greed, Lust, Envy, Gluttony, Wrath and Sloth.* How did he get mixed up with Roger? Deep down, he felt that he probably knew that Roger was like this. He allowed this because they had become successful, and his work filled a void in the technology market. This gave him as much time as he needed to investigate and explore any of the latest technology he wanted. The one question that he still has not figured out was the "why?". He looked at clock and saw that he should head downstairs to the lobby, to meet Belinda – no he must remember it's Lindsey.

As soon as the elevator door opened into the lobby, he looked over at the glass doors opening and saw Lucy and Belinda coming into the hotel.

Lucy gave him a big hug and Belinda did the same. Then, she said to head over to the hotel restaurant where she would book rooms for herself and Lucy. They went over to the little restaurant and got a table at the back of the restaurant. To Lucy Gary said, "Belinda is booking a room for you? So, you are staying down here? That's great. How are you managing with Freddie?"

Lucy smiling said, "Freddie is great. Peter is home for a couple of days to help with him. Also, I met Bert to see if he could be a backup for Freddie, if Peter or I are not able to get him. When I spoke to Bert and asked him, he just looked at me and said '**No!**'. He said that he would not have any part of it. He told me that Freddie will stay with him through the day and if we wanted him in the evening to come by around 6 when he was closing the store."

Lucy continued her story, "He's kind of a funny character. He listened to me very patiently. When I had finished, he just looked at me and said, "No!! It totally threw me off balance."

Gary laughed, "Freddie is in good hands with Bert. I'm sure at this point one of the Sophomores or Juniors will be taking Freddie to the park to get some exercise and cleaning up his 'Freddy-burgers'. How is everything else going?"

Lucy paused a second, "Well I decided to take the Christmas break from teaching early. I will go back to school on January 7th. Belinda called me yesterday. She told me more about some of the things going on. About Joseph in the hospital, and you abruptly flying across the country. I'll be honest I'm a little scared about this. Roger is nowhere to be found. Barry, we suspect is responsible for severely hurting Joseph. And 'oh yeah', I found out that I have a shitload of money in the bank!"

Gary recognized this hurried, breathless tone from Lucy. She was signaling that dealing with Freddie, leaving the college early, Joseph getting hurt, and the windfall of money were throwing her world into chaos.

Most times people feel that they have some control of their lives. Everyone is different. But family can throw a monkey wrench into this. There is no choice. You do it, whether it's quiet or kicking and screaming the whole way. She was angry at Gary. Not just a little angry but pretty pissed off. At this time, she was angry at Gary, but he knew it wasn't 100% Gary that she was angry at. He suspected there was a lot of fear and uncertainty of the immediate future.

Lucy stopped herself from getting more worked up. Thankfully before Lucy started to wind up and spiral into a pit of despair, Belinda came to the table and sat opposite him. The waitress came over to offer coffee or juice to start off. She also mentioned the buffet on an opposite wall. They all ordered the buffet and went over to fill their plates. As usual, Gary filled his plate with at least one kind of everything. The food would be enough for two people. This happened a lot with him.

After they had eaten and the waitress took the plates away and filled their cups with fresh coffee, he asked Belinda if there was any more information about Joseph.

She said, "right now, he's somewhat out of the woods. Having both arms broken at the same time is very difficult. They operated on his kidney and were able to restore it to normal functioning without having to remove it."

She paused again and said, "My father and uncle have spent a lot of time investigating the location of three people, Roger Tillson, Barry Parker, and Joanne

Druci. We found out recently that Roger has a new identity. His name is Paul Schneider."

He had to stop her at this point, and asked, "Belinda, did your father say that it was Barry? I strongly suspect that Barry did this. Is there any information from the police?"

"My father is still unconscious. They did perform the surgery for him, but he's still recovering and will probably be in intensive care for the next couple of days. I will be flying back to Boston tomorrow morning. I hate leaving him, but I can't just sit there at the hospital. My uncle will let me know if there are any changes. The police said they will notify me if they get any new information."

Belinda continued, "We had two leads on this There're a Paul Schneider from Ontario, Canada. This lead has come to a dead end. My uncle found out one possibility. He has worked with a woman and her family for several years. She's from Connecticut and my uncle did a lot of legal work for her. Michael brought several corporations into a legal fight for patent infringements. She created a special more efficient solar panel. She asked my uncle to do a little digging about a person in New Zealand that was hosting a huge fundraiser. Some of the causes they were asking for was money were simply ridiculous."

"What are some of the different charities that the sponsor was asking for?", Gary asked.

"The first one seemed legit because it asked for any dollar amount that would be donated to the children's cancer unit of Wellington Hospital. The other charities they were just crazy. One is called F.E.E.L., which stands for Federal Ecological Empathy for Lobsters. They want lobsters to be totally removed from the Australian and New Zealand diets. Apparently, the person organizing this fundraiser was asking for donations of $100,000 or $500,000 to donate to a charity. She thought the fundraising for these charities were very suspicious. These functions are all about being seen. They somehow give you a reputation among your peers as a 'philanthropic donor'."

Gary's interest piqued when she said this was about lobsters. It was probably nothing. Roger hated lobsters. I don't know why but I'm sure he paid some therapist a lot to get at the root of that phobia.

Belinda paused at this point to take a sip of her coffee.

She continued, "I suppose that being seen at these parties gives a visible gain and an advantage that can be used later with your peers. She sent my uncle a picture of the hospital and the person who was sponsoring this event. One picture showed the hospital staff in front of the hospital and on the side was a person that they thought was out of the picture. My father swears that this is Roger. So, my uncle is going down there again to gain more information about this person that was apparently from Wellington, New Zealand. It sounds far-fetched but it might still be something."

Gary looked at Belinda, "Joseph's right!! I guarantee that this person is Roger. The reason I say that is that Roger despises Lobsters. If he sits down in a restaurant, and if one of the entrées on the menu is lobster, Roger won't eat at that restaurant. He's afraid the other entrées will be ruined by the smell or something. I always thought this was weird. I like lobster but, I can take it or leave it."

"Gary, you should give Michael a call later tonight and tell him about this. It will be tomorrow morning in New Zealand time. Here is a card that has Michael's cell number on it. It also, has my father's cell phone and mine."

She handed a card to Lucy also. Lucy thanked Belinda and then asked, "I know I'm trying to play catch up here, but you mentioned three people. There's a watch out for Barry right now. The person in New Zealand might be Roger. Who is the third person, Joanne?"

"Joanne was Roger's assistant. She was someone that got a lot of pleasure from hurting other people. Rose told me some stories of how badly she treated others. In the beginning, Roger and I agreed that if we hired an executive assistant, then we would need to hire two admins. One reporting to me and the other reporting to Roger. It had to be this way so that it would not be a conflict of interest. If something between them could not be resolved, then Roger and I would meet them to sort it out. Rose couldn't stand Joanne. Rose was not the only person to feel that way."

Lucy asked, "did I ever meet her at one the company functions?"

"I don't think that you did. I was thinking that Rose probably knows Joanne better than any of us. I think she might be able to help with this. Lucy, would you mind working with her if I ask her to come to New York?"

"Does she need to come out here to New York? Can't I go back to Boston and work with her?"

Belinda jumped in at this point and said, "I would agree that it doesn't make a lot of sense doing this in New York. But the one thing that worries me is that Barry is still somewhere in the Boston area. This is just an assumption, and we don't have proof to say otherwise. My father was nearly killed. He was also responsible for my father losing his leg during his college years. And Gary was left for dead on the bottom of the Coral Sea. So, no I don't think that you or Gary are safe to go back to Boston until we have a bead on Barry. At least for a couple of days to see if anything more develops. My father is tucked away in the hospital under a fake name so Barry will not be able to reach him there."

Gary added, "Lucy I know this is a big pain, but Barry is a really a dangerous person. He's liable to look for you - even Freddie for that matter. Bert will take good care of Freddie, I will give him a call and let him know that Peter and Patrick are nearby if he needs help. I doubt he will, but I can at least give him their numbers to call."

"Ok I get it and it does make sense." Lucy said reluctantly.

Gary added, "Before I left for Australia, I remember that there were several accounts that were not being reconciled correctly. I was trying to sort all of this out. Roger convinced me to put it down and go on my vacation to Australia. I think I made Roger very nervous because I was getting close to figuring out that these accounts were not adding up correctly and I would uncover his fraudulent stealing of money from our company."

For the next 30 minutes he explained further. It's a simple formula any company uses. Money coming in were credits to different accounts. Any bills for general overhead and salaries etc. were subtracted from the amount that was coming in. These represented profits for the company.

Gary explained, "I got a call first thing in the morning of the day I was heading to Australia. I worked with this one customer a lot over the years. He was one of the first that helped us get established. So, it was important to make sure he was well taken care of."

Gary went on to explain that the owner of this company became good friends. He called to tell him that his accounting department was seeing a lot of errors in the account using invoices from our software. He told me that our company was over charging his company twice the amount that was agreed upon

Most of that morning Gary was looking at different accounts and was trying to see where his company was charging customers twice.

The issue that he found was that each month twenty different new accounts were created. That in and of itself isn't an issue but those accounts were never used as internal or external accounts. Every dollar that was received by the company was logged as a journal entry. If that journal entry was from an active customer a new account would be created. This account would take a percentage of the money that was sent to them and deduct that amount from the journal entry. The amount it deducted was anywhere from 15% and up to 30%. As the month went on it always maxed out at creating 20 new customer accounts. As an example, if they received payment from 21 different customers, it would only deduct from the first 20 payments in that month. The strange part of this was that every month each one of those new accounts was zeroed out and the account was removed and deleted. The strange part of all this is that he couldn't find a single trace of anything being withdrawn or sent to an account outside the company.

Gary continued to explain what irregularities he found that morning. He said, "A few items that are relevant here. First, I am certain that our software was being used to do some of this. Secondly, I also believe whoever was doing this, was able to go through our firewall. I can only think of three other people besides Roger and I having the rights to do this. I am pretty sure that Roger wouldn't have the skill to do something covert like this. The last thing that was strange about this, was those new accounts that were created were in alphabetic order. I would have never known this, but I accidentally hit the sort button when I had one the spreadsheets open on my screen."

Lucy and Belinda listened in disbelief.

"For example, the first twenty accounts started at customers that have a company name started with the letter 'D'; and ended on the letter 'L'. I went back several months and found this similar pattern. The month before it started with the letter 'A'; and the last account created began with the letter 'C'. Every month after this, I was surprised that it used this pattern to create those accounts. To me it seems like a trick that an inexperienced software engineer might do. They probably thought that they were very clever, but it left a signature of the person doing this. If you want to do something very covert, then you need to make sure that it doesn't leave a trace." Gary seemed relieved to unload this information.

"I remember that before I left, I sent your father one of the spreadsheets that were not adding up properly. The little notebook he gave me had all these account numbers and the amounts of money sent to it. This kind of business tactic that someone was trying to do was not new, but it is illegal. This is classic bait and switch activity."

Gary sat back and looked at the bottom of his empty coffee cup. He said, "One of the senior developers that worked with me on these products was Alexi Restorz. He and I worked day and night on these products. If there was anyone who knew the code and where to look for errors, it is him. I need his expertise to help unravel this and find out where someone put this code into the product. I can give him a call. I know that he has no love for Joanne or Roger."

Belinda said, "Gary if you can convince them to come down here that would be great. I can have someone fly down here or if they would rather drive down that can be arranged also."

He said, "I'll give them a call from my room. I hope that I still have the right contact information for them. What rooms are you both in?"

Belinda said that they were on the same floor that he was on, "If I remember correctly, I think, this hotel has a bunch of conference rooms that can be used for hotel guests conducting business while they are traveling. Let me find out about that and we can meet later today. I think we should block out a couple of days so we can establish a "war room" to operate as a central base. I'm sure the hotel can provide us anything we need for computers or A/V equipment."

Belinda looked at Lucy and asked her how she was doing. It was only 10:30 AM but both Lucy and Belinda looked tired. So, they decided that Lucy and Belinda would head up to their rooms, unpack and take a nap. They agreed to meet here in the lobby at 3:30 PM.

Gary walked into his hotel room and slept for a few hours. He awoke thinking about how he and Alexi spent a lot of time working late nights and weekends to produce the first version of our product. At first it seemed very straightforward; but once you were down in the bowels of the core part of the application it got very complex. We were trying to create a bitcoin wallet and allow it to make financial transaction of Bitcoins. Eventually we covered all the pieces of these features. The other big part of this software was that it allowed your computer or any number of computers to act as a node on the internet. Once they were registered properly you could tap into your computer's ability to perform complex calculations and act as a data miner.

By doing all these complex computations you can determine if a transaction for the general ledger would be unique; then, your data mining produced a reward in a small amount of a Bitcoin given to the owner of the of the computer, or computers, that conducted these computations.

This part of the software code was very complex. Alexi had a style that made him perfect for a partner in this type of application. Gary and Alexi used to get into heated discussions about *what-if* scenarios. As usual, Alexi was very good at always thinking about what might happen if 'X' gives you back this. For example, what if you are data mining and you lose your network connection; then, what happens? What if someone enters a character and the form is expecting a number? He always thought about those conditions, that, maybe one out of a million times, would blow up unexpectedly. Those are the moments that you would say, "oh shit" I never thought about that.

Alexi's wife had developed an advanced breast cancer and as a result he needed to spend more time with his wife. Gary understood this and made sure that anything Alexi needed, then Gary would do "whatever he could" to make it happen. At one point, he saw that Alexi's work with the company was something that he desperately wanted to hang on to, but it became more and more obvious that Alexi's wife needed him. Gary sort of fired him one day when they were out to lunch together.

He told Alexi that tomorrow was his last day in the office. His only job now was to take care of his wife and support her. No job is ever more important than that. If Alexi had not left, then he would still be trying to juggle work and his time with his wife. Alexi understood why Gary told him to stop coming to work. But Alexi just didn't feel right if he couldn't contribute for his work. It was an ingrained habit that he always needed to protect his job for both financial reasons and for medical insurance. The one thing that really got Alexi to understand this was to use his own logic on him. Gary told Alexi that his wife with breast cancer was an "oh, shit" scenario. He had never thought about this being any kind of probability. No one does. Then Gary promised Alexi that his wife would have full medical no matter what. Alexi would still receive his monthly salary so there should be no reason he couldn't take care of his wife. Gary said that he wanted this for Alexi, but he wanted this to be quietly done. Rose has all the paperwork for this arrangement.

Gary reiterated, "Rose and I will be the only ones that know about this arrangement. Roger does not know about this, and I want to keep it that way."

With these memories in mind, Gary went over to the phone and dialed the last number he had for Alexi. After three or four rings he was afraid it would go to voice mail. But Alexi answered the phone. After Alexi got over the surprise of hearing from Gary, Gary asked him if he had some free time saying that he could use his help. He could just hear Alexi smiling through the phone.

"Gary it's so good to hear from you. I didn't know what had happened to you after the company shut down and closed the office. Roger and Joanne just up and disappeared. No one really knows what happened. Rose has been an angel for me and my wife."

He was afraid to ask, "How is your wife doing health wise?"

Alexi laughed a little before saying, "She is doing absolutely fantastic. She is the bread winner now. She went back to work after the difficulty with the breast cancer, but she's in full remission. She also told me that if I ever see you again, she wanted me to give you a big sloppy kiss thanking you for firing me. It was tough the next couple of months after I left the office, but I learned something that day you and I spoke about my situation. These **what-if** scenarios are not just for software but are helpful in a lot of situations. You said I need to apply my own logic on this with the breast cancer. My wife and I both focused all our energy to make sure that we were protected or covered if something came out of left field.

We had a doctor that was not really helping us move towards getting better. She was focused on managing the pain. My wife and I decided to always play the "what if" this doctor is not helping move us forward; then, go to another doctor. We did and found one of the best in the field. You gave me an adjustment to my thinking. It wasn't just ones and zeroes, but it was persistence to never accept an incorrect input, or in this case accepting that it was about pain management. You gave me and my wife courage to not accept just the "so-so" doctor but find a superstar."

"Alexi, you have no idea how good that makes me feel. I'm not sure if you knew this, but after you left the company, I had a bad scuba diving experience that put me in a hospital for three years. I am physically doing well though. So, this is where I need your help on parts of the codebase that might be doing something wrong - and it looks like it is stealing money from users. I don't suppose you have a copy of the old code handy?"

"Gary how can you ask me something like that. Of course, I have a copy of that codebase, I never delete code that was completed. I can help you in any way you want. Where are you right now?"

"I'm in New York city near Grand Central Station staying at the Westin."

"Well, I'm not too far from you. I moved to Connecticut just south of Hartford. I'm only about two hours away from you. When do you need me to help? I can be there tonight if you need me to be."

"Really? Well yeah, I could. What about your wife? Is she going to let you just take off like this?"

"Gary don't worry about Carol. Sometimes I think she likes you more than me."

"Ok, that would be fantastic. When you get to the Westin, go to the front desk, and give them your name and they will have a room reserved for you. If Carol wants to come down, then she is very welcome here also."

As he hung up the phone. He was excited to see Alexi again, but he had not anticipated that it would be so quick.

Now he needed to contact RoseMary Pilantez. He called one of the last phone numbers that he had for her. The person that picked up the phone was a man's voice. Gary asked if he could speak to RoseMary. The guy asked who this was but before Gary could answer a woman's voice said "This is Rose"

When he said who he was, he could hear the sharp intake of her breathing. After she heard his voice, she exclaimed "Thank God! Gary I was so worried about you. Where are you? Are you OK? What happened?"

She pelted him with a half a dozen questions strung together and not letting him answer any of them. He laughed and said Rose, "Slow down a bit. I'm doing

302

good and I'm currently in New York City. I was in the hospital for a long time after that scuba diving trip in Australia. I'm calling you today to see if you might be able to help me."

"Of course, I will help you. Why would you ask me such a silly question?"

Gary smiled to himself as he remembered Rose to be someone that didn't hold anything back. She just says what she feels and does not edit herself.

He said, "Rose, I'm sure you already know this, but Roger and Joanne disappeared after the office closed. This was only a couple of weeks right after I had the problem in Australia. You are probably one of the people that knows Joanne better than anyone. I need your help with tracking her down. I was wondering if you could meet me in New York city for a couple of days to work with my sister, Lucy. To dig her up."

Rose said she could do that with no problem. She asked him if it was ok to bring her husband along.

Now it was time for him to use her own retort against her. He said, "Of course, he can come with you. Why would you ask me such a silly question?

"That was nicely done, Good comeback line. It needs a little sarcasm and then it will be perfect. You are finally learning from me!" Rose quipped.

"We can probably get there tonight if you want. We are close to South Station in Boston, and we would probably take a train. Where are you exactly?"

"I am at the Westin Hotel at Grand Central Station. We are maybe two or three blocks from Grand Central Station. When you get here the reception will have a reservation for you."

After he hung up with Rose, he called down to the front desk. He asked the woman on the phone to reserve two rooms on the 33rd floor for tonight and the next 4 days. He also told her to charge these to his room. He was pleased to get everything in motion, and he was also excited about seeing his old friends.

Later that night, Rose and her husband, Joe, Alexi, and his wife Carol arrived at the hotel. Once they had all checked in, they all met in the lobby around 6:30 PM. Everyone was a little hungry, so they went to a nice steak and seafood restaurant not far from the hotel. They had a table for seven in the back.

Alexi and Rose had a lot of questions for him. They wanted to know what happened, who was with him when it happened, and all the details of his absence. They were not happy about Barry hurting Belinda's father. As they talked through dinner, a plan started to formulate.

The next day, Belinda left to go back to Boston. The hotel had reserved two conference rooms on the 5th floor. Lucy brought her laptop to use with Rose. And Alexi brought his laptop and a second one for Gary. He wasn't sure if he would have one with all the development software on board to run and debug the code. He smiled and was glad to have it.

Rose and Lucy started to discuss a few areas where they could track Joanne down. Carol announced to everyone that if they were not needed then she had a date with Joe to go ice skating at Bryant Park.

"After that we might go to Rockefeller Central to spend ridiculous amounts of money on tourist trinkets. Don't stay up we will be back before midnight."

Joe looked at everyone and then announced, "Yeah, what she said."

Everyone laughed and Carol very dramatically turned around saying, "Come on Joe, let's go skating."

Gary and Alexi went into one of the conference rooms and started to write on the whiteboard. They wrote out what areas they would start looking at. Rose and Lucy went into another conference room and started to do the same thing. They also started to draw out a list of items and places that might be possible locations where they might track Joanne down.

After about three hours, they ordered some room service. As they were eating lunch, everyone shared the progress they had made. Gary started off by saying the accounts that he was looking at on the day he went to

Australia all had funny account names. The only common thread in the account names were two words, jade, and unicorn.

"Every time I looked at an account, I could see interlaced in the account name were those two words, they were all different. Sometimes it was those two words but altered, like J1A2D3E4U5N6I7C8O9R10N11. It also showed up in an account that the two words were spelled backward, like NROCINUEDAJ. I found there are about 6 other patterns that were used. This was someone that used it because they felt it was clever and it would not be figured out. Usually if someone really wants to be covert then they need to make a pattern that is random and not repeated.

Another part of the code was collecting customer payments and siphoning a percentage of the money coming in. This amount was put into a different account and then the account was deleted. I couldn't find anything that helped me find out where that money went. It went into the account and then was deleted. I think that someone was accessing this account from outside of the firewall for the company. We still have many other things to look at.

Rose said they had figured out a couple of places that they were planning to look for Joanne, "We suspect that she bought a new house or condominium because of the purchase and sale document that Rose had seen come out of the copier one afternoon. It was from a company called LE Real Estate. Another clue was a place called *The Golden Mile*."

Rose continued excitedly, "When I heard that I immediately thought about the Magnificent Mile in Chicago, which is sometimes referred to as the Golden Mile. Lucy and I did not see anything in the United States for a company call LE Real Estate. We did find a couple of mentions of this in several countries in Europe, like Spain, Greece and Portugal."

Rose asked Gary, "What's the name on those accounts you said were all similar. Did you say Jade Unicorn?"

"Yes, it was. Why?"

"One of the only personal things I ever saw on Joanne's desk was a Jade horse. When you said unicorn, it made he think about it and in fact it was not a horse but a Unicorn."

Lucy asked, "What is Joanne's last name?"

Rose said, "Her last name is Druci."

Lucy said, "You said the account all had the words Jade and Unicorn interlaced in the account names. Jade Unicorn is an anagram for Joanne Druci!"

Everyone was stunned as this information started to set in.

Gary's eyes went wide, "Your right! Wow, I never even thought about that angle. I think if we start looking at her accounts this might be the string that unravels everything. I know Joanne was difficult to work with, but I didn't think that she was part of this. I think this is how the money was being taken out of those accounts. One of the bigger questions is why?"

Alexi said, "About one week before you fired me" Alexi grinned at Gary because no one knew the reason why Alexi left. "We had contracted out some engineers to help us push through the last part of tidying up everything before we released the final version to of the product" he began.

"One of the junior engineers, Kimberly Ambrose, was having problems getting her latest changes into the main source code branch. It was late in the day, so I didn't think much about it, but I logged into her computer and let her get the changes in with my credentials. I suspect that she made code changes that would send money out of those internal accounts to a personal outside account."

Rose said, "I think Alexi is right. I saw Kimberly in her office, and it looked like Joanne was berating Kimberly. That is typical Joanne though. In that month before you went to Australia, I saw Joanne spend a lot of time in and out of Roger's office. The strange part was that it was to look at something; and, then Joanne would sign a document and give it to Roger. It makes sense though. If money was going to be embezzled out of the company, then it's smart for Roger to make sure that his hands were clean, right?"

Lucy said, "You realize that the only way we can get to Roger is probably through Joanne. So, if we find out where she is, maybe we could trick her to reveal where Roger is. At the very least make her a little worried about someone looking for him."

Rose and Alexi all nodded their heads, looking at him.

Rose said, "In all the time I worked there I could tell that Joanne was totally driven by money. Money to her, was this insane drug that she could never get give up, or ever have enough. Do you remember after that big blow up you had with Roger? She was in a rage. She slammed drawers and kicked the couch. She was so mad at Roger. I think she was mad at me as well. She kept giving me these evil eyes when she looked at me. Roger came into her office and asked her to go somewhere. I saw her leave at 1:00 and she never came back that day. I don't know what happened that afternoon with Roger, but she came in the next day. The strange part of this is that she seemed to be in a good mood."

Everything was starting to come into focus a little more. Gary had not shared anything about the meeting he had with Roger. He remembered when he and Roger had a meeting with a customer and in that meeting, Gary was supposed to give a demo. When he started to do the demo, it crashed. He was able to recover from this incident by swapping the laptop that crashed with his laptop and doing the demonstration again. So, it was just about three or four minutes of awkwardness as the customers waited for Gary's laptop to boot up. For some reason, he thought that the demo blowing up was done deliberately to make Gary look like a foolish technology guy.

Later that night, Gary went through the code base and found out where the crash was happening. When he matched it to the exact line of source code that was the problem, he looked up the change history. The last change done on this part of the code was changed by Alexi. He looked at it and instantly knew that Alexi had not made these changes. It was just not Alexi's style of writing software code. The person making these changes was sloppy and looked like they were doing trial and error to make it crash.

Gary and Alexi have been writing software code side by side for the last 9 months. Alexi was a perfectionist. He also carried that trait into his software code. Alexi's style was to always guard against the worst-case scenario. This slowed us down but even though he would not admit this to Alexi, it made the quality of the software much higher. Several times these worst-case scenarios saved the software from crashing, or any other kind of bad state. For instance, if something in your code is expecting a number, then what happens if you give it an alphabetic character? What if you put in a symbol like a dollar sign or a percent symbol? Many times, Alexi's style of planning for the worst helped save us by not crashing.

Gary remembered clearly what actually happened. The next day Gary came into Roger's office and confronted him. Roger denied it but eventually gave in and admitted to it. He also blamed Joanne. The only thing that seemed to drive both Joanne and Roger was money so Gary thought that money would be the right penalty. Roger had to donate $5000 to the American Kidney Fund and $5000 to St. Jude's Hospital. Additionally, Joanne's salary would be reduced by $5000 which would also be donated to The Salvation Army. He told Roger that if he did not do this then he would quit.

Now Gary looked at Rose and asked her if this was around the time that Joanne came into the office with a brand-new red BMW. Rose thought about this for a second and then smiled.

"Gary, I think you're onto something. I remembered that Joanne, for a couple of days after that meeting with Roger, seemed happy. This scared me a little because this attitude was so foreign coming from her. At the end of that week, she drove to work in a beautiful Candy Apple Red BMW. One other thing was I got a peek at something she sent to the copier machine.

The document, sent to the printer, looked like it was a Purchase and Sale agreement from LE Real Estate company. I just saw it briefly before Joanne walked into the copy room. That might help us track her down quickly. How many Red BMWs are there in Europe? Of that number of Red BMW's, how many had transactions with LE Real Estate?" Rose concluded.

It was about 3:00 PM when Carol and Joe came back to the hotel. They came up to the conference rooms to see how everything was going. He relayed the progress they had made so far, and they said that they were looking for a way to trick Joanne into contacting Roger.

Joe asked what kind of car she likes to drive or own.

Rose said, "Candy Apple Red BMW. Why?"

Joe said, "That's easy. Make her think that this guy, Roger, is lying to her. If he really wanted to show his appreciation, why didn't he buy her the i7 model? It was so much nicer than the i5 that she was getting. When I was a car sales guy, this trick was easy to start the customer feeling that they weren't getting their fair share. Some would get angry and do one of two things. Many said to wait, and they needed to talk to the person or the company that they were getting this car from and squeezing more money from them. Sometimes, this worked. But either way they always came back and either financed the 30K or 45K for the upgrade to an i7, or they grudgingly settled with the i5. Not all, but many of the people buying the expensive BMW were very arrogant. Find a way to exploit that then, I think you would have a good shot at getting the information you wanted from her."

Rose looked at Joe in a very lovingly way and smiled. He could read Rose very well, but this was a side he had not seen before. It was nice. He realized he was lucky to have friends like this.

Carol was listening from the side of the group. She started to giggle, and said, "I just don't understand why this isn't so obvious. Promise her jewelry, gold, diamonds, emeralds, rubies or sapphires and you will be able to get her to say anything you want her to say. Especially, because of what Joe said. Plant that little seed about how she is not getting what she thinks she should get, and the bonus is rare stones. That is one hell of a motivator."

As Gary was listening to both Joe and Carol, he was idly doing a search for Red BMWs in Europe that also had a transaction with LE Real Estate. The screen came back with 11 hits. Eight of those were in or near Germany. That makes sense. Those eight hits had no transactions with LE Real Estate. He found that the other three were in Greece, Spain, and France. Greece and France were both males and had no transaction with LE Real Estate. The one in Spain bought a villa in Malaga Spain and more importantly it was in a part of Spain that

313

was called the 'Golden Mile'. He couldn't really tell from the name on the public records if it was male or female. This was largely because the record keeping in Spain had not kept up technologically with the rest of the world. But this had to be it.

"Hey, I think I found out where our friend Joanne is hiding. Does anyone speak Spanish?"

Chapter 17 - Joanne Druci

In Spain there's the king –

and then there's Antonio Banderas.

- Melanie Griffith

The Golden Mile,

Marbella, Málaga, Spain

"¡Mierda! Hijo de puta!"

A tall, thin, young Spanish man hobbles around in the dark, searching for his pants. His shin hits the edge of a grey marble coffee table. His curse breaks the total silence. Everything that was still before is now very alert. The sound kept echoing and rippling through the surrounding area of the house from where it originated. Little birds were just starting their morning hunt, green Gecko's and lizards froze in place, and little rodents all heard the noise as it echoed and reverberated through the trees around the large villa.

The man finally found his pants and shirt on the sofa exactly where he had taken them off last night for that nice, and very rich, one-night stand he had met at the casino. Actually, it wasn't last night, it was only four hours ago. Now, he quickly grabbed everything, and quietly rushed out the front door. He wanted to make a quick escape so as not wake his little friend from the night before. Thanking the Gods above for his stealthy escape, he revved up his little car and quickly drove away.

The woman on the bed woke up when he got out of bed and was trying to find her clothes from the night before. She smiled a little when she heard him curse from hitting the living room coffee table. She let him think he had made a clear escape, but she didn't care. She wanted him to leave. She was just done with him now. Most people don't usually look at "a night out" as a simple contract deal. But she got what she wanted, and he got what he wanted. Simple as that!

Still reeling from all the red wine from last night, Joanne Druci was glad that she could sleep some more. She drank a lot last night. Usually when this was the case, she did things that she regretted. Her payment for last night was the pounding and throbbing head she felt right now. A little nap and then maybe take a short walk to the beach and go to her favorite restaurant for some lunch. Yeah, that's what I'll do, she thought as she slipped back into sleep.

Several hours later…

The Marbella Marina Club hosted a comfortable open-air bar and restaurant. The pleasant breeze from the sea had an indelible smell to it, almost like a memory tattoo. Memories of sand, sunshine, cold ocean water, waves, or surfing immediately come to mind with the tangy, salty smell of ocean air.

The bar, made of a very long piece of mahogany with a super glossy finish, was classy. Many of the patrons of the Club were owners, or renters, of the sailboats and yachts in the marina docks. Currently there were only a handful of people eating or drinking in this small quaint restaurant.

Joanne was sitting at the bar enjoying the ocean breeze coming through the open-air Marina Club's restaurant and bar. The bartender, like most good bartenders, never lets a customer's drink remain empty. She was a familiar face here, so he knew exactly what she wanted to drink. He put a drink on the bar in front of Joanne. The first drink of the day was always Café bonbon con hielo, or Iced Coffee with sweetened condensed milk. She often wondered how he was able to intuitively know what she wanted before she even knew.

Then, the bartender brought over some finger sandwiches for her. It was only about 10:00 AM, so it was a little early for lunch, or Almuerzo as it is referred to in Spain. She was trying to decide what she was going to do today. Shopping? Beach? Casino? She decided to go to the beach.

Joanne picked up a bottle of water and headed to the beach area behind the club. She picked up a couple of towels and walked over to one of the cabana's dotting the golden, sandy beach. Two lounge chairs were placed half inside of the cabana to shade her upper body. In an almost routine manner, Joanne put her bottle of water on the little table between the lounge chairs.

The day like almost every day is Marbella Spain was perfect. Not a cloud in the sky, temperatures about 85°F and the Mediterranean water temperature averaging about 80°F. A pleasant light breeze and the loud crashing of the waves on the beach. To Joanne, this was heaven! Surrounded with famous and ultra-rich celebrities, she considered herself as elite, and rich. This was just a perfect place for her to live!

The young pool boy, working for the club, walked over to her cabana, and nervously asked if she'd like something to drink. The teenager was nervous because she had utterly speared him about a week ago. She had ordered a Bloody Mary and the boy forgot the celery stick. The poor kid was almost in tears. She tossed the Bloody Mary at him with a repulsed cry. He tried to catch the drink but failed. His white shirt took the brunt of it and the poor kid was covered in the red tomato juice.

She was tempted but decided she wouldn't order a Bloody Mary today. She ordered a large glass of Sangria. That should be easy enough, right? A few minutes later he brought her the Sangria with a large glass of ice. He put those on the little table next to the bottle of water she had on it.

She said sternly, "I didn't ask for the glass of ice cubes. Was this idea yours?"

The poor kid's face dropped as he cast his eyes intently on his sandals.

Finally, Joanne said, "Well it was a nice thought to bring that. I can keep the Sangria nice and cold. Thank you." She mused to herself about why she said Thank You. She never does that. Maybe she's losing her edge.

The kid's face lit up, almost as if he had just found a $20 bill on the ground. Ear to ear grin. He asked if he could get her anything else.

"Come back in a half hour with another glass of Sangria."

The young man turned, and half ran back to the bar area.

After a couple of Sangria's, she decided that she'd had enough beach for the day. She walked back to her villa and took a couple of hours siesta nap. She awoke from her nap when her cell phone rang. Her friend from last night wouldn't be able to meet her tonight at the casino. She wasn't surprised. Anyway, she really didn't want to be with him again so soon. Maybe later in the month they could have a repeat of last night.

It was good that he called. It was about 6 PM so she started to wash up and "beautify" herself. She planned to go to the casino a little later but was undecided whether she should get a taxi to the casino or drive there. If she drove, she would need to keep her drinking to a minimum. Last night was a combination of drinking and gambling. Joanne was a so-so gambler, but if she drank, she was horrible. Well, that answered that.

A little before 8 PM she got into her car and drove to the casino. When she arrived, she gave the keys to the valet, and he gave her a ticket.

The valet said, "Thank you Ms. Sue. When you're finished give us your ticket and we'll have your car ready as soon as possible."

She was very careful to keep her real identity a secret. The name she goes by in this place is Sue Joy Kono. Joanne established this identity before Roger sold the company and the office closed. She and Roger sold the company for $20 million. Roger had to pay her $10 million dollars because her name and her signature was on all the documents When she came to Spain, her identity was already established as Sue Joy Kono. It was also a little amusing that she used anagrams for her identity. Joanne Druci was for 'Jade Unicorn' and Sue Joy Kono was an anagram for '*Jokes on you*'. It was silly but at the time it seemed like a good idea.

The casino also only knew her by Sue Joy Kono. She wanted to keep both her fake, and real name, out of any government tax liability. No traceability back to her! Many banks, and casinos, will stash this money into offshore accounts, or in accounts that wouldn't in any way be noticeable. Of course, it was expected to give the bank a nice "kick back" for services rendered.

It amazed her sometimes by how easy it was to cover, or hide money, in banks all over the world. Many banks have a couple of accounts that only exist as a way to categorize different money. So, for example, a bank could take money that was in a normal, or business account, without any activity for a long time, and deposit this into a special account for abandoned money. But the bank doesn't necessarily need to deposit it into that account. Sometimes that money just vanished with no record of its existence. Many casinos would also be amenable to taking money in, or paying money out, of hidden accounts when customers didn't want any scrutiny.

Before going to the tables, she decided to get something to eat. Since Joanne had been in Spain, she had adjusted her eating schedule to the Spaniard's mealtimes. Four or five meals a day sounded great. Many in Spain use these mealtimes to socialize - or go home and have a nap. Even though she was overweight, the five meals a day were too much food for her. When she finished eating, she walked over to the 'craps' table.

She found out that Craps is a game that's very fast. You could win big on one bet or lose a ton on another. After about an hour, she wasn't seeing any winning action on the table, so she walked over to the "Texas Hold-em" table.

This was usually her game of choice. It wasn't too long before she was sitting at a large table of other players. The hand she was looking at had a possibility for her cards to get a stronger hand. So, it was worth staying in the first round of betting before the "flop" - when the first three cards, which could be combined to make the best hand of any five cards, were shown. The hand she was dealt with was *King* and *Four*. The table was made up of six players, 2 woman and 3 men. She decided to stay with this hand and see where it led her. Betting started with the guy across from her raised it $1000 plus the big blind of $250. The person to his left was the other women who pays in her ante, or the small blind of $125. This woman decided to stay in and put $1000 to match the current bet. If she wants to see the flop, she needs to fold or match the $1000 raise. Joanne also stayed and put in $1000 to continue playing. She threw $1000 to match his bet. The two players to her right all folded.

The dealer dealt three cards to the middle of the table, A **King**, **Jack**, and a **Four**. The man across from Joanne, was first to bet or fold. He raised and added $2000 to the pot. The woman next to him folded. So now the players were Joanne and the handsome guy across the table from her. She decided to stay in and met his raise of $2000 and then re-raised him an additional $1000. He matched the re-raise.

Now this was getting interesting! She couldn't tell what this guy was going to do. She was pretty good at determining a player's body language 'tells', or when they bet. Was it a good hand or was it just a bluff? The dealer put down another card and it was a six. Both Joanne and the man across from her, checked the bet.

Now the final round of betting would begin. The dealer put down a King. The guy across from her raised another $1000. She matched his bet and called. The dealer turned over the last card which was a King. She won the hand with a full house, three **Kings** and two **Fours**. She smiled at the gentleman across the table. He nodded politely. She liked this guy, and he was good looking. She thought Maybe she could have some more intimate time with him back at her villa, or at his place.

He was collecting his chips and leaving the table. She looked at the dealer and said that she would be right back. This kept her money on the table holding her seat at the table. She walked over to the guy and introduced herself.

'Hi, I'm Sue."

"My name is Joe. That was a nice round. Just thought I should quit while I was ahead", he said.

"Would you like to go to the bar for a drink?" she asked him. As Joanne said this, a woman came towards Joe. Joe politely introduced his wife, RoseMary.

Joanne was shocked to see Rose here. Of all the places in the world? The odds of that were astronomical. Rose is very good at keeping a stone face, but Joe was relieved that she was there to carry out their plan. He hated like hell to lose that hand of poker. He knew any money that was spent, or lost, would be reimbursed by Gary. Joe also knew Joanne is a very sleezy, clever person. The plan was for Joe to play at her table and to lose to her. Then, to introduce himself and wear down her defenses so that her guard would be down a little. The plan was to innocently drop a little bait to see if she would take the bite.

"Joanne, how are you? We haven't seen each other in such a long time. I never heard anything from Gary after he went on his trip to Australia. I tried calling him several times, but got nothing," Rose said in a cheery voice.

"Well, Rose, I'm also as mystified as you are. I went back to the office after my vacation, and it was all locked up. I tried calling Roger but like you I got nothing. I went into the building and used the office key to see what was going on. The key for the office didn't work and the locks were all replaced. I finally got one of the building maintenance guys to open the office door. It was completely empty. No desks, computers, or anything. In the front part of the office, I found two boxes. One box had my name on it and the other box had your name on it. I had one of the building guys ship that to you. You received it right?"

She didn't fool Rose. Rose remembered how she hated farms, and farm animals, because everything smelled like shit. She was emanating this "bullshit" right now. Joanne had that "icky, too sweet" tone in her voice. Rose was not new to the game and her *kung-fu* was stronger than Joanne's.

"Yes, I did receive that and thank you so much for sending it. By the way, have you heard anything from Roger?"

Joanne didn't like this line of questioning. She didn't know where Roger was. Her only link to him was through Barry Parker. Barry could forward a message to Roger if she wanted. She got what she wanted from Roger which was, the villa, the money, and a new identity. There was no real reason to reach out to Roger, or Barry. She thought that was a lifetime ago.

"No, I haven't heard from anyone at the company. You're the only person I've seen from that office. Why, is there something that you need Roger to help you with?"

Ah-huh, finally she asked the question Rose was waiting for.

"Well, Joanne, I'm not sure if Roger could help. But it's the strangest thing, and I'm not sure if it's real or not.", Rose said with a veiled sarcasm.

"Really, well, run it by me and maybe I might have heard about it." Again, that "icky, too sweet" tone of just fake bullshit. Well, if you want them to dance then you need to start dancing too, Rose thought sardonically. Rose carefully thought about her response.

"I'm not sure if you're aware of this, but Gary came back from Australia a different person. He lives with his sister, and she takes care of him. You wouldn't recognize him if you saw him now. He's not the same man I knew at the office. He's still trying to recover his senses. He called me last month, so I went to visit him a couple of weeks ago. His memory is almost completely gone."

Joanne appropriately turned her face to concern about Gary's wellbeing. "I'm shocked by that. I thought he'd died on a Christmas scuba diving trip. He's so lucky to have come out of that coma."

Rose smiled and thought to herself, 'I gotcha! I never mentioned he was in a coma.'

She continued according to plan, "Gary called me to see if I had one of his notebooks that was in his office on the day he left for Australia. This notebook was his "to do" list that I wrote down for him, daily. It was always going from his office to my cube, or the other way around. Now here is the weird part. He told me that he had written down a set of coordinates. I did have the notebook and the only thing I saw was on the last page. It said, Cyprus and then some numbers 33.3N and 33.3E. When Joe and I looked it up, it was in the middle of the Mediterranean Sea and south of Cyprus. I really don't know what it is, but Gary seemed to imply that it's crucial. This place at these coordinates contains a lot of money. He said that there were Golden Bitcoins and bunches of diamonds and jewels worth a ton of money. Also, to reinforce the image she was painting, she told Joanne that she thought he was dead broke and that is the reason for his call.

Joanne thought of how unusual it was to bring something like this up from four years ago. She would have to talk to Barry and get a hold of Roger.

"So, are you having fun in Spain?"

"Yes, we're having a fantastic time. We jumped off a cruise ship and decided to stay a couple of days in Spain and then just take our time and meet up with a cruise ship in Lisbon, Portugal. This part of the world is just fantastic. How about yourself?", Rose asked.

"I've been here many times. My mother lives here. She recently fell and hurt her hip so I'm here to help her get around after her surgery."

Joanne looked at Joe and thought, what a shame that he was married to Rose. Well, his loss. At this point, the conversation was starting to bore her.

"I'm meeting my date here in twenty minutes. Think I can get in a couple more hands of poker before he arrives,", she said gesturing towards the table.

Rose and Joanne did the phony goodbyes and how great it was to see each other after so long as Joanne headed back to the table. The only thing that Rose had in common with her was that they each hated to be in the same room.

Joanne went back to Texas Hold-em table. She sat through one hand and lost. Her mind was not on the game, so she cashed in her chips. Seeing Rose out of the blue like that was strange and suspicious. Getting in her car, she took the long way home to think about what to do next. When she got back to her villa, she had made up her mind to call Barry.

The person that she considered as a wild card is Gary. Would he do something like this? It wouldn't be that unusual for him to keep a stash somewhere if he wanted to stop doing what he was doing. If this is on the bottom of the Mediterranean Sea, it made perfect sense since Gary was an avid scuba diver. But if he was infirm and physically not able to go to the bottom and retrieve it, she was certain that someone could be hired to get this. She needed to get to Barry and Roger involved.

She called the number she had for Barry. She didn't want to sound really urgent, but she wanted to impress on Barry that she needed to talk to Roger soon, if he wouldn't mind relaying this information to Roger.

Barry answered on the third ring. "Hi ya Barry. This is Joanne Druci. I just had something strange happen to me. I bumped into Gary's admin. Rose. She was asking me some strange questions about Roger. I didn't tell her anything, but I wanted to give Roger a heads up. Do you have Roger's contact information?"

Roger told Barry not to give out his contact info but that was just for nosey people. He'd never told him to not give it to Joanne. As far as he knew, Roger had already given Joanne his contact details when he disappeared. Roger had changed his identity a couple of times, but Barry had recently talked to him and had his information for where he was in New Zealand. Besides, this did make Barry curious.

Barry continued in an overly familiar voice, "Hi, honey. Nice to talk to you after so long a time. How have you been? Are you still in Spain?"

She was hoping this familiarity would not be there when she decided to speak to Barry. At one time, Barry and Joanne had a little one-night thing after many, many gin and tonics. It was just that one night and neither of them spoke about it again. Barry sometimes would call her "honey" and she would cringe inside. Now, she didn't really have any choice but to play along in this charade.

"I'm doing great. I am still in Spain and the one drawback is that there's so many tourists here all the time. I'm thinking of moving to get away from all of them. How're you doing?"

Barry in his usual gruffness said, "I'm doing swell. Been working hard getting my gym to keep making some half decent money. The little snot nosed gym-rats are assholes. Occasionally, I have to *thump* one of them on the head, but, hey, it's Boston, right? Hold on a sec, let me get that info you want. Ok here it is. He's in New Zealand now, so the time difference is a pain."

"Thanks Barry, I really appreciate it."

"Ok, good night darlin."

She always felt dirty anytime she talked to Barry. When she got home, she pulled out a big bottle of expensive white Pinot Grigio. Joanne booted up her laptop. Wellington, New Zealand is exactly 12 hours ahead of Marbella Spain. It was only about only about 11:00 AM there now.

She needed to think a little of why she wanted to talk to Roger. Something about bumping into Rose tonight was strange. She examined it turning it over in her mind. She was hard pressed to see any flaw in her exchange with Joe and Rose. But it just didn't sit right. The odds of them bumping into each other is astronomical. This had to be staged. It just had to be. Nothing made any sense. I don't know why Rose did this though. She must have some "sweetheart" deal with Gary. It only made sense that way. What a smart-ass Rose was. She thinks she can play me for a fool. Good Luck!!

Chapter 18 - Barry Parker

Misfits aren't misfits

among other misfits.

- Barry Manilow

Barry was walking out of Milly Howard's apartment around 4am. Everything was quiet, the only sound was his footsteps echoing in the parking lot. He wanted to be away from this place as soon as he could. Almost running to his car, he got in, started it, and drove away as quickly as he could. He was sweating even though the car air was cool when he got in. His body was pumping more adrenalin than blood at that moment.

His meeting with Milly did not go as planned. He showed up at her door. When she opened it, he went in. He was carrying the wooden bat that he'd used during Joseph's beating. When Milly saw the bat in his hand, she knew that this was going to be very bad.

Barry sat down and asked for a drink. She quickly, got him a scotch and water. She also got one of them for herself and downed it quickly. Then, she poured a second glass for herself. She brought both drinks over to Barry.

"Milly, where's Gary McKeown?"

Milly responded quickly, "He's still at Ashwood, where he's always been."

"Milly it's time to tell the truth to me. Come closer and sit with me, nothing's gonna happen, I just want to know so that I can tell my father exactly where he is. Come on, sit next to me."

Although she regretted doing it, she went over and sat next to him anyways. He repeated his question. Milly's answer was that she didn't know where he was and that was all she knew.

Barry said, "Ok that's what I'll tell my father. He's no longer at Ashwood.

"Do you know where he went?"

Milly was on shaky ground as it was. She said Gary's "bitch" sister took him home about a year ago.

He said, "See that wasn't so bad. My father will be happy to know exactly where he was. Hey why don't you and I go into the bedroom and have a little fun?" He did not sound as dangerous as he was, so she felt a little more at ease with him now.

When they got undressed. He asked her why she lied to him? She said "His sister wanted no one to know that he wasn't there. She paid me a couple of hundred dollars."

Bit By Bit

Barry said that it was ok. Milly got on the bed, and he got on top of her. As they started their familiar routine, he put his hands gently around her neck.

With the same familiar rhythm of past sexual encounters, Barry put his hands around Milly's neck. At first, Milly didn't mind but as they continued, Barry's hands got tighter and tighter around Milly's neck. Milly's eyes were darting all over as it dawned on her that Barry was going to kill her. She was scared. Milly was kicking her legs and doing everything she could to get him off her.

He released his tight grip on her neck and let Milly breathe again.

After Milly stopped coughing, she said, "Barry, are trying to kill me? Don't choke me, you asshole! Better yet, get out of here now or I will call the police."

He wasn't moving. Milly screamed as loud as she could. He looked down at her with a stupid silly grin. Using all his force he punched her in the face. Her nose immediately started to bleed. Again, he punched Milly in the face as hard as possible. Milly eyes rolled back in her head a little. She begged him to stop.

He was not going to stop. He continued the rhythm that they were into moments before. Barry put his hands around her neck and choked her more and more.

"They told me he was taken out after the first year there. That was 3 years that you've been lying to me.

Three years of making me your fool. **WHO'S THE STUPID FOOL NOW?"**

Milly kicked and scratched. he kept going even after she was dead. Dead or alive it didn't really matter to him. He took his time until he was totally satisfied. He left her apartment now with his heart beating and adrenalin coursing through his veins. There was no high better than this.

He quickly got into his car and drove away. Milly and Joseph both got dealt with tonight. He thought he deserved another drink for that. But he would have that drink at home. When he got home, he was so tired he barely got his clothes off before he passed out on his bed.

The next day he woke up at noon because his cell phone was ringing. He was still hung over when he answered the phone. It was his father because it had that ominous Darth Vader - *"Luke I am your father"* ringtone.

He answered, "Hi pops. What's going on?"

Barry's father, Henry or Hank as most people called him, began, "I guess you hurt Joe Daly pretty badly. He almost died which is good for us because we can use him again. I got a call from the scumbag that owes us big. He said that he would meet you at the Four C's tonight at 6 p.m. He'll pay what he owes for this month plus the interest. Don't let him give you anything less than $8,500.00. You can keep $500 but make sure he gives you at least the 8G. Good job last night. I take it you played 'baseball' with Joe."

"Yes, I did. He almost got away but putting that UBER sticker on the windshield was the thing that got him caught. Ok I'll meet him at C's at 6 PM."

"Give me a call when you get the money from him. Ok? Bye"

After his father hung up, he remembered that the baseball bat he used on Joseph Daly was left at Milly's apartment. Shit! Now he was going to have to go over there and get it. He didn't have Milly's keys, so he was going to have to break her door or a window to get inside.

It wasn't till about 3 PM that he got showered and shaved and got into his car. He was pissed that he forgot the bat. Now he had to schlep all the way from Medford down to Weymouth which is south of Boston. It was hard to say which town around Boston that he hated more than Weymouth. He hated Quincy and he hated Braintree equally because he got the shit beat out of him in each of those towns. Weymouth sucked but Hingham was by far the worse. Hingham is the first place he got shot at and it was the first place he had killed someone. Barry was no friend of the Boston Cops, so he always gave them wide berth. He knew he stood out in the crowd, so the police usually stopped him to ask questions. Profiling was just a fact of being a street brawler. You just had that look.

He arrived at Milly's at 3:30. The apartment complex parking was filled with police cruisers and vans and other official looking vehicles. His first thought was that Milly was found. His bat would connect him with many different crimes. He'd used that bat many times hitting people, or at least roughing them up if they were late paying. Shit!

Milly's apartment was on the second floor. Maybe the police were here for other reasons or for people on different floors. He thought he would just wait this out a little before going in there. Then he saw a kid, probably 12 or 13, riding his skateboard on the sidewalk behind the parking lot. Getting the kid's attention, he got the kid to come to him, and asked him if he wanted to make some easy money. This kid grew up on the streets, so dealers came up to him all the time asking him to deliver a package.

The first thing the boy said, "Hey man, I ain't carrying any of your shit to someone else. My Mom's on the Methadone plan and she is still messed up. Got it!"

He could respect that. Barry said, "No kid that is not what I want you to do. Promise. I need you to go over to the apartment building and go to apartment 202. If there are no cops there, then come back and tell me. I'll pay you $20. Will you do that for me?"

The kid was named Charles, but he preferred Chuck. The name Charles was saved for his mother- and only his mother. Chuck looked at Barry with a deadpan face.

"How dumb do you think I am?" Chuck wanted to be careful here. This guy was a street guy so he could probably kick his ass if he wanted to. The guy didn't say anything.

Chuck continued, "Listen bro, if you are going to pay me $20 and cops are involved it's gonna cost more. I'll give you this week's special of just $100"

He almost slapped the kid in the face but then he thought that when he was this kid's age, he did something like this for a dealer that thought the cops were in his place. Back then he charged the dealer $50 so this is a steep price to pay. He would put another condition in it.

He added, "Ok you little prick, I will give you $100, but in that apartment 202 there's a bat that I left there last night. If you grab the bat and get it to me, I will give you $300, ok?"

The little kid asked, "What if someone is in her apartment?"

"Just knock, if no one answers then I'll give you the $100 but if you can get in, I 'll give $300 for the bat. You probably know this already, but do you know how to use a bump key?"

"Ok, I grew up in Southie. We are born with a bump key and a manual of every lock out there and how to crack it. What'd you think?"

Barry has used bump keys since he was this kid's age. A bump key is simple and quick. You take a key that is sort of like a blank master key. If you hit the end of the key, it will disturb the pins inside the lock and if you're able to catch them falling in the places, then turn the key. It's a trick for most locks but the newer locks are very sophisticated, so a bump won't work.

He had to admit to himself that he liked this kid's attitude. Most shady deals you make are done in a certain way. Taste in, Taste out. Kind of like a deposit or Lay-a-way. He gave him the twenty and Chuck gave him his skateboard. The skateboard was worth a lot more than $20. His entire life is pretty much in that board. This was the deal. Full payment when product was delivered or forfeit the "taste in" part.

Barry sat in his car and watched the kid walk right through the group of Weymouth and Boston Police talking in huddled groups. He looked back once. He went up to the second floor to Apartment 202. There were some police at the far end of the hallway, but no one was there in front of the apartment he wanted. It took about four tries using the bump key to gain access to the apartment. Something inside smelled. He wasn't sure of what it was, but it smelled gross. He saw the bat by the couch. He quickly grabbed it and walked out of the apartment door. As soon as he opened the door, it was blocked by a huge piece of muscle in a police uniform. Not sure why the random thought popped in his head now right now, but this guy looks like the hulk but blue rather than green which is the signature of the hulk. Officer Watashe pushed his way through the doorway like a bull and commanded Chuck to tell him who he was.

Shit, I'm caught. There was no way he could escape. If he got out of the building, he would never make it to the guy in the parking lot. He tried to lie to the cop telling the cop that he was looking for his friend Eric who lived there. Halfway through this lie he realized this guy wouldn't buy it. Chuck was a street kid so as slimy as some people can be, you never ever gave up or ratted on someone. Even in times like this, it was a code that you didn't break. This wasn't some ABC or CBS crime show that they will dramatize for their brand of rough and tough urban life. People watch that and they think they wouldn't have any problem. No, this was real life, and this is real pain. Oh, I don't need to lock my car door; no one will steal my crappy car. Don't start balling when you get back and your car is gone.

If you've ever walked into an alley to use as a shortcut, you might come across a dead guy in between garbage cans. Chuck came across one while he was going to his friend's house. When he got to his friend's house everyone was talking about the guy that ratted to the cops about his DD (Drug Dealer). Everyone knew except the police. So, in the city you kept your mouth shut.

His brain was working overtime. He might be able to get away and not rat on the guy. He gave the cop one of his fake identities. You never wanted to give your real name. Occasionally, he and a friend from school used to share their identities. B&E were minor so no biggie. He told the cop that he was just trying to see if he could get some pills, or pot that a friend told him this woman dealt. He told the cop that he couldn't find any drugs just the alcohol. This cop was not buying one word of it.

Chuck told the cop that he just wanted to get out of here, and not be in any trouble.

"Can I leave?"

The cop thought about it. He knew he wasn't going to get anything more out of him. He decided to let the kid go but the bat had to stay. This kid had nothing to do with the blood on the bat and the dead woman in the apartment.

The kid walked out of the apartment building and turned 90 degrees to the left from where he came in. He did this to not give the cops anything to be suspicious of. To stay clear of the car that was about to pay him. He looked at the guy in the car but made no hand movements. But to just say "not here, follow me".

Barry caught up to the kid at a McDonalds's down the street and away from the cops. The kid told him that he got in and was walking out of the apartment when the cop stopped him.

"I told the big cop that I was looking for pills, pot or booze. I tried the best I could to get out of there with the bat. Chuck said breathlessly. " I don't think the cop believed me."

When he finished, he told Barry that he needed to be paid the $300 he promised. He was about to renege on the deal they had but, he told the kid he'd pay $200 for going in there and not ratting on him. Chuck was about to protest but on principle he agreed. It's not the full boat but it wasn't shit either. He accepted it. Then he told Barry that he was pretty sure the cops were checking the direction he was going, so he should probably get out of here. Barry agreed. He gave the kid his skateboard back and thanked him. Barry held out his closed fist turned with the thumb on top. Chuck did the same thing and vertically punched Barry hand down. It's called different things, but it was traditionally called a "donkey konged" deal. In other words, your deal is officially ended.

As he drove away, he felt something he had not felt in a long time, guilt, and remorse. It felt like he was in a room that was too hot, and he wanted to escape but couldn't. Trapped. He knew the significance of that bat being traced to him. This time around the courts might have just enough to have him end up doing time in Walpole.

He headed over to the Four C's a little early. At 4:30 PM, he sat down at the bar and ordered a scotch and water. Some of the stress from the last couple of days started to ease as the alcohol spread through his body. Now, it was 5 PM with no one else at the bar. Usually that's not the case at any time here. He was working on his second scotch when a guy came up and sat on the stool next to him. Every bar stool was empty, and this guy pulls up and sits next to him. This is like that urinal etiquette crap.

The guy that was sitting too close said, "Hi."

Barry just looked at the guy.

He hated this when people invaded his personal space. He got up and told the bartender he would like another drink after he came back from the bathroom. He did have to go so it wasn't really his way to enforce etiquette. When he came back to the bar, the guy was sitting where he was seated before. Barry moved his drink down about sat down about 3 bar stools away from the guy. The bartender delivered his next drink in front of him and put the tab or receipt into an empty shot glass. This bar never let you owe any money at the end of the night. If you over drank what your wallet could support, it's the same on the streets, "taste in, taste out". This simply meant that you left the bar without something of yours, or some pain that had to be endured. Like other bars in the area, you made sure your tab was paid. This unfortunately is the "taste out" part. The owner has a reputation of being very psychotic (that's not an exaggeration). He would nearly piss himself when his tough "bar keeps" broke every finger on your hand. One finger for every hundred dollars owed. Taste out sweetie pie. A finger is a finger and so if the finger was black, brown, white, red, or with pink nail polish, he didn't discriminate.

For Barry, the guy that was bugging him was about to get a punch in the face if he didn't stop looking in his direction. Finally, the guy said "hello" again.

"I'm sorry to bug you but you're a dead ringer for my old friend, Micky."

He picked up his drink, took a big gulp, and felt it burn every muscle, joint, cartilage, and tendon in his body. As he was putting the drink down, he mumbled to the guy that he didn't know anyone named Micky. The drama was palpable.

What a dumb ass question that was he thought. Micky? This guy doesn't know anything about South Boston.

In "Southie", a large majority of people here are either Irish, or Irish born, living in the USA. If you were not Irish in Southie, all the neighbors watched closely, looking to see if you were an enemy, or an ally. If you were an ally, then you were brought into the neighborhoods. no, this guy is clueless, he thought.

In South Boston, in summertime there were a lot of BBQs, Boston Sports parties, and anything that could be rationalized a need for a big party. If you were asked to come, then "you are in like Flynn". If you were not brought into the communities and neighborhoods, then nothing overtly bad would happen to you. They just ignored you and let you do your thing. Just like he was avoiding the guy at the bar.

Then he thought of the winters in his neighborhood. Boston gets pummeled with snow every year and it has strict laws regarding where to park and what times are ok to park. The plows are working on narrow streets, and they can only go so far. If the plow didn't come down your street, because your car was not moved; then, usually, but not always, any snow not removed was all piled on your car. The kids made a killing in winter shoveling cars out, but they wouldn't shovel one bit of your car if you weren't one of the neighbors.

Every person in every neighborhood knew everyone else. That 70-year-old sweet looking elderly lady put two guys in intensive care when they tried to grab her pocketbook. They were not from Southie. Or, once a teen age girl got out of bed and sleep-walked around the streets in her underwear. Everyone knew that.

One story came to mind. It was at 1:00 AM in a darkened alley, when a shady deal with a prostitute and her "john" was happening. It was the financial part that was the riskiest part of any deal. Robbed, raped, or killed was not out of the realm of reality in a big city. However, when the prostitute saw the girl. She needed to act, she needed to get this girl home, now. Tony is gonna be pissed if she doesn't come back with the cash to give him. She gave the guy a very sloppy kiss. She told the guy to give her his jacket. She told him she'd be right here at exactly 3 AM to complete their transaction.

She said, " It's not free but if you give me your coat for a couple hours, I'll greatly discount the service. I will make it worth it." Then, the prostitute, who was already wearing next to nothing, grabbed the naked sleepwalker and put the coat around the poor girls' shoulders.

She walked away from the alley to get the girl home.

"Where are her parents?" she muttered angrily.

She knew that the parents had put special locks on the doors, and just about everything else, but once again she was caught in her underwear walking around the neighborhood. If Tony finds out he might make the girl's parents pay for the money I'm losing for him.

However, sometimes and some days he can be sweet. I just hope he's in a generous mood. South Boston was just like that. The big cities just bred these types of neighborhoods. Different zip codes but the same rule existed, "taste in, and taste out"

Barry picked up his drink and finished the rest of it. He probably knew about 15 different people named Mick or Micky. He looked at the guy a little astounded that he asked the question. How many John Smith's do you know? Stupid question. He said, "you're in Southie, so yeah, I know a bunch of people called Micky. Why?"

"Well like I said you look like a friend of mine."

Barry's "Spidey sense" started to alert him. He needed to be careful. Out of the corner of his eye he saw that most of the bar stools were filled now.

His brain took control and said, "It was nice meeting you, but I got to meet some friends who are waiting for me."

The guy came over to the bar stool that was directly next to his again. He was approaching a point of no return. What is it with this guy and personal space boundaries?

The guy continued, "So do you ever play any baseball? Oh yeah, my name is Ben Costello." When he said that, he moved his jacket open a little and there, clipped to his waist, was a badge.

Barry was still thinking that he could make it out of C's, but that was not the case tonight.

The asshole with the badge pulls out his cell phone. On his phone was a live video of Henry, his father. Ben said, "Say hi Pops!"

That was it. Whatever control he had was totally out of control now! He put on his game face even though it was that stupid silly grin. He started punching, kicking, and doing as much damage as he could. The Four C's bar was an old-time place. They were going to be mighty chaffed about the damage, but they will get reimbursed from someone. His father had connections everywhere so they knew that they would get their "*taste out*" eventually.

One guy standing at the bar was only at the bar because he wanted to order a drink. Somebody pushed him and then someone pushed him in a different direction. Crash his new White Russian was now on the floor. This was a tough bar, so it was not usual to see someone with a gun or a knife. This guy had both. He pulled his knife out and another person pushed him again. He almost sliced his thumb off. In his younger days, this bystander would join right in and punch or kicked anything in his way. The bartender noticed the guy's drink was now on the floor. He nodded his head as if to say I will get you another after this craziness stops. The guy slowly backed away.

The bartender was getting a little pissed at the mess he was going to have to clean up. Under the counter he kept two guns. One was a starter's pistol. The other was a real gun if someone tried to rob or hurt him. The first shot of the starter's pistol got everyone's attention.

In a loud thunderous booming voice, he yelled, "Out! Everyone in the bar area, Out! Now! This gun makes noise to get your attention, but I also have a real one that will put you in the hospital, or dead. Either way it doesn't matter. **JUST GET OUT**!" The bartender's face at this point was blood red and sweaty. People quietly picked their stuff up. Some made a half-hearted effort to straighten bar stools or clean up. In about 20 seconds the bar was empty.

Ben grabbed Barry's arm and said that they were not finished. He took his arm and guided him to Ben's car. He pulled the phone out again with the live video feed of his father.

He just said, "Hey".

His father saw that he was watching Barry's on Facetime video chat, so he yelled, "Barry call Brent. Remember faigheann stiallacha greamanna!

Did you get that? Call Brent and keep your mouth shut." Loosely translated from Gaelic, Henry's words meant "snitches get stitches"

Barry yelled at the phone," I will pop. I promise."

Ben turned him around and said more forcefully, "Do you like baseball?"

As he said this, he produced from the backseat of his car, a garbage bag that contained Barry's "Louisville Slugger". The bat that was left at Milly's. That stopped him cold.

At this moment, Barry was stunned. Ben took advantage of this to get him into compliance. Ben decided to go full forward while he still could. He took his left arm and his right arm bringing them together behind his back. Ben as quickly as he could, he snapped handcuffs on him. Most of Ben's training with the government involved training to quickly put handcuffs on a suspect. They practiced, over and over.

Once handcuffs were on him, he was pushed into the back of Ben's black, unmarked government car. Barry hit his head rather hard on the top of the door frame of the car as he was pushed in. Ben didn't feel bad at all about this. Not one bit.

Ben breathed a sigh of relief with Barry cuffed in the back of his car. Now is when the fun starts to happen. Is Barry as tough as his father? We will have to see.

Ben Costello

Boston 8:00 PM Thursday…

After almost 4 hours of interrogating, Barry Parker was booked and arrested on suspicion of murder of Milly Howard, and attempted murder of Gary McKeown. He was also charged with assault and battery of Joseph Daly.

Ben was tired, but he needed to make one final call. He called Belinda Daly to tell her that Barry Parker was being arrested right now. He could hear the long sigh on the other end of the phone.

She was very relieved to hear that. He asked about her father.

"He's improving but it's going to take a lot of time. Right now, he is being given a lot of pain meds, so he's comfortable. He's sleeping a lot. I am glad to hear about Barry. It's funny you called right now. I just booked myself a plane ticket to Cyprus. We might have a strong lead on Roger Tillson. Gary set a trap for Roger to entice him with money and diamonds. We think this will bring him out in the open. I contacted the US/UK NATO base and they said that they would help us in anyway they can."

"That's fantastic but it sounds a little dangerous if it's just Gary and his sister. You said there is a NATO base, and they will help?"

Well, yes that is what they told me. But now that I think about it, I am a little doubtful that they were just telling me what I wanted to hear," she answered.

"Belinda, I'm sorry if this sounds ignorant of me, but where is Cyprus?" Ben said sheepishly.

After a moment of hesitation, before Belinda answered, Ben could hear her laughter even though he knew she was trying to hide it.

Ben was thinking of a polite way to escape his '*ignorant*' question. Lucy broke the silence first and said, "Ben, trust me I am not laughing at you. I'm laughing because I asked the same thing. I thought Cypress was a type of tree. I knew nothing of an island called Cyprus. I thought I was flying to a town or city called Cypress that was in Canada or Maine. The Republic Island of Cyprus is in the eastern part of the Mediterranean Sea."

"Oh, OK. I might have been napping in my geography class when this was talked about."

"Ben, I just had a great idea. Would you like to go with me to Cyprus? This situation could get a little dicey. It would be a huge help to have you there. Your experience with the law and also your scuba diving experience could be a life saver," Belinda said this, knowing it might be laced, and promote a guilt-ridden response.

He almost said no, but the scuba diving didn't seem right. His response was a question more than a statement, "Scuba diving?"

"Well, now that you say it, it does sound a little strange", she added.

Belinda started to lay out what she knew of the plan. Ben saw a couple of weak areas in this plan. Maybe it was just the investigator part of himself.

"No, No. It's not strange. I guess I look at things cynically. If Gary puts something on the bottom of the sea, what happens if they decide to leave Gary there? That is almost as bad as just killing him outright. What if they put a leak into his air supply somehow? All these types of scenarios are exactly why people dive in pairs. Gary and I, would methodically go through these types of cases every time we make a dive."

"Ben, I'm getting on a plane in about 4 hours, I know this is a big *ask* but this is where your experience of scuba diving would be crucial. Just think about it, Ok? Sorry to put you into this kind of position. I will shut up now."

This would be an interesting trip. Ben was glad he would see Gary again. He felt very guilty that he didn't reach out to him sooner. I hope we patch things up and maybe do some more diving.

"Belinda. Wait. Let me talk to my boss and see if I can get time off and permission to expense the flight. How long is this flight to Cyprus?"

"Seriously? That would be such a huge help. It's about 12 hours. Don't worry about the cost of the ticket or anything else. We will be flying in First Class, by the way."

Ben chuckled a little and only said this because he felt that she would get the pun. "Did you really just say, we are flying First Class. *By the way?"*

It took a second for it to register on her, but she replayed it over in her head. She started to giggle so hard she couldn't speak. After her giggles started to calm down, "Your right, that did sound funny. I keep thinking of that classic movie 'Clueless' where the girl is in school and says, '**as if....**' I admit that sounded snarky."

"Well, I am definitely not going to tell my boss that. He will want to come too. Let me call you back in about 15 minutes?"

Once Ben updated his boss on the recent developments with Barry. His boss agreed and said it was ok to go to Cyprus.

Ben called Belinda back telling her he could only be away from work for one week, but he was excited to go. Belinda told him that he would get a call in about 10 minutes from a woman named Betsy. She was the person that handled all of the logistics of any travel for Trinity Trust Holding.

She mentioned that Betsy was exceptional at handling every little thing that you might need when traveling. Simple things like a converter for a laptop or anything, "I am going to tell Betsy to give you a call in a minute." she said.

"Ben, I am very appreciative of this. I don't even think it has registered yet, but Barry's done so much damage to my father. He rarely talks about what happened in College. Neither Gary nor my uncle will really give me all the facts. My grandmother told me, once. She asked me to not to say anything about it. She told me that my father was a person that did not want pity or charity from anything or anyone. That's just his way. She also told me that this was the way my father was. Your arrest of Barry is a big win for me today. Unfortunately, though it's not over. Now we get Roger!"

He heard just the slightest crack in her voice. To him Belinda is a strong person. This is an emotional side of her that he was not familiar with. Understandably, anyone experiencing the hurt of a loved one, especially a parent, would be emotional. How can anyone with a pulse not be vulnerable in a situation like this?

"YES! Now let's get Roger and put him in a prison for the rest of life. First drinks on me when we catch him!!"

After Ben, got off the phone, right on cue, Betsy called. He gave her a couple of details and she was processing the ticket securing a seat on tonight's flight. The flight leaves at 11:50 PM tonight. They would like him to be there at 11:00 PM. She also told him that a car would pick him up at 10:30 at his house in Malden.

After he hung up, he realized he needed to get going to pack and get ready for tonight's flight.

An hour and a half later, he was just bringing his suitcase downstairs to put it by the door, and he spied the limo driver outside. She was ten minutes early. Perfect timing. He arrived at the gate in terminal E with a couple of dozen people already in the gate area.

Ben saw Belinda off to the side of the gate area, away from where everyone else was. She was reading a travel book on Cyprus. He smiled when he saw that. She reached into her carry-on and handed him an additional travel book about Cyprus.

They both laughed at this.

Chapter 19 – Zoom Zoom

"Arrive before you leave."

- British Airways' slogan for the Concorde

After the fund-raising event, the last month has kept Roger in a deliriously happy mood – a mood that he desired his entire life. He worked very hard in his life planning, scheming, stealing, hurting, and manipulating people for over 40 years. The single reason for doing all this was the goal of "more". He was never satisfied. He always wanted more. And when he got more, he still wanted more. It was a vicious cycle for Roger. For him, this form of addiction was almost identical to other addictions like drugs, alcohol, gambling, sex, and on and on. The signs were all there, but he continued to keep obsessing about money even though it was hurting him emotionally and physically.

Roger's ego and his sense of self were intimately tied to how much money he could make, or steal, and get away with it. The chemistry of his brain, over years of this type of a cognitive pattern, had changed. The neurotransmitters in his brain were sending too little or too much. The neurotransmitters, amongst the hundreds of billions of neurons in his brain, kept him high or dropped him into depression. He was on a high for almost a month after the fund-raising event took place.

Then, he would become depressed if he didn't have a money-making scheme in place. The Bitcoin bit mining was a huge boost to his money addiction. Even though he was making money every single day, the shine quickly peeled off. It was just not enough. He needed something in addition to that automatic process of making money from the bit mining places where he was taking from old customers.

It was about 10 AM on Friday morning when his phone rang. The caller ID said *unavailable*, and he almost didn't answer. But he answered it spontaneously holding the phone to his ear. Calls like this he never spoke first. When the other person spoke then he would decide whether to talk or not. Silly but he didn't like it when people he didn't know called him.

The voice from the other phone said, "Roger? Are you there? Roger?"

Ok this was a call from Joanne, his old administrative assistant.

"Hi Joanne! How are you doing?" he asked.

"I'm doing great. Really good. I just had a very strange thing happen and I wanted to give you a heads up on it. I bumped into Rose Pilantez here in Málaga. She asked me about some information that Gary McKeown desperately wanted. It was a set of coordinates from something he wrote in a notebook. Rose said that Gary was going crazy looking for this information because he confessed to her that it would solve all his money problems. He had a hidden a stash of gold Bitcoins and rare jewels worth millions. She said the information he was looking for was a set of coordinates, or at least that's what Rose thinks. In addition to the coordinates there was also the word Cyprus. Do you recognize any of that?"

Roger thought for a second before replying. "This is the first I've heard of this. What were the coordinates she gave you? Do you think it's real or is it just odd ramblings of a broken man?"

"At first, I thought the same thing, but I did look up the coordinates. They were 33.3North and 33.3East. They point to a spot in the middle of the Mediterranean Sea. This spot ironically is about 33 miles south of the Republic of Cyprus. I'm going to get on a plane in about 4 hours to fly there. I'll let you know if I find anything. OK?", Joanne replied.

Roger quickly answered, "Hey, Joanne how long is your flight to Cyprus? Maybe I could meet you there. I know a friend that will let me take his yacht for a quick overnight in the Mediterranean Sea. We could go there in style and maybe make some money, or just have a laugh and relax. Let me call Brent and he will set things up. What do ya say? It will be a lot of fun."

He heard silence and then Joanne said, "Roger you are in New Zealand. That is a long, long flight. It's 10PM here and I touch down in Cyprus at 9:30 AM"

Roger seized the opportunity, "Joanne, that is the beauty of living down under. It's like traveling back in time. Even though it's afternoon here, If I go now, I can probably get there at about 11:00 AM. It will be like old times. What do ya say?"

"Yeah, I guess I never thought about that. It would be nice to go there in a nice comfortable yacht."

To seal the deal he said, "The lower class do Glamping, but the rich like us go Yamping! Right? I will let you know when I arrive."

Roger went on, "This could really be just something Gary was imagining he had. But I've known and worked with Gary for a long time and one thing I do know, is that he shows everything, and nothing is left secret. It's a weird goody-goody guy thing with him."

"Well, I agree with you about Gary always showing his cards. Do you think you can get to Cyprus by Saturday afternoon? If you can get there by Saturday afternoon, I'll wait for you. I'm staying in the Crown Plaza Hotel. The marina is a couple of miles away. It's called Limassol Marina. We can go out on Sunday to that location in the Sea for the "supposed" goldmine Gary left out there. Roger, just like it was before when we were in Boston, any money that is found must be shared equally, ok?" Joanne added.

"Joanne my sweetheart, of course it will be 50/50. Why would I do anything different, besides, it might be nice to have my partner in crime back again. You got to admit that it was a sweet deal we had back in Boston. We had a lot of fun too. To be honest, Joanne, I think Rose might be trying to hurt you. Gary told me a lot about how Rose couldn't stand being in the same building with you. A building? Really why not a City? If this is her trying to be mean, then we can meet and have some fun out on the sea like we had before. Sound good?" Roger seemed convinced.

"Ok, I will meet you at my hotel. Talk to ya later."

Roger hung up. he sat there for another minute thinking about how he was going to get to Cyprus so fast. His laptop was nearby. He punched in a search for how long to fly to Cyprus and was surprised that it was approximately 24 hours of flying, not to mention any time for transfer or flight layovers. The one thing that worked in his favor is that if he left today at 6:00 PM he would arrive in Cyprus at 7:00 AM tomorrow - a total of twenty-four hours of flying. He had a lot of work to do. He thought flying first class would be better but even though he loved first class, now time was the most important part of this. He wished the Concorde aircraft still flew.

The second it popped into his mind about the Concorde not flying anymore, he immediately remembered a conversation he had with one of the wealthy guests at a party Roger organized. Occasionally you would bump into someone at a party that you had seen at other parties. I wouldn't say he was a friend but a more of a familiar person that Roger had several conversations with. One conversation they had was about the time wasted when traveling to various places - where they needed to conduct business. Many deals and meetings required that they be there in person. He'd found a solution that he shared with him. A company in France was trying to resurrect the Air France Concorde line of aircraft. It wasn't official yet, but these new supersonic aircraft were flying almost 24 hours a day going all over the globe for testing purposes. This testing was just the final check before it became commercially available. They are safe and they also have a base in Auckland. He suggested that the next time he needs to fly somewhere quick to give them a call. "You might be able to catch a ride with them."

This idea intrigued Roger, so the guy wrote down his contact at this company saying, "Just ask if they are doing any supersonic flights. Don't tell anyone else but if you mention my name, they will help you out."

Roger went into the house and retrieved the information. After he talked to the company representative, he was dumbfounded by his good luck here. In fact, they were excited that they could go to someplace new. They were running out of new places to fly that they hadn't done before. There was a plane leaving Auckland, New Zealand in 3 hours at 1:30 PM and they would be glad to take him to Turkey. The plane could not land in Cyprus because the airport runway was not long enough. So, Turkey was his closest option. It would take the plane just 10 hours to get to Turkey. It would normally be 24 hours trip on a commercial plane. The cost was surprisingly cheap. It was about equal to a first-class ticket price.

Roger scrambled to pack a couple of things especially those items necessary for international travel. Thirty minutes later he walked into the Wellington Airport and took the next flight to Auckland. The flight was short, so one hour later he was in Auckland.

He went to the part of the airport that the girl told him to go to and saw a small logo of a company called "Zoom-Zoom."

The person behind the desk told him about the flight he was taking, "The co-pilot on today's flight is Zack Carmichael. In addition to Zach, there will be an additional eight other people onboard. These people will be conducting several tests to look at different things about the flight. Things like how cold the air was outside, what was the air pressure, or how long it took to reach 70,000 feet plus many more tests to collect data. There will be no other civilian passengers on board the aircraft. This is a very normal flight and there will be a lot of food for the crew and yourself. Many drinks like soda but no alcohol. If you have a dietary need, we might be able to help."

After he talked to the woman behind the desk, she said, "You can wait here or get a quick bite to eat. Zach will come out in about 45 mins when everything is ready, and he will bring you over to the plane."

Roger thanked her and said he was going to get a cup of coffee and maybe a quick snack.

He found a decent coffee bar and sat down on one of the chairs that were provided in this small space. While he was sitting there, he called his accountant and friend, Brent Fisher. He looked at his watch and thought it would be late in Boston. This was important so he called anyway. Brent's phone rang several times but just as Roger thought it would go to voice mail, Brent answered the call.

"Hi, Brent. Sorry that I'm calling so late, but I needed to talk to you." "Don't worry. So, what's going on? I'm not in Boston right now." Brent said in a sleepy voice.

"Oh, ok. Sorry if I woke you up. Where are you now?"

"I had to care of some business in Cape Town, South Africa," Brent lied. He hated giving people too much information. He didn't want to tell Roger that he was in Spain right now.

"I just talked to Joanne Druci. She called me right out of the blue and said that she bumped into Rose Pilantez. She was Gary McKeown's administrative assistant. Rose said that he might have millions of dollars in Bitcoin and rare gems that were put in a secret stash. Rose asked her if she knew about a piece of paper that had longitude and latitude coordinates - and the word Cyprus on it. Joanne looked up those coordinates and found that they were in the middle of the Mediterranean Sea, about 33 miles south of Cyprus. Joanne is going there to check it out. I convinced her to wait till I got there, but I wanted to run it by you."

"Well, Gary did have a reputation in technology circles, and he was being asked to speak at huge conferences. He also had a book that he published. I doubt that it was bringing in millions. He could have been setting aside money for a little rainy-day account. Hey Roger, didn't he go on some trip to Israel to work with their government and military to protect themselves from all kinds of electronic hacking or sabotage. He was over there for about a week, right? I remember this because we had to wait to sign some documents until he was out of the country."

"Your right. Cyprus is not far from Israel, I think."

After a slight pause, Roger continued, "I convinced Joanne to wait for me. I'm heading to Cyprus now. I told Joanne I could use one of my contacts to let me take out one of their yachts. I have done this before. It's been a while since you were skipper of a boat. It's supposed to be nice out there now this time of year. Do you want to go?"

The silence on the phone extended into an awkward silence. Brent said, "I was thinking of just going home. South Africa is almost halfway there. Sure, why not? I'll get the next flight out. Where are you staying?"

Roger gave Brent all the details that he was doing on the fly, literally. He was able to book 2 rooms at the Crowne Plaza Hotel near the Limassol Marina. He called the Marina and they said would be able to charter a medium sized yacht from the Marina for him. It was planned to leave tomorrow and stay overnight. Once he was done talking about the arrangements for this trip, he went back and got his coffee refilled and picked up a meat pie for himself. He continued waiting in the designated waiting area for Zoom-Zoom planes as he started to read the newspaper, he just picked up on his way back.

After about 10 minutes a person came over to him and asked him if he was Daniel Ortis.

Roger Tillson aka Daniel Ortis nodded. The guy introduced himself as Zack Carmichael. Zach brought him to the hangar area and in front of the hangar was the aircraft which had a set of stairs that went up to a door to enter the body of the plane. This plane was a super long, slim, swept back wings, a very sleek looking plane.

The first third of the plane was painted a beautiful Royal Blue starting at nose tip then fading into a solid white. The second third of the plane was solid white. This white then faded into a solid bright Fire-Engine Red for the remaining last third of the plane. Another striking feature was that on the tips of the wings, the winglets, were a solid Fire-Engine Red. On the body and on the vertical stabilizer was the plane number in white. The scheme of blue, white, and red represented the colors of France.

The color of the plane was stunning and whoever designed it was exceptional. If they were looking for a design that people would notice, or just stop and take it all in, then they had far exceeded that.

Once Roger got inside, Zach started to tell him about the flight. They would be flying at an altitude of 70,000 feet. The plane will get to that altitude slowly by doing a sort of "porpoising" up to that altitude. As the plane's fuel in the front of where the fuel is store is used that will make the weight of the rear of the plane heavier, which forces the plane to go higher. The reason that this plane flies at such a high altitude is to take advantage of the fact that there were very few other aircraft at this altitude and because less fuel is used flying at that altitude.

Zach continued to tell him all about the flight today," 'The speed was at Mach 3.5 which is approximately 2,500 mph. There are six people in the back of the aircraft here with you. They are performing different tests and have a lot of data to collect."

Zach said in a louder voice, "If they do not have something that is taking up their time up, they might be playing Solitaire like Jim."

Jim was the person sitting across the aisle with a computer in front of him. He said, "Don't worry about him, mate. We are very friendly here; we are just unfriendly to Zach. Solitaire helps to keep your mind strong; you prat."

Zach continued and told Roger about where he was going to be sitting. "Keep your seatbelt on as much as you can. We will not be putting "seatbelts lights" on so try to keep it on. Turbulence in this plane is unusual but it can happen. If we do encounter turbulence, it will be a lot worse than any turbulence you would have on a regular commercial airliner. The altitude helps a great deal on the turbulence, but it can happen."

He told Roger that he had only experienced it once and if he did not have his seatbelt on, he would have been seriously hurt. He continued, "The bathrooms are in the rear of the plane. If you want some soda or juice, you are welcome to take some. There are also sandwiches and various snacks in this cabinet. We should have enough food for all of us and more. So, help yourself. "

Roger followed attentively.

"The trash goes here. I don't know whether you are prone to air sickness or not, but I can give you some motion sickness pills. To be honest the first time I flew on this plane I got a tiny bit queasy. Motion sickness pills only really work if you take them before you get sick. If you take them after you feel sick, they won't help. If you want some before, we take off I can give you some now. If you do get sick the bags are here and can be used for that. It does happen sometimes though."

He began to feel a little sick already.

Jim said loud enough to hear, "Zack mate, we only get motion sick when you fly. Please don't fly today."

Roger told Zach that he would take the motion sickness pills before they took off. He also said that he's not prone to get motion sick; but agreed with him that it's good to take it just-in case.

Zach said, "The pilots come out of the cockpit at different times. Sometimes just to stretch their legs or go to the loo. If you are interested the pilots can bring you up front when their workload is minimal. They don't mind it and it helps pass the time. The trip is about 6 hours, and we are traveling approximately 11,000 miles and will land in Turkey at 10:00 AM today. It feels like going back in time."

Finally, Zach said they would be leaving in about 10 minutes, and he also asked Roger if I had any questions.

Roger didn't. He thanked Zach for the introduction about the plane and the do's and do not. He still had his coffee in his hand, so he took the 2 motion sickness pills Zach had given him. He decided that he would use the bathroom before the plane got going. After doing that Roger sat down and buckled his seatbelt and again pulled out the newspaper he had picked up.

In a few minutes, the plane started to roll towards the runway. One of the pilots put on an overhead speaker and announced that they were next to take off. Runway 23L.

The plane started to roll faster and faster. When it seemed that they were going as fast as they could it went even faster. Gracefully, it slowly started to the leave the runway. WOW! Roger was impressed but ironically, the person who would probably most enjoy that take-off was his previous business partner, Gary.

At 10:30 AM Roger was checking into the Four Seasons Hotel in Cyprus near the Limassol Marina.

Chapter 20 - Cyprus

"Put money in thy purse."

William Shakespeare's Othello (Iago, Act 1 Scene 3)

New York City, Westin Hotel Tuesday - four days earlier…

After Gary, had made the connection of where Joanne was, now he needed to figure out a way to bait Joanne. Joe was right. We need to make her think she was cheated out of money. Carol was right also. For Joanne, money was a great motivator. She loves to buy expensive things and is always looking for a way to get money with the least bit of effort on her part. Joanne would need to hear certain suggestions that would make her suspicious and more importantly give up Roger's location. That fund-raising event that Belinda talked about had to be Roger. He is also probably traveling under a new identity. Hopefully, Joanne will take the bait and contact Roger. It was a gamble to see whether Roger would show up or not. The premise of this is based on their greed. It was hard to imagine Roger or even Joanne wouldn't try to get this.

Carol answered Gary's question about speaking Spanish. She said to everyone a little sheepishly, "I can speak a little Spanish. I'm not exactly 100% fluent but I know enough to get by."

Gary asked, "Rose do you think Joanne would suspect something was fishy if we were to '*bump*' into her in Spain? You know her better than anyone."

"Are you saying 'we' as in everybody here, or are you saying me?", Rose insinuated.

Off to his side, he saw Joe smirking. To Gary, it seemed obvious that Joe had been on the receiving end of Rose's rhetorical affirmations before. None the less, he unabashed, responded, "Yes, but I thought you already knew that?"

Now Joe looked at him with a smile and silently told Gary that his response was brilliant.

Rose looked at everyone and let out a big dramatic sigh and said, "The bumping into her is a little bit of a stretch. Hey Joe, do you remember that cruise we talked about going on? One of the stops was in Málaga Marbella Spain, right? We were going to jump off the cruise boat and skip the Strait of Gibraltar part and spend a few days in Marbella. We would meet up with the cruise line in Lisbon, Portugal."

Joe jumped in at this point, "You know this might be the place. This place has a lot of casinos and from what I read about it's a hot spot for the rich and famous."

"Joe, you're right. This sounds exactly like the place she would go to. She loves to gamble, and I would bet she probably goes to the casino every night", Rose agreed with Joe.

"It looks like we have two scenarios possible here. The first is obvious, is she actually living there right now? I think she is, but we might be wrong. The second scenario here is that if we confirm that she is there, then the reward needs to be enough to make her contact Roger. We have to make sure that whatever it is, it will not raise an alarm for her.", Gary said.

The second he said this to the group, he thought about the day he moved into his apartment. That coffee table which held all the clues, and the money was what started this adventure. The items were enough to convince him to go to Boston to see Belinda. Hidden money or hidden advantage was the trick. Convince Joanne that I forgot where I left a lot of money. Maybe?

Everyone around the table, was looking at him to answer his own question. Rose wasn't about to wait for him.

"I got it. Joe your gonna be my wingman. I want you to introduce me to Joanne if we spot her on one of the tables. Gamble a little at a table that she is on, flatter her a little and flash her your devilish smile. That should lower her guard. At the right time, I will come over and surprise you. Two games that she likes to play are *Craps* and *Texas Hold-em*. I think that we could pass that off as an "accidental" bumping into her in Spain. What do you guys think?" interjected Rose.

Lucy who had been sitting there quietly said, "I'm sure that we could find a store that would sell some nice cheap, jewelry pieces. There is probably some little "rinky-dink" shops near the hotel that would sell things like that. I saw in the gift shop; they had some mesh bags of chocolates gold coins."

Gary looked at Lucy for a moment and caught a slight look on her face that he knew was trouble brewing. Rose announced that she was tired and wanted to take a nap for a little while. Everyone around the table nodded. Probably as good a place as any to break for a little while.

Great progress on this. Everyone agreed to meet back in the lobby around 7:00 and go out to dinner.

As everyone was walking over to the elevators, Lucy caught Gary before he went up to his room. She asked if he could talk to him for a little bit. He agreed and they found a spot in the bar area that was quiet. They sat down in a booth and ordered some coffee.

Lucy said, "Gary you know I want this as much as you do. My emotional side is saying loudly, Roger and Barry need to be brought to justice and held responsible for the physical abuse and attempted murder on both you and Joseph. Barry tried to murder you and it was Roger pulling the strings. He also was doing the same thing with Joseph. He nearly killed him in college and now again he nearly killed him in Boston. Roger is a dangerous person."

Continuing, "The ripples of Roger and Barry also affected other lives too. My life, your two nephew's, Belinda, and Michael's life were affected deeply by this whole mess. Also don't forget Freddie was affected by this, too. Poor little guy just wanted you back. When you were staying at my house, I would leave in the morning and Freddie would be right there at the foot of the bed, hoping every day that you would wake up. I would come home, and he would still be there."

There was a silence that developed and hung in the air between them. He could tell that this was not the end of what she wanted to say, so he listened intently.

"I am pretty certain that both Roger and Barry will be exposed for all their corruption and attempted murder. I am not saying forgive Roger or Barry, but I am saying that it doesn't necessarily mean **you** have to *bring them to justice*. Belinda said that Ben Costello has been tracking this a long time and maybe we should step back and let him take care of the "bringing to justice" part."

Lucy paused a second to take a sip of coffee and continued, "I can't tell you to go or not go. You are the only one that can answer that question."

"Lucy, in my mind I have been wrestling with something similar too. I'm alive, healthy, my mind, and the weird wiring of my memories are nearly the same as before I took that trip. I have you and the kids, Freddie, friends, and more money than I know what to do with, and a lot more to just be thankful for. I keep coming around to one question of Roger though. I need to know **"Why"**. Why did he try to murder me?"

Lucy said, "so what is keeping him from having a second try at killing you or Joseph? Your anger might be making you need to find Roger. I'm not saying that it is wrong at all to be angry with someone that tried to kill you. All I am saying is just make sure you are honest with yourself about what is driving you here."

"I am angry at Roger and probably a little angry at myself for being taken advantage of and being naïve. I know I'm playing with a stick of dynamite here. I can walk away right now go back to Boston and just start over. We both have a bunch of money, and we can both just do whatever we want to do. That is not a bad picture at all to have. The one thing that stops me from doing this is it would always be in the back of mind to know *"why"* Roger did this. Things were going well at the time. The company was good and on track for more success, I could jump into whatever technology I wanted to play with. Roger could be the Sale's guy and both of us would make some substantial money. That question will not leave me until I find out *why*."

Bit By Bit

Lucy smiled at Gary, reached across the table, and put her hand over his saying, "I understand that. I just wanted you to know exactly what is driving you so hard to catch Roger. That's all."

Later that night they all went out to a restaurant for some fabulous food. After they had finished their meals, the topic of Joanne came up again.

Rose started it off by asking, "What is the bait we are going use on Joanne if we do bump into her? We talked earlier that we could get some really cheap costume jewelry that could be passed off as real diamonds, rubies or emeralds."

Carol added, "I was with my sister and my niece a couple weeks ago. Well, my niece is young, and we were in some store, and she spied these plastic rings that have this huge hard candy to represent an enormous Emerald or Ruby. I think it was called a jewel pop. That would be fun to see Roger's reaction to this." Everyone laughed at this as the picture came in mind of Joanne or Roger getting these.

Gary looked at everyone and said, "We hear the buzzword of *Bitcoins* a lot today, but most people are basing their concept of cryptographic currency as a tangible item. Even though a lot of things, like checking accounts, allow you to pay your bills without writing a check or going into to bank. Bitcoins are entirely electronic. I would bet that Roger or Joanne would think that it is tangible and that they could steal something like cash or other items."

Joe jumped in and said, "Carol and I were in one of the super expensive candy stores at Rockefeller Center. On one of the shelves, they had small bags of chocolate gold coins. They were pieces of chocolate that were shaped like a gold coin and were wrapped with gold tinfoil paper. In my life I will admit that I have had my fair share of chocolate gold coins."

"That's brilliant" Gary said to Joe.

They continued to talk more about this. After about fifteen minutes, it became clear to him that everyone was taking a stake in each part of the plan. Joe was going to flirt with Joanne and then Rose would "bump" into Joanne while Joe was talking to her. Carol was going to help with the Spanish translations, and Alexi would keep digging into the code to see if he could find out where the flaw in the source code that was stealing money from our customers. Lucy, Joe, and Rose volunteered to go out tomorrow morning and find some costume jewelry that would look like it was super expensive. They were also going to pick up some of the chocolate gold coins. Joe was not allowed to go in the store that sold these.

Gary finally asked the question that seemed obvious. "I asked all of you to come down to New York literally at a moment's notice. Each of you came here and I am very grateful for this. The next part of this mystery is to fly to Spain. This is a lot to ask. I don't want anyone to feel they are obligated to go. Before you answer, just remember this is a long flight into a foreign country. Please, don't do this because you feel pushed into this."

Joe asked, "I think Lufthansa goes to Spain. I can get us some nice executive lounge passes with my airline miles. I'm pretty sure, I have enough airline miles to get Rosie and me some tickets to fly to Spain."

At this point Gary jumped in, "Joe, hold on a second. No one is paying one dime to fly over to Spain. You are all doing this for me. No discussion, this is final. This is going to be First Class all the way. Besides, Joe already said he is buying the first round of drinks for everyone in the executive lounge. The next item is a little trickier, we can't fly unless we have passports."

With the prospect of going to Spain, Rose and Joe talked a few minutes alone and they shook their head and smiled. Rose and Joe both had their passports with them. They were in the backpacks they brought with them to New York. They were still in there from the last time they traveled out of the U.S.

Alexi and Carol were at a good time and did not have any commitments for the next couple of weeks. Carol and Alexi have been thinking about taking a vacation soon. Alexi looked at Carol and said that they would need to go home to get their passports. They planned to go home early in the morning and can be back here around noon .

The plan was set.

Gary wanted to make a toast and said, "Lucy, Rose, Joe, Alexi, and Carol. I really appreciate your help with this. I will cover all costs no matter what it is. Ok, well I wouldn't go as far as buy you an Ostrich lined coat but pretty much it is whatever you want to do, I'll cover it. I think this trip could be a lot of fun. I have not been to Spain before, but I've always heard good things about Portugal and Southern Spain beaches. Thank you all so much." Everybody picked up their glasses and toasted each other.

Later that night Gary booked 5 tickets to Spain leaving tomorrow at 6:00 PM nonstop to Málaga arriving at 8:00 AM Wednesday morning. While he was at it, he booked three rooms at the Four Seasons Hotel and Resort in Marbella right on the beach.

It was late and he felt completely drained of energy. It was great seeing Rose and Alexi. It felt very familiar and grounding for him. He had not met Carol or Joe before, but he liked them instantly.

Wednesday…

The next morning, he got up at 6 AM. After getting dressed, he went downstairs to get some coffee and a light breakfast. Alexi and Carol were in the lobby doing the same thing. He went over to sit with them. He told them the flight was at 6:00 PM.

"Are you sure you want to make this trip? He asked. I'd love it for you both to be with us, but this is all of a sudden. If you want to maybe take a vacation in Spain at a later time, I still have some great airline tickets for you."

Carol spoke first, "Gary it's not that at all. We want to go with you. We just hope that we won't get in the way and not be able to help. We were hoping to hang out with you guys in Spain and try to help in any way we can."

Alexi nodded in agreement. He smiled to himself. Alexi has not changed. He is steadfast and his work ethic is so strong. Alexi is ready to dive into anything he can do to help.

Now it was Gary's turn to speak. He said, "First of all, you are both dead wrong. You're both going to be a big help in this next part of the scavenger hunt. We still need to find exactly where Joanne is. Carol, you mentioned last night that you could speak and read Spanish. Whatever your level of Spanish, it's a lot better than me."

Carol said, "My Spanish is only barely understandable, but you're right I do know enough to get around."

"Well, Carol that could help us tremendously. I was thinking about this yesterday, and I think that you, Joe, Lucy would be a great team to scour this part of Spain. Would that be, ok?"

Carol's eyes brightened and nodded.

Gary continued next with Alexi, "I started to think a little about this before I fell asleep. You know Roger has been doing the "*what-if*" scenario right in front of us for a long time. Our code did not protect us from this scenario. What if we adjust the code a little and see if this could be traced back to Roger and take away the money he was stealing and drain those accounts. This might be something as simple as changing a couple of formulas to a minus from a plus. So instead of stealing from the customer, it would do the opposite and take money out of the accounts Roger owned, and replace the amounts that were stolen from the other accounts. I started to think about it last night. I fell asleep when it got more complicated. What do you think?"

Alexi agreed, "I think you're right about protecting from this happening. When we designed this, we never thought about stealing Bitcoins. We probably wouldn't be good thieves. I think this is a good angle and we can map it out and see how we could do this."

Carol said, "I think that is great for you guys to rip into. I will definitely get out of your way

Then Carol thought of something, "In TV shows and movies when they are looking for someone, they always have someone that can look up where their credit cards are used or check calls that are made on cell phones so they can find out an approximate location of someone. Maybe she goes to some place or store frequently. We may get lucky."

Gary smiled at Carol. "That's a fantastic idea. I never would have thought of that. I think Belinda might have some contacts she knows who could do this. Carol, are you trying to be team captain on Day One?"

"Don't mess with mama bear, you might end up in the hospital." Alexi said before Carol could answer. Carol playfully hit Alexi's shoulder with a magazine she had been looking at before he came over.

Alexi looked at the time. They were taking the 7:20 train back home to pack and then drive to JFK. Carol hugged Gary to say goodbye. She gave him a hug and big red lipstick kiss on his cheek and said to him quietly in her ear that she was so grateful to him for firing Alexi that day. Gary and Alexi shook hands saying they would meet at JFK around 1PM or 2PM based on the traffic.

Gary decided to get a second coffee to take up to his room. He wanted to call Belinda and he wanted to talk to Lucy. With this second cup of coffee in hand he finally got into his hotel room, then, with a sigh of relief, sat down on the little couch by the window. This view would never be boring he said to himself.

Belinda answered her phone after two rings and said "Hello" in a quick way which sounded like she was busy. She asked him to hold on for a second. He heard a lot of background noise. Someone said very gruffly, "the usual?" He heard Belinda say, "you bet, thanks Minnie."

She picked the phone back up and said thanks for holding on.

Gary said, "You're at Morissi's aren't you?"

Again, he heard in the background Belinda saying, "thanks Tony. Yes, as a matter of fact, I am. What gave it away, Minnie?"

"Yes, it did. I was wondering if I could talk to you about a couple of things."

Belinda said, "Let me call you back when I get into the office, in about 15 minutes. ok?"

"Sure, whatever works best for you. I'm in my room so it's probably easiest to call my cell. Talk to ya in a few."

Fifteen minutes later Belinda called him on his cell phone. Her father was still recovering, but he was getting better day by day. He talked to her for about 30 minutes to catch her on the progress they were making. He also wanted to see if she had a contact that could look at someone's credit cards, or also any other nonpublic information about the villa, linked to Joanne that they got a hit on yesterday- the one that was in the Golden Mile, Marbella, Málaga, Spain. She told him that she would give her contact a call and let him know if she hears anything new.

It was about 8:30 AM and he was feeling a little hungry. He called Lucy's room to ask if she wanted to go for breakfast.

"Sure. Perfect Timing. I was just about to call you."

Twenty minutes later they were in the little breakfast dining room with a large breakfast buffet. As usual he came back to the table with enough food for two people.

When they sat down, Gary broke the ice and said, "How are you feeling about this trip to Spain. I wanted to ask you because I was thinking about how insane this was. I can intellectualize that this is something that I should just back away from thinking that it's the wrong decision. The problem is that I won't feel closure until I know *why* Roger did this."

Lucy replied, "Well I'm kind of glad you asked that. I tried to imagine how you would feel, and I know that if it were me, I would probably want the same thing."

She paused slightly, to make sure she said this is in the proper context, and said,

"Gary you're my brother and I care about you a lot. This is not the older sister saying this. We're always stronger together than apart. We have been through it all, right? We both have lots of great memories and some painful ones too. Gary, I never thought you would wake up from that coma. That was really tough on me. I kept hearing in the background Mom saying, 'God will provide'. You will be given only as much as you can handle, nothing more or nothing less."

He thought for a second and replied, "Lucy, I'm deeply sorry I pulled you into this. I understand that it's not easy to live each day with uncertainty of what is next. In a lot of ways, I feel that way too. Each day I feel that my life is being revealed one bit at a time. I wish that I could see the whole picture, but I can't."

He looked at Lucy and continued, "I am really blessed with some great things in my life. I could just drop this and go home and chock it up to a fun trip in New York City. The fear I have is that if everything out there goes back to normal, we will let Roger and Barry just disappear into the background. What will stop them from coming back at us again? Obviously, Barry didn't hesitate to try to kill Joseph a second time and he almost succeeded again. Roger and Barry came close to killing me. So now what? We hope that they're done and will leave us alone. They wouldn't try to hurt us again, right? My fear is that they will come back again. You've become a target, Patrick and Peter have become targets, Belinda, Joseph, and Michael all have become targets. It won't end and we will always need to keep looking over our shoulders. This needs to end now."

"You know I have to admit I really had not thought this all the way through. You're right, this does need to end now. It will be difficult to do this. There is no easy way out. Ok, what is the next step? Do we all go to Spain, now?" Lucy said.

"Well yes and no actually! I was thinking about this last night. and everyone is ready to go to Spain, but it might not work until I set a trap someplace else. Rose is going to Spain to try and push Joanne into giving up Roger, or Barry, or both, right? Something needs to be seductive enough to make her reach out to Roger or Barry. Something believable."

He took a sip of this coffee and continued, "I was flicking through the channels last night and saw some few commercials for a couple of shows that are on Broadway. Shows like Hamilton and Wicked are really popular right now. I don't know why but it made me think about one of Shakespeare's plays. In school we had to read many of his works but there was one that stuck out to me. It was Othello. The whole play revolves around revenge, jealousy, and murder. There's a lot of similarities that parallel Roger, Barry, and Joanne. It would take a lifetime to figure that one out. What I really thought about was the locations that were used in the play. It starts in Venice, but it eventually leads to

Cyprus. I think I need to go to Cyprus to plant the trap," Gary ended.

Lucy smiled at him, because she had no idea what he was talking about. He recognized that glazed look on her face that she did sometimes when he talked about computers or cryptography.

"Ok so if you're going to Cyprus, then where in Cyprus are you going to hide this. I don't know enough about Cyprus to even begin to offer any help on this. I think you have already thought this through, right?"

"Yes, I have. I don't want to bring anyone else into this. It needs to be a neutral place. Irony has a fickle way of showing itself. This started on the bottom of the Pacific Ocean, so I think it needs to end in a somewhat similar way. So where? Almost all boats on the ocean use GPS coordinates to navigated by. You can navigate without GPS but navigating with it is considered more precise. The boats that I have been on for scuba diving, use GPS to navigate to the various dive locations."

"Do you already have the coordinates picked out?", Lucy asked.

Gary was quick to reply and said, "Yes, I have. You may think this is crazy, but I happen to be very fond of the number three. There's no reason or any logic to why I like the number three. I looked on a map last night and approximately 33 miles south of the Island Republic of

Cyprus was a spot in the Mediterranean Sea and it is 33.3 North longitude by 33.3 East latitude. Crazy right?"

"So that is the trap?"

Gary concluded, "I thought about what Joe and Carol said earlier and the chocolate Bitcoins and the rare jewels. This would cost less than a $200. You saw that steel case I brought with me. I was thinking of putting that at that location in the sea, putting the case on the bottom and then marking it. What do you think?"

Lucy replied trying to take it all in, "I get it. Does anyone like Roger, Barry or Joanne know how to scuba dive?"

"Roger does, but that was a while ago. Barry does also. They both are very inexperienced. Diving lower than 30 feet they are liable to hurt themselves or drown. They could also hire someone to dive for it."

He smiled at Lucy but neither of them would ever admit their thoughts.

"When are you planning on doing this?"

Hesitantly, he said, "Today. I bought 5 first class tickets to Spain last night and booked three rooms in Spain. That flight to Spain is at about 6PM tonight. I asked Frank Douglas if he could file a flight plan to take me to the Republic of Cyprus. I suspect that it will be a couple of hours after the flight to Spain tonight. The time of takeoff depends on the FAA. I suspect we will be in a long line of planes going towards the Mediterranean."

While he was saying this to her, a storm was brewing behind her face. Gary has seen this before. BEWARE.

Finally, in a measured voice, Lucy announced to him, "You bought one too many tickets to Spain. I am going to Cyprus with you. Gary, you need to hear me on this. I'm not going to go through this again. I understand the reason you feel compelled to go to Cyprus. I know, I can't change your mind about this. You said it yourself yesterday. It's not just you that has to worry about their safety. Your nephews, Freddie, Joseph, Belinda, Michael, and me are all in a little bit of danger with Roger and Barry still at large. If this is going to end in Cyprus, then I will be there. Gary, I am more stubborn than you so the sooner you get over it, the better."

"Ok, well then I guess I need to call the airline and get you on the flight with me to Cyprus.," he winked at Lucy as he said this.

When they got up to pay for their coffee he said, "I'm way more stubborn than you. I just let you think you are more stubborn."

Chapter 21 - Curium Palace Hotel

"people change places, and

places change people."

- Unknown

Larnaka International Airport, Cyprus – 15 hours later.

Gary and Lucy exited out of the custom's area to a huge throng of people waiting for friends or relatives. After their long flight and going through customs they were met with complete chaos. So many sounds and so many smells can be overwhelming. Especially for someone like Gary with an eidetic memory. But now, he has been able to regain his control of the overwhelming rush of sights, sounds, smells, taste, and feelings.

Once they pressed through the throng of people anxiously looking for their loved ones, they found their own way through to the front curb to get a taxi outside the airport. Twenty minutes later they were both checked into the Curium Palace Hotel. When he made these reservations, he also looked for a shop where he could rent scuba gear. He was scheduled to go out with someone from that scuba shop around noontime. They agreed to go out to that precise longitude and latitude. It was now about 10:00 AM. Lucy said that she was going to take a dip in the gorgeous pool at the back of the hotel and then go up to her room and nap.

"Ok. I am gonna be out there for several hours, so I probably won't be back here until about 6 or 7 tonight. Why don't you go take a nap or swim or whatever and when I get back, we can go out and get some dinner together," Gary said.

"Sure, that sounds great. See you later"

Later that night, after an incredibly long day, Gary walked into the Curium Palace Hotel lobby. Before he went upstairs to his room, he went to the front desk to ask if they had an electric converter. The person at the front desk said that they would have someone from the hotel staff bring it up to him. The desk clerk told him she had a message for him as she handed him a small envelope. He thanked her and took the envelope up to his room. When he got there, he called downstairs to ask them to connect him to Lucy. The phone rang and rang. He hung up after no one picked up. Maybe the message he received was from Lucy. He opened the envelope to read the message.

What he read was just too unbelievable to comprehend. The message said in large, printed letters.

WE HAVE LUCY –
IF YOU WANT TO SEE HER UNHURT
BE AT THE COORDINATES
33.3 NORTH BY 33.3 EAST.
BE THERE AT NOON.
TELL NO ONE. COME ALONE

Gary called Belinda who was at the airport now with Ben. She said that she would call when she got to the hotel. Gary was sitting in the hotel lobby waiting for Belinda and Ben. He was a wreck. His nerves at this point were so tense, it wouldn't take much to make him snap. How many hotel lobbies has he been in the last week? Too many. It's been only a week, but he keeps waking up in different parts of the world. He missed Freddie. He knew that Bert was probably spoiling him rotten. Freddie has been through a lot with me in the hospital, then adjusting to Lucy's house and now with Bert. I'm glad that I can count on his being safe and well treated.

Ben and Belinda walked into the lobby. They spotted Gary and walked over to where he was sitting. When Ben said "Hi" to him, Gary stood up and gave his friend a big hug. "I would have rather dived with you than that shithead, Barry," he said.

Ben was relieved. He apologized for not being there for him.

Gary just smiled and said, "No worries, we're all good."

He gave Belinda a hug. In a panicked voice she asked, "What about Lucy? What does the message say about Lucy?"

He gave the message to Belinda and told her that he had just gotten back from putting the case down at that location. Then, he looked at Ben and Belinda and said, "I need some help on this. I'm almost positive that this is the work of Roger, Barry, and Joanne. Back in New York, Lucy, and I, just talked about getting Barry, Roger, or Joanne to be out of our lives. I am alive, physically, and mentally doing ok. This stuff was over four years ago. We could have just stopped and tried to go back to a normal life. I agreed with Lucy, but I said that I just needed to know why Roger started this. Why did Roger, through Barry, try to drown me?" Listening to himself relaying this information, objectively he noted that his voice was rising. His words were coming out of him as if they were daggers or darts being thrown at a board. Now is not the time for this.

Ben and Belinda had an empty expression on their faces. They cared about what Gary was saying, but they were not sure of what to say. Being there and just listening was enough.

Gary took a breath to just slow himself down a little and said, "I just wish I could press a button to rewind time back to the day in my office when I agreed to go scuba diving with Barry. I should have been suspicious that Roger could arrange all the travel, visas, and bookings in twenty minutes. Ben, we have done dozens of scuba dives together. Every time we went underwater, if there was anything not right, or if one of us was feeling sick, without any hesitation we would abort the dive. We never pushed it. Well, what is done is done. Sorry for venting a little here."

Ben looked at Belinda and smiled as he said, "Gary, I arrested Barry Parker last night for assault and battery of Joseph Daly. Also, he was charged with the murder of Milly Howard. His father was also arrested for money laundering and racketeering. This is not his first time so he will receive the death penalty. Barry will be in jail for the rest of his life. The death penalty might be taken off for his father, if Barry gives more information of Roger Tillson and Joanne Druci. Barry and his father will be celebrating Christmas and Birthday's in MCI-Walpole prison for the rest of their lives.

"Ok the first thing is to make up a plan for this. You said that you left the case on the bottom of the sea at specific coordinates.", Belinda said, changing the topic to rescue him from the downward spiraling frame of mind.

"Yes, I left it on the bottom with some chocolate coins that look like Bitcoins and a bunch of hard candy *Jewel Ring Pops and a bunch of fake looking rubies and emeralds*. I also put a bottle of emergency air in the case. I wasn't sure if Roger or Barry would dive for it. Unless they want me to do it and then what?"

"Gary, have you talked to Frank today? He left a message for me on my phone and said that you and Lucy were safe, and he had checked into this hotel with you."

"All three of us were really exhausted, so I assumed he went back to his room and crashed." Gary said.

Belinda suggested, "Let's get Frank in on this. I want to go up to the room and change. Let's meet down here in about 20 minutes. There's not that much privacy in the lobby, so how about we all meet at one of the tables in the bar area?"

Ben said that he would also like to go to his room for a minute. He wanted to check in with his boss.

Gary called Frank and asked him if he could come down to the lobby and meet Belinda and Ben. He said sure. When he came down from his room, he came over to the corner table in the hotel bar and saw Gary sitting at a little table. Soon, Belinda and Ben came down. After a long discussion everyone decided to meet here in the lobby at 8:00 AM.

Ben asked Gary if he could stay behind for a moment.

Ben said, "Gary, I'm really sorry about your sister and the fallout from Roger and Barry. I never told you what I did for work, I never really thought about it. I only heard about you from one of the books you published regarding network security. There was a big company in Boston that was hacked and stole a lot of customer financial information like Social Security numbers, credit cards info etc. I read the bio in the book, and it said you were an avid scuba diver. When I met you, it really was to go scuba diving. I've had some great times scuba diving with you. I just wanted to tell you that I wasn't doing that just for work, or a case. I really considered you a friend. I'm ashamed that I didn't look in on Lucy when you were sick. I just wanted to tell you that. I promise we will get Lucy back and finally put an end to this once and for all.

Chapter 22 - Mediterranean

The average depth of the Mediterranean Sea is 4900 ft, but the deepest point is 17280 ft. The name of this deepest point is Calypso deep, which is in the Ionian Sea, near Greece.

Frank and Gary are at an altitude of four thousand five hundred feet above the Mediterranean Sea, flying south from Cyprus. They are navigating to a GPS coordinate of Longitude 33.3° North by Latitude 33.3° East. The Mediterranean Sea has a long ancient history with the beginning of human civilization.

The Mediterranean Sea was formed through movements of the Earth's plates. When the ancient landmass of Pangaea broke apart about 250 million years ago, a huge ocean, the Tethys, evolved around its middle. This ocean extended to the north of today's Alps and to the east as far as the Ural Mountains. When Africa and Europe started moving towards each other this ocean became smaller. The Mediterranean Sea is what is left of this large ancient ocean.

Geologists think that the Mediterranean dried up several times in the last few million years because the Strait of Gibraltar closed and reopened, allowing water from the Atlantic to flow in.

Looking out across the vast sea in front of them, it was hard to not feel the prehistoric history and the raw starkness of the Mediterranean Sea. The blue water was a special hue that was in between the typical Atlantic Ocean blue and the Caribbean Sea blue. One color that is used to describe the Mediterranean Sea is Aegean Blue. However, this is not quite accurate.

The Mediterranean Sea is made up of many different seas, the Aegean Sea being one that lies between Greece and modern-day Turkey. The Sardinia Sea has France and Spain on its shores. The Tyrrhenian Sea favors the western parts of Italy. On the eastern side of Italy, the Ionian Sea has rule. The Aegean Sea covers much of the northern countries of the far eastern portion of the Mediterranean Sea which covers Turkey and Greece. Finally, the island country of Cyprus is truly surrounded by just the Mediterranean Sea.

In the horizon, a large boat is resting at anchor. As they got closer to the location of the boat, Gary's anxiety increased. Anxiety is like a snowball that you roll down a hill. The more it rolls down the hill, the larger and larger it gets.

This is his second time visiting this specific location in the last 24 hours. He is just wearing a 3 mm shorty wet suit which is a one-piece garment of 3 mm neoprene. It was short sleeved and short legged specifically for warmer waters.

Watching the boat ahead getting larger was a realization of the final part of this opera. He stayed silent. All of his attention right now was on the boat. It was important that he marshal his mind to focus. Keep fear at bay. He thought stay anchored and look only at what is in front of you right now. The end of the day is not here but the "now" is in front of you.

Frank started to set up the sea plane for his final approach. He needed to calculate the direction of the wind and the direction of the waves on the water. A landing like this is never just a walk in the park. Pilots might want you to think that, but it requires an extreme amount of concentration. There are adjustments that must be factored in. This is also not an XBOX Flight Simulator game where if you crash you say, "Oh well let me try that again." Frank slowly descends and lands gently on the Mediterranean Sea, about a hundred yards from the boat.

Gary opened his door and he jumped into the water. That familiar calmness, and tranquility seeped into his body. Listening to his breathing and making each breath less forced and easy. He was wearing a yellow life preserver. As he came up to the surface of the water, he looked behind him at the Otter Seaplane that Frank was flying. He waved to Frank and watched him turn the plane 180 degrees and taxi back to the spot where he landed. When Frank had turned the plane 180 degrees, the passenger door was out of sight. Ben came up from

403

the back seat of the plane with his full scuba gear on and silently got into the sea without being seen. Frank continued to taxi down to the spot where they had landed and turned the plane another 180 degrees to take off into the wind.

As Frank raced in the direction of where Gary was, he could see the floats of the landing gear magically lift off from the surface of the ocean. Without the friction and drag of the ocean on the plane it could accelerate and start to gain altitude.

On his left was a small private yacht. Gary swam towards the boat. In these waters 100 yards is not really that difficult provided there's no current. Thankfully today there was no current.

He swam to the rear of the boat. There was a metal ladder used to get up onto the ship. As he climbed the stairs it brought him to a small platform where divers took off their scuba gear and a shower head so that they could clean the salt of the ocean away. A second set of stairs brought him to the main boat area covered with a blue sun awning.

The main deck area was not overly large but was comfortable, not cramped. At the opposite end of the main deck area was another set of stairs that led to the areas below decks. In the middle of the main deck area was a small table that could be unfolded to a larger table area for dining. It was usually folded into a small table to hold a couple of drinks, or anything that would spill. There were four recessed drink holders for drinks, or appetizers. On the left and right of the main deck area were two long couches which were built into the boat. Each couch was similar with long seat cushions and many comfortable back pillows.

Suddenly, Gary took in a deep breath. Caught by surprise.

There were two people on the couches. On the couch on his right, he immediately saw Lucy. He also saw that her mouth was covered so she could not speak. Her hands and legs were tied together with tight nylon ropes. From the look of Lucy's ankles, he could tell that her skin was getting red abrasions from the friction of the tight ropes. Her eyes were full of sadness.

He winked at his sister and gave her a small curt nod. She understood Gary's body language and she felt a little better. Probably, Lucy and Freddie were the only ones that could decipher his body language knowing what he felt.

Now was not the time for analysis. He needed all of this focus on the other person on the couch on the left side of the boat, Roger Tillson.

"Gary, it's so nice to see you again." The sarcasm dripping off of that statement was palpable.

"Roger, I wish I could say the same thing about you.", he kept repeating over and over in his mind that he needed to focus.

"Well, I guess you are right. I suppose I have been quite a bother to you. The whole coma thing and all. The funny part is that if you were dead, I would never have known where this cache of Bitcoins and rare stones that you hid are located."

Roger looked at Lucy, and said, "*Suzie* don't you think this is funny? Come on *Suzie*, surely you must find this funny?"

Lucy turned her head to look at Gary. Confused. She wondered, '*who is Suzie?*'

Roger continued, "Ok, Gary we are at exactly the coordinates that Rose told Joanne. Latitude 33.3 North by longitude 33.3 East. This is what the GPS is telling us. So, I guess that since we are in the middle of nowhere, the gold Bitcoins and the jewels are down below on the bottom of the sea. I anticipated that and I brought you some scuba gear. Actually, this scuba gear I have here is your old scuba gear. The diving boat you were on in Australia sent it back to me. I hope you haven't put on any extra pounds since you last wore it."

Anyone who scuba dives, knows that a dive computer is very helpful to have on a dive. Scuba diving is a combination of times and depths. Typically, before you dive you should use the diving tables to manually compute the times and depths of your planned dive. It's important to do this manually so that you don't rely solely on just the computer in order to have a safe dive. It's very helpful to have a computer that will give you times at different depths. Otherwise, you must write it down on something that is waterproof or commit the information to memory. About 99.9% of people opt for the dive computer.

Roger was correct that it was his scuba diving suit. Surprisingly, Roger had overlooked one important feature of his scuba suit. One of the four hoses of the regulator was a hose that connected to the brick sized computer that displayed depth, how long to stay at a depth, or the total time of the dive and displayed it on a small LCD. On the back of the computer case, it also had a holder for a diving knife. Dive knives become important if you ever get stuck or tangled in huge kelp forests or nylon fishing nets. It can also be used to provide a bit of protection. Large predatory fish such as a shark or a manta ray - this knife wouldn't be able to kill a big fish like that, but it might surprise them and give you an opportunity to escape. His diving knife looked like it was still in the knife sheath on the back of the computer case.

"Roger, I mean Paul Schneider, or is it, Daniel Ortis? I don't know what name you are going under now.", Gary said sarcastically.

"Roger is fine. So, what I want you to do is to go to the bottom and get me all those wonderful gold coins. I think I will melt it all down and make a beautiful gold watch or some nice gold jewelry. What do you think, Suzie? Should I make a gold ring for you?"

This was getting weirder and weirder. Gary had an idea, "Roger, you're right? There are a lot of gold Bitcoins on the bottom, but it will take me hours to retrieve them all. Each gold bitcoin weighs about 5 pounds. If I grab 10 of those Bitcoins, that is 50 lbs. plus the 20 lbs. of lead I need to just get to the bottom. That is about 70 lbs. and I about the maximum I can handle. Do you have an extra tank? I won't be able to do this on one tank."

Roger was really trying hard to figure this out. He thought that he had thought of everything. While Roger was thinking about this Gary picked up the hose that the computer was attached to. Roger glanced at him quickly. Gary said he just wanted to make sure it was working ok. Roger didn't notice that Gary took the knife from the little sheath on the back of the computer. He sat down next to Lucy. When he sat down, he turned to Lucy and gave her a hug, and said he was glad that she was ok. What Roger did not see, because Lucy had to face him, was her right side that was blocked from sight. Gary had the knife in his hands and put his left hand down to slide the dive knife under Lucy's right leg. Lucy understood.

What was baffling to him is that Roger really thinks and believes that on the bottom of the sea were 100's of "solid" gold Bitcoins. What was really on the bottom was about 200 pieces of chocolate that are in the shape of a coin with a gold wrapper. There was also a bag of lollipop ring pops with ruby or emerald shaped candy on top.

He could see the rage building in Roger. This was going to blow up and soon. One thing that he learned was that the person, Suzie, had either made him a fool, or tricked him. It was a guess, but he figured maybe he could use this building rage.

"Roger, do you have some kind of container? I might be able to tie a rope to the container and haul them up that way? Hey, what about that cooler over there? I'm sure we could pull up maybe half of them, in one dive."

"Gary, I'm losing my patience here. Put the gear on now and get me those coins. I'm going to add a little incentive here."

Roger told Lucy to stand up. Then, he put a 10-pound lead weight belt around her waist making sure that the clip to release the belt was in the middle of her back. He gave her a face mask and untied her legs.

Roger turned to Gary and said, "Suzie is going for a swim. Her feet are untied so if she can kick hard enough, she may be able to float for a while. So, the quicker you go down and come up, the quicker it will be for her to stop treading water."

Gary had his gear on now and was heading to the back of the boat to go into the water. When he got to the bottom of the stairs, he stepped onto the flat platform that sits just above the water. He turned around to face the stairs and was about to jump off when he saw Roger pushing Lucy overboard.

Gary was shocked and terrorized by this.

Roger turned to him, and he said, "Better hurry! I don't know how long she can hold her breath."

Gary wanted to say something, but he stopped himself and jumped in the water. Lucy was kicking her legs in vain. That weight belt keeps pulling her down. She's in trouble. She wasn't able to clear her sinuses. Gary caught up with her descent and took hold of Lucy's arm. He ripped off the tape over her mouth and put on the mouthpiece of his emergency secondary air supply. She resisted at first but realized it was her brother helping her. She couldn't really see much, since being pushed off the boat caused her face mask to fill with sea water. Everything was blurred. He reached around Lucy's back, unclipped the weight belt, and watched it fall to the bottom of the Mediterranean.

Gary kicked his legs as hard as he could while he inflated his Buoyancy Control Device or BCD. An internal air bladder filled with air from his air tank helped to pull them both up toward the surface. He headed to the keel of the boat. As he got closer, he saw Ben holding onto a makeshift pole that was fastened to the boat using suction cups.

Ben swam over to Gary and Lucy and helped to bring them both to the little bar to help keep them stable. He reached over to Lucy to put the mask the correct way on her face. Ben took his secondary regulator and tilted Lucy's head down a little and pressed a button on the mouthpiece that expelled air. Ben pulled the bottom part of the mask away from her face. The water in the mask was forced to be replaced with air. With the mask on correctly, Lucy could see Gary and Ben clearly now. Lucy was surprised but very relieved. Using his knife, Gary cut the rope that bound her hands.

Ben pulled a small Emergency Spare Air tank from his waist and gave this to Lucy. Lucy gave back Gary's secondary breathing mouthpiece. Lucy was relaxing to control her breathing. Ben pulled out a writing tablet to communicate with Gary and Lucy. Ben wrote down, "Gary to the bottom. You Stay with me"

Lucy nodded her head and understood.

Gary gave Ben an OK hand signal and then gave him a thumbs down signal. Gary pushed the button on his vest to release the air in the bladder he put there earlier. He was making a rapid descent, so he had to keep clearing his sinuses at about every 10 feet. At one point, he wasn't able to clear his sinus passages using the normal Valsalva technique. This was expected at the rate of descent that he was going. He remembered, another way to clear his sinuses was to bite down and move his jaw around almost like he was swallowing or chewing gum. This helped. He was at 65 feet and needed to go down another 40 feet. He pushed the button to put a little air in his BCD vest. This helped to slow his descent and let his body adjust slowly.

Gary spotted the blue case that he had put here last night. It was sitting on the bottom about ten feet from him. He picked up the blue case. He had not locked it, but he put a decent size rock on top. If someone came by and found it, they would take the contents that were inside. It was only $200 so it was not something he needed to stress over.

Inside was a loaded pistol wrapped in a ziplock bag, a small emergency bottle of O2 and two boxes. One box had a big plastic bag that contained a couple dozen of the candy ring pops and some very good fake jewels. The jewels looked like a collection of diamonds, rubies, sapphires, and bright green emeralds.

There was also a bag of chocolate coins covered with a gold colored wrapper in the other box. There was a little surprise if someone opened either bag. He took the pistol and tucked it into his vest. With case in hand, he headed slowly to the surface by adding or releasing air from his BCD to swim up to the surface. He swam over to Lucy and Ben. It looked like Ben was making motions to control her breathing. Lucy is not a scuba diver, being underwater in scuba gear can be a little frightening if you have never done it.

It didn't make any sense to stay down in the water. Gary handed the pistol to Ben. He also gave Ben the second O2 Emergency Spare Air bottle he brought from the bottom. Ben clipped this to his side. He gave Lucy his secondary air regulator. She took the one that Ben gave her and took Gary's secondary air. Gary took the tablet and wrote, "Gary + Lucy go up – Ben wait 5 mins. Then up."

Gary looked at Lucy and she nodded that she understood. Gary looked at Ben and he gave the OK signal. He and Lucy swam over to the ladder hanging a few feet from where they were with Ben.

He wasn't sure what he was walking into, but this seemed to be one way to end all of this. To finally close this chapter. If Joseph and Michael had not helped him over the many years of their friendship, he couldn't even imagine where he would be. Being able to completely trust another person is a rare find in this world today. The one thing that keeps nibbling in the back of his head was still the same question he has yet to find an answer to, Why?

Gary and Lucy walked up the steps onto the main deck for the second time. The surprises just never seem to end here. Now Roger had company with him. Sitting on the built-in couch was Joanne Druci.

Joanne chimed in, "Fantastic! We're all together again, just like old times. If feels like a high school reunion. Everyone hating each other but this is much more boring. At least at a reunion party, I could concoct stories about who slept with who, or just make some shit up. Watching how catty those girls were and pretending to be a pillar of virtue. It was so phony." Joanne started to laugh in her signature cackling laugh.

"Hey, look 'Gar-Gar' has a present for us. Can we open it up, pretty please?" Joanne said in a voice about 2 octaves above her normal gravelly voice. The sound of her gravel voice reminded Gary of Fred Glynne as Herman Munster of the Munster's TV show from the sixties.

He was not surprised to see Joanne here. His hope had been that she would relay the message to Roger. Her attendance today was a nice little bonus of sorts. In all the years of working with Roger, he knew that money was a drug for him and her. It makes sense. Roger and Joanne were driven by material and money. That was their master.

Lucy is behind Gary, and she senses that Ben is coming out of the water. Her left hand was not visible from where she was standing. Very nonchalantly, Lucy casually put her hand behind her side and motioned for

Ben to hold and not to come up the stairs yet. Ben stopped and crouched down on the flat platform, quietly waiting.

Gary put the blue case on the center table and put his eye close up to the mini eye scanner. This scan completes and one of the two little green lights come on to indicate the scan was positive. There was one additional thing that needed to be done. The last security measure is for Gary to put his thumbprint on the fingerprint scanner. He takes a step back from the case. Both Roger and Joanne, are on the edge of their seats. Anxiously waiting for this case to be opened. Maybe they were expecting fireworks or money just falling out of the sky.

Joanne just glared at Gary. Absent-mindedly he thought of how many times Joanne looked at him with just absolute, complete hatred. Hopefully, today he can get some closure on "why?" Roger and Joanne tried to murder him and Joseph. None of it makes sense.

"Roger before I unlock the case, can you tell me why you wanted Barry to drown me in Australia? My friends and family all thought I would never recover from that coma. I've been struggling every single day to get back to the level of who I was before that day in Australia. We both made a lot of money together. Surely, you would have enough money to retire several times over."

Gary didn't wait for an answer; a random thought jumped in his head and took over his voice. Joanne is not as clever as she thinks she is. "Joanne, I was expecting you to show up sometime. It's nice to see you once again, groveling at Roger's feet for any little scrap of money he throws to you. Joanne, are you sure you made a good deal with Roger? When we searched for you, we found you were living in a very chic location. The Golden Mile in Málaga, Spain. That is where all the rich and famous go, right? Joanne, you paid $3 million for that villa. I would have expected that Roger would have given you a 50/50 cut in the selling price of the company. I hope he told you the truth. Roger walked away with over a 100 million. I don't think you got a good deal."

As he said this, he walked over to the case and did the final fingerprint ID to open the case.

Now, both Gary and Joanne glared at Roger. Before Roger could get to the case Joanne had it in her hands. She opened it up to see the two boxes. Roger quickly grabbed one and Joanne was unable to get it, but she had the other box. It was at this time that Ben made his entrance.

That stopped both of them. They went completely still, cradling their respective boxes. As expected, Joanne looked at Ben and said, "Who the hell are you? This is starting to turn into a shit show."

Ben looked at Roger, "Surely, you remember me? You canceled the trip I had scheduled with Gary to go scuba diving. You even downgraded the seat from first to coach saving $3,500 by doing that you put Barry in coach class and used that money to secure a birth on the scuba boat in Australia. I think Barry was very uncomfortable on the 17-hour flight."

"Big deal. You caught me." Roger conceded.

While Ben was telling Roger how he manipulated the trip to Australia, Joanne started talking about how much she was supposed to get from Roger. Everyone except Lucy was all talking at once.

Gary yelled as loud as he could, "**STOP**!!"

Well, that stopped everyone, and all eyes were on him.

"Enough is enough. No one says another word until I hear from Roger why he tried to murder me."

Roger, having the temperament of a four-year-old said, "I didn't do anything! You are lying! What are you talking about?"

He was done dealing with Roger and his games, "Roger that's bullshit. I made you very wealthy. Can you tell me what I did to you? I let you do just about anything you wanted, and I never said no or asked you for a thing. Please, tell me why?"

Unfortunately for Gary, "please" is about the worst thing you could say to Roger. It gives him an advantage. "Gary, ok so you want to know why? It sounds corny, but I did it because I could. Plain and simple I really got a charge out of stealing from you without getting caught. I came close a couple of times. It was so easy to steal from you and what is even better, stealing from the customers we sold this software to. I had one of the young developers put in a backdoor so that we could break into their internal network and map and catalog every computer or server in the company. This girl that I asked to do this, was very discreet and buried it in a part of the code no one would look at too much. It worked beautifully every time."

Gary said, "Kimberly?"

"Give that man a prize! Yes Gary, she put the backdoor into the product. I could go into any of those customer's internal networks. It would catalog every computer in their network. When it came across some of the accounting servers, it skimmed a little money off their accounts payable ledger. The last product was the most fun though. A cryptographic currency just in the name alone, says 'we can't be hacked'. The reality is that I didn't have to hack them. All I had to do was change their math a little. Kimberly was clever. Somehow, she set it up so when they mined for Bitcoins, they got one piece of a Bitcoin, I took two.

"Roger you still aren't answering me. Why?"

"You came very close to messing up all my plans after I was just about ready to do the disappearing act. Then you started sniffing around those accounts. So, I called "my friend" to help me get the airline tickets and a spot on the boat. I don't think you have actually been introduced before."

Roger got up and yelled down to the galley and sleeping area for this mysterious person to come up top.

He looked at Ben and silently told him to be alert. Ben nodded.

It seemed like this day of surprises would never end. As the person was walking up the 5 or 6 steps up to the main deck, everything just slowed down as Gary tried to believe what he was seeing. Off in the distance he heard Roger identifying the person as Brent Fisher. Gary's mouth dropped to the floor.

The person coming up from below was Michael Daly!!

Ben said, "Who the hell is Brent Fisher?"

Chapter 23 - Irukandji

Life is a beautiful, magnificent

thing, even to a jellyfish.

- Charlie Chaplin

Gary was too incredulous to speak.

Ben was the first to speak. "Brent, is that the name you are going by now? Ok, now it all starts to make sense."

Gary looked at Ben with total confusion.

Ben motioned to Gary and Lucy to take a seat on the empty couch across from Roger and Joanne.

"Let me bring everyone up to speed. Roger, your fix-it man, Barry Parker, was arrested yesterday or was it the day before. Not sure," Ben said mysteriously.

Then Ben spoke directly to Roger, "Roger, did you know who Barry's father was?"

He went on, "Barry's father was Henry Parker, or Hank. His father is a big-time bookie in Boston and Rhode Island and had a lot of guys that would collect debts owed to him. They would severely beat anyone to an inch of death if they didn't pay. It also helped Hank to reinforce his reputation of getting money owed to him. His son was Barry Parker."

Roger was stone faced. Not one bit of surprise or concern.

Gary had a question. "Who gave the order for Barry to tie Joseph to that lamp pole when we were in college. Joseph lost his leg. I know that Barry did this but who ordered that?"

Ben smiled a little at that question. "Gary, you have your question a little backwards. It wasn't *who* ordered that, but the question is *why* it was ordered. Maybe our friend here can tell us. Michael?"

Michael had not spoken at all since he came up from below. Gary also didn't say anything.

Roger looked at Ben, and said, "Buddy, I don't know who this fool Michael is. This is Brent Fisher. He's been a friend of mine for the last 25 years. I think you got your facts wrong."

Gary jumped in at this point, "Michael, you've been working with Roger all these years? You were with me that morning at the hospital when Joseph lost his leg. Now he's lost his second leg because of you. I highly doubt that Barry would do this on his own."

Gary was now nearly yelling out his anger, "Why did you have Barry beat the crap out of Joseph all those years ago? Why did Barry try to murder me!"

Michael remained silent. Ben took an opportunity to add more to the discussion.

"OK, let's start at the beginning."

Ben started to tell everyone the full story. Roger and Barry met in college. They both cheated on a paper they needed to write. Barry got caught. Unfortunately, he wasn't the sharpest knife in the drawer, so he dropped out. Now, Michael loved to gamble on sports and horses. He started to accumulate a hefty debt to Hank Parker when luck was not in his favor. Hank ordered his son, Barry, to beat the crap out of Michael. This is where it gets weird. Barry thought that the person he was beating up was Michael Daly, but it was Joseph. Michael and Joseph are very similar looking. Since Hank was willing to hurt his family, ultimately Michael somehow was able to gather the 20K that he owed Hank.

As expected, Michael stopped gambling for the most part, but he did keep gambling at a much lower level. Again, he started to get behind and make huge risky bets. Word started to get around Boston. Michael changed bookies thinking that it would be better. It wasn't. His new bookie, 'Papa Joey', didn't beat people up for late payments, he killed them. Hank decided to buy the debt from 'Papa Joey'. Hank only did this because he owed 'Papa Joey' a favor.

Once he bought the debt, Michael eventually paid the debt to Hank. The gambling was a vicious cycle for Michael. As soon as he got his debt paid off, he would start making bets again and then the cycle would just start over again.

About five years later, Roger needed to hire a tax attorney. Roger had so many different grifting schemes going on at the same time, the IRS started to demand a lot more documentation of his money coming in and coming out. That is when Roger and Michael met. Trinity Trust Holding was just starting to show profits. Primarily, it was generated by the patents that were fought in court and also a moderate residual from the 3 books that Gary wrote. Both Michael and Joseph dove straight into contract law and started to build up a client base from all over the world.

Michael presented himself as Brent Fisher when he met Roger. He knew Roger was friends with Barry, so he gave a fake persona. On a couple of occasions, Michael and Barry were at the same function. When he met him face to face, he was meeting Brent Fisher.

A couple of years after Roger and Gary's company was established, Roger hired and became friends with Michael aka Brent Fisher.

Ben turned and looked at Roger and said, "Roger, did you know that Michael was siphoning about 50% of the money that you were making in your various schemes of laundering money, and also stealing from many of your customers?"

"Bullshit!!" Roger snorted. "I have checked each and every account that was created. I also paid Brent handsomely, at about 20%."

"Ok, well we can agree to disagree, but let me ask you one more question, Ok?" Ben continued.

Roger just looked at Ben with utter disgust. He looked like the petulant 5-year-old that wasn't interested in any of Ben's questions.

"Roger, didn't it look at a little funny that each bank account was exactly the same number? If you logged in on a computer, the web pages are almost identical. If you ever needed to talk to someone at the bank that held your account, you spoke to the same person, Michael's wife. You didn't have anywhere near the money you thought you had. All of the webpages of the different banks were coming from a server in Michael's basement."

Roger's face started to turn red. He spun around to face Michael, and venomously said, "Brent or Michael, is this true?"

Michael said, "Roger, come on. I wouldn't do that. You have been very generous with me. We have worked together for a long time. Why would I need to create different IDs for you?"

Observing this interaction Ben smiled, "Roger who convinced you and finally pushed you into selling the company? Who convinced you that you needed to leave the country and obtain citizenship in Canada? You see, Gary was starting to snoop into accounts that would incriminate you and eventually come back to bite you in the ass. Isn't that right Michael?"

Ben took a deep breath and continued, "Ok, Michael doesn't want to answer this question, but I think I have it figured out. Trinity Trust Holding would have been the jackpot Michael wanted. Except there was one part of this he forgot about. The *contingency plan* that he, Gary, and Joseph signed. Michael tried several times to withdraw money from the account that was holding Gary's money. He was a primary signatory now, and he mistakenly thought he could just make a huge withdrawal. The bank refused to give him any money from that account, unless Joseph also signed the document to withdraw money. Is that about right, Michael?"

Everyone on the boat, except Ben and Michael, was dumbstruck. Total silence.

Ben continued, "Gary, if we come back to your original question of the '*who*' and the '*why*' Barry tried to kill you in Australia. The answer of the '*who*', was Michael. Michael aka Brent convinced Roger that you, *Gary*, needed to disappear or the whole plan would fail. Roger, paid Barry some money to go to Australia and drown you. The '*why*' of your question is again Michael. You were in the way of many, many millions of dollars. Michael was going to get that money using anything he could to get it. He misled and misdirected his brother on the search for Roger. Barry went overboard when he attacked Joseph, he almost killed him."

Everyone was looking at Michael at this point. Michael just let out a long sigh.

Joanne became restless with all this talk, "Yeah, yeah. You are boring the crap out of me. I don't care, I want to see what is inside these boxes", Joanne whined.

Gary was about to say something and then changed his mind.

Both Joanne and Roger, opened their boxes and reached in to get their treasure. Roger grabbed two fistfuls of gold coins. He smiled ear to ear. Joanne also grabbed a fistful of ring pops and some of the other fake jewelry. She smiled but it looked phony like someone trying to do a 'selfie' might look.

At this moment, Michael walked over to where Joanne and Roger were sitting. He put each hand into both boxes and grabbed as much of the golden coins and the costume jewelry and jewels as possible.

"Hey, Gary, why do these things feel so slimy?", Joanne said.

Michael said, "What is this bullshit, Gary? This is fake shit. I know you have a stash of gold coins, somewhere."

Not 100% sure that all of the coins and the jewelry were indeed fake, Roger put all of it in his pockets. From somewhere behind him, Michael brought out a silver gun. When Ben saw that, he also brought out his gun. It seemed like it was going to be a standoff. Michael shot the gun straight up in the air. He wanted Ben to know that he was deadly serious about Gary giving him a stash of money.

When Michael shot the gun, Joanne and Roger were so startled that they lost their grip of the boxes. All the slimy water that was in the boxes fell forward and fell directly into all their laps and stomachs. It was warm today, so Joanne, Roger, and Michael all wore light shorts and unbuttoned shirts. There was a lot of exposed skin.

The faces of Michael, Roger, and Joanne, almost at the same time, became bright red. Like a very bad sunburn. Michael started to sway back and forth, but not because of the boat. Michael came over to the couch where Roger and Joanne were sitting. None of them looked good. They were starting to feel intense pain. Michael dropped the gun on the floor as all three of them were writhing in pain.

It was difficult to talk but Roger asked, "What did you do, Gary?"

Gary said, "Hey, you guys don't look so good. You guys are burning up. Maybe, a glass of cool water will help". They all nodded yes.

He went down the steps to the little kitchen, got some glasses and filled them up with cold water and a couple of ice cubes. Gary was still wearing his "*shorty*" wetsuit. On the inside of the wetsuit, it was common to

428

have a little pocket to put a car key or a credit card in - so if you surface in a different place than where you submerged it would have your car key or whatever. Gary retrieved the small bottle he put in there earlier before he dove in to help Lucy. Inside it contained powder of several heavy-duty pharmaceutical pills for sleeping. It would only make them more pliable under the circumstances. He put equal amounts of powder in the cold water and stirred it up.

When Gary, came up from the kitchen, he handed each of them a tall glass of water. Ben had retrieved Michael's gun and sat with Lucy on the opposite couch.

Joanne almost screamed her question at Gary and said, "Gary, what the hell did you do?"

At first Gary didn't say anything. He just looked out to the horizonless sky. When he turned back, he noticed that all three glasses were empty.

Gary looked at the three of them and said, "One of the most consistent rules, under the water, is that the more beautiful something is then the more deadly"

Roger interjected, "Gary what is this?

Gary was almost enjoying this. He said, "Yeah, ok I did do something but before I help you, I need to know why Barry beat the shit out of Joseph, this last time?"

Michael said, "Barry hurt Joseph because my brother was digging into accounts that you were looking at before you left. Over the last several years, Joseph was starting to piece things together. That little notebook he gave to you was a detailed listing of all the accounts that were being used to take money from customers and showed where those accounts shifted the money. There is one last document that he did not include that is the key for all these accounts. Barry started to follow Joseph. He almost got away once, but Barry put an UBER ticket on his windshield."

Michael gasped in pain, "Ok so that is all the information. Now, Gary what have you done to us."

Gary looked directly at Michael and said, "Why would you do this to your brother?"

Michael's face was contorted in pain. It appeared unlikely that Michael was going to answer him. "Ok everyone, the sickness and pain you are feeling is from a couple of jellyfish. Unfortunately, they are very potent and extremely deadly. For my protection, I put in those boxes, a bunch or Irukandji jellyfish, and some small Box jellyfish. Their venom is potent and deadly."

Gary continued, "Now, I'm quite tired. I'm just going to sit here and watch all of you die!"

Gary added, "I almost forgot, Frank, who was piloting the seaplane that I came in on, is going to have a couple of UK/USA NATO boats from Akrotiri arriving here very soon. If you're still alive, you might be able to go to jail. If not, then you'll die right here in about 30 minutes."

Gary looked at Ben and asked if he was able to get everything. Ben smiled and nodded yes and pulled out the little camera and microphone that was inconspicuously attached to his snorkel tube. This camera and microphone recorded everything since they were on the boat.

He then looked at Lucy and said in a very low voice so as not to be heard by Roger, Joanne or Michael, "This is a bluff. They won't die. I put a strong sedative in the water they drank."

The next morning...

Ben, Lucy, Belinda, and Frank arrived in Málaga at about 9:00 AM. Frank was getting the plane refueled and Belinda and Frank were going directly back to Boston. Belinda had spoken to her father last night. He was in a lot of pain, but he was feeling better. One day at a time.

Once everyone got settled into their hotel room, they planned to meet everyone for lunch at the Marbella Marina Club. Ironically, this was the place that Joanne visited only a few days ago.

It was great to see everyone together again. Lucy looked like she enjoyed hanging out with everyone that she has met over the last few days. Gary could see the tension draining from Lucy's face. She needed to just stop and relax.

Laughing and joking with his friends was also allowing him to relax. He was just glad that all the tension and the uncertain feelings of "why he was targeted", was finally done. Now was the time to move on from this and look to the future, to the new areas of technology he could look at.

Ben who sitting across from Gary said, "When we were underwater in the scuba gear it was great. I haven't really done that much diving since you were in the hospital. I'd like to do some more diving with you if you're up to it?"

Gary smiled and said, "I would love to get into diving again. We should plan a trip sometime."

After an amazing meal and a great desert, everyone started to get up and make their way out to the parking lot. Alexi asked him if they could talk for a minute.

Alexi said, "I looked at our software code yesterday. I found a couple of changes that we could make and then push it out to several companies that Roger stole from. The best part of this is I found a way to track the money back to Roger's bank accounts and also track the deposits going into the accounts Michael set up"

Excited, Alexi continued, "Gary, I'm not saying that we can get a few of Roger's bank accounts and his investments. We can get *every* account. The one thing that Kimberly forgot to do, is to delete the logs that were saved in our Cloud Drive server. These logs are everything that tells us who, what, when, and where. Really Gary, this is a goldmine. I think that if you and I dove into this, we could pay back all the people that Roger and Michael stole from in a short amount of time. This is a lot of money. I am pretty sure I know the answer, but we are returning the money, right?"

Gary wasn't expecting to be asked this question. He smiled and said, "I have always wanted to own an island in the Caribbean. Maybe buy two. I can call it *Gary Land.*"

"Ok, now you are pulling my leg."

"Alexi you know I would not do that because I know that you would never do that. However, Alexi-Land or Gary-Land does have a nice ring to it. No that will not happen on my watch or yours I suspect."

"I would like to get started on this soon, if that is, OK? Maybe in a couple of weeks? I don't know about you, but I don't like this money hanging around."

"Alexi, I feel the same way, I really want to get rid of this money as much as you do. One extra thing we need to do is to bring Ben into this problem. Even if we paid back some people, they might be a little 'miffed' before we pay them back. They might assume that we stole it. He can help smooth things over and help us to return the money in the right way."

"I almost forgot. I found an audio tape that Kimberly recorded. It was a conversation that Roger had with her, where he told her to make a backdoor to our customer's networks and steal money from their accounts. Just on that alone you could, have Roger go to jail. I'll give these over to Ben too."

Gary nodded and smiled at that. Trying to think of Roger or Barry or Joanne in orange jumpsuits.

Alexi responded, "I'll be happy when we get this all done. Then he added joking, "Can we get something different this time if we do "take out"?"

Gary laughed and said, "Yeah, those pizzas were not very good for the cholesterol."

For the next couple of days everyone took advantage of the beautiful beaches and sunshine. Joe, Rose, Carol, and Alexi all decided to go exploring to see some of the sights in Spain.

When Ben, Gary and Lucy arrived in Boston, it felt good to be home. Ben went home and "crashed" for another day before going back to work. Lucy dropped Gary off at his apartment. It was about 4:30 PM and Gary was anxious to see his companion again. He walked down the street to go to Bert's store. Bert saw him and brought Freddie outside to Gary. As most dogs can be, Freddie was beside himself with happiness.

"Bert thank you so much for looking after my friend here. I can't tell you how grateful I am. If there is anything, I can do just let me know. This was a big ask for me and I'm very thankful."

Bert said, "Freddie is a great dog. I really enjoyed having him here. He is so well mannered. A lot of the regulars that come down are also very fond of him."

Gary reached in his pocket and pulled out a key to his apartment. He said, "Bert I will make a deal with you. Anytime you want Freddie to hang out with you then here is my key. He likes you a lot, maybe even more than me, but I know Freddie is very social. He likes to be around a lot of people and dogs. Anytime you want just to give me a call or come over to the apartment and get him. Is it a deal?"

Gary didn't think it was possible, but Bert looked at him and was surprised. Bert said, "Are you serious? If so, then you definitely have a deal. That really makes my day!"

Gary walked back to his apartment with Freddie. He got some food out for Freddie and went over to his couch. Being home felt good as he reflected on the past week's escapades. His relationships with his friends and his family are so important he thought and he's very grateful to have them in his life. Alexi's question in Spain, was something that he was not expecting. Do you give the money back or keep it? It was a fair question. Maybe he would ask Alexi the same question. He knows that his answer wouldn't change.

Ever since his meeting with Belinda at Trinity Trust Holdings, he never really thought about the amount of money that he has in the bank. For most of his life, he has never been obsessed about material things or the power that money can give you. Gary's needs were very simple. If there was something he wanted like a car or a TV, he always believed that you worked and saved for the things you want. With that feeling of having worked toward a goal or accomplishment, the reward was so much sweeter.

Along those same lines, the feeling of being able to help someone or lessen their load in a significant way, always gave him a lot of joy. The interesting part of this is that it happens everywhere you turn. Holding the door open for someone; saying thank you to the person getting your coffee ready; helping a person put their luggage on the top row of a plane; and just thousands of acts of kindness. It might not be apparent at first, but sometimes it can be significant.

Along the way of his travels, he thought about Tim Triton. Tim's exuberance when he won the money from the scratch tickets made Gary smile. Tim reminded him of his earlier youth and getting started. One of the strongest feelings that he felt back then was confidence in himself. There is always uncertainty in the path you are following. No one can honestly say for certain of where they might end up. Two ingredients were required in most everything. Give it your best shot and also don't take yourself too seriously, if you fail. It always worked for him, and he could see that in Tim.

Freddie awkwardly decided that he wanted to come on the couch and lay down next to Gary. The couch barely fit Gary and Freddie. Gary laughed a little at this.

If there was any lesson to be learned from the past month's experience, it was that he had a choice of the type of person he wanted to be. The unbridled greed and corruption with Roger, Joanne, and Barry, showed him that he would do whatever he must do – to make sure he was not on that same path. As simple as that. He realized a person can be rich or poor, brilliant, or slow, hero or villain. But he also realized to never forget that he alone had the choice to be whatever kind of person he wanted to be.

Gary looked down at Freddie. Freddie just looked at him and Gary could tell that the only thing he wanted was to be near his friend.

It was good to be home again.

THE END

www.ingramcontent.com/pod-product-compliance
Lightning Source LLC
Chambersburg PA
CBHW071732110726
47908CB00006B/1576